THE SUGAR BARON'S RING

THE LEEWARD ISLAND SERIES - BOOK 3

LORRI DUDLEY

WILD HEART
BOOKS

For my boys,
I love who you are,
and I'm proud of the young men you're becoming.

"I will guide them in paths that they do not know.
I will make darkness into light before them
And rugged places into plains.
These things I will do,
And I will not leave them abandoned or undone."

Isaiah 42:16

CHAPTER 1

By day, the ocean blue sparkles with life, and sails fill
with promise. Under the black curtain of night, the
crewman fill tankards to cope with the monsters lurking
beneath, the ones within and the ones below.
~ *Journaled the 4ᵗʰ of April, 1829*

*I*f he lost his journal, he lost his future. Bradlee Miles
Granville's hand grasped thin air as the leather-
bound book slipped from his fingers. His writings were his only
chance to prove he wasn't an irresponsible disgrace to his
family name. The journal landed with a thud and skidded across
the weathered floorboards, dangerously close to the spilt
tankard of ale. His shoulder slammed against the ship's rail, and
he winced. The hull emitted a groan followed by the crack of
splintering wood. The eerie sounds raised the hair on the back
of his neck and tingled his scalp, distracting him from the pain.

"Hound's teeth!" Colin Fitzroy pushed himself up from off the deck and frowned at the black stripe from the contents of Bradlee's inkwell, now staining his white muslin shirt. Whether his impeccably groomed grand tour companion swore due to the ship hitting bottom or over his ruined shirt was still to be determined.

The scraping of the ship's bottom as it ground against what must have been a coral reef held the same pitch as fingernails down slate and continued for almost a full minute. The stench of ale and rum wafted under his nose, blending with the briny air. Inebriated sailors cursed as the contents of their tankards puddled about their feet. The billowing white sails deflated, and the familiar whistling of the wind ceased, along with any forward progression.

The contents of one of the spilt tankards ran down a seam in the planks toward Bradlee's journal. He snatched it up and examined the pages to make certain the ink hadn't smeared, breathing a sigh of relief when his research notes from his travels appeared unaffected. He slid it into his knapsack for protection.

The ship could merely be stranded on a reef, or it could be capsizing.

Blood surged through Bradlee's veins, quickening his pulse. He hooked Colin under his arm, dragging him to a stand.

Colin's eyes widened. "The ship didn't just... Please tell me..." He raked a hand through his windblown hair and groaned.

"Sink me!" The captain cussed from the helm. He fumbled with his hat and plopped it back on his head. It fell over one eye. With his other hand, he wiped the ale off the front of his shirt. "We've run-agrounds." The captain slurred his commands, "Goeth below tah see if her keel hasth been breached." He grabbed the first mate's lapel and shook him, but in his foxed state, lost his balance and toppled the crewman in the process.

The panicked screams of the crew and passengers permeated the deck like a gale of wind. In the chaos, the crew bumped into one another. A couple of drunken sailors sprawled on the deck snorted and tipped back the last of their bottles while the halfway-sober men clambered to their posts on unsteady feet.

Colin's face paled whiter than the sails. "The ship is sinking, and the captain and crew are as drunk as wheelbarrows." His fingers dug into Bradlee's forearm. "We're going to die."

"No, we're not. Look." He pointed to the dark shape on the horizon and speckled lights. "We're in sight of land. We can always swim for it."

"It could be ten miles away."

"Try to be positive."

"Fine." Colin stared at the melee ensuing on deck. "I'm positive we're going to die."

Bradlee looped the strap of his satchel over his head and shoulder. "Stay here. I'll be right back." He raced below deck to gather their belongings from the cabin. He couldn't afford to leave behind another one of his journals. They were his only hope of graduating, and he was not about to let them sink.

The ship groaned and tilted toward the port side. Bradlee grabbed the rail to keep from missing the stairwell. Men spilled out of the crew's quarters, pouring onto the deck. Bradlee pressed against the wall to squeeze by the outflow of people.

"We're taking on water, captain!" a sailor yelled.

Sure enough, below deck, an inch already filled the hold. The stamping of running feet splashed through the large puddle. Bradlee pushed through the narrow passage. Men brushed against him, knocking him back a few steps. He reached his cabin door and slid into the room as the ship tilted further.

Hurry!

He grabbed his journals from his bunk and a few spare clothes from the dresser and stuffed it all into his knapsack. He felt under his mattress for his meager change purse, but came up empty. As he flipped up the bedding, a piercing whine followed by a loud crack split the air. Bradlee slipped on the wet floor and whacked his head on the hanging oil lamp. He grunted and grasped the writing desk for support. His textbook on agricultural studies glared at him—a reminder of his father's expectations.

Confound it.

He disregarded the book and climbed uphill out of his cabin. Fewer men filled the passage now. The ocean trickled in through the cracks and seams like the Grecian fountains he'd seen on the Continent. The water now sloshed halfway up his boots. He turned the corner and mounted the stairs leading above deck.

"Help!"

He froze.

"Someone, please," a brittle male voice said. "I don't want ta drown."

It sounded from the galley. Bradlee turned. The elderly cook clung to the pot rack on the far side of the splintered deck, unable to pull his weight up the steep incline.

Feet pounded above deck, and flashes of people passed by the opening of the hold, but no one stopped for the man's cries.

"Help!"

Bradlee picked his way over the cracked boards. The wood scraped against his boots and breeches. He grabbed hold of a beam and leaned over as far as he could. "Give me your hand."

The man stretched but couldn't reach.

Bradlee scanned the area for a rope or something to grab hold. Rations and utensils lay strewn about the floor, but nothing useful for aiding the trapped cook. Bradlee blew air past his lips. A loud groan echoed through the empty hold. The gap between them widened.

"Colin!" Bradlee yelled up the stairs.

No response.

His hand rested on the strap of his bag. He glanced down. It might work.

He unlooped his knapsack from around his head and shoulder and dangled the strap down to the man.

An inch short.

"Colin! Get down here this minute!"

After a long pause, Colin's face peered into the stairwell. "You told me to stay put."

"Since when do you heed me? Get down here. I need you."

He glanced back toward the upper deck. "We'll lose our place in the lifeboat."

"Dash it all. We'll be fine. Get over here."

Colin clamored down the stairs, grumbling under his breath.

Bradlee fashioned the strap of his bag around the beam. "Get a good grip and lean me out." Bradlee locked arms with Colin and swung over the splintered boards. Beneath the rift, crated cargo floated in the ship's hold. "Take my hand."

The cook clutched Bradlee's outstretched palm.

"Hold fast." Sweat broke out across Bradlee's forehead. He strained with all his might and heaved the man over the divide. The cook didn't waste time thanking him, merely dashed up the steps. Colin handed Bradlee his satchel, and they followed in the man's wake.

"I'd heard being a hero was a thankless job," Colin hissed in Bradlee's direction.

His companion's aptitude for sarcasm didn't change even in a crisis.

They chased the cook up the stairs. Bedlam had erupted on the top deck as men pushed and shoved to claim a spot in the few remaining dinghies.

"Stay close." Bradlee pried away from the crowd and found a

spot near the rail. A warm breeze flapped the loose sails. He sucked in a deep breath and blew it out past his lips. Stars twinkled brightly in the night sky and stood in stark contrast against the pandemonium that surrounded him on deck. The moon reflected off the water, shimmering in the rise and fall of the waves. Lights shone in the distance, a beacon of hope. "That must be one of the Leeward Islands. I knew we had to be close."

Bradlee searched the deck. "Here." He grabbed a small barrel full of rum and opened the stint. The golden liquid spilled over the wooden boards, wafting the scent of spiced vanilla through the air.

"What do you plan to do?" Colin snorted. "Toast to our demise?"

Bradlee ignored him. "Use this or anything else you can find to help you float."

The stream lessened, and Colin closed the stint. "Can't hurt to save some. After all this, I might need it."

"If we have to jump…" Bradlee gripped Colin's shirt near the collar and locked gazes. "Swim as fast and far as you can away from the ship. The suction might pull us under."

Colin nodded, and they both turned toward the rail. The sea seemed calm compared to the mayhem on board. One dinghy rowed toward land with slow, steady strokes.

"You realize this is your fault." Colin didn't look in his direction.

"My fault?" Bradlee's mouth dropped open. "You can't blame me for the captain dipping too deep and running the ship aground."

"It's your spirit of adventure that keeps getting us into these messes. Before this, I lived a peaceful life as a humble Servitor at Oxford."

"You hated serving the professors and students. You complained about dull discussions regarding the crop rotation of turnips. I saved you from boredom."

"Indeed, and you have excelled to an extreme. There is no time to be bored when you're caught in the middle of a Spanish bar fight, dodging Indian arrows, or clinging to a sinking ship."

Off the starboard side, a dinghy heavy with passengers tipped and plummeted its occupants into the black water below. The zip of the line hissed as it flew through the winch, and the rowboat toppled after them. Another loud groan reverberated the boards beneath their feet.

"Grab ahold—" Bradlee's boots slid as half of the ship upon which they stood pitched forward, dipping its bow into the ocean.

He gripped a metal cleat bolted into the decking. His satchel dangled in the air and bumped against his side. Colin clung to a rail post with one hand and the rum barrel with the other. Below them, men splashed in the water, stirring up white foam at the bow. Grown men screamed like children as the dark water swallowed them whole. Others grabbed barrels or masts as lifelines.

The sight made the confident words he'd uttered earlier seem foolish. This couldn't be the end. What about his family? Would they remember him only as their foolhardy son?

God, get me through this. I promise I'll go back and take my final exam—even if it kills me. I need to redeem myself in my father's eyes before I die.

Bradlee adjusted his grip to ease the ache in his fingers. His strength waned. He couldn't keep hold much longer.

Colin released the rum barrel to grasp the rail with both hands. It rolled down the steep slope of the deck, splashed into the water, and submerged. A second later, it bobbed in the waves.

A blood-curdling scream howled above the wails of the drowning men. A man frantically slapped the waves. His scream muffled into a gurgle. A moment later, he disappeared.

An eerie hush fell over the water.

And then someone else shouted, "Shark!"

~

$\mathcal{H}$annah Rose Barrington ducked out her bedroom window into the humid night air. Her Uncle Reuben's rantings pounded her ears. Miss Albina Kroft's screeching fury followed. Hannah cringed. The bickering between her uncle and his frequent guest had, as of late, exploded in full-out battles. Their tension permeated the house, easily spilling under Hannah's door and stirring her sleep.

She inhaled the salty air and the sweet smell of molasses drifting on the light breeze from the neighbor's boiling houses. Her feet knew the path down to the beach by heart. Small crabs raised their pinchers but posed no real threat. They darted into their holes before she passed by.

She crawled up onto her favorite spot, her uncle's over-turned rowboat, careful not to obtain splinters from the weathered underside. Flakes of peeling paint poked at her skin as she tucked her skirt under her feet. The warm night hadn't allowed the sand to cool completely from the scorching heat of the day. The ocean breeze played with her hair, and the rhythmic breaking of waves washed the day's tension away.

It's unsafe for a lone woman to be wandering the island at night. Lady Clark, the reverend's wife, warned after Hannah had mentioned slipping out in the evenings to escape her guardian's quarrels.

Hannah glanced over her shoulder at the house. The silhouette of Uncle Reuben tossing back the last of the rum in his glass showed in the lighted window.

She released a sigh and turned back to the tranquil ocean. Was it evil to find comfort in something that had taken everything from her? Twelve years next month. That's how long it had been since the sea stole her parents. She swallowed against the lump that still formed in her throat. Her hand moved to her chest and fumbled for the gold ring that lay hidden under her gown—her father's ring.

An unsettling sound drifted across the waves, raising the fine hair on the back of her neck.

A ship sailed into the harbor, its white sails illuminated by the moonlight. It was not an uncommon sight, but most ships came in on a different angle to avoid the coral reefs. Distant cheers split the air. The crew must be having a boisterous night, or perhaps they were celebrating reaching their destination.

Strange. It didn't appear to be moving.

She rose onto her knees and squinted at the black outline of the ship. It seemed to bend in half. She blinked to clear her vision, but the masts continued to tip in opposite directions.

Her heart stilled, and her veins turned to ice.

Merciful heavens.

The ship was breaking in half. Those weren't cheers. They were screams.

She scrambled down to the sand and pressed her hands against her ears to block the sound. Bile rose into her throat, strangling out her breath as she was drawn back to her six-year-old self, the night she'd run away from her nursemaid as the squall hit. The sailboat her parents had navigated toward the Isle of St. Kitts had been much smaller than the ship now fighting its battle. Her parents' skiff had sank fast, faster than any fishing boats could get there.

She had stood on the shore, screaming for her mama and papa, while they drowned.

Hannah pivoted back toward the house. Should she run into town and sound an alarm? By the time she got there, it could be too late. What of her uncle? Would he be sober enough? Not likely. He'd probably pass out on the side of the road, or worse if he rowed out. He'd likely drown.

Hannah plunged her fingers into the sand, grasped the edge

of the rowboat, and heaved it over. With a strength she didn't seem capable of on her own, she dragged the dingy to the ocean's edge.

This time, she wouldn't be helpless.

CHAPTER 2

A whale blew its spout off the port side. Its massive tail fanned out of the waters. It measured half the length of the ship. Examples of God's miracles–the powerful sea creature and the fragile thin hull of our ship still afloat alongside it.

~ Journaled the 21ˢᵗ of March, 1829

"*H*old Fast!" Bradlee yelled.

Colin's fingers were white on the wooden rail.

With a loud groan, the ship swung to the side. Colin screamed as the boat shook him loose. He slid down the deck's steep slope. His arms grasped for anything to hold, but he missed the rail, tumbling through a broken section. He disappeared into the inky water.

"No!" Bradlee released his grip and followed his friend. Splinters from the wooden planks snagged his clothes. The ship tilted, redirecting his path to the right of where Colin submerged. Bradlee leaned left, but obstacles arose as the railing approached. A rolling cask hit him square in the arm and ricocheted. He spun and flipped over the edge of the ship headfirst.

His foot caught between something, and the rail wrenched it in an awkward position. He dangled in the air above the water, pain shooting up his leg. Another barrel slammed into the railing knocking his foot free. He plunged into the deep.

The rush of water surrounded him. Down and down, he plummeted. His arms and legs flailed in the pitch black as he gathered his bearings. If only he'd thought to remove his boots. They impeded his swimming as if the soles were comprised of lead. He struggled, clawing his way to the surface. The journals in his bag weighed him down like a millstone, and his lungs compressed, aching to draw in air until they burned. He followed the rising bubbles until he broke through the surface, gasping in deep mouthfuls of glorious air.

Screams and shouts surrounded him from all directions.

He spun around in the water. The vessel was underwater up to the helm. It's mast and withered sails draping into the sea. The swirling water dragged him closer to the corpse of the ship as if gathering occupants for its watery grave.

"Colin!" he yelled.

People splashed about all around him, fighting against the ship's pull. Where was Colin?

Bradlee kicked and cupped his hands over his mouth. "Colin. If you can hear me, swim toward the shore. Get away from the ship before we're dragged under."

A passenger nearby struggled to keep his head above water.

Bradlee spied a large drifting board and pushed it toward the man. "Grab hold and swim toward the distant lights."

The man wrapped both arms and a leg around the wood and heaved in deep breaths.

Bradlee shifted his satchel around to his back and swam with all his might toward the dim light in the distance. Something bumped against him, probably debris from the ship, but when he turned his head, it was a man's body floating face down and partially submerged. Bradlee said a quick prayer for the man's soul and kept swimming toward shore until his breathing grew labored. A swell of a wave lifted him, and he peered back at the ship, searching for Colin. The ship's crow's nest, the only part of the ship remaining above the waves, teemed with rats. As it slipped under, the creatures paddled to keep their heads above water, searching for something else to climb.

"Colin!" he screamed.

The shadowed head of a man floating on a plank answered, "You'd be lucky ta find anyone in this mess. Best ta keep swimming." The man jerked in the water. "Somethin' bumped me." He frantically paddled his arms and legs toward shore.

Moonlight glistened off of a silver fin emerging from the water several yards away. Bradlee stilled. The fin glided past him, picking up tremendous speed.

The man holding the plank barely released a yelp before a flash of white jaws yanked him under.

Other cries pierced the air. Bradlee's body trembled, rattling his teeth, but not from the tepid water. He'd known there was a chance of dying, but it never seemed so real until this moment. *Heavenly Father, please, help!*

A wave crested, and he caught sight of the bow of a rowboat, its oars straining up over another wave and sliding down the other side. "Over here!" a woman called.

Bradlee's arms propelled him through the water with long swift strokes. He reached the boat and grabbed hold of its side.

"Take my hand," the woman said. Her slender arm extended toward him. "Careful not to tip us over."

She braced her legs against the side and leaned back as they worked together to pull his shoulders over the edge.

"Can you kick a leg over and hoist yourself in while I stabilize the boat?"

"I—believe—so." He gasped in between breaths.

Something large brushed against his breeches. Bradlee clambered up the side and rolled into the safety of the dinghy. He lay scrunched in the hull, panting, his satchel laying on his chest, and both of his legs draped over the bench seat. The woman didn't waste any time maneuvering back behind the oars and rowing toward the cries for help.

Bradlee shifted onto the opposite seat, careful not to rock the boat. It was smaller than a wagon bed, but its two benches might allow for five people to pack tightly together before capsizing. He scanned the water. Two dark objects bobbed on a wave. "Over there. Two o'clock." He pointed. "You balance the boat, and I'll reel him in."

The woman adjusted her stroke, and they moved alongside a man with spectacles still perched on his nose.

"Help!" The man clawed at the side of the boat.

Bradlee reached over into the shark-infested water and gripped the back of the man's shirt and waistband. His muscles strained to drag the fellow over the ridge. The man's boots still dangled over the edge as the woman resumed her rowing.

"Over here." Another man waved.

With the help of the man in spectacles, they pulled in the other survivor.

Bradlee kneeled on the seat and cupped his hands to his mouth. "Colin!"

"I be Colin!" a distant voice said from the waves, but it wasn't Colin's voice.

"Colin!" Bradlee called again.

The rowboat reached Non-Colin, and Spectacles helped Bradlee heave him aboard.

"Help!" a voice cried from the other side of the dinghy.

Bradlee leaned over and scooped the man under the arms, reeling him in. Water from all the drenched souls puddled in the bottom of the boat as the men huddled in the center, shivering in the tepid night air.

"Colin!" Bradlee yelled again.

"We can't take any more," Spectacles said. "It will be too much weight fer the boat."

"Granville?" a faraway voice called.

Bradlee whipped around. "Colin?"

A barrel floated on the water about fifteen yards away. "There! Over there!"

The woman picked up the oars and grunted as she dragged them through the water.

"Here," Bradlee said. "Let me take over."

She hesitated a moment, then slid to the back of the boat.

Bradlee climbed over the huddled men and assumed the rowing position. His whole body ached as he propelled the small craft toward Colin.

"More to the left." The woman motioned with her hand. "There. Straight on for five yards."

In the cramped vessel, the woman's scent of coconut and molasses surrounded him. Her figure was concealed by a baggy gown, but her arms were deceptively strong for such a small frame. Her hair, which hung wild and loose about her shoulders, whipped in the wind and hid the view of her face.

"Stop." She held up a hand.

Bradlee released the oars and twisted in his seat. Two of the men leaned over the bow and hoisted Colin over the side.

"Praise God. You're alive." Bradlee patted his friend's leg. "You are a welcomed sight."

"I daresay, if I make it back to England, it's God's divine intervention that got me there. Had I known this grand tour was going to be one death-defying adventure after another, I would never have come." He shook off his jacket and wrung it out over the side of the rowboat. "By Jove, I'm asking for an increase in wages immediately upon my return."

"Ah, Colin. What would you have done without me to add spice to your life?"

"Probably had a better chance of making it to the ripe old age of thirty."

The woman cleared her throat. "I hate to break up your touching reunion, but there are others still in need of our help."

Bradlee resumed his rowing. The rescued men squished together in the little boat like pickles in a jar. Colin sat on the bench next to him and rowed one oar while he rowed the other. They found a rhythm and picked up two more men before they had no other choice but to head to shore. The pleading of his shipmates struggling to stay afloat gnawed at Bradlee's conscience, but the boat stood too low in the water. One more would surely capsize the dinghy.

"How did you find a rowboat?" Colin asked.

"I didn't. It found me." He nodded to the woman. "And I don't believe I have adequately thanked you."

"Nor I, my lady." Colin inclined his head.

She lowered her head and tucked her hair behind her ear, revealing a profile of high cheekbones and a delicate jawline. "There's no need."

Her voice held a captivating lilt—a mix of English and French.

"You saved our lives," Bradlee said with a grunt of exertion as he pulled back. "Without your aid, we certainly would have died." He strained forward. "Either from drowning or from being eaten by sharks."

The mere word sent a collective shudder through the men.

"We are forever in your debt." Colin paused to keep the rowing in tandem.

"Please excuse our poor manners. My name is Bradlee Granville, and this is my companion, Colin Fitzroy. May I ask the name of our saving grace?"

She turned to stare out over the waves and chewed her bottom lip. "It's Hannah." Her voice cracked on a husky whisper, and she cleared her throat. "Hannah Barrington."

Hannah. The name rolled off her tongue.

In the moonlight, Bradlee thought he saw the glistening of tears in her eyes.

~

*S*he'd saved so few.

The cries for help and pleadings for mercy of the dying men squeezed the air from Hannah's chest. What if they had families? Would children stare out at the horizon, forever waiting upon their father's return? Who would now provide them with food and shelter?

How could she leave them to die?

There was no choice. They had to unload. Her fingernails dug into the underside of the rowboat to keep her from screaming. Had her parents, worn and exhausted, slipped silently into the deep? Or did the sharks strike them, tearing at the very flesh that had kissed her and tucked her into bed each night? She blinked away tears and pushed the image from her head. Her parents would have wanted her to help, to save as many as she could. Her fingers wrapped around her father's ring and the thin leather strap that bound it to her person as if it could renew her strength.

The strenuous trip back to shore felt as if it lasted a year, even though it was probably mere minutes. The first man she'd aided—Bradlee something or other...oh yes, Granville—and his companion rowed the entire way. She was grateful for the reprieve. Rowing out had sapped her strength, and she must do it again and again, as much as necessary. She couldn't rest until every breathing man was rescued.

The boat rode the breakers catching a wave into shore, and the men jumped out, tugging it to the beach. Weary passengers filed out and lined up on the sand, uncertain what to do or where to go.

"If you follow the path, there"—she pointed—"between those dunes and seagrass, it will take you to the main road. Turn left, and in ten minutes you'll be in town. The mayor lives in the house with the weather vane. Knock on his door, and his wife will see to you."

They thanked her and started in that direction.

Mr. Granville hung back.

Hannah ignored him. There was no time for chatting. She pushed the rowboat back into the water.

He grabbed the other side and aided her. "My man, Colin, and I will go back out. You should get some rest." His voice strained over the crashing breakers.

How could she sleep with the echo of the men's screams in the distance? She shook her head. "I'm not tired, and besides, I'm responsible for the boat and must see it returned."

"I can make certain it is…"

She hopped into the dinghy.

"Fine. Then we all go." He braced as a wave crashed against his legs.

"No. Three will mean less men will be rescued. Only two of us are necessary—one to row and the other to reel in the men."

Mr. Granville hesitated, and another wave pushed him back.

Hannah grabbed the oars and began rowing. There was no time to lose.

"Colin." Mr. Granville hopped in the boat. "Stay here. We're going back out."

"What kind of companion am I if I let you go off without me?" Colin held the boat but eyed the water as if a shark might dive through the next wave. "What would your father say?"

"Father isn't here. We'll be fine."

"Every time you say that, something bad happens. I'm beginning to take it as a bad omen."

"See to any injuries. I'll be back before you know it." Bradlee turned and stilled her hand on the oars. "At least let me do the rowing."

"I'm perfectly capable." She struggled against his grip. "I got to you the first time, remember."

"You did, indeed, but I'd prefer to row."

His warm fingers slid over the tops of hers, and her stomach leapt. His touch somehow felt intimate. She withdrew her hands.

"Besides"—he scooted her aside with his hip—"you're a better spotter."

She scrambled out of his way, flustered by his proximity. "Why would you say that?"

"You have a better gauge of distance in the water than I do."

Truly? She had grown up on an island. Hannah gripped the side for balance and tried to pretend she received such compliments all the time.

He strained against the oars, sending the boat over the crest of a wave. "Where is it that we've—ah—landed or, I guess, shipwrecked?"

"Nevis."

"Nevis? Is that near Montserrat?"

"By sailboat Montserrat is about a four-hour ride south." The cries for help grew louder as he rowed. Perhaps, his chatter could keep her mind off the task ahead. "Why were you traveling to Montserrat?"

"It was a stop on my grand tour."

"I thought grand tours consisted of young bucks gallivanting around Europe?"

"Indeed. However, my research is less in the art and architecture of the past and more in the wilds of the present. I chose Montserrat as a stop because of its Soufrière Hills Volcano. I'm researching soil content and wildlife in order to finish my schooling. I'd also heard of the great adventures and pirates in the Caribbean from back during the sugar boom, and I wanted to come and see for myself."

"If you were looking for adventure, you certainly found one."

He snorted. "I've always craved excitement, but I admit, this was a bit much."

"Rightly so." She half stood for a better view. Floating in the center of a pile of debris was a man. "Over there. Off the port bow twenty yards."

Mr. Granville grunted and lifted his body with each row. In the dim moonlight, she could tell he was tall and slender, of athletic build, with a broad chest and a narrow waist. His hair was a bit long, as if in need of a cut, but his beard was trimmed tight to his face—or perhaps he was cleanshaven and in dire need of a shave.

She forced her gaze to focus over his left shoulder on their target. The man in the debris called to them and waved. He'd somehow managed to hold together various floating remnants of the ship to keep his body above water. "Five more yards. One more stroke will do it."

"Praise God!" the floating man called. "I don't know how much longer I could hold." As if to prove his point, a fin emerged and bumped into one of the planks upon which he floated. The man's leg dipped into the water, and he yanked it out, clambering to get back on his makeshift raft.

They couldn't get to him with the debris in the way. Hannah scratched the bridge of her nose and scanned the area. Pieces of the ship's wooden sides bobbed in the water, mixed in with chunks of wood, the bodies of dead rats, and random items from the ship—a ladle, a hat, an apple. "Hand me the oar."

Mr. Granville shimmied the pole out of its brace and placed it in her open palm. She carefully pushed each piece of debris aside while Mr. Granville paddled the boat closer. He begged her pardon when water dripped from the oar onto her gown, but she ignored the cold sensation and focused on her task.

The man grabbed the side of the boat and attempted to pull himself aboard, but lost his balance, and the lower half of his body splashed into the water. Hannah reached for him, as did Mr. Granville. The man thrashed about, churning up the water. She reached down to grasp his pants. With all her strength, she yanked him over the side as a pair of jaws lunged out of the water.

She screamed and jerked backward. Mr. Granville flipped the man's legs over the edge. The shark's nose slammed into the stern and shot the rowboat backward.

Hannah's fingers ran over her other hand, feeling to make certain everything remained intact. Mr. Granville's arms twisted around her and held her tight to his chest. "Hound's teeth, that was close."

Hannah's entire body shook, not from cold but from her frayed nerves.

Mr. Granville stroked her back. "It's all right. You're safe." He repeated the words over and over, but a tremor coursed through him also.

The rescued man struggled to an upright position and made the sign of the cross. "Merciful Mother Mary full of grace."

Hannah couldn't recall the last time someone had held her this close. Lady Clark—perhaps years back when she was still a pupil at the school. She fought the desire to turn her face into his hard chest and weep. Instead of relenting to weakness, she pushed his arms away. There was no time for comfort, even if her heart, soul, and even her flesh longed to be held by a stranger. When had she become so weak?

More men needed saving, and the sharks smelled blood.

CHAPTER 3

Mediterranean Sea farers speak of a phenomenon of blue fire illuminating the night sky guiding them through the storm into calmer seas. They call it St. Elmo's fire after their patron saint.

~ Journaled the 3rd of November, 1828

"We're wasting precious moments." Hannah pushed out of Mr. Granville's embrace, ignoring the sudden chill, and struggled to rise in her half-drenched gown. She scanned the waves, distributing her weight as the dinghy rose and fell. The clouds shifted, and moonlight splashed upon the waves. She caught sight of the tops of four heads, their matted hair plastered to their foreheads. The men clung to the top of a crowded, overturned dinghy. She pointed. "Over there."

Mr. Granville slid the oars back into place and resumed his position. They continued aiding men until the night sky faded from deep indigo to a lighter lavender. The first glimmer of morning's light would soon creep over the horizon. A sailboat joined them in their efforts. Hannah recognized the mayor's rigid shape at the helm. The sweep of his arms was as dramatic as if he were presenting behind a podium, much as he had the day the islanders determined her guardianship.

After four trips, Hannah lost count of how many they'd rescued. This time, as Mr. Granville rowed into shore, the boat remained only half full. They'd called out, but no others responded. They'd searched, but only debris remained. The mayor's boat had already sailed into shore, and Mr. Granville decided they'd done all they could.

The waves rocked them as a hand might a child's crib. She rubbed her tired eyes and stifled a yawn. Her weary body could sleep for days, but she would only have a couple of hours before her uncle would awaken. She'd lose at least fifteen minutes to ensure the rowboat was returned exactly to its original place and another five to clean herself up. She must look a fright. Her fingers caught in her knotted hair as she pushed the strands out of her eyes, and she shook the water from her soaking wet gown to keep it from clinging to her skin. It would be a miracle if she got any rest before her day began.

Mr. Granville rowed them close to shore where Colin awaited. A couple of men hopped out and pulled the boat up onto the sand. Hannah attempted to soothe the thin man with sunken eyes, one of the last they'd rescued. "You're safe now. We're on land."

He shook uncontrollably, clinging to the wooden bench, and refused to get out of the boat. "N-n-n-no. No water. I-I-I c-can't swim. S-sharks!" His glassy eyes stared blankly ahead while he rocked back and forth.

Mr. Granville crawled next to the man. "It's all right, Mr. Fennish. There are no sharks. We've reached the island. You're going to be fine."

The man didn't budge.

"Colin?" Mr. Granville pried the man's fingers from the bench, pulled him to a stand, and guided him to Mr. Fitzroy.

Mr. Fitzroy hooked an arm around him and drew him up

the beach. "The mayor's wife is here, and she's got food to fill your belly and coffee to warm you."

Hannah's muscles groaned as she stood in the damp bottom of the boat.

"Here, let me." Mr. Granville jumped over the side. His face winced, and he grunted as his boots sunk into the wet sand. He hopped on his right foot and extended his hand to assist her out of the boat.

"You're injured?" She pulled her hand back and wouldn't allow for his help as she stepped over the side.

"I hit something when I fell off the ship. I knew it pained me, but with all the excitement, I didn't have time to consider it." He shrugged. "I probably bruised my ankle. I'll be fine."

"Do you think you can help me drag the boat further up the beach where it's kept?"

"Of course."

He grabbed the bow and attempted to pull it himself, but he hissed each time he put any pressure on his left side. She grabbed the other side, and they were able to make it halfway before Mr. Granville cried out in pain and dropped to all fours.

She scooted around the boat and knelt beside him in the sand. "Let me look at it."

He sat and tugged at his boot. After several tries, he let out a grunt. "I can't get it off. It hurts too badly."

"It might be swollen."

"Indeed. It's throbbing with my heartbeat. That's usually not a good sign." He patted the sand next to him. "We'll have to wait until Colin returns."

Hannah hesitated. Her gown was a mess. At this point, it wouldn't hurt to get it sandy. She sat down beside him and tucked her bare feet under the hem.

The first rays of light illuminated the sky, coloring them in an orange glow. Mr. Granville wiped the sweat from his brow with his arm and rolled his sleeves up past his elbows. Unruly hair curled up at the ends and fell across his forehead. Sooty lashes framed the impish gleam in his eyes and conveyed a boyish look. His relaxed demeanor only accentuated his rugged appeal. However, his straight nose and square chin reminded her he was English gentry—prone to proper etiquette and an endless, unwritten list of do's and don't's—even if his angular features surrounded a generous mouth.

He rested his forearms on his bent knees and met her gaze.

She pushed her damp hair back behind her ear and wrapped her arms around her middle to hide her gauche appearance.

"You're much younger than I originally thought," he said.

She snorted and stared at the fine grains of sand, filling the distance between them.

"I didn't mean to offend." He shifted to face her, gingerly moving his sore ankle. "I couldn't get a good look at you in the dark, so I based it on your actions. I would never have imagined someone so young could act with such courage."

Her pulse fluttered. He thought she was courageous?

"I'm eighteen." She pressed her lips together. Why would she blurt out her age? Proper English women like her mother and Lady Clark didn't do such things.

One side of his mouth raised in a playful half-smile. "Ah, just a babe. I'm surprised they let you out of the nursery."

"Almost nineteen," she murmured, then sent him a sideways glance. "You can't be much older yourself. Your beard has hardly grown in."

His hand flew to his jaw and rubbed over the stubble.

She fought a smile but failed.

"Touché." He broke into an infectious grin. It transformed his face into warmth and light. "I am in need of a good shave and a week's worth of sleep." He covered up a yawn. "You must also be tired."

"I'm fine." She locked her jaw so as not to catch his yawn, but one flared out through her nostrils anyway.

He chuckled. "Yes, indeed." He twisted back toward the island. "Do you live close by?"

"Up the path on the left." She nodded in the direction with her chin. "You can see the corner of my house just above the top of that palm tree."

"Is there someone who'll come looking for you?" His eyes locked on hers. "Your husband?"

"My uncle."

His eyebrows hitched.

"He's my guardian."

His lips turned down a tad at the corners. "Your parents?"

"My parents died in a shipwreck when I was young."

Lines creased his forehead. "I'm sorry."

She drew swirls in the sand with her index finger. "It was a long time ago."

"It explains why you worked so tirelessly to save every last soul. I've never seen the like of it, especially for a woman."

Heat rose to her cheeks, and she dusted away the swirls she'd made with her fingertip.

He lifted her chin with his knuckle. "You are exceptionally brave."

The bright rays of his smile warmed her from the inside out. The intensity of his gaze held her as if it had reached out and cupped her face with two hands. Her stomach somersaulted, picking up speed. Her breath matched its pace.

She tore her gaze away.

He dropped his hand.

"I must head back before my uncle notices." She dusted the sand off her hands. "He'll become unreasonable if he finds I've been speaking to strangers."

"I'm sorry to have delayed you." He rubbed the top of his ear, "I—we—owe you our lives. I would hate to repay you with more trouble."

Mayor Simmons disappeared up the path, guiding the dazed

man toward town, most likely to his home, where Mrs. Simmons and their six children could aid with the men's care. Likely, survivors would fill the town hall tonight.

Mr. Fitzroy flopped down on a blanket in the sand and closed his eyes.

"Colin," Mr. Granville called.

He didn't respond.

Mr. Granville frowned. "There's no time for sleeping."

Mr. Fitzroy didn't open his eyes. "I'm merely training for dying since you seem determined to send me to an early grave."

"Ignore my companion." Mr. Granville's gaze flicked to her and back. "Sarcasm is his way of coping in unfortunate situations." He beckoned him with his hand. "Get over here. I'm in need of your assistance."

With a groan, Mr. Fitzroy rose and sauntered over.

"Dreadfully sorry, milord. May I recommend your kerseymere waistcoat with a matching frock coat." He raised his index finger to his lips. "Oh, I forgot. I'm no longer your valet. I've been promoted to your companion, which entails defying death daily." He lowered down onto his haunches and leaned in. "I guess it's for the better, considering your trunks have sunk to the bottom of the ocean."

"Do not fear. I packed us a change of clothing in my knapsack." Bradlee winced as he extended his swollen ankle toward Mr. Fitzroy. "I need assistance getting my boot off. It seems I may have injured my ankle in the fall."

Mr. Fitzroy dropped to his knees in the sand. Lines of concern marred his brow, and he gently handled his master's foot. The truth of his devotion to his employer was apparent in his face and actions. "It's swollen, all right. The only way this boot is coming off is if we cut it."

Hannah stifled a gasp and stared at the fine quality of his Hessian boots. They would have brought in a good amount of coin if she had them to barter. Perhaps even allow her to upgrade to a faster ship once she obtained the funds to purchase passage to England.

Mr. Granville flipped opened his satchel and dug out a small knife. "Best get on with it then."

Mr. Fitzroy sliced through the fine leather, and Hannah closed her eyes, unable to watch.

"Are you squeamish?"

She opened her eyes to discover Mr. Granville's amber eyes studying her. "It's a waste to destroy a perfectly good boot." She sighed. "But what other choice do you have?"

He examined his boot. "If it helps, the saltwater spoiled their value long before the knife did."

Mr. Fitzroy finished cutting and peeled the boot away. "Now we shall know with what we're dealing." He pushed up Mr. Granville's pant leg to reveal purple skin. "Can you wiggle your toes?"

Hannah glanced away. A proper English woman wouldn't stare at a man's feet. She exhaled. Half the island walked around barefoot, including herself. Why was she worrying herself with such concerns?

"I daresay it's a bad sprain if not broken. The only way you're going anywhere is with our help." Mr. Fitzroy stood and offered his hand. "The main road is not far, but I'm not certain where to go from there. The mayor's house is overrun with survivors."

"I know where you may stay." She straightened her back, scraped her hair into a twist, and tied it into her usual topknot. "Reverend and Lady Clark would think nothing of offering up their home to those in need. I'll show you the way."

Mr. Fitzroy grasped Mr. Granville's hand and hauled him to a stand. Mr. Granville hopped about to steady his footing, bumping Hannah. "I beg your pardon. I'm a bit clumsy this evening–er–morning."

She merely shrugged, uncertain how a lady should react in such a situation, and led the way up the path.

Mr. Fitzroy followed with a firm grip on Mr. Granville, who struggled to balance on one foot. The sun climbed above the horizon. It had to be at least half-past six if not already seven. They needed to move faster if she was to return before her uncle discovered her missing and flew into a rage.

She willed Mr. Granville to hobble faster.

CHAPTER 4

The cries of men drew them like the clang of a dinner bell. Their empty black eyes as unforgiving as death. The razor rows of their teeth sliced through flesh and bone and showed no mercy.

~ Journaled The 5ᵗʰ of April, 1829

"*H*ere." Hannah stalked to the other side of Mr. Granville and looped his arm around her shoulders. "You'll move faster if I help."

The three of them trekked up the rest of the path. Mr. Granville's hops kicked sand upon her bare feet and the hem of her skirts. His heat permeated his damp clothes and warmed her side. A metal scent like mineral water flowing fresh from a spring clung to him. Or perhaps, she merely imagined it due to her increasing thirst. She tucked snugly under the crook of his arm and could tell he tried his best not to put his full weight upon her. By the sound of Mr. Fitzroy's grunting, he received the brunt of it.

They reached the main road. Her home, with its drawn shutters, stood on their right behind the thick hedge of sea-grape trees. Mr. Fitzroy begged for a rest. He wiped the sweat off his brow with the back of his hand.

She could borrow her father's mare. It would aid Mr. Granville and speed their arrival. But if her uncle knew she'd taken Shadow without his permission, as she had the rowboat, she would be in even greater trouble.

The rowboat. She bit her bottom lip. With all their attention diverted to Mr. Granville's injury, they'd forgotten to return the rowboat to its proper place. She mustn't forget to right it before she returned home.

Mr. Granville wobbled on his good leg and gripped Mr. Fitzroy's shoulder for balance. He was taller than his companion by a couple of inches. His lean but muscular physique must weigh at least a couple of stones more than Mr. Fitzroy's scrawny frame. Mr. Granville didn't complain, even though clearly his ankle pained him. And while he may not have shown it, he must have been shaken, considering the pair of them had survived such a horrific ordeal and now found themselves stranded on a strange island.

Hannah puffed out a breath of air, decision made. "I will be right back." She ducked under the canopy of sea-grape branches and darted into the small stable. Her papa's once beautiful mare's back had swayed under the weight of her uncle's heavy build, and a cloudy film blinded her in one eye, but she was rideable.

Shadow's ears perked up at Hannah's soft murmurs of encouragement, and the horse stamped her foot to show her delight. Hannah wished her uncle would allow her to ride, but he didn't like her traipsing off into town. He believed she drew too much attention riding astride like a man. Of course, if he hadn't misplaced her mother's sidesaddle, she wouldn't have to do so.

She didn't dare take Uncle Reuben's saddle. He'd surely notice and go into one of his fits. Fortunately, she still had her mother's reins. Shadow accepted the bit in her mouth and quietly clip-clopped out of the stables as if she knew not to wake Uncle Reuben. As they approached Mr. Granville and Mr. Fitzroy, Shadow's muscles twitched, and she neighed.

"It's fine, Shadow. They're friendly." Hannah stroked the horse's mane to calm her. "This is Shadow. She's old but steady and should get us there at a better pace. Can you ride bareback?"

Mr. Granville slapped Mr. Fitzroy on the back. "I told you our adventures would come in handy someday."

Mr. Fitzroy harrumphed.

Mr. Granville grinned at Hannah. "I was taught by a Sioux Indian. That's how they ride." He hopped to the horse's side, grabbed Shadow's mane, and in one fluid movement, pulled himself up, kicking his bad leg over the horse's back.

Shadow snorted and moved sideways, but adjusted to his weight and her new rider's gentle commands. Mr. Granville tightened the rein and sat proudly upon his mount. His natural control and confidence made the elderly horse appear like a high-stepper. Shadow trotted in a circle as if five years younger.

Hannah smiled. "I do believe she likes you."

"I think it's been a while since she's been out for a good canter." He slowed her to a walk.

"Sadly, it's true. She deserves better, but my uncle only rides her to inspect the fields." *On the rare occasions when he does so.* Hannah headed in the direction of Reverend Clark's homestead, straightening her shoulders and imitating Lady Clark's graceful stride instead of her own lengthy one. Mr. Fitzroy fell into step by her side, along with Shadow and Mr. Granville.

Questions about her homeland bubbled up like a hot spring within her, but to ask too many would make her seem green. "Have you heard of Sir Charles Barrington of Bristol?" she asked.

Mr. Granville's lower lip raised over his top, and he shook his head. "I don't believe we're acquainted."

"How about any Barringtons of Bristol? Or perhaps Rosewood Manor?"

He frowned. "I'm afraid I've only been to Bristol on a few accounts. My travels have been more abroad than domestic, unless of course we consider traveling to London for the season." He glanced at Mr. Fitzroy, who merely shrugged.

Blast. She'd been hoping he might be able to connect her to some of her lost relatives. If only she could remember her mother's maiden name, he might have made their acquaintance in London. The more clues and contacts she had, the better her chances to reunite with lost family.

Sunlight streamed down on the stone church on the hill, illuminating its façade in a white sheen. She directed them to the left. "Their cottage is close. This way."

Hannah squinted through the sun at Mr. Granville's form, illuminated in an orange halo. "You've ridden with Indians?"

"Indeed. I wanted to journal their culture and rituals as part of my grand tour."

"It must have been a wonderful adventure."

Mr. Fitzroy snorted. "If you like arrows whizzing by your head and that sort of thing."

"If you hadn't offended the chief's widowed sister—"

"How was I to know she was the chief's sister?" Mr. Fitzroy crossed his arms. "She entered my tent and began setting up house, not the other way around."

Mr. Granville eyed her with a sardonic twist to his lips. "She made advances, and Colin couldn't get away fast enough."

Mr. Fitzroy's pitch raised to a squeal. "Not when the rest of the tribe deemed me to be her newly betrothed husband."

"At least I was able to document a few of their rituals before we were run off their land." A reminiscent smile teetered on his lips. "I even have a few sketches if you'd like to see them sometime."

"I would enjoy that very much." Hannah tightened her lips. What was she thinking to say such a thing? Her uncle wouldn't allow her to gallivant around with an Englishman. Over the past few years, her uncle's controlling nature teetered on the extreme. Whereas he used to take her out with him to inspect the fields, on hikes, and for daily walks, now he frowned upon her going anywhere other than school, and typically followed with a barrage of questions about where she went and to whom she spoke.

A slow, easy smile spread over Mr. Granville's features, and her pulse escalated. His presence radiated through her like the electricity in the air before a storm.

Little geckos skittered out of the way as they meandered up the drive, and monkeys chirped in the canopy of trees. She grew reluctant to part company with the Englishmen, but it was necessary to return. If she gauged the sun correctly, it must be close to eight.

Mr. Granville slipped his satchel off his shoulder and passed the bag to Mr. Fitzroy. "See if you can find the illustration of Kasa. She was Colin's betrothed squaw. Her name means dresses in furs." A wide grin spread across his face. "Unfortunately, she was a tad too rich for Colin's tastes."

Mr. Fitzroy opened the bag and pulled out a dripping journal.

Shadow abruptly stopped. Mr. Granville's hands held tight on the reins. He stared wide-eyed at the book in Mr. Fitzroy's hands.

Mr. Fitzroy opened the journal and quickly turned one page after another, the creases in his brow deepening with each flip. He peered up at Mr. Granville. "It's ruined."

∿

ot his journals. His chance for a future.

Bradlee's blood pooled in his feet, which only caused his ankle to throb harder. Those journals were his only chance to skip parts of the verbal examination. Sweat slicked his palms merely thinking about standing up in front of the dons.

Hannah's steps slowed, but she peered down the lane and inched in that direction as if needing to hurry.

Colin held the soggy book for him to see. A page of smudged black spots that used to hold a semblance of writing lay between his fingers. He flipped to the next page, but it revealed more of the same.

"Blast!" Bradlee's hands grasped the sides of his head, and his palms slid over his eyes to block the sight. His life was over. He could see the repugnant look of disappointment in his father's gaze. "Check some other pages. They can't all be ruined." He peeked through the cracks of his fingers.

Hannah studied his expression and stepped closer, probably either out of pity or curiosity.

Mr. Fitzroy peeled apart the damp pages, and black ink ran toward the crease darkening the valleys of the wavy edges.

"This can't be happening." His future had sunk along with the ship. It may have been better if he'd gone down with it. Then, at least, he wouldn't have to face his father. "Journaling was my only chance to avoid taking the great go."

"The great what?" Hannah asked.

Mr. Granville lowered his hands, and his shoulders slumped forward in a defeat. "It's a required exam one must pass to graduate from university."

"I see," Hannah said, however the furrow didn't leave her brow.

"Look." Colin passed the journal for him to view. "The notes you took in pencil are still readable."

He accepted the book and stared down at the pages. It was

something. He flipped through a few pages, fighting down the bombardment of disparaging thoughts. He'd survived a shipwreck. Surely he could figure another way out of his exams. "At least part is salvageable." He held out his hand. "May I have the pencil?"

Bradlee balanced his journal in his palm and jotted a note about monkeys.

Hannah rose onto her toes and stared curiously at the writing.

Could she read? He'd heard of the islands having schools, but did they teach women? He nodded to her. "They have monkeys in Africa. I'm merely noting that Nevis also contains the pesky beasts."

"How are you writing without an inkwell?"

Ah, she was a curious little thing. "It's the lead in the pencil." He held it up. "Have you not seen one?"

She shook her head.

"Here." He passed her the writing utensil.

She examined the long, pointed cylinder and weighed it in her hand. "It's heavier than the light and hollow quills to which I'm accustomed." She held the point in front of her face. "It appears they wrapped charcoal in wood."

"It's graphite, but the same concept." He accepted the utensil back and tucked it in his jacket. "It was given to me in Boston as a gift. Even though we have pencils in England, this one is by far the strongest."

"I hate to break up the chit-chat, but someone has noticed our arrival." Mr. Fitzroy nodded ahead.

An elderly couple rose from their rocking chairs on the porch and waved to Hannah. She waved back.

"Good morning." The woman beamed as she descended the short set of stairs.

The man padded along behind her. "Who have we here?"

Bradlee straightened. He looked like a cad. Here he was

sitting atop a horse while he made a young lady walk, and now he was about to intrude upon strangers. His mother would swoon at his lack of decorum.

⁓

*H*annah cleared her throat and concentrated on the hazy memory of her mother's instructions on formal introductions. "Mr. and Lady Clark, may I make Mr. Granville and his companion, Mr. Fitzroy, known to you. The ship upon which they had passage wrecked near the bay. They are in need of your generous hospitality." Her words didn't flow as well as her mother's once had. Hannah swallowed down the notion that she'd bumbled the introduction and faced Mr. Granville. "Mr. Clark is reverend of the church we passed on the hill. He and Lady Clark also teach the local children at the school there."

"Guests. How lovely." Lady Clark clapped her gloved hands. "Welcome. It's a pleasure to meet you." She bobbed a curtsy.

Mr. Granville slid off Shadow's back and hopped on one foot. His relaxed posture straightened into proper English fashion. "The pleasure is all ours, Lady Clark." He bowed using the horse for balance. "Mr. Clark."

Mr. Fitzroy bowed also.

Heavens. Should she have curtsied?

Mr. Clark stepped forward. "Most unfortunate to hear about your ship—"

"Indeed. How dreadful." Lady Clark, never at a lack for conversation, rambled in her endearing way. "How fortunate you weren't harmed. Or were you?" She frowned at his unclad foot. "Is that a limp I see? Poor thing. Come inside and rest. I'm certain you must be exhausted, and thirsty—oh, and probably famished. Whenever I sail, I can't keep a thing down, so when I reach land, I'm starving and devour everything in sight."

Mr. Clark slipped his hand around her arm and ushered her toward the house. "Why don't we let them settle in a bit before we start a conversation."

"Yes, indeed. Why don't you see the men inside? I'll run and inform Hattie to prepare food to break their fast." She scurried up the stairs in a swish of skirts.

"Pardon my wife," Mr. Clark said. "She can be a bit excitable and a tad hard to follow when she flits from topic to topic as a bird flits from branch to branch."

"We appreciate your hospitality and shall be in your debt for your kindness in our time of need." Mr. Granville passed the reins to Mr. Fitzroy, who frowned and glanced about, uncertain as to what to do with the horse.

Hannah pulled the reins from his fingers and peered at Mr. Granville's ankle. She would only stay a moment to see them settled. Shadow seemed content to munch on the grass below, so she hooked the leather straps onto a nearby branch.

"Please, follow me." Mr. Clark started up the stairs. Lady Clark, in her excitement, left the front door open, so they marched, or rather in Mr. Granville's case, hobbled with Mr. Fitzroy and herself on either side, into the front foyer.

Mr. Clark ushered them into the salon, which had always been Hannah's favorite room. A tufted sofa sat under a cheery window that received the morning sun and faced the ocean's view. Across from it sat two low-backed King Louis X chairs with a tiny end table between them. On the table rested two Bibles. Mr. Clark's spectacles sat on one of the covers, and Lady Clark's teacup perched next to the other. She imagined the loving couple read their Bibles in those spots every morning before they began their day. The room emitted the same feeling of comfort and safety that she remembered in her own house back when her parents were alive.

Mr. Fitzroy eased Mr. Granville onto the couch and offered

her the other spot. "It's the least I can do for someone who saved my life."

"I must be go—"

"Miss Hannah rescued you?" Mr. Clark stopped in the process of bringing in another chair for Mr. Fitzroy.

"What's this, I hear?" Lady Clark swept into the room, her head cocked to the side like a bird's.

Mr. Granville tapped his thumb and his pinky back and forth on the side of his thigh. "She rescued us out of the ocean as the ship sank."

"My goodness." Lady Clark blinked, sank into her regular chair, and focused on Hannah. "Whatever were you doing out on the ocean at night?"

"I heard the commotion from the shore and dragged Uncle Reuben's rowboat out to sea." *Remember to put the boat back in its place.*

"We believed we were done for until she propelled in like a Saint Elmo's Fire." Mr. Granville's eyes beamed at her.

Hattie carried in a tray of fresh fruit and biscuits, followed by another servant holding the tea service. "Miz Hannah, how lovely of you ta visit wit us dis mornin'." Her graying hair peeked out from under her cap, and her smile stretched the length of her face. She opened her arms.

Hannah walked into Hattie's embrace. She slid her arms around the buxom woman's waist.

Hattie squeezed Hannah tight. "How's my precious girl?" She rocked Hannah back and forth until the prick of tears stung the backs of her eyes. Hattie's hugs were notorious for welling up emotions, and Hannah was not immune. The beloved servant released her, and Hannah stepped away, swallowing around the lump in her throat while she returned Hattie's smile.

"I'll let ya all be, seein' yah have guests. But Miz Hannah, I know ya see da Clarks at da school, but don't be a stranger around heah." She unhooked a small basket from her arm. "Dis is my loaf of banana bread fer you ta tak home with ya." Hattie patted her arm and ambled back toward the kitchen. "Mek certain you stay and have a bite. Dos biscuits are hot—straight from da oven."

Hannah's mouth watered at the mere thought of Hattie's famous banana bread. She knew she should be getting back, but her stomach rumbled at the delicious smell of freshly baked biscuits. Besides, there was a chance Uncle Reuben wouldn't rise early after a night of drinking.

Lady Clark poured tea. She asked the gentlemen how much sugar, but she already knew Hannah's preference. Plates were passed loaded with fruit and a biscuit the size of her hand.

"Were there many survivors?" Mr. Clark cleaned his spectacles with the tail end of his shirt before sliding them back around his ears.

Mr. Granville washed down a bite of biscuit with tea. "I'd say we rescued thirty or so. Miss Barrington recognized the mayor's sailboat out there also. I'm not certain how many they saved."

Mr. Clark blinked. "Is that where they are now, at the mayor's house?"

Hannah nodded. "I believe so. Mrs. Simmons was behind the dunes, passing out blankets and coffee and leading them toward town."

"If you'll excuse me, please." Mr. Clark rose. "I'll ride down and offer my services, in case anyone needs prayer or an extra pair of hands."

"Yes, of course." Mr. Granville nodded. "We don't mean to be in the way. I wish I were more mobile. I'd join you, but perhaps Colin—"

"No, no," Mr. Clark said. "You have been through quite an ordeal. Eat and get some rest." He dropped a kiss on his wife's forehead and removed his hat off the hook in the foyer before strolling out.

"I must hear all about what happened." Lady Clark leaned forward. "Please, do tell and leave nothing out."

Mr. Granville started from when the ship hit the reef. Hannah relaxed her aching muscles into the soft cushion of the sofa and listened, for she hadn't heard this part. As he spoke, Mr. Fitzroy added his perspective, and Lady Clark peppered them with questions. Hannah found peace in Mr. Granville's British accent, his rhythmic baritone voice similar to how she remembered her father's. The sun warmed her skin, and the fruit and biscuits satisfied her belly.

"Hannah, darling." Lady Clark's voice called her out of the deep. "Hannah, wake up."

She forced her heavy lids open and raised her head. A pair of good-humored brown eyes with little golden flecks peered into hers. One dark brow tilted slightly higher while the other angled down toward a slightly crooked nose.

Merciful heavens. Had she fallen asleep on Mr. Granville's shoulder?

"The hour is growing late." Concern laced Lady Clark's eyes. "Won't your uncle be wondering where you are?"

She bolted off the sofa. "What is the time?"

The men shrugged. Mr. Fitzroy lifted his pocket watch attached by a chain to his jacket. "Unfortunately, mine is no longer ticking. Water seeped in and stopped the gears."

"It's quarter past eight, my dear." Lady Clark clicked her pendant closed. "I must ready for lessons."

Hannah's stomach tightened. Her uncle would plague her with a hundred questions regarding her whereabouts. "I must go." She scooped up the basket of banana bread. "Thank you for your hospitality, Lady Clark, and I—um—I might be a bit late for school."

"Take your time, dear. Get some rest and come in after the noon meal. I can manage this morning."

Hannah smiled her gratitude.

The gentlemen rose to their feet, Mr. Granville balancing awkwardly on one foot. "Wait. I can escort you—"

"I can manage faster alone."

Mr. Granville leaned forward as if to catch her before she made her escape. "May I call upon you to thank you properly?"

Hannah pleaded with her eyes for help from Lady Clark.

Lady Clark rose. "I'm certain Miss Hannah will stop by to see to your well-being tomorrow. If not, you may see her at school." She smiled. "She assists us by teaching in the mornings."

Hannah opened the door and waved good-bye. "It was a pleasure meeting you." She turned and dashed down the stairs, but not before catching the look of concern on Mr. Granville's face or the exchange of glances between him and Lady Clark.

CHAPTER 5

We have not reached our intended destination, but I do
not despair. The Leeward Isle of Nevis offers much
appeal and many sights to behold.
~ *Journaled the 6th of April, 1829*

*H*annah pushed Shadow as hard as the old mare
could go. When the house came into view, she half
expected Uncle Reuben to be pacing the yard, but, fortunately,
all seemed quiet. She hopped down and walked the horse into
the stables, hoping not to draw attention. Shadow's nostrils
flared, for she was in poor physical condition, thanks to Uncle
Reuben's neglect. As Hannah removed the bit and rubbed down
the mare, she kept her ears open for any stirrings within the
house.

Finished, she swung the stable door closed and tiptoed past
her uncle's window around the backside of the house to where
her bedroom window remained open and the shutters lifted.
Her white curtains blew in the breeze, and she crawled into her
room to discover a mess.

The empty bottle she used as a candlestick lay on its side on her nightstand. Her washbasin had been knocked over. Its water puddled on the floor, and dripped into her pried-open unmentionables drawer. Two furry critters froze in the process of tossing about what little undergarments she owned.

Monkeys.

Dreadful nuisances. "Shoo." She waved her hands at them. One of them hissed at her, baring its tiny teeth. She grabbed a pillow and swatted it. The little creatures scurried out the window. Thank goodness she'd kept her bedroom door closed. If they'd gotten into the rest of the house and awoken her uncle...

She quickly cleaned up the mess and glanced at the time. Quarter past nine and still no sound from her guardian. *Praise God for small miracles.* She pulled a clean gown from her wardrobe and quickly undressed.

"Hannah," her uncle called. "Bring me my elixir."

How close she'd come to being discovered. She fumbled with the buttons on the back of her dress. Uncle Reuben needing his elixir meant he'd be in the foulest of moods this morning. In the last six months, his drinking had become more frequent, his mood swings more pronounced, and his strange obsession to know her every interaction more prevalent. She loved her uncle, but when she tried to convey her fears for his well-being, he merely shrugged her off and said he had it all under control.

Miss Albina Kroft's influence didn't help the situation.

"Coming." Instead of finishing the tiny row of pearl-sized buttons, she wrapped a shawl over her shoulders and scrambled down the hall to the kitchen. When she stepped in, she watched as Blandina hacked off some slices of bacon and tossed them into a frying pan. Hannah greeted her with a smile, but the slave girl focused on her task. She and Hannah were close in age and had been friends and confidants as children—until Uncle Reuben had begun to disapprove of their association.

Blandina hadn't spoken much in the past year. Hannah had

asked her about the slave boy from the adjacent Renier Plantation who used to come around. She'd seen them talking on several occasions while Blandina washed the laundry in the creek that ran between the two properties. However, Blandina refused to speak of him, and now he'd run off. Over the past year, Blandina's eyes had grown hard as her belly grew with child. Hannah's heart ached for her friend and the dwindling of their friendship. She'd tried to get Blandina to open up as she used to do, but to no avail.

Hannah yanked dried beetroot powder off the shelf, added it to a mug with coconut water, coffee, and two heaping tablespoons of sugar, and mixed it with a spoon. She set it outside Uncle Reuben's chamber and tapped softly on the door.

Back in the kitchen, the delicious aroma of bacon filled the room. She poured coffee for herself and another cup for her uncle. Blandina set a piece of bacon and egg on a plate and handed it to Hannah, along with a second larger portion on a bigger plate for her uncle. Hannah started toward the dining room, but stopped. She'd already broken her fast. Perhaps there was better use for her portion of the food.

She turned back to Blandina. "I'm not very hungry this morn. Why don't you have my plate?"

Blandina eyed the bacon and glanced at Hannah with hopeful eyes. The tension in her face melted away, and she swallowed as if already salivating for the blessed treat.

"Go ahead. You're eating for two."

Her eyes shadowed, and her jaw set. She dropped her gaze, refusing to meet Hannah's eyes, but she accepted the dish anyway.

Hannah strode into the dining room. The large silver candelabra, which had graced the center of the table, was missing. She set Uncle Reuben's plate on the table and glanced about for any sign of where her mother's prized possession had disappeared too.

Uncle Reuben lumbered into the room, clutching the mug of elixir like a life source. He gulped back the rest of the drink and dropped into his chair. The slight movement wafted the smell of stale spirits in her direction. He pushed the empty mug away and rubbed his temples. His eyes were bloodshot, his round face red and splotchy. His reddish-brown hair stuck out in all directions.

"What took you so long to bring my elixir?" His bloodshot eyes narrowed on her. "I had to holler for you three times."

Hannah floundered for an explanation. "Monkeys." She flipped open the Bible to where they'd left off in their daily devotional, her throat thickening at her half-truth. "I-I accidently left the window open, and they made a mess. I was so preoccupied tidying up I must not have heard you the first time."

"Pesky little beasties." He picked up a greasy hunk of bacon and gnawed off a bite.

"Have you seen Mama's silver candelabra?" She eyed the center of the table.

He finished chewing and swallowed. "I put it aside for fixing."

Hannah stilled with one hand on the back of her chair. How could he be so careless with the precious items that remained of her mother's memory?

His glaze lowered, and he pushed his eggs around on his plate. "Things got a bit heated last night." He peeked up at her. "I said some things I shouldn't have, and she retaliated in kind. Somehow, the silver was damaged."

Hannah stared at the empty spot. She'd polished the piece yesterday. Mama used to frown upon it showing any tarnish, and Hannah kept up the same regimen as if she could still make her mother proud.

"You know how I feel about Miss Kroft's presence at the

house." She leveled Uncle Reuben with her gaze, but he looked away. "My parents wouldn't approve."

He ignored her statement, as usual. "I'll take it to the blacksmith and have him fix it. You'll never know the arms were bent."

Bent! She gritted her teeth. "You said you'd have Mama's chipped serving platter fixed, but it still hasn't been returned."

He wiped a hand over his face. "There was nothing that could be done for it. The chip turned into a full-blown crack. It couldn't be restored."

Hannah pushed back an arm's length from the table. "So you did what? Threw it away?" Her fingertips pressed into the hardwood. "It was my mother's."

"Hannah." He winced at the volume of his voice. "My head aches too much to discuss this right now." He pressed a hand to his forehead. "I'll be buggered if Albina's rantings didn't drive me to the bottle, but a good woman is hard to find on the islands. Especially, for a misfit like me." He glanced at her. "Like us." He stuffed a spoonful of eggs into his mouth and leaned on his forearms over his plate.

She slowly sat, hating being lumped into the category of misfit, but her uncle wasn't wrong. After all these years and countless letters, none of her relatives had ever come to claim her.

Yet, she still wouldn't accept it. A notion, so deep inside she couldn't explain it, argued that something wasn't right. She had no proof—no logic, or reasoning—yet she still believed she had relatives who'd accept her. She just needed to find them.

He ate in silence as Hannah stared at the blurring pages of the Bible beneath her fingers. A silver candelabra couldn't bring Mama back to life, nor did it take her place, but the possessions did bring fond memories of her laughter and smile when she'd entertained their guests. Memories were all Hannah had left of the vibrant lives that were her parents'. If she lost those reminders, would her memories fade completely?

Uncle Reuben's eyes sagged with woeful regret. "I know our quarrels are tough on you, but it don't mean nothin'." His sausage fingers patted hers. "Everything's goin' to be fine."

She issued him the barest of nods. He'd gotten her through the blackest days of her life. How many nights had he heard the screams of her nightmares and rocked her until the darkness receded? She'd refused to let him out of her sight for fear he too would disappear. She dogged his every step, trailing him to work and into town. He'd turn around to tell her to go back to the house, but then his face would soften, and he'd scoop her up onto his shoulders and carry her with him.

Those days had long passed.

"I'm expecting a letter from England. Has anything arrived fer me?"

Hannah shook her head.

His eyes shifted to his plate and back. "It's important business, but nothing to fret over."

Nothing to fret over? Her stomach twisted into a knot. *Please don't let it be a notice of termination.* Her uncle only had one property left to oversee.

He must have noticed the concern on her face, for he mumbled, "Potential client—er—something like that."

She perked up. "How splendid." Another property to manage could ease some of the financial strain.

He shoveled more egg into his mouth. "Don't open it, and don't get your hopes up." Bits of egg sprayed the air. "It's merely a prospect." He pointed the upside-down prongs of his fork at her. "When the letter arrives, I want you to notify me straightaway."

"Where shall I find you, at the Maynard plantation?"

"I can't be bothered with work today. My head's splittin'."

Her jaw tightened, but she was too weary to argue. "Time for the day's devotional. We're on First Peter chapter two. She looked down at the Bible and read. 'Wherefore laying aside all malice, and all guile, and hypocrisies, and envies, and all evil speakings—"

He waved his hand and groaned louder. "Can it not wait until tomorrow?"

She eyed him. He did look haggard with deep bags under his eyes and a couple days' worth of stubble on his beard. "Fine. This evening before supper, then." She flopped the Bible closed.

He grimaced. "What about your whereabouts today?" His bloodshot gaze held hers.

"School of course, and I have an errand to run in town."

His lips twitched. "Yer gettin' a mite too old to be wandering into town on yer own."

Since when had he become concerned about keeping up appearances?

"Where exactly are you goin' in town? What business have you there?"

She shifted in her chair. "To the general store. We've run low on some of the ingredients for your elixir." Her courage left her before she could state that she was also selling her poultices. He'd want to know why, and she wasn't prepared to do a round of battle.

"Fine, but don't talk to anyone. Get yer supplies and get back home. We'll discuss this further later when my head's not aching." He closed his eyes. "I think a hot toddy might also help the ache. Be a good poppet and run make me one." He pressed the fleshy part of his palms into his eye sockets.

"Wasn't it partaking of spirits that put you in such a state?"

"Just a smidge to take the edge off."

"I won't contribute to your list of sins, Uncle." She rose. "Give the elixir a few more minutes to take effect. I must water the garden, but then I'm off to the store and to help at the school."

The scraping of her uncle's fork against his plate could be heard through the window as Hannah knelt in the garden. Her plants lifted their leaves toward the sky in worship, and she stooped beside them to pray her morning prayers. As she prayed, she dug up some yucca roots and picked a pot full of beans. Before the sun grew too hot, she stole into the kitchen and wrapped them in cloth. Her uncle shuffled past the open doorway on his way back to bed.

Blandina dried Uncle Reuben's plate and put it away before slipping out into the yard with her head down to tend to the other chores.

Merely thinking of laying her head down on a pillow made Hannah's eyes water, but there was still much to do. A pair of warm brown eyes flashed through her mind. Was Mr. Granville sleeping, or was his ankle paining him too great to rest? Maybe she could make a poultice to ease some of the swelling, but did she have enough ginger root? She opened the canister to find only a small remnant.

She'd pick up more. Mr. Maroon had sent word that her poultices were selling and needed replenishing. While in town, perhaps she could trade the yucca root for some ginger. She ground up the other ingredients with the mortar and pestle and scooped them into small round tins. Mr. Maroon would be more likely to trade if she brought him some tooth powder. She opened the cabinet and seized another tin.

A low groan and the creak of Uncle Reuben's bed meant he was done for the day. If only he would take her advice and visit the one remaining plantation that still compensated him to oversee the sugar crops. Its absentee owners paid little attention to their bookkeeping, for the plantation's proceeds had dropped significantly in the last few years. She figured the only reason Uncle Reuben was still receiving pay was thanks to the owners' neglectful oversight.

Hannah slipped her satchel off the hook, stuffed the tins into the front pocket, and exited the kitchen.

Blandina stood in the yard feeding the chickens and pigs as Hannah left the house. She waved, but the girl stared at the ground, unseeing.

Hannah headed toward the school, but passed the turn and kept going down the path to the beach. Uncle Reuben was being unreasonable. Why could she no longer talk to the same people she once conversed with daily? Why was he becoming so controlling of where she went and to whom she spoke? Whenever she tried to question him about it, he'd contradict himself, proclaiming he'd never limited her whereabouts or social interactions.

A weary sigh blew past her lips.

At least, she's found a way to market her poultices anonymously, thanks to Mr. Maroon, who offered to sell them in his store for a cut. Her steps grew lighter, and weariness rolled off her shoulders. She bit her lip to keep from smiling. If islanders continued to buy her poultices, she could have enough money to pay for passage to England within the year. A few months more, and she'd have some petty cash to ensure her lodging and travel until she could locate her extended family in Bristol.

Her weariness returned like a heavy anchor. She mustn't get her hopes up. She had yet to broach the topic with her uncle, much less convince him.

Shouts floated on the ocean breeze.

Her steps slowed as she rounded a bend.

A bunch of men and women of color scoured through items dotting the shoreline. Smiling faces rolled barrels up through the sand. Trunks were pried open, and hands rifled through them. Shouting and arguments broke out over the treasures. Two women fought over a pair of men's breeches, while another woman grabbed a pair of boots and sped off down the beach.

The taller of the three women dropped the pants and set out chasing the woman with the boots, shouting words in Creole.

These were the shipwrecked crew's personal belongings. How could they take advantage of another's misfortune?

Hannah spied a box floating in the tide and darted toward it. If she could salvage a few items, she could leave them with the mayor's wife, who could return them to the rightful owners. Another man beat her there. He straddled the small box. "Dis here is mine. Get, you redleg." He waved his arms to shoo her away. "Go on now. Get, you white beggar."

She drew up short. Her spine stiffened at the names.

"You betta get before I lick ya." He curled his fingers into a fist and drew back.

Would he strike a white woman? It could mean his death.

His nostrils flared, and his chest heaved.

Hannah backed up, not willing to risk it. Maybe Uncle Reuben was right. Maybe her safety was a justifiable concern.

As she wandered down the beach farther, the men and woman paused briefly to stare at her as she passed. Their eyes questioned, *Redleg, what are you doing here?* Her jaw clenched until her teeth ached. This was her lot in life. After the death of her parents, she no longer belonged with the elite white planters, what few of them remained on Nevis, nor did she belong with the working blacks who banded together against their white rulers.

She may be an orphan who lived off the benevolence of her uncle, but she wasn't a beggar. Her gown may be well-worn with the tears repeatedly fixed, and a few inches too short, but she was still her parents' daughter. She had a roof over her head, and the sale of her poultices brought in a few coins each week. She'd make a way.

A smooth turquoise stone caught her eye. She bent down and plucked it from a bit of seaweed. Perhaps she could make the gem into a necklace to sell. Two curious faces eyed what she'd picked up, deemed it nothing of worth, and continued to fish the treasures out of the ocean with sticks. They stood on the shore because they were fearful of water. She'd overheard slaves native to Africa talk about sea witches that would drag people under and drown them.

Hannah held no such qualms. At least not about witches. Sharks were a different story. However, the predators became more active at dusk and usually patrolled the waters beyond the reef, where deeper tide made it easier to feed.

Uncle Reuben taught her where to swim when he used to take her out in his rowboat. A smile spread across her face. Maybe there was still a chance she could return some of the lost items to the rightful owners before they were scavenged.

She waded out into the waves. The saltwater swirled about her skirts. Thankfully, she'd donned a light day dress. Then again, when was the last time she'd donned a corset or heavy petticoats? In this humid weather, it seemed ridiculous to wear such garments. Her break from proper attire also differentiated her from the English women who traveled to Nevis for its healing hot springs or visited the plantations with their husbands.

She strode toward the breakers, keeping her satchel above the water. A school of fish zigged and zagged under a nearby wave. A flash of light reflected through the clear water. Hannah inhaled a deep breath and plunged under the surface, holding her bag above with one hand. Bubbles tickled her skin, and the salt burned her eyes and blurred her vision. A conch dragged its heavy shell along the bottom past the item. The sun hit the treasure once more, revealing its location. She scooped up the round object—a pocket watch—and pushed up for a breath. She tucked the watch deep in her satchel.

Hannah wiped the water from her eyes. A thin, lanky slave on the beach stared at her and shook his head. She pushed farther out, careful to stay where she could touch. A dark object caught her eye. She waited for a small wave to pass before she reached under again, collecting her treasure and storing it in her sack.

When the sun rose higher in the sky and her muscles protested like rusted gears, Hannah let the current drift her down the beach, away from the beachcombers. Once no one who might steal her findings remained in sight, she dragged her tired body back out of the water. Her fingers had wrinkled into raisins, and her lips were swollen and tasted of salt. She collapsed on the beach and opened her heavy knapsack to peer at her treasure. A bottle of men's cologne, a pocket watch, a complete razor set, and four bottles of unopened Madeira.

Her most substantial find was an ornate box. It was locked, and she didn't find the key, but she imagined it holding something of value—a locket with a cameo of a man's wife, an engagement ring, or a special family heirloom. She touched the box but didn't dare pull it out of the sack in case someone was watching. Even though the only signs of life other than her came from the seagulls crying overhead.

A large wave pounded the beach behind her as she rose and dusted off her soaked gown. It clung to her curves, and she hoped it would dry before she reached town.

She understood the precious value of mementoes from those who'd passed, like her father's ring. On days like today, when others called her *white beggar* and *red legs*, the ring became her lifeline. It kept her from forgetting her true identity.

Her hand moved to her chest, unable to rest assured until her fingers fell upon the leather strap and the round object that always hung there.

Her heart seized. *Nothing.*

CHAPTER 6

Sugar cane fields blanket the area in green waves,
merging into the thick foliage of Nevis Peak. However,
the summit could be bathed in orange or purple for all I
know, since its crown is forever cloaked by clouds.
~ *Journaled the 7th of April, 1829*

*T*he fine hairs on Hannah's arms jumped to attention.
Where was the ring?

Both hands moved to her chest, frantically patting and
feeling about her neck. Her finger touched upon the leather
strap and she traced it back to a lump entangled in her hair.

The air whooshed from her lungs, and her shoulders
slumped. She hadn't lost it.

Thank God.

Pushing to her feet, she dragged herself into town. The edge
of her heavily-loaded satchel dug into her side and weighed her
down. She yawned, but her limbs were too tired to raise a hand
and cover her mouth. Thankfully, no one witnessed her ill
manners.

The market clamor and the thrill of haggling for a good deal revived her a bit. Men and women called out their wares and held them up to entice people to buy.

"Pretty gal, let me braid yer hair." A slave woman called.

Hannah strode past the persistent vendors until she reached Mr. Maroon's general store. Shells jingled as she entered. Mr. Maroon stepped out of the back room and dusted off his hands. "Miss Barrington?" A puzzled expression twisted the free man's face. "Tell me ya didn't go swimmin' wit yer clothes on dis morn?"

"Did you hear about the shipwreck?"

He pressed his hands together and glanced heavenward for a brief moment. "God rest dere poor souls."

"Thought I could take some of the possessions washing up on shore back to the survivors."

"Dat's mighty thoughtful of ya." He rounded the counter and faced her from the other side.

She unbuttoned the side pocket of her satchel. "How did my poultices sell?"

"We've had a few purchases. A little slow, but not a bad start."

"You're telling them to add it to hot water like they do with tea?"

He nodded. "I have."

"And that it helps with fever?"

"I did."

"If they complain that it's bitter, they can add sugar to ease the bite. If they know what's good for them, they'll drink it down."

He folded his arms. "I've been sayin' all dat."

She sighed. "I merely want it to sell."

She removed a tin of sour orange leaves. "This one will ease a sore throat." She handed him the herbs to smell before removing a container of mint. "And this will help with a stomach ache."

Mr. Maroon lifted the tin of mint to his nose and sniffed.

"How much ya lookin' to sell dese fer?"

"A shilling for each, except for my special elixir." She pulled out several tins of elixir used to clear the head after a night of heavy drinking. "These are two shillings each."

He reared back. "Dat be too much. Wat fool gonna pay tat much?"

"I want you to give away the first few. Pass them out to tavern patrons holding their heads the next morning."

"Give tem away? Have ya lost yer mind?"

"You'll see. Soon they'll be flying off the shelves." She licked her lips and met his gaze. "I also want half the cut."

"Half?" He shook his head. "All ya have ta do is crumple up some leaves into a tin. I have ta bring in da customers and man da store."

She raised her chin. "I have to tend the garden, research the recipe, and test the product."

He pursed his lips. "You drive a hard bargain. Yer cut can be half, but if dey aren't selling"—he grimaced and rubbed his jaw —"I drop the price."

Hannah had heard him on several occasions mention his sore tooth. "Word's going to spread. You'll see."

"Two shillings a tin." He whistled. "If dey sell fer dat, I'll be happy to tek half the money." He opened his cash drawer and handed her a coin. "Dat's yer cut of the sales from last week."

"May I have a couple ounces of ginger and a jar of yeast?"

Mr. Maroon measured out the ginger into a bag and handed her a jar of yeast.

She slid the coin back across the counter.

He waved her off. "I'll tek da price out of next week's sales. Ya go and get yerself somethin' nice."

Hannah smiled her thanks. "Pleasure doing business with you." She tucked the coin in her satchel and pulled a small tin from her side pocket. "For your tooth. Good day, Mr. Maroon."

He held the tin as if it were precious. "Yer a good soul, Miss

Barrington."

She curtsied and left, avoiding the temptation of the market. Every coin saved brought her closer to England and to finding her relatives.

A mulatto woman dressed in purple-dyed linen bumped Hannah's shoulder as she passed. She stopped and eyed her. "Watch yerself, white beggar."

She grimaced.

Bradlee hadn't treated her as such. He'd treated her like a lady, offering to row and to escort her back home, even in his injured state. Would he still think of her as a lady after he heard the names she was called? Would the intensity in his gaze fade? Surely, she was being fanciful, believing she saw a spark there in the first place. She could imagine the fine ladies with whom he'd made his acquaintance.

Like the fancy women who used to parade into the Artesian Hotel. Their expensive gowns and elaborate hairstyles reminded her of cockatoos primping their feathers. They swept in with their beaks—er—noses in the air. She held out a side of her gown, stiff with dried salt. Compared to their sophistication and grace, she must appear like a beggared pot licker.

On the way to help Lady Clark at the school for the afternoon, she stopped by Mrs. Simmons's house to see how they fared with the injured men from the shipwreck.

"Why, Hannah." Mrs. Simmons greeted her with a weary smile. "It has been an age." Lines of concern creased the folds on either side of her eyes. "Tell me that wasn't you in the rowboat last night?"

Hannah dropped her gaze to her bare toes.

Mrs. Simmons placed a hand on Hannah's shoulder. "You should leave such work to the men."

Hannah met her gaze.

Mrs. Simmons' voice softened. "I know it must have been personal for you."

Hannah blinked back the sting of tears. "How fare the men?"

"Dr. McLaughlin has been here to see the patients and has administered bloodletting. Thankfully, it has calmed most of the patients. Mr. Clark has been a dear, praying and giving them hope."

Hannah opened her sack and removed more tins, which she hadn't given to Mr. Maroon. "I made some chamomile to put in their tea to help calm their nerves. I also was able to retrieve these from the ocean." She removed the ornate locked box, shaving kit, and other small treasures. "Perhaps you could help find the rightful owners?" Hannah handed them to Mrs. Simmons and retrieved the watch from her satchel. She held it up. "I'm going to keep the watch and see if I can repair it, but if anyone asks about it, I have it for him."

"How kind of you. Many are still reeling from shock." Mrs. Simmons passed the goods to a nearby servant and took Hannah's hand in hers. "Would you like to come in and have a cup of tea?"

"I don't want to be a bother. I know you're busy. Plus, I need to get to school."

"Tell me, how is Mr. Huxley?" Mrs. Simmons frowned.

Her uncle, as of late, had become an unpleasant subject. Uncle Reuben's troubled mind fueled island gossip. She cleared her throat. "He's well."

Mrs. Simmons's knowing eyes searched hers. "And how are you faring? I heard from several of the rescued men of a beautiful woman who rowed up like St. Elmo's fire and saved them from the deep. It is a brave thing you did, especially knowing your uncle's moods. Is he aware of your good deeds?"

Hannah's breath stopped. She shook her head.

"You may want to inform him. Some of the men have been wandering into town to the local haunts. Drink loosens the tongue, especially when it's a good tale."

Hannah bit her bottom lip and nodded. "Good day, Mrs.

Simmons."

"Hannah." A deep sorrow filled Mrs. Simmons's eyes. "I'm sorry. I wish…" She blinked away tears. "We should have fought harder to find you a good home, searched longer for your relatives." Her voice tightened. "Governor Vaux had the final say."

"You have been a support to me over the years. I'm grateful to your family and the Clarks."

"I wish we could have done more."

Hannah turned away with a gentle smile and headed up the lane to the schoolhouse.

She, too, wished they could have found her family, but that was not God's plan—not yet anyway. Besides, Uncle Reuben needed her. Who else would pray for his soul and continue her parents' work?

Dark clouds passed over Nevis Peak and shaded the sun. Warm raindrops sprinkled as she strolled up the lane to the small one-room school where the Clarks taught. Hannah tilted her head back to let the rain splatter on her face. She didn't mind the shower, for it washed the salt from her skin. Inside, the children repeated Lady Clark's phrase, "M—the moon shines bright in time of night." The rain picked up, hammering the thatched roof. Hannah yanked the door open and found Lady Clark waiting with a towel.

"I saw you coming. Dry yourself off before you catch your death." Lady Clark handed her the cloth and addressed the class. "Trace the next letters on your primer with your fingers."

Rows of young dark faces bowed their heads together in pairs, while groups of three shared a hornbook primer.

Hannah wiped her face and blotted her hair dry. "Would you like me to work with the children on their math or continue with their reading?"

Lady Clark pursed her lips and studied her. "There are purple smudges under your eyes. Have you not slept?"

"I slept a few winks on your sofa."

"That's entirely too little." She tilted her head and tapped a finger to her lips. "After the storm passes, you should go home and rest."

Hannah scraped her hair up and tied it in a topknot. Sleep sounded wonderful but elusive. "I brought a poultice for Mr. Granville's ankle. How are he and Mr. Fitzroy faring?"

"Delightful fellows. They were resting when I left. Hattie has doted on them, but I daresay Mr. Granville is not a good patient. He keeps trying to put weight on his foot. Maybe you could talk some sense into him." Lady Clark tapped a finger to her cheek. "With Mr. Clark in town for the day, it might be best to end school a mite early. Perhaps, you can visit Mr. Granville on your way home to offer him the poultice and some good sense."

Hannah's pulse quickened. She'd only met Mr. Granville a few hours ago—well, more like eight—but why did the thought of seeing him excite her so? She agreed to the plan, then set to work, strolling up and down the aisles, peeking over the children's shoulders, and helping them on any words causing difficulty.

Hannah sat next to Katie, the youngest student, and had her read aloud. The mulatto girl's small voice stumbled over the letters. Hannah helped Katie sound them out, but her mind drifted to the strong arms that had snatched her out of the shark's jaws and held her tight as she trembled in fear. Would Mr. Granville be pleased with her visit? She rubbed her eyes. It was wrong to wonder such things about a man she barely knew.

An hour later, the rain stopped, and wet palm branches shimmered in the sun. Hannah stared at the old weathered clock on the back wall. Would Mr. Granville still be sleeping?

"All right, class." Lady Clark clapped her hands together. "That's enough for today. The sun is out. Go and enjoy the nice day." She turned to the eldest child. "Robert, would you like to lead us in prayer?"

The entire class bowed their heads.

"Blessed Heavenly Father, thank you for today's teachings. Please bless Mr. and Lady Clark for teaching us Your ways. Aid our parents in their toil and labor and watch over us as we go home. Keep our hearts and minds on You until we meet again tomorrow. In Jesus's name we pray. Amen."

A shuffling of feet scuffed the floor, and the children filed into the yard. Hannah assisted Lady Clark in cleaning the room and a quick preparation for tomorrow's lesson. Before long, they returned to Lady Clark's home.

As they stepped onto the front porch, a loud thump sounded inside the house.

"I don't have to be sarcastic." Mr. Fitzroy's voice floated through the open window. "But you give me so much material. I don't want to be wasteful."

Lady Clark opened the front door and swept into the foyer. Hannah followed, then stopped at the sight before her.

Mr. Granville lay on the floor with an end table toppled onto his waist. He held Lady Clark's framed miniature portrait in one hand and a glass vase in the other.

"Miss Barrington." Mr. Granville tried to move, but couldn't in his odd predicament.

Hannah pinched her lips shut to keep from smiling.

"My heavens." Lady Clark's hands covered her heart. "What happened here?"

"Good afternoon, Lady Clark, Miss Barrington." Mr. Fitzroy bowed. "Mr. Granville insisted he didn't need my help." He arched a sardonic brow at the man still lying on the floor. "Apparently, he did."

"Take these so I can wring your neck." He held the glass objects higher.

Despite the threat, Colin commandeered the vase and the portrait from Mr. Granville's fingers and set them on another table.

Hannah aided Mr. Fitzroy in righting the end table.

Mr. Granville scooted into a seated position, and Mr. Fitzroy lifted him to his feet with Hannah's assistance. His biceps flexed under her grip. Mr. Granville's slim frame was deceiving. Beneath his billowing white shirt, raw power resided. She pushed the improper thoughts from her mind as they lowered him onto the couch.

"In my defense"—Mr. Granville raised his chin—"my companion here left me unsupervised."

"I was fetching you the cup of tea you requested."

"I grew tired of waiting. What were you trying to do? Turn it into wine?"

Mr. Fitzroy waved. "Nothing of the sort. Hattie merely showed me how a cup of tea goes lovely with a slice of banana bread."

"Did you bring me a slice?"

"You didn't ask for one."

"Did you bring me the tea?"

"I would have, but it went nicely with the banana bread."

Mr. Granville met Hannah's gaze. "You see with whom I'm dealing? He's completely mad."

Mr. Fitzroy sank into a nearby chair. "Mad and maddening are two different things." He laced his fingers across his chest and raised his eyebrows. "Besides, the voices in my head tell me I'm entirely sane."

Laughter burst through Hannah's lips, and she covered her unladylike display with her hand.

~

*B*radlee's heart slammed into his ribs. Miss Barrington's laughter invigorated him deep inside, more so than all the reckless endeavors he'd ever risked. Her smile transformed her face into youthful sunlight. The same woman who'd tirelessly hauled men out of deep waters until the early morning hours also seemed to enjoy his and Colin's unusual sense of humor.

He settled back into the sofa. After three hours confined to a couch with only Colin's company to entertain him, his day was finally looking up. His newest challenge solidified in his chest. He was determined to conjure her smile and laughter as frequently as possible.

Lady Clark watched the exchange with a twinkle in her rheumy gray eyes. Strange that she'd be silent now when this morning she'd rambled on endlessly.

"You're smiling." Colin frowned.

Bradlee's face twitched. He hadn't realized he'd been smiling. Miss Barrington seemed to have that effect on him. He redirected his smile at Colin. "Is that a problem?"

The furrow in his brow deepened. "It frightens me."

"Why would his smile scare you?" Miss Barrington angled toward Colin.

"Usually, it means he's developing a plan." Colin pursed his lips. "One that typically requires scaling mountains, introductions with hostiles, or sailing into uncharted territory."

Bradlee snorted. "Your exaggerations are unnecessary."

Colin wouldn't acknowledge him, but instead addressed Miss Barrington. "At least his injured leg works in my favor. He won't be daring any stunts in his current state." He exhaled a sigh. "Heaven knows, I could use a holiday."

She dug through her bag. "I almost forgot. I brought a poultice to ease the swelling."

Truly? Her concern for his wellbeing pushed aside the dark cloud of worry regarding his exams. "How thoughtful of you."

Colin grimaced. "And here I presumed Miss Barrington might be on my side."

"I shall ring for tea." Lady Clark stood. "Mr. Fitzroy, Hattie is probably busy preparing supper, would you be so kind as to assist me with the tea tray?"

"Indeed, my lady." Colin stood and followed her.

Lady Clark left them unchaperoned, but, then again, Miss Barrington had little to fear with an injured gentleman. He glanced at her. He would remain such—a gentleman—not injured. The sooner his ankle could heal, the better.

She pulled a tin from her bag and a small rag. "I'm sorry my cloth is a little damp." With graceful fingers, she removed the lid and dipped the rag into its contents. The mint and spice scent permeated the air. Her head tilted, and the makeshift topknot holding her hair loosened. Light-brown tresses stained golden by the sun fell down past her shoulders. The scent of sugared vanilla wafted around him. His fingers raised, but before he caved to the temptation, she brushed the silken strands behind her ear. A pair of straight teeth bit her bottom lip as she worked the paste over the cloth. Her pouty bottom lip beguiled him. Its fullness appeared swollen, as if she'd just been kissed.

She glanced up at him. "What?"

"Nothing." He averted his gaze. *God forgive me.* What had gotten into him? He shook his head and raised his palms. "I'm merely admiring your medicinal skills. How did you learn the trade of apothecary?"

"My father was a sugar baron, but my mother came to the island to help the natives and teach them the gospel."

"And you learned from her instruction?"

Her cheeks reddened to a beautiful rosy-pink. "Unfortunately, my mother passed before I was old enough to learn. She did, however, leave behind a plethora of books on the topic." She wiggled her fingers on the hand closest to his leg. "Let me see your ankle."

If her parents had books, then they must have been well-inlaid, and she did mention her father being a baron. However, being an English baron was a lesser title and may or may not be associated with money. From the look of her well-worn gown, it appeared they may have fallen upon hard times. He shifted back in his seat and gently propped his leg over her knees, fascinated with the young chit.

She rolled down his stocking. Her touch felt cool and soft upon his fevered skin. His breath stalled at the intimate moment, but he made much out of nothing. She behaved as if it were common for men on the island to need such assistance.

Starting with the middle of the cloth strip, she wrapped the poultice and bandage around his swollen ankle several times with gentle fingers, before tying the ends neatly in a knot.

His lower leg began to tingle. "Is it supposed to burn?"

A trace of a smile formed on her lips. "Not burn, but it leaves a tingly feeling. It may turn a bit red, but the swelling should go down."

"Will I be able to see the red behind the black and blue?"

"Let's say purple, then." She smiled fully.

Bradlee's stomach tipped like a drunken sailor. A ballroom full of London's marriageable cream of society didn't intrigue him the way this winsome woman did. Had island life stoked her bravery? How could she be so tough one moment and so gentle the next? Did the loss of her parents at a young age develop her independent qualities?

He rubbed the back of his heated neck. "I hope it does the trick, for I'm afraid I'm an insufferable patient. I despise sitting for long periods. While Colin laughs at my immobility, I find myself devising creative ways to strangle his scrawny neck."

She scratched the bridge of her nose. "Let me think about a solution. I'm certain I can come up with something to aid you."

"Then, it will be the second time you have saved my life, and you still haven't told me what I may do to repay you."

"Mr. Granville you need not—"

"Please call me Bradlee. After the turmoil we survived

together, it seems silly for you to refer to me in such a formal way. I already consider you as a sister."

The light in her eyes dimmed.

A poor choice of word.

A faint blush appeared behind her golden tanned skin, but she held his gaze and cleared her throat. "Bradlee, then. You need not—"

"I do not mean to be so forward, but may I call you Hannah? At least when we are not in mixed company?"

Her lips parted. "I—"

"Here we are." Lady Clark swept into the room, followed by Colin as the stand-in butler carrying the tea service.

Hannah startled at the sound of Lady Clark's voice and pushed his foot off her lap.

It hit the floor, and a bolt of pain shot up his leg. She turned her back on him to face Lady Clark. He ground his teeth against the pain. Did Hannah's nervous behavior mean such intimate ministrations weren't normal?

Lady Clark poured a cup. "One lump of sugar for you." She passed Hannah her tea. "And if I recall properly, no sugar for you, Mr. Granville, but three lumps for you, Mr. Fitzroy."

Mr. Fitzroy accepted his cup and sat. "It's why my disposition is so sweet, and Mr. Granville's so sour."

Bradlee scooted forward in his seat to take the cup and saucer offered to him.

"Miss Barrington not only was a star pupil." Lady Clark perched on the edge of her seat and sipped her tea. "But now, she assists Mr. Clark and me in the school."

Another selfless attribute and another clue to the enigma that was Miss Barrington.

Lady Clark's eyes sparkled as she regarded Hannah with a motherly fondness. "She is wonderful with the children."

"Truly?" He studied Hannah.

She drew back her chin as if offended.

"I didn't mean to sound dubious." He shook his palm. "It's merely that at Oxford, the professors are stodgy, old, and dreadfully dull. If I'd had a teacher as interesting as you, I might have been more attentive."

Hannah's eyes searched his as if trying to determine whether he spoke the truth or teased her.

"Perhaps." Colin crossed one leg over the other and eyed Bradlee. "You might even have shown for the exams."

Bradlee glared at Colin before clearing his throat. "I had hoped to explore the island of Montserrat until our ship ran aground, but the topography of Nevis is similar. Once the swelling subsides, I hope to document some of the wildlife and fauna."

Lady Clark's eyes widened. "If you do, make certain someone who knows the island like Hannah is with you. Some areas are hazardous to venture." She tilted her head. "Does Montserrat hold a particular interest to you?"

Hannah stared at Lady Clark under heavy lids. Had she not yet slept?

Bradlee said, "I was hoping to peer down into the volcano and note the wildlife living at its peak."

"Our Mount Nevis may not be an active volcano, but we do have similar rainforests and hot springs." Lady Clark sipped her tea.

He leaned forward. "Hot springs, you say?"

Hannah's head lolled beside him. She jerked upright and blinked her eyes.

"Yes, Nevis has several. They boast of healing qualities to the water. Many visit the renowned spring at the Artesian Hotel. I do believe Mr. Rousseau has entertained the likes of Lord Nelson, Lady Wentworth, and Prince William, the Duke of Clarence. You can also find natural hot springs on the trails up Mount Nevis, but the trek can be dangerous. There's the threat of mudslides, fall from steep inclines, poisonous snakes, and—"

"Please, my lady, you're only enticing him to go." Colin's nostrils flared.

True. Bradlee's limbs itched to scale Mount Nevis and record his adventures. His blood pumped faster at the mere thought. *Blast this inconvenient injury.* He did not want, nor had he the patience, to be an invalid.

Hannah nodded off. Poor girl must be exhausted. Her teacup tilted, and the liquid hovered near the edge of the brim. He righted it with his finger to prevent it from seeping onto Lady Clark's sofa.

Hannah jolted and blinked several times before setting her cup down. "I'm afraid I must go."

"So soon?" Bradlee fought to keep the disappointment from his face.

She stifled a yawn. "It was a long night. I need a nap before supper."

"Poor thing." Lady Clark rose. "I don't see how you're functioning without any sleep."

Weariness lined Hannah's eyes. "The nap on your sofa this morning was quite refreshing." She smoothed her skirt. "I do apologize for my ill manners."

"Think nothing of it." Lady Clark waved.

Colin rose to his feet, and Bradlee stood and leaned on the sofa's arm.

"Miss Barrington," Bradlee said, "shall you be coming by on the morrow?"

Her lips parted, and he heard the slight intake of her breath.

"In case I should need more of your poultice?"

"Of course."

He hobbled forward. "Perhaps if you could spare the time, I could show you my journals? At least, what is still legible from them."

The light returned to her exhausted eyes. "That would be lovely."

He acknowledged her with a nod. "Splendid."

"Splendid, indeed." Lady Clark escorted her to the door. "We shall see you tomorrow. Farewell, dear."

Hannah's feet flitted down the steps. She rounded the bend and drifted from view.

Bradlee turned to find Lady Clark's gaze darting from him to Colin. Colin watched Hannah's retreating form with similar interest.

Lady Clark pursed her lips as if to suppress a smile.

Bradlee's ears burned. There was nothing wrong with showing Hannah his journals. Lady Clark should be glaring at Colin for ogling Hannah longer than was proper. He hobbled back to his seat, and the others returned to theirs. "I noticed Miss Barrington wasn't wearing shoes. Is that common on the island?"

"Things are different here than in England." Lady Clark stared into her teacup. "The dreadful humidity and scorching sun make keeping up with propriety challenging. You'll find servants and children often run around in their bare feet."

He frowned. "Miss Barrington doesn't appear to be a servant, and she certainly is not a child."

"I'm afraid that tale is a bit complicated."

"I'd like to hear it." Out of the corner of his eye, he caught the sardonic arch of Colin's brow. "Er... In case there is a way to be of help."

Lady Clark glanced out the window as if contemplating whether to confide in them.

He issued Colin a warning look to cease the misguided direction of his thoughts. "We owe her our lives."

Her eyes clouded. "I never knew her parents. They died before I arrived in Nevis. Theirs was a tragic death."

"Miss Barrington told me their sailboat capsized."

"Indeed. We're not certain exactly what happened, for there were no survivors. Young Hannah, their only child, was orphaned at the tender age of six. Letters were sent to London to inquire about family and means for the poor child, but the governor at the time, Governor Vaux, I believe, claimed there was no reply."

"Claimed? You believe there's reason to doubt the man's word?" Bradlee tapped his thigh with his thumb. "Perhaps the letters never reached the proper hands."

Lady Clark shrugged. "There's a lot of hearsay and no way of knowing. Hannah stayed with the Simmons family while the Nevis council paid a hefty sum to one Captain Phelps to dock in Bristol and inquire into the Barrington family and holdings. Rumor has it, Captain Phelps got caught up in a smuggling ring with pirates off Grand Terre and was never heard from again. The council was still reeling from all the damage caused from a storm and couldn't be bothered with the fate of a young girl. During one of the meetings, Mr. Huxley stood and claimed to be the child's uncle. Governor Vaux approved of the guardianship. Despite several objections, the governor's decision remained firm and final."

Her voice lowered. "I do not believe Mr. Huxley is her true uncle. According to my husband, Sir Charles, Hannah's father, never introduced him as such." She clicked her tongue. "My husband believes Sir Charles was being charitable and attempting to lead Mr. Huxley to the Lord, but I had often wondered if Mr. Huxley took advantage of the Barrington's misfortune." Her gaze and voice lowered. "He moved into the sugar baron's estate that same night, and there are rumors he has been bleeding Hannah's inheritance ever since."

Bradlee rubbed his lower jaw to hide the tight clenching of his teeth. "How could they leave her in the hands of a blackguard?"

"It is merely hearsay and, Lord forgive me, I shouldn't be perpetuating gossip, but I've grown concerned for Hannah's future." She exhaled a long breath. "Mr. Huxley has fallen upon hard times. He used to oversee multiple lucrative plantations, but he lost most of the accounts after they were sold to local bankers."

Colin steepled his fingers. "I don't mean to be forward, but couldn't she stay here?"

"We've tried, but the governor's ruling stands. Huxley holds full custody until she marries."

"Why hasn't Miss Barrington married?" Bradlee shifted his tingling ankle.

"Hannah is stuck between the classes. She's a baron's daughter, which puts her above much of the common folk living here. However, she's orphaned and without any means. She doesn't attend fine gatherings or consort with the social circles due a woman of her station."

Lady Clark clicked her tongue. "To add to that, it's hard to determine who is an honest chap or a scoundrel. Many plantation owners returned to England years ago. Bankers and overseers were left to make decisions about properties in which they have a minimal investment. Many have become dishonest, skimming off the top, and underreporting earnings to their rich overlords. Being a white overseer has become unpleasant and dangerous. Blacks outnumber whites significantly, and that has created a power struggle. On St. Kitts, there have even been uprisings. Even the British Naval officers who are here to protect us are foxed more often than not." She sighed. "I cannot name a man with whom I would trust an innocent like Hannah."

Colin leaned his elbow on the armrest. His index finger wrinkled the skin at his temple as he glanced in Bradlee's direction.

Lady Clark's gaze drifted, once again, out the window. "The people of this beautiful land are not what they once were. It's no longer safe here for a young woman. Hannah desires to return to England and search for her family, but Mr. Clark and I live off the church and don't have the funds. Not to mention, she'd also need a companion."

Bradlee scratched his stubbled jaw. "How does she know she even has family in England?"

"She found a letter from her mother's brother tucked away in a book on their shelves. She's been trying to save money ever since, but there's more to consider than just the fare. Someone must champion her. It is unsafe for a woman to travel alone."

The solution wasn't simple. The vibrancy of Hannah's natural smile flashed in Bradlee's memory, haunting him. Lady Clark didn't mention who would care for her once she reached England. Where would she go?

He had connections. Perhaps his family or one of his professors would sponsor her. He would speak to them upon his return. Unfortunately, that begged for an answer to another question. How would he raise funds for his and Colin's return passage? In the past, whenever he'd overspent his allowance, he'd worked odd jobs for earnings. But what good was he with an injured leg?

"Why have you stayed?" Colin interrupted Bradlee's thoughts.

Lady Clark smiled. "Because God has called Mr. Clark and me to the Leeward Islands. The good Lord is calling Nevisians and St. Kittians to forsake the idol of sugar and return to Him. There is still much work to be done, but the hearts of the people are turning." She peered at Bradlee as if reaching deep into his soul. "God has a plan, and He has started putting the pieces into place. And if there is one thing I have learned, it's that the arm of the Father is never too short."

He certainly hoped so, for he needed God to work a miracle, not only to get him back to England, but to help him pass his exams and not pass out from fright.

CHAPTER 7

The roar of the lion echoes for miles. All stop and take note, from the lowly field rabbit to the mighty African warrior, for they tread within the big cat's domain.

~ Journaled the 12th of September, 1827

*H*annah stifled a yawn as she slipped quietly into her room. Her feather pillow and horsehair mattress beckoned, but she still had work to do. In the far corner of her room, she pried up the loose floorboard and removed the locked chest. Her earnings shined up at her like a ray of hope. She added her most recent coin and returned the box to its spot for safekeeping.

A knock sounded on the door.

Hannah pushed the loose floorboard into place and spun on her heel. "Come in."

Blandina entered, rolling the soaking tub.

She wanted to blurt out the events of the day to Blandina, and tell about the wonderful man she'd met, along with his witty companion. She wanted them to sit cross-legged on the floor, whispering so her uncle wouldn't hear them, like they used to do. But Blandina kept her gaze lowered, refusing to make eye contact. Hannah swallowed around the lump in her throat. Her heart broke for her friend. Didn't she miss their friendship? Didn't she feel lonely too?

Hannah followed Blandina to the kitchen and gripped the wooden handle of the bucket of water, lumbered back to her room, and poured the steaming liquid into the metal tub. Two more trips for the both of them brought the bath to the proper level for a nice soak. Blandina aided her with the buttons on her walking dress, but her silence screamed in Hannah's ears.

"I can bathe myself. Why don't you get some rest?" Her eyes dropped to the heavy load of her protruding stomach. "You must be weary."

Blandina nodded and slipped from the room.

Hannah undressed and collapsed into the lukewarm tub. It felt wonderful to wash the remainder of the itchy salt from her skin, and the warm water eased her aching muscles. She washed her hair with a sugar scrub and soaked in the tub until her eyes drifted closed.

Her mouth slid under the water.

Hannah awoke with a start and jerked upright. She dragged her weary limbs from the tub, and donned her chemise. Too weary to call for Blandina or bother with her dress's buttons, she crawled under the covers.

Through her bedroom window, the ocean breeze ruffled the branches of the palm trees, and the sun hung low in the sky at the evening angle of approximately five o'clock. If she shut her eyes until half-past, she'd still have enough time to help Blandina prepare supper and join Uncle Reuben at the appropriate time. She rolled to her side and allowed sleep to overtake her.

Images of men drowning, dark waves, sharks, and her parents' voices crying out for her to save them tormented her until warm brown eyes offered solace. She clung to his strong arms for comfort, but a voice called to her. She tried to block it out and hold onto the dream, but the voice became insistent and angry.

Her eyes sprung open.

Uncle Reuben stood over her. He held the oil lamp high over his head. His gaze raked down the length of her.

"Uncle? What are you doing here?" She pulled the covers to her chin. "It's improper for you to be in a lady's chamber."

His eyes narrowed. "Are you ill?"

She shook her head.

"You've slept through supper."

She struggled to sit up, but the covers remained tucked under the mattress and wouldn't move with her. She lay trapped by her uncle's presence. "I'm sorry. I merely meant to rest my eyes. It was a trying day at school."

"Then you should stay home."

Hannah sucked in a breath. "I'm fine, truly. I hadn't slept well, so the smallest things became a trial. Tomorrow I'll be back to normal."

He lingered, shifting his weight. "I'm going out for the night."

"Did the letter come?" She yanked the covers out and sat up. "Did you get another property to oversee? Is that how you have the funds for a night on the town?"

"It's none of your business." He barked the words through clenched teeth.

She shrank back.

His gaze lowered.

She swallowed. Her uncle's temper flared over the slightest remark. She missed the days when they rode in the wagon, talking about how the plants grew and what lay beneath the ocean.

Those days were long gone.

He strolled from the room and slammed the door behind him.

⌒

*T*he following morning, Uncle Reuben didn't appear for breakfast. After their odd exchange the previous night, Hannah felt relieved.

Blandina appeared almost her old self this morning, except for her bulging stomach. She mustered a weak smile when Hannah strolled into the kitchen.

Hannah pulled the ingredients to make Mr. Granville another poultice while Blandina washed the dishes. She shook the water from her fingers before excusing herself to collect eggs from the hen house.

Hannah scraped the concoction into her tin and returned to her room. She opened a trunk that held clothes she'd outgrown but were too worn to sell as scrap. A calico print caught her eye, and she tore off a fabric section. She held it up for inspection before tucking the material, cotton batting, and medicinal tin into her satchel. Satisfied, she burst out the door into the warm sunlight. It would be a hot day, for the morning sun already shone strong. Sweat beads formed on her forehead as she scanned the sea-grape hedge along the road for the perfect branch to configure into a crutch.

Halfway to the Clark's home, a branch that ended in a Y caught her eye. Hannah hung her bag on a bush and climbed onto the low tree limb. Twigs poked her skin as she held the branches above her, pushing and bouncing on the lower branch until a resounding snap split the air. She continued to weaken its hold until it broke off completely. Sea-grapes rained down on her head as she dangled in the air a few inches above the ground.

Hannah let go, landing softly on the sandy soil. She tested the branch on herself, sticking the Y end under her arm and hobbling a few steps. Its length was too high for her, but since Bradlee was almost a head taller, the height should do well for him. Her chest fluttered like hummingbird wings as she raced up the Clarks' steps a few minutes later. Would Bradlee appreciate her contraption to aid his walking? Would he be pleased to see her?

Hattie opened the door, and Hannah thanked her for yesterday's gift of banana bread. After missing supper last night, she had devoured several slices of the delicious bread and grabbed a couple more to break her fast this morning. She'd left the remaining slice for Blandina. "Is Mr. Granville available? I've brought him another poultice." She bit her lip and raised the stick. "And this to aid his walking."

Hattie's belly shook with her laugh. "Mr. Granville and Mr. Fitzroy, dey be out on da back porch. Lady Clark is still readying fer the day, and Mr. Clark is in his study preparin' his Sunday sermon."

"Please inform Lady Clark of my arrival. I can show myself the way." Hannah strolled down the hallway through the back parlor. She paused at the entrance to the back porch.

"I'm sorry." Colin's voice carried through the open door. "Did the middle of my sentence interrupt the start of yours?"

Both men sat in rocking chairs facing outward with their feet propped up on the railing. They stared out at the ocean, its watery blues blending into the pale sky through a break in the overarching tree canopy. Monkeys and birds chattered among the branches.

"Such impertinence." Bradlee raked a hand through his wavy hair. "I'm merely saying, there must be something we can do."

"Good morning."

Both men jerked around to face her.

Colin jumped to his feet while Bradlee struggled to rise.

"I come bearing gifts." She held up the stick. The leaves she hadn't plucked from the ends shook.

"A tree branch?" Colin's lips twisted. "How thoughtful."

Bradlee gripped the railing to aid him around the edge of the rocking chair. "It's a wonderful gift. Obviously, Miss Barrington understands my pleasure in local flora samples." He frowned at Colin. "By Jove, have some tact."

"Tact is for gents who aren't witty enough to use sarcasm." Colin leaned against the rail and crossed his arms. He bowed in welcome to Hannah, and his eyes glinted with mischief.

Bradlee's warm gaze met hers and remained there. "I'm pleased you've joined us this morning."

Her heart turned over in response.

He motioned with his hand at Colin. "Pull up a chair for Miss Barrington."

Colin dragged over another chair.

"Please, be seated." Bradlee gestured to the middle seat.

She propped the branch against the rail and sat. The men followed suit, treating her as if she were a gently-raised Englishwoman.

"How fares your leg this morning?" She settled her skirt about her as she'd often seen her mama do, wishing her gown wasn't so frumpy.

"Right well, thanks to your tendings. It still hurts to put weight on it, but the swelling is much improved."

"Which is why I brought you the tree branch and some more poultice."

"You are a dear." Bradlee flashed a devasting smile.

"I'm a woman of my word." And she'd thought of little else.

"Indeed." He studied her face with an unnerving intensity.

She reached for the branch, and her hand shook. "It doesn't look like much now, but we can trim the branches." She marked a pretend line with her hand. "And—wait." She snapped off the remaining branches with leaves. "Hold this." She passed the stick to Colin and opened her satchel. "We'll wrap the cotton batting around it like this with the cloth." She rose and tucked the stick under her arm. "Then you'll be able to move about like this." She limped a few steps, leaning on the crutch.

"Ingenious." Bradlee tapped his thumb and pinky back and forth on his thigh, creating a drum beat.

"Brilliant." Colin snorted. "She's reinvented the crutch."

Bradlee speared his companion with a steely look. "This one is innovative. She's added padding to see to my comfort." He gazed at her, and the corners of his eyes crinkled. "Frankly, I find it delightful. Ignore Colin. Mornings make him cranky."

"You're not a morning person?" She turned his direction.

"I am a morning person." Colin's expression remained solemn. "I merely choose to sleep through them whenever possible."

Hannah covered her mouth to hide her smile.

Bradlee rose and stepped between her and Colin. He stood so close that her head tilted back to peer up at him. She inhaled his unique scent, which reminded her of minerals fresh from a spring, with a hint of citrus.

"Let me give it a try."

His fingers brushed hers, and she relinquished the crutch.

He tucked it under his arm on his bad leg side and leaned his weight upon it. He wielded a couple of trial steps and nodded. "It works."

"It should be trimmed with a saw." She gestured over the railing. "I believe Mr. Clark has one in the shed."

He limped around the porch area before resuming his seat and passing the crutch to Colin. "See to cutting off an inch or so for me."

Colin took the makeshift crutch and leaned it against the rail.

Bradlee glared at him.

"Oh, you mean right this moment?" He stood and, in a wry voice, said, "Well then, let me be off." He grasped the stick and carried it down the steps.

They were alone—without a chaperone. Such things were not done. Perhaps he didn't see her as a proper lady. Her heart twisted, and the ache spread through her chest. Hannah scooted to the edge of her seat and eyed the door. She should excuse herself to find Lady Clark.

"I'm a morning person."

Her attention snapped back to him.

The breeze rustled his hair. He peered at the distant ocean through the break in the thick canopy of trees. "I enjoy the sweet morning air, the dew glinting with the haze of colors from the first sun rays. The birds' chirping seems louder, more cheerful. Everything is peaceful. It makes me want to shout."

A bubble of laughter erupted, but she quickly stifled it. "Shout to disrupt the peace? Like a rooster?"

"No." He shook his head. "I mean, yes." He pivoted in his seat to face her. "I merely feel exhilarated in the morning. It's the thrill of the moment. I want the world to know I'm alive."

She envisioned him jumping out of bed, throwing up the sash, and yelling to any passersby, *Good morning, old chap. Lovely day, fair lady.* "I can picture it."

"Indeed. I want to roar as the lions do on the plains."

The image in her mind switched to the old chap and the fair lady fleeing from a madman roaring out his window like a wild beast. She clamped her mouth shut, but her laughter escaped in a snort.

"You don't hold the desire to roar like a lion?"

"I've never heard a lion's roar."

"It's magnificent." He stared toward the ocean. "You can hear a lion's roar from five miles away."

"My goodness."

"I've written quite a bit about lions in my journals."

"I'd like to read them."

"Yes, but first." He pulled her to a stand. His other hand held the railing.

Her nervous laughter flittered through the air.

His eyes danced with mischief. He encouraged her to lean against the railing. "Are you ready?"

She scrunched her face. "For what?"

"To roar." He beamed a wicked smile at her. "You cup your hands over your mouth like so."

"No really, I couldn't." She tried to step back, but he caught her elbow and pulled her to his side.

"It's simple, and it feels delightful. You must try it. I'll go first." He leaned over the railing, cupped his hands around his mouth, and bellowed toward the ocean in a loud, ragged note that extended on for several seconds.

From the canopy, the monkeys' and birds' chatter ceased.

He turned with a smile. "Your turn."

Her grip tightened on the rail. She peeked over her shoulder. "Do I have to cup my mouth?"

"Only if you want to."

She swallowed and concentrated on the ocean's distant thunder. "All right. Here I go." She inhaled a deep breath and roared toward the horizon until her lungs had no breath left in them.

Below, Colin poked his head out of the shed with the saw in hand and peered up at them as if they'd taken leave of their senses.

Laughing, Hannah scooted back under the protection of the porch and fell into the chair.

Bradlee did the same. "See, didn't I tell you it would feel good?"

She wiped a tear from the corner of her eye. "Indeed, you did."

"Is everyone all right?" Lady Clark burst into the doorway.

Hannah sobered and jumped from her chair. She shouldn't be alone with a man, especially a handsome one like Mr. Granville. Lady Clark would never approve.

"What was that racket?" Lady Clark's gaze bounced between them. "And what happened to Mr. Fitzroy?"

Bradlee stood. "Colin has gone to trim the crutch Miss Barrington made for me, and I was merely teaching Miss Barrington about the lions of Africa."

"I must ask for a warning, next time. You scared the life out of me." Lady Clark raised a hand to her breast. "My heart cannot bear it."

Hannah straightened her shoulders and fashioned her hands in the same manner as Lady Clark to appear more cultured.

Bradlee bowed. "I beg your pardon. Next time, we shall give you fair warning."

"Good." She turned. "Come along now. It is almost time to leave for school."

Bradlee raised his arm, offering for Hannah to take hold.

She dropped her gaze to his bad ankle and raised her elbow for him to grasp instead, wearing what she hoped was a playful smile.

He threw back his head and laughed. "This goes against every gentlemen's code of ethics instilled within me back in England." Nevertheless, he accepted her arm.

Hannah issued him a sideways glance. "You, sir, are not in England. Nevisians are different. Although we acknowledge propriety, islanders are not sticklers in its adherence."

The white of his smile flashed in her periphery, and his warm gaze fluttered her heart.

His voice melted over her like molasses. "I do believe I like different."

CHAPTER 8

My companion complains he needs funds to attend
university, to attend university to become a physician,
and to become a physician to obtain funds. I find myself
wondering who the mastermind is behind this system?
~ *Journaled the 18th of October, 1828*

*B*radlee sat in a Nevis single-room schoolhouse
reviewing vocabulary and wondering why in blazes
he was there. Indeed, he needed to better understand the
culture. He'd grown bored sitting in one spot listening to Colin
snore the day away. The more experience he had with teaching,
the better perhaps he could see himself as a professor in the
future, as his father so desired. However, he suspected his
appearance might have to do with the captivating sun-kissed
beauty before him. She paced the room, aiding the children with
their reading. Occasionally, her gaze drifted his way.

School had never been his forte, but he'd lumbered up the
path early this morning out of curiosity. Hannah hadn't come
by the Clark's bungalow in a couple days and, the fact was, he
missed her presence.

84

"Good reading, Alice." Hannah smiled at the pupil.

Under the desk, Bradlee bounced his good leg. The young mulatto boy to his right stared out the window, much like Bradlee used to do as a child while his tutor droned on. Outside, the sun shone brightly and the waves gently crashed in the background. A bright-colored bird landed on a branch. It tipped its head and used its beak to help pull its way up to another limb. If only he'd thought to bring his journal. He would document the creature for Professor Gillis.

"Mr. Granville? Is there something the class should see outside?" Lady Clark asked.

All eyes were upon him, including those of the young lad who'd also been staring out the window. Even Hannah's crystal gaze regarded him, although she appeared inquisitive instead of reproving.

"I've never seen such a fascinating bird."

The class snickered.

What compelled him to endure this punishment? Hadn't he suffered enough ridicule from his professors at Oxford?

Lady Clark smiled. "Indeed. Parrots are not native to England. Perhaps you'd like to share with the class some of the differences between their motherland and their homeland?"

Get up in front of the class? Not likely. One more reason why he loathed the idea of becoming a professor. He broke out in a sweat thinking about a room full of expectant eyes peering at him, waiting, evaluating, sneering. He couldn't bear to face a panel of five professors without feeling faint, even when his graduation depended upon it. "Another time, once I've seen more of what Nevis has to offer."

"Later in the week then." Lady Clark turned to Hannah. "Miss Barrington, why don't you begin the math lesson?"

Hannah strode to the front with her head high and not a hint of nervousness. "Let's all stand."

She was the bravest woman he'd ever met.

"Only if you are able." She glanced his way.

He rose to stand on one foot, using the back of the chair to balance.

With all eyes upon her, she smiled at the class "Very good. Let's begin with our ones tables."

The room filled with sound as the children slapped their legs, clapped their hands, and snapped their fingers while repeating their tables. The distracted boy next to him joined in with a smile.

Hannah waved for Bradlee to participate. Slap, clap, snap. His rhythm was delayed and rather awkward until he could do the motions without thinking about them. The tables he'd learned from his tutors took on a whole new perspective. It felt great to move, to use his body and his mind. How much easier would it have been to learn like this?

After finishing the twelves tables, Hannah moved on to real-life multiplication examples by grouping the children into active math problems. "Now say each person in this group holds five mangoes." She pushed a group of four children together. "How many mangoes do they have in total?"

A young girl in braids lifted onto her toes as she raised her hand and wiggled her fingers.

"Yes, Lydia."

She dropped her hand and raised her chin. "Twenty mangoes."

"Correct. Good work."

Bradlee enjoyed watching the interactive lessons almost as much as he enjoyed watching Hannah direct the class. Her face shone as she praised the kids or encouraged them to think about a problem in a new way. As the class and Lady Clark stepped out for recess, she slid onto the bench seat next to him. The scent of vanilla sugar wafted around him.

"Did you learn anything today you didn't learn at university?" Her lips twisted into a teasing smile.

He shifted to face her and draped his arm over the back of the bench. "I learned you are a remarkable teacher. If only I'd been so lucky as to have you as a governess. I might have enjoyed school."

"You didn't like your classes?"

Bradlee struggled to find the right words. "I prefer learning in real-life situations. Fortunately, my instructor, Professor Gillis, saw my struggles and still believed I had potential. He invited me to do a year abroad in Africa. The adventure opened up a whole new world. It was difficult to return the following year to the classroom to complete my studies." He scratched his arm. *Almost complete.* "Who would have thought British history, Shakespearian literature, and mathematics would all be easier to learn under an open sky instead of in the confines of a musty, dimly-lit classroom?"

Hannah said, "I couldn't help but notice you tapping your fingers and squirming in your seat. Do you struggle with sitting and listening when you're in a lecture?"

He chuckled. "It's that obvious?"

She nodded. "I teach restless little boys in a land where the weather is always warm and beautiful. It's a constant distraction." Her eyes widened. "Not that you're a boy. You're obviously a man." A light blush stained her cheeks discernably beneath her tan. "I mean—"

"It's all right. I've struggled with what the Eton headmaster called, 'ants in my breeches.'"

She drew back wide-eyed. "How horrid."

He pinched his lips to hold back his laughter until it came out in a snort. "You misunderstand." He shook his head and wiped a tear from his eye. "I never actually had ants in my breeches. I merely wiggled as if I did."

"Wiggled? I would run screaming from the room. Ant bites are painful."

His shoulders shook as laughter rolled out of his mouth. The way she eyed him, questioning whether he'd completely gone mad, only made it worse. "Perhaps the analogy only works in England. Up there, the ants are rather harmless."

"Here, they're beastly little creatures." She folded her arms. "I may have some tricks to help you calm your ants."

"Would you now?" He raised his brows. "Doesn't it involve snapping and clapping? Because my professors may frown upon the disruption."

"Snapping and clapping work when everyone is doing it."

"I witnessed that today."

"There are other means I use to keep boys with ants busy."

"Such as…?"

"I have them doodle on their slate while they listen. I merely ask that they draw something we're discussing."

"Interesting."

She sat up straighter. "I have them twiddle their thumbs and fingers."

Bradlee laced his fingers and circled his thumbs. "Like this, you mean?"

"Yes, but now try to do it with different fingers. It takes more concentration. I find circling the ring fingers the most challenging."

He tried. Challenging, indeed.

"I'll also have them take frequent breaks to stretch or have them chew or suck on something. Sugar cane works well. They enjoy the sweetness, and the reed is crunchy and tough to chew. I'll bring you some to try. Do not swallow the reed. Only suck out the juice." She paused, and her clear blue eyes studied him under those dark, sultry lashes. She sighed and shook her head. "What a pea goose I am. If you're on your grand tour, then you are finished with university. You don't need to sit through lectures anymore."

Bradlee stared down at the worn wooden space on the bench between them. The all-too-familiar sinking feeling weighed his shoulders, and the top of his ears burned. He rubbed his left ear. "I may have gone on my grand tour a bit prematurely."

Only Colin knew his shame. Why would he confess his sins to this slip of a woman?

She didn't say anything, merely waited with those bright eyes searching his. The sounds of children's laughter floated in through the open windows.

"I left before taking the public examination." He swallowed. "My parents don't even know. My father knows I left for my grand tour, but most students don't travel until after they finish the great go. He would be livid if he found out."

Her brows drew together. "Why would you go through all those years and hard work to not finish?"

He peered out the window at the carefree children racing in the schoolyard. "I can't..." He sighed. "I can't do what you do." He met her gaze. "I can't speak in front of people."

"You're speaking to me now?"

"One-on-one and small intimate groups are fine, but something happens when I stand up in front of a larger group, like this classroom." He glanced at all the empty seats. "I start to sweat. My mouth goes dry, and my tongue gets thick. I can't control my shaking, in my hands, knees, and even my voice." His voice pitched higher. "Everyone is looking at me, and I fear I'm either going to cast up my accounts or faint like a woman in hysterics."

Her hand slid over the top of his.

Bradlee swallowed and inhaled a deep breath. Even thinking about speaking in front of a group sped his heart rate.

"What do you intend to do?"

"I don't know." He ran a hand down his face. "I made an excuse about a family issue that needed my attention to extend the retaking until the end of summer. I thought if I researched foreign lands and wrote a dissertation, they'd allow me to forgo the public exam, but I don't know now if it's possible."

"Why not?"

"You saw the pages of my journals. Very little of my notes are legible after my swim, and I was forced to leave one of my journals behind when we made our hasty escape from the Indian village." He exhaled a deep troubled breath. "If I don't return before the end of the extension, I will have to take the year over again. And if I do return without a dissertation or an ability to speak to the panel, I will be plucked."

She stared at him with clouded eyes.

"It means I'll fail."

Her blue eyes cleared.

"Either way, my father believes I've already graduated."

"You misled your family?" Her lips remained parted.

"Not exactly. They knew I planned on traveling. It's merely that most students don't go on their grand tour until after they pass their exams. I, however, needed this voyage in order to substitute my written findings for parts of the oral exam. He closed his eyes and exhaled. "If my father finds out I didn't graduate, he'll believe his second son is an irresponsible imbecile. I'll have confirmed what I've always seen in the depths of my father's eyes—that I'm a disappointment." He met her steady gaze. "I guess I was delaying the inevitable. Now, I'll be lucky to make it back for the exam at all."

"Maybe I can help."

"Do you have a ship that can sail me back to London?"

"Tsk, tsk. Sarcasm is only becoming on Mr. Fitzroy." A slow, crooked smile lifted one side of her mouth.

He grinned. "Don't start. I barely tolerate Colin as it is."

"I do not have a ship, but I can help you research the island." She perked up. "My parents had a book on speaking in public. From what I remember, it holds suggestions on how to deal with nervousness during a presentation."

He leaned back. "What I have is more than nerv—"

"Perhaps you could practice presenting here in the classroom to prepare you." She tapped a finger to her lips. "I might also be able to help you find employment to earn your fare back to England."

"Truly?" He couldn't hide the skepticism in his voice.

She lifted her chin and leaned forward with her hands on her knees. "I shall take it as a challenge. By the time you've earned enough money for your passage, you'll have enough information about the Leeward Islands to write a book." She nudged him with her elbow. "It will be fun. I, for one, am excited."

The class filed back in, and Hannah stood to assume her place by Lady Clark.

The rest of the afternoon passed quickly. From his seat on the wooden bench, he observed Hannah interact with the slave children of all ages. She laughed over a comment a small boy made, and Bradlee felt the sound pulse through his being. What was this connection that drew him to her? Even the tilt of her eyes intrigued him, especially the way she glanced up at the ceiling when contemplating a problem. Delicacy and strength coincided together in her slender frame. She was a host of contradictions, playful with the children yet composed with intelligence. She was unpolished and yet refined. She was honest and open, yet her eyes were shadowed with trouble.

She was the opposite of Miss Radcliff.

Not only had his father planned out Bradlee's profession. He'd also planned for his future wife. Alice Radcliff had been groomed as a child to marry into the family. Since his eldest brother, Samuel, was supposed to marry within the peerage, it meant the duty to marry Miss Radcliff, who was an advantageous match with substantial wealth but no title, fell to him, the second son.

He held the utmost respect for Miss Radcliff. She was an exemplary gentlewoman. She could hold a trite conversation for hours with princes or paupers, knew all the latest fashions, and was skilled at playing the pianoforte. Her pale blonde hair, pale skin, and exquisite manners cast her as the epitome of a proper lady. But compared to Hannah's freshness, she struck him as stale and dreadfully dull.

Hannah's hair slipped out of its bun, draping over her shoulders in long graceful waves. Without the aid of a mirror or concern for her appearance, she used her fingers as combs to pull her hair back, twisted it into a long inverse cyclone, and tied it into a topknot.

His heart pattered a quick two-step rhythm. He forced his eyes away with the sudden feeling that he was entangling himself in a dilemma. Documenting Nevis was his only hope, and if doing so meant he had to spend more time in Hannah Barrington's presence, so be it.

He never shied away from an adventure.

CHAPTER 9

I discovered a red ant upon my windowsill and allowed
my curiosity to get the best of me. The initial sting
burned as if I'd used my hand to snuff out a candle, but it
faded quickly. I did not foresee the persistent itch that
followed.

~ Journaled the 14th of April, 1829

"*L*et's see how you get about." Hannah handed Bradlee the
neatly padded crutch she'd finished for him. A cool
ocean breeze scented the air, and the only clouds in the
sky were the ones that perpetually hung around the peak of Mt.
Nevis this time of morning.

"Tally-ho." Bradlee crutched his way toward the Clarks'
wagon. He paused and tapped the end of the stick on the
ground. "It works splendidly. Time for us to start earning our
keep."

Colin aided both Bradlee and Hannah into the wagon before
climbing onto the wooden bench.

Hannah sat between the two men. "I believe it's best to
begin…" She hesitated. Her uncle's disapproving voice nagged

at her, but she'd promised Bradlee before her uncle made his ridiculous demands of not speaking to anyone. She understood his concern, but certainly Bradlee and Colin could provide for her safety. She raised her chin. "Let's begin in town."

Colin snapped the reins, and the wagon pulled onto the main road.

Bradlee stretched his legs and extended his arm around the seat's backrest. A wide grin flashed a set of even white teeth. "Ah, the great freedom of the outdoors—sun on your face, the trade winds in your hair." He leaned out of the wagon. "Look at the size of the fruit. What are those? Yellow oranges?"

Hannah giggled. "Those are grapefruit trees."

"Interesting." He noted it in his journal

She pointed at a narrow path leading up the mountain. "Nelson's spring lies up the hill. When you're able to walk better, I shall take you to the hot spring. It's supposed to have curative abilities." She glanced at his foot. "I do believe it's more for ailments than for sprains. If we could figure a way to carry you up the path, we could determine the hot springs' best use. You might be able to document the results. It could be an experiment."

His eyes twinkled. "I like the way you think."

She fanned herself with her hand, trying to pretend it was the warm sun heating her face and not the effects of his compliment. As they bumped along the washed-out dirt road, she answered Bradlee's questions regarding the island. He possessed an insatiable curiosity. *What does coconut taste like? Why does she think the land isn't producing as it had in the past? Have there been any slave rebellions? What does her uncle do to earn a living?*

He shifted on the seat to face her after the last question.

"He's an overseer." Hannah searched for a change of topic. "Over there is the Mountravers, owned by John Pinney. He returned to England and now lives in Bristol."

"Is that one of the plantations your uncle oversees?"

She dropped her gaze. "Not exactly."

"What does that mean?" He ducked his head to force her to look him in the eyes.

She stared at her folded hands. "He did at one time but was let go."

"What plantations does he manage?"

"Sherbrook Manor."

"And…"

She could feel his gaze boring into her. Her hand raised to her father's ring and fiddled with it under the neckline of her bodice. Why must her uncle be such an embarrassment? "That is the only plantation he oversees."

"Is it a large plantation?"

Her jaw clenched. "Must we discuss my uncle?"

He drew back at the sharpness of her tone.

"My apologies. I did not mean to pry."

"Oh yes, he did." Colin muttered under his breath.

Bradlee eyed her hand, still fingering her necklace. "What hangs around your neck?"

Her fingers stilled. "It's nothing."

"It must hold some significance. You toy with it whenever you're nervous."

"I do not." Did she?

The clip-clop of the horse's hooves upon the dirt road grew louder in her ears as Bradlee waited for her answer.

She dropped her hand back to her side. "It's my father's ring. I was upset they were leaving, so he gave it to me for safe-keeping and as a promise of their return. It was the night they died." She could still feel the warmth of her papa's hand as he curled her fingers around the ring.

The memory stood in stark contrast to the swollen and life-less hand strewn with seaweed she'd witnessed the next day poking out between the boots of the gathered crowd. Their hushed voices still echoed in her memory, along with the wailing sobs of her nurse as Hannah had pressed her face into the woman's skirt on the sandy beach that horrid morning. She could feel the clench of her stomach as the wind whipped the linen material and afforded her a glimpse of her father's naked form. The beachcombers had already stripped him of all his possessions down to his unmentionables. Hannah swallowed back the lump growing in her throat. "He'd told me to keep it close to my heart." She patted her chest where the circle of gold lay hidden. "And so, I have."

"I'm sorry." Bradlee cleared his throat. "I can't imagine..."

She picked at a ragged edge of her fingernail. "It was a long time ago."

"Still, an ache lingers."

Lots of children were orphaned. It didn't make her anything special. It had taught her at a young age to lean on God. "Psalm 146 says, 'The Lord protects the foreigners among us. He cares for the orphans and widows.' I believe God is looking out for me. I'm fortunate to have had a relative living on the island. God also brought Lady Clark to Nevis at the right time. She and Mr. Clark have become like family."

Bradlee searched the depths of her eyes. "Perhaps it was God's hand that brought me to Nevis?" His voice rumbled in a husky whisper.

She lowered her voice also, but she couldn't reason why. "God wouldn't have sunk a ship."

"No, but He has a way of using bad situations to turn them around for His purposes."

The intensity in Bradlee's tawny brown eyes awakened her like the smell of a cup of morning coffee. How easily her heart rode with the tide when it could be dashed upon the rocks and left as weathered as sea glass.

She tore away from his gaze and nudged him with her shoulder. "As I recall, it was you and Mr. Fitzroy who were in need of my rescuing. Perhaps, God's hand brought me to you?"

She didn't see his smile, but she felt it.

"Indeed," Bradlee said. "It wasn't St. Elmo's fire. It was St. Hannah's fire illuminating the darkness."

Colin shifted in his seat. "Who needs to study a bunch of dead poets and philosophers when we have the great romanticist, Mr. Bradlee Miles Granville."

Hannah perked up. "Miles, is it? Very fitting for such a well-traveled man."

Bradlee snorted. "I hadn't thought of that connection. Miles is a family name. My great grandfather's name was Miles." He flashed her a challenging grin. "What is your full name?"

"Hannah Rose Barrington."

"Rose." He rubbed his chin. "Also fitting. A lovely flower."

She shrugged. "I don't recall having seen one, only sketches drawn in books. They don't grow on the island."

"In England, you'll see them in all sorts of gardens and sold in the market."

"I plan to see them firsthand someday."

Bradlee draped his arm over the wooden backrest, and his hand rested so close it almost grazed her shoulder. "You think you'll return to the homeland?"

Her fingers fiddled with her father's ring. "I wasn't born on Nevis, but I was raised here, and I'm blessed to live on a beautiful island, but I've always felt like an outsider. Deep down, I know I don't belong. I long to return to my people—my family. I merely have to locate them."

"If it's God's will, then I'm certain you'll find them."

Hannah smoothed her worn skirt. Was it God's will? Did He have greater plans for her life than merely being an orphaned island girl? She could still hear her mother's voice, even though her face had grown hazy in her memory. *Remember who loves you, whose child you are.* Hannah used to square her shoulders and reply, *I'm Hannah Rose Barrington, child of God.*

Back then, the words fell easily from her lips. Her parents

loved and doted on her, but after their deaths, her identity changed to orphan, Huxley's unfortunate niece, or white beggar. She craved the confidence she once had as a child, so certain of belonging, of her value.

Hannah stared at the threadbare fabric of her gown until it blurred. She quickly blinked back the haze of tears.

Bradlee's knuckle stroked her shoulder. It was barely a touch, but it woke her from such dark thoughts. She felt his gaze upon her, warming her like the morning sun.

"I'm terribly sorry. I shouldn't have pried. It was not my intention to upset you."

She exhaled. "I'm saving money to return."

Bradlee's brows lifted. "How so?"

"I'm selling my poultices at the general store. Not much has sold yet, but it will."

His eyes danced. "I like your confidence, and I can attest to their benefits. I will make certain to spread the word. Soon enough, it will be all the rage."

Warmth spread through her midsection. His compliment stirred the urge to roar like a lion as they'd done the other day, but she subdued it into a smile.

It wasn't long before Colin turned the wagon onto the main street. Shops lined both sides. Colorful shutters swung wide, and shopkeepers stood amongst their wares calling out to passersby. Hannah kept her head down as they walked the streets and quickly popped into stores. She introduced Mr. Granville and Mr. Fitzroy to Mr. Maroon at the general store. He had no work for them but passed Hannah a half penny for a cut of a sale.

Next they visited the postman, the butcher, and several shopkeepers. All of them shook their heads, especially after spying Bradlee's injured leg.

Hannah hid her disappointment, but Bradlee impressed her with his gregariousness. He spoke to every person as an equal and inquired not only about open positions but also how their business fared, what drew them into the industry, and how their ancestors settled on Nevis. He listened intently to their stories and even wrote notes in his journal, which made each stop take longer than expected. More often than not, they parted bearing gifts or samples of the shop owner's wares. Colin's arms soon became overloaded with goods.

When he could carry no more, Colin said he'd meet them at the pier and lumbered back to the gig. Hannah pushed open the door to the dressmaker's shop. Seashells chimed above the door as she and Bradlee entered the small, stifling room filled with colorful fabrics. Mrs. O'Dell emerged from the workroom and peered at them above her wire-rimmed spectacles. Perspiration dampened the dark hair at her temples.

"Good day to you, Miss Barrington, and you, good sir."

"Mr. Granville, may I present Mrs. O'Dell. She is Nevis's highly skilled dressmaker, par to none."

Mrs. O'Dell's cheeks colored a deeper pink. "Miss Barrington, you are too kind."

"Mr. Granville is looking for temporary employment to pay for their passage back to the motherland. I thought perhaps you might need help inventorying or lifting the heavy bolts of material."

Bradlee bowed. "Indeed. My companion, who stepped out for a moment, and I are seeking to help in any way possible. We are both familiar with London's fashions."

Mrs. O'Dell's gaze flittered over Bradlee's form. "Indeed, your shirt is well made and of the finest quality. The thread count alone speaks for itself. May I?" She lifted a hand to feel the sleeve of his coat.

"Most certainly." He nodded.

Her hand slid over his forearm and squeezed. "I see." She glanced Hannah's way. "A strapping young man."

Bradlee cleared his throat and tugged on the bottom of his

sleeve. "We're not afraid of hard work. My father always said, 'the industrious shall never go hungry.'"

"Why are you looking to return to England? Does a young miss await you in London?"

Bradlee smiled and shifted his weight. "Nothing of the sort."

Mrs. O'Dell waggled her brows at Hannah.

Hannah inwardly groaned at the dressmaker-turned-matchmaker. "Do you have any employment?"

"I'm afraid not at the moment." She leaned in and whispered so only the two of them could hear. "I'm struggling to keep the staff I currently have. Sales have decreased. We aren't getting the foot traffic we once had. Planters and their wives have returned to London and their visits to the island are fewer and farther between."

Hannah sighed. "If you hear of anyone looking for workers, please keep us in mind. Mr. Granville and Mr. Fitzroy shall be staying with Reverend and Lady Clark."

"Oh, I will." She eyed Bradlee, and her eye twitched. *Merciful heavens.* Was that a wink? Bradlee would believe islanders to be most improper.

"You do well to have Miss Barrington as an acquaintance," Mrs. O'Dell said. "She is very resourceful. In fact, I don't know what I would have done without her saving the day."

Bradlee nodded, and his warm auburn eyes slid to Hannah. "Indeed, she's exceedingly good at coming to the rescue."

"We were in a complete fix." Mrs. O'Dell gestured toward the workroom. "My loom stopped working, and no matter what I did, I couldn't get it operating again."

Mrs. O'Dell raved about how Hannah had fixed it. She made it sound as if Hannah had saved them from utter ruin when, in reality, she'd only traced the problem back to its source and untangled the yarn preventing the wheel from spinning.

"In fact..." Mrs. O'Dell drew in the extra material of Hannah's gown and held it. The material tightened around her curves. "Maybe now you'll accept my offer to alter your gown. With a few darts, it would be much more flattering. Don't you think so, Mr. Granville?"

She stepped aside with a firm grip on the folds and pushed Hannah forward.

Hannah gasped. Her mortification knew no bounds as Mrs. O'Dell held her for Bradlee to inspect like a young sow at market.

Bradlee averted his eyes.

Hannah's jaw tensed, and she tried to bat the woman's hand away.

When his gaze returned hers, his eyes had darkened into thick molasses. He rubbed the back of his ear and shifted his weight.

The door opened behind them, tinkling the chimes. In walked Mrs. Marchmain, a sugar baron's wife and a plantation owner from New Castle. The peacock feathers in the woman's hat danced alongside the tiny bells and contrasted with the woman's dour expression. Her frown deepened as her gaze bounced between Hannah, Mrs. O'Dell, and Bradlee.

Mrs. O'Dell quickly dropped her hands, and Hannah backed out of Mrs. Marchmain's way.

"Mrs. O'Dell, such cavorting is simply not done in a proper establishment." Mrs. Marchmain's lips pursed.

Mrs. O'Dell curtsied and offered Mrs. Marchmain a seat and some tea. "I was merely showing Miss Barrington how I can alter her gown." She folded her hands. "I'm certain you've had the pleasure of meeting Miss Barrington, but may I introduce you to a new visitor to the island, Mr. Granville?"

Mrs. Marchmain fluffed her skirts and lowered into a chair by the window. She tilted her head to inspect Bradlee. "Granville? Are you related to the Earl of Cardon?"

"Indeed." Bradlee nodded. "He is my father."

Mrs. O'Dell excused herself to retrieve fabrics from the workroom.

Hannah stiffened. Why did that surprise her? Of course, his family was part of the peerage. It would explain his manners, why he had a companion and had traveled on a grand tour, which the average gentleman could never afford. Her gaze dropped to her worn slippers and drab gown. It was the way he regarded her as if she were a part of his world that had muddled her thinking. As if they'd been childhood friends, and that friendship transcended borders and social status.

If only her parents were still alive. Her father had been titled, only as a baron, but it was a title. At least there would have been a small possibility that she and Bradlee might have run in the same circles.

"My niece attended a ball at Willowstone Manor," Mrs. Marchmain said. "Perhaps, you were introduced? Her name is Miss Lucile Edwards?"

"Hmm." Bradlee rolled his lips. "I'm afraid the name isn't familiar. However, I've been away at Oxford for the last four years."

"Oxford, how lovely." Mrs. Marchmain's gloved hand patted the chair next to her. "Please, do have a seat. I'd like to hear more."

He glanced back at Hannah. "I beg your apologies, but Miss Barrington and I are meeting someone."

Mrs. Marchmain ignored Hannah's presence. "My husband and I shall call upon you to finish our conversation. It's lovely to have members of the *ton* visit our island. I'd love to hear news from London and introduce you to our daughter. She'll be having her coming out this season. We return to England after the harvest." She crossed her wrists over her lap. "Where are you staying?"

"Lady and Mr. Clark have kindly opened their home."

She blinked. "You're not staying at the Artesian Hotel?"

"No, but I've heard splendid things about their healing springs."

"Rightly so. There is nothing like them in the world."

"Miss Barrington has graciously offered to show me the island and some of its springs."

Mrs. Marchmain's nostrils flared, and her gaze appraised the length of Hannah, right down to her ragged slippers. "Indeed."

Much could be read into the way Mrs. Marchmain spoke that single word. *How could this pathetic, improper, unladylike mess give a tour to a gentleman of the peerage? She's not even chaperoned.*

Heat flooded Hannah's face, and her feet propelled themselves out the door as if of their own will. "Good day to you, Mrs. O'Dell." She rambled before the door closed. "Mrs. Marchmain," she murmured after.

CHAPTER 10

I hide from the sun's wicked rays that burn the skin red
in under an hour's time, but when I see it burnish her
hair in gold like the touch of King Midas, I find myself
singing the sun's praises.
~ *Journaled the 16th of April, 1829*

*H*annah heard the door's hinges swing open again,
and Bradlee hobbled to catch up with her fast pace.
He threaded his arm through hers and yanked her to a stop.
"Blast. What is the matter?"

"It's nothing. I merely felt we needed to be on our way."

Bradlee winced as he put weight on his bad foot.

"Pardon my thoughtlessness. I completely forgot about your
ankle." Hannah steadied his uninjured side while he readjusted
his crutch.

"I despise being lame."

"Your ankle will heal with time."

His normally warm eyes hit her with a cold, hard stare.
"When?" He stopped to massage under his arm.

"Do you need to rest? We've been going all day."

He blew a rush of air past his lips and closed his eyes. "No. It's..." He balanced on his good leg and raked his hand through his wavy hair. "I'm merely discouraged. If I don't gain employment, then I won't get back in time for the exam and my family will know I'm a disgrace."

"Let's have a rest." She gently tugged on his sleeve. "I know just the spot."

They rounded the street corner, and Hannah stopped. She pointed ahead, and Bradlee followed her gaze to a banyan tree, with its low thick branches and long finger-like roots extending into the ground. It not only offered shade, but also some privacy in case anyone passed with whom her uncle may consort.

His lips parted, and his eyes widened with wonder. "What kind of tree is this?"

"It's a banyan tree, similar to your fig tree."

He limped with his crutch for a closer examination and touched the bark. "Look at these branches. It's magnificent." He dug through his satchel and pulled out his journal. "I need to document this."

She laughed and shook her head. She should have known he'd want to chronicle everything.

"Look at that canopy. Are those different leaves?"

Tilting her head back, she saw the tree through his eyes. "That's the original tree."

"Original?"

"Its seeds land on a host tree and sprout." Her fingers wrapped around one of the tree's prop roots. "It sends roots into the ground and eventually takes over the host tree."

He pulled out two journals and handed one to her. "Here I brought this along in case you wanted to read about my visit to Africa. Flip to the middle where it's still legible. It will give you something to do while I sketch."

"How splendid." She rested against the tree's thick trunk and opened the book halfway.

September 5, 1826. An azure sky stretches for miles, only inter-rupted by the distant haze of purple mountains...

September 8, 1826. We wouldn't survive without the thorough knowledge of our guide, a scantily clad African man. He walks thirty miles without growing tired, and his keen eyes can follow the tracks of an animal who traveled over fifty miles.

Hannah gripped the prop root for leverage and scooted up onto the low branch as a seat. She crossed her ankles and flipped the page.

September 9, 1826. The reverberation of the lion's roar woke us from a deep sleep. Our guide appeared nonplussed. He merely added another log to the fire and lay back down to sleep. Despite my weari-ness, I spent the rest of the night counting stars. Fortunately, there were more than plenty to count. I can imagine this was the sight Abraham must have beheld when God told him his descendants would be as numerous as the stars.

∽

*B*radlee sat upon the mix of grass, packed dirt, and sand and rested his open journal on his lap. He roughly sketched the outline of the tree and jotted down a few notes. Before long, his interest in the tree strayed to the woman perched upon its trunk. Her hair had fallen from its usual topknot and flowed over one of her eyes and past her shoulders. Her slender fingers raked through the golden-brown strands and tucked a few behind her ear. She occasionally sucked on her bottom lip. Perhaps it was her habit. His pencil traced the line of her jaw, the pouty fullness of her lips, and the fringes of her dark eyelashes.

He shaded in the folds of her sturdy cotton dress and pressed a tad too hard on the utensil. Blast her uncle for dressing her in such rags. If Bradlee had any coin, he'd march back into the dressmaker's shop, demand her measurements to be taken and a new gown started immediately.

However, he didn't have coin, nor would it be proper for a gentleman to buy a dress for someone who wasn't his wife. And although he admired Hannah's generous spirit, courage, and industriousness, marrying an islander was out of the question. His father would never approve. He'd determined the second Bradlee had breathed his first breath that this second son would marry their neighbor and close friend's daughter, Miss Alice Radcliff.

Did Bradlee have no say in his own life—in his own dreams?

The point of his pencil broke.

Thankfully, he'd already finished sketching her covered feet. He felt a twinge of disappointment when she'd arrived wearing slippers, but it was for the best. He fought the occasional glimpse of her tanned toes and ankles. A gentleman didn't stare at a woman's bare feet. She was a lady, born of good British stock. He must conduct himself in a proper manner.

She licked the tip of her finger and flipped the page.

Hannah deserved better than what her uncle provided. What could he do to aid her situation? He sighed. The only means for a woman to improve her surroundings was to marry well, yet the advantageous matches on an island were limited, and Lady Clark didn't seem pleased with the prospects.

There must be something Bradlee could do. Someone who'd appreciate Hannah's impressive qualities.

Colin.

Bradlee swallowed. A tide of emotions warred against the idea, but in his mind, it made perfect sense. Colin was a gentleman bachelor, studying to be a physician. Hannah showed promising talent with poultices and desired to return to England. They were of a similar age. Colin didn't hold the same restraints, being from the upper middle class, as Bradlee's family held as members of the peerage. And Hannah seemed amused by Colin's odd sense of humor.

A dull ache formed in his chest, but his mind was set. He'd do everything in his power to play matchmaker between Hannah and Colin. Bradlee ignored the constricting of his ribs and inhaled to expand his lungs.

Hannah glanced up. "You must turn your journals into a book." The excitement in her liquid-blue eyes squeezed the band around his torso tighter.

"Your verbiage is incredible... and your use of description. I feel like I'm there alongside you. Not to mention, you have an eye for details. I can see the antelope's twisted horns and the patterns of the zebra's fur."

His stomach somersaulted at her compliment, and he craved more. Her proficient use of the English language certainly separated her from a common islander. He flicked his journal closed with the end of his pencil and rubbed his chest to ease the tension. "It doesn't even begin to describe the beauty of those creatures." Leaning heavily on his crutch, he rose and limped to Hannah's side.

"You are a masterful writer." She studied his journal. "Nevis must seem boring in comparison."

He leaned the crutch against the banyan tree and peeked over her shoulder to see which page she was reading. The sweet scent of vanilla permeated the air around him.

Did Colin like the scent of vanilla? Bradlee must ask him later.

Her bare shoulder peeked out above the capped sleeve of her frumpy dress. His voice grew hoarse. "There is plenty of beauty here to hold my attention."

"But the wilds of the savanna..." She glanced his way. Her seated position on the tree trunk brought them eye to eye.

Her bright expression renewed his vigor. He stared at her pert nose and parted lips. Colin would appreciate such beauty.

She held completely still, but her eyes questioned him.

He cleared his throat and looked away.

"We should continue our walk. Colin is probably now waiting for us."

Hannah laid his journal upon the branch and whipped her hair back into its tight knot.

He forced himself to recall his new objective as his hands slid around Hannah's narrow waist, and he lowered her to the ground.

She retrieved his journal and handed it to him. "I meant what I said about writing a book."

He mentally shook himself to clear his thoughts.

"My parents had many memoirs in their collections," she said. "Your writing is as good, if not better."

He ran his thumb under his jaw, where stubble already grew, even though Colin had shaved him this morning with Mr. Clark's razor. "What are some books you've read?"

"The *Bible* of course. *The Federalist Essays*. It's author, Alexander Hamilton, was born on Nevis, so I'm assuming that is the reason it ended up on our bookshelf. I've also read Thomas Paine's *Common Sense*. However, my favorite was *Pride and Prejudice* by a woman named Jane Austin."

"Ah, my mother reads her works. She, too, enjoys them."

She frowned at him. "You've yet to tell me much about your family."

"You haven't asked."

"I've been remiss."

He strolled in the direction of the pier. "There's not much to tell. I have a brother, Samuel, who is two years my senior. He's the reason for the proud gleam in my father's eye. Samuel is your typical first-born son—poised and responsible, a masterful student. I love my brother, but it's hard to live up to the comparison. I'll always be the disappointment."

"I don't see how you could be considered a disappointment.

Look at your writings. How could they not rave about your talent?"

"My father has never read them."

"Whyever not?"

"He can't be bothered. He's busy training Samuel up to be the rightful heir. I don't mind much, for when his attention is on me, it's to remind me of how I need to focus harder on my studies to become a professor at Oxford. Those are the times I want to go back to being forgotten."

She gently touched his arm, and they both stopped. "I'm sorry. I know what it's like to be forgotten. It cuts deep and leaves scars."

He frowned. "Were your parents inattentive?"

"I was loved." She sighed. "But, after they died, I felt forgotten. They hadn't planned for my future. There was no will, not even a stipend. I still have nightmares about the endless days where I waited, hoping a relative would claim me, until my uncle stepped up to be my guardian. I might have been remembered when my parents were alive, but I was forgotten upon their deaths."

A guffaw of cheers rose from farther down the road. A cluster of men huddled around a cockfight and held up money to place their bets.

Bradlee turned to Hannah and waited for her attention. When she focused on him, he said, "I won't forget you."

A melodious laugh burst from her lips. "I will be long forgotten once you return to England, and I'm an ocean away." Her eyes widened. "Perhaps if you mention me in your book, then others may ask about me." She rubbed her chin and narrowed her eyes as if to impersonate him in the future. "Oh yes, I do recall an island girl who once saved my neck from a horde of sharks." Her face lit. "Perhaps, you could make me seem heroic, and I could be remembered as an islander Joan of

Arc." Her eyes sparkled like the sun reflecting off the ocean's waves.

His creative mind swirled with possible plots. "I think that's a splendid idea."

On their left, a fisherman tied nets to sticks to dry them in the sun. The webbed drapery hung all around, swinging in the ocean breeze.

"Hoy there." Bradlee raised his hand.

The weathered and bent man weaved through the maze of nets.

"Are you in need of two able-bodied workers for some short-term employment?" Bradlee refused to recoil at the potent smell of fish and body odor emanating from the stranger.

The man's gaze lowered to Bradlee's injured leg. "I'd hardly say yer able-bodied. Ya need two good legs to heave heavy nets over the side of a boat." He wiped the sweat from his brow with the back of his sleeve. "But try Captain Dailey. He's getting' hisself some grog over at the Dolphin."

Bradlee tipped his hat. "Many thanks, kind sir."

"Anytime, gov'ner."

"I know Captain Dailey." She smiled and glanced at Bradlee's injured leg. "He may be more sympathetic to your plight. He sails into port often and is a good sort of fellow, even though he imbibes a bit much." Hannah rose on her toes and waved. "Look. There's Colin."

Sure enough, Colin stood on the pier, leaning his forearms against the railing and watching a rowboat unload.

Colin must have heard his name, for he glanced their way and perked up. "Tell me your short jaunt took all this time." He sauntered toward them with his arms crossed. "Did he stop to consort with every person in the market?"

Hannah laughed. "We haven't even made it to the market yet."

Colin shot an exasperated look heavenward.

"We do, however, have a lead on a means of employment." Bradlee inclined his head toward the Dolphin, and they all strode in that direction. "I'm going to meet with Captain Dailey. Why don't the two of you stay here and get to know one another better. I daresay, you have much in common."

Colin's eyes narrowed and issued a *what plan are you hatching now?* sort of look.

Bradlee ignored him and mounted the steps to the entrance. With a prayer for God's favor, he opened the tavern's door and recoiled at the dank air with the overpowering stench of rum and unwashed male, tinged with vomit. He waited a second for his eyes to adjust to the dimmer lighting before crutching his way to a burly man standing behind the bar. The man's gaze slid over Bradlee's clothing as he dried a mug.

Bradlee leaned on the counter. "Kindly point me in the direction of Captain Dailey."

The publican inclined his head toward a man emptying the last of his tankard into his tipped-back mouth. He slammed the glass on the table and wiped his beard with his sleeve. Weathered lines intersected in a cross-hatch pattern on his tanned face, and wiry gray hair protruded from his head and his beard, except for several sections that were streaked white. He pushed back his chair and rose, tossing coins on the table.

Bradlee hobbled his way over, wishing for the hundredth time that day his foot wasn't injured.

The man turned toward the back door.

"Captain Dailey, hold a moment."

The captain stilled and eyed Bradlee over his shoulder with dark, suspicious eyes.

"I was told you might have work?" He stood as tall as he could on one leg. "My name is Bradlee Granville."

His gaze dropped to Bradlee's injured leg. "I know who ye are."

~

*H*annah sat on the stone steps to wait. Across the way, the chickens squawked and the men laid down their bets.

"I don't see how you can stand another second of the sun." Colin leaned against the stone wall in the alcove of the tavern's door, where the tiniest bit of shade offered him relief. "My skin screams in agony. It doesn't bother you?"

"I don't know anything else." She peered over her shoulder at him and shrugged. "I've overheard the military men speak of the gray clouds of England, but I barely remember anything other than the island." She shifted sideways on the step and wrapped her arms around her knees.

A fond smile tugged the corners of her lips. "I do remember a few things, like running through green grass alongside a rectangular hedge that seemed to extend on forever. And I remember a large bright window near a stone hearth with a roaring fire, and people who slipped in and out of rooms quietly."

Colin snorted. "Servants, probably maids, footmen, and such."

Shouts erupted as one of the cocks won its fight, and money exchanged hands.

Hannah shivered at the pooled feathers around the men's knees and the bloodied lump of the bird whose penalty for losing was death.

"You better have my money," a voice growled behind her.

CHAPTER 11

...An unsavory, ne'er-do-well. My fist was ready to draw
the man's cork.
~ *Journaled the 17th d of April, 1829*

*H*annah's head whipped around.

The tavern owner placed his booted foot on the
pleat of her skirt, pinning her in place, and glared down at her
with incrimination in his eyes.

Colin straightened.

Hannah's blood pooled in her legs at the man's angry
glare. What money? She forced what she hoped was a calm
expression. He must be mistaken. "Good afternoon, Mr.
O'Halloran."

"Yer uncle best not be inside runnin' up another tab he
cannot pay." He moved to the door as if to check.

She brushed the dirt from his boot-print off her gown.

Colin stepped aside to let the man pass. "We are merely
waiting for a friend."

Mr. O'Halloran ignored Colin and twisted to scowl back at
her. "If you don't have what's owed to me, then get yer white-

beggar-self off my front stoop. I don't want you blocking paying customers."

Heat poured into Hannah's cheeks. She knew Uncle Reuben's drinking had worsened in the last few months, but merciful heavens, she had no idea he'd been racking up a tab. How could he do that to them? Didn't he realize the shame they would face? She fought to keep her shoulders straight as she rose with as much dignity she could muster. "I was unaware of any debt. I'm certain my uncle will be by to pay you shortly."

Colin glanced her way. The sympathy in his expression increased the lump in her throat and drew the sting of tears.

"Didn't you hear me?" Mr. O'Halloran stepped up to Colin. "I said no white beggars on my stoop."

"There's no need to repeat yourself." Colin widened his stance. "I ignored you quite well the first time."

Mr. O'Halloran's nostrils flared, and he leaned in closer, as if about to release a flurry of his temper on Colin. Hannah grabbed Colin's arm and yanked him down into the street before the men came to fisticuffs.

The tavern door closed behind Mr. O'Halloran with a bang.

"Delightful fellow." Colin's voice dripped with sarcasm, and he glowered at the tavern entrance.

"I'm sorry you had to witness such a display." She peeked back over her shoulder as they strolled toward the shade provided by the mercantile building next to the tavern. Hannah dared not move any closer toward the cockfighting. "I hope Mr. O'Halloran is mistaken. My uncle partakes of spirits, but he knows better than to spend beyond his means."

"Mr. O'Halloran should take it up with your uncle and leave you out of it."

Hannah searched for a different topic, one to distract Colin from his anger and her from the hurt of humiliation. "How did you end up employed by Mr. Granville?"

A glint of mischief shown in his eyes. "Now, that is a tale." He wiped the sweat from his brow with his handkerchief. "I too attend Oxford University, but obviously not as a nobleman or a gentleman commoner such as Bradlee. I fell in just below commoner, what they aptly call a servitor, for we are expected to serve the other students in exchange for a lowered tuition. I was assigned to Bradlee's older brother, Lord Samuel Russet, the Viscount Russet, future Earl of Cardon, as his valet."

The titles sounded so formal. It seemed strange for Bradlee, who wore an easy smile and whose laughter flowed freely, to be the brother of a future earl. "What is he like, the viscount?"

"The exact opposite of Bradlee. He's studious and a rule follower who, by his birthright, feels obligated to be in charge of every situation, including the tending to his younger sibling."

"I doubt Mr. Granville responded well to an overbearing brother."

"Quite right." Colin heaved a deep sigh and glanced heavenward. "They argue constantly over Bradlee's reckless behavior."

"Did his brother assign you to keep him out of trouble?"

"I wouldn't put such an act past his brother, but no. I was awarded to Mr. Granville at the loss of a horse race."

Hannah's brows shot up. "Truly?"

"I would cry if I could spare the moisture." He blinked his eyes. "It's indecent to be bartered off so, but until I graduate, I might as well be an indentured servant."

The wafting ocean breeze cooled the beads of perspiration on her forehead. "Mr. Granville challenged his brother to a race?"

"Indeed, in Hyde Park. Lord Russet is well known for his equestrian skills. No one thought Bradlee stood a chance."

Feathers and chicken squawks filled the air.

Colin's gaze flicked to the fight and back. "Lord Russet was in the lead but chose a safer route, not wanting to injure his horse. Bradlee rode like a fiend, jumping park benches and low walls. Lord Russet was in the lead the entire time, but Bradlee had some nodcock plan. His brother had just rounded the side of the hedge and was in the straightaway to the finish. He even slowed his horse, sensing a victory. Bradlee, however, urged his horse to jump the high hedge as a shortcut. Lord Russet waved him off, but Bradlee spurred his horse, determined to reach the finish directly on the other side. At the last minute the horse balked and skidded to a stop. Bradlee flew over the hedge past his brother and across the line."

Hannah gasped. "He could have broken his neck."

"He broke his wrist." Colin shrugged. "And received a nasty bump on his head, which may explain some odd behavior, but I have a feeling he was born nicked in the nob."

"You shouldn't say such things." She pinched her lips tight, surprised by her need to defend Bradlee.

"It's the only explanation for his madness. Truly, I'm certain angels exist because they somehow keep Bradlee Granville alive."

The cockfighting ended, and the local men dispersed.

Hannah crossed her arms. "Surely, he's not as bad as you say."

"Ask him how many bones he has broken and then tell me I'm overstating."

Slow footsteps from the direction of the cockfighting drew Hannah's attention.

"Who dat wit ya, red legs?" The local man she'd seen on the beach the other day slapped the arm of his friend and pointed at Colin. "Did ya find someone who'll buy ya nice tings so ya don't hav ta scavenge da beach wit da rest of us?"

Colin stepped in front of Hannah as if his body could block the insults from hitting their target.

"Hey, English," the friend yelled. "Ya better take yer spoils and git out quick before the duns come fer you too." The men burst with cajoling laughter.

Duns? Hannah peered around Colin. Why would creditors

be coming for them? Mr. O'Halloran's voice echoed in her mind and joined with the taunting from the beach. Was this why Uncle Reuben didn't want her coming into town? My word, what had her uncle done, and how bad was it?

The tavern door swung open, and Bradlee exited with the captain.

Bradlee spied the men across the street and eyed Colin's stiff pose. His gaze slid to her.

Her cheeks went up in flames. *Please, God, don't let Bradlee find out my shame.*

"I tip my hat ta ya, white beggar. Ya know how ta catch 'em." The beachcomber lifted three fingers and dipped the brim of his straw hat.

Too late.

Bradlee lunged, but the captain restrained him by grabbing the back of his shirt. "Watch yerself now." He waited for Bradlee to calm himself before he released him. "The crown believes the magistrate has things under control, but on this isle, we're vastly outnumbered by African slaves." He exhaled a deep breath. "It's only a matter of time. Ya don't want to be known as the man who launched Nevis into an uprisin'."

"The mayor is going to hear about this." Bradlee's eyes flashed. "How dare they speak so to a lady."

"It's not somethin' of which he's not already aware." Captain Dailey patted Bradlee on the shoulder. "Calm yerself, now. I need you alive to start work in the morning."

Hannah perked up. "Captain Dailey has work for you?"

Dailey slapped Bradlee's back, causing him to hop on his good leg for balance. "Our families go way back. Sat under his great uncle's tutelage at Oxford, meself. The blasted man almost plucked me twice." He peered at Bradlee with a twinkle in his eye. "Now, I get to seek me revenge on his great nephew."

Colin's face blanched, but Bradlee remained unfazed.

"Granville here is very convincing of speech." A wheeze of a laugh rattled deep in his throat. "This bloke tells me you don't need legs to dangle over the side of a ship and scrape barnacles." He sucked on his front teeth and winked at Hannah. "You should have seen his face when I pulled off my foot and used it to scratch my head."

"You didn't." Hannah crossed her arms. "Here you go and tell me never to bring up your leg to anyone, and yet, you pull a stunt like that." She helped Bradlee hobble down the few steps. "And, don't believe his tales of sharks or run-ins with pirates. That's not how he lost his limb."

"Naw." The captain grinned so wide his eyes disappeared into the folds of his skin. "It was living the good life that did me in, rich sauces and bottles of rum. Gout in my leg pained me to perdition. I had the surgeon take the whole blasted thing off." He wheezed out more laughter. "I lived well off the white gold until the land tuckered out."

Colin and Bradlee exchanged a glance that clearly stated they thought the captain quite mad.

"Be at the docks two hours before sunrise." Captain Dailey chucked Colin on the shoulder. "I'm lookin' forward to takin' my revenge startin' tomorrow."

CHAPTER 12

White planters hold power but make up a small minority.
African slaves wield no power but are the majority, and
the mulattos hover somewhere in between, dependent
upon the number of generations blended.
~ Journaled the 18th of April, 1829

*A*t the fork in the lane, Hannah insisted Bradlee and
Colin pull the wagon over. She'd manage the rest of the
way on her own. A lady would have them walk her to the door,
but if Uncle Reuben were home, she'd be exhausted by his
inquisition. She did however have a few questions for him.

She strolled around the sea grape hedge into the drive that
had once been lined with crushed seashells. The grand home
her parents once built now lay in shambles. Half the shutters
hung on one hinge, and weathered clapboards curled against
the sun in desperate need of paint. She rounded a corner, and a
rusty nail caught the material of her gown, tearing a small hole.

"Drat," she whispered and unhooked the fabric. It was almost
ready for the rag bag anyway. Her bare toes peeked out beneath
the dirty hem an inch too short.

She'd cried as a young child when her gossamer dress had been caught in a thornbush. The memory was hazy, but she could still feel her childhood distress. Mama had instructed her to stay put, but the blackberries were ripe and beckoned her. Funny, but she must have still been in England, for blackberries did not grow on Nevis. Her younger self would have been horrified at the sight of her current dress.

Hannah sighed and reached for the side door.

"You." Uncle Reuben's voice startled the seagulls on the rooftop into flight.

She jumped at the gruff sound of his voice and spun around.

He jabbed a finger through the air at her as he weaved up the path from the beach to the house. He wiped the sweat from his brow with a white rag, and his breath huffed out in deep gasps from the short trek from the beach.

"Where have you been?"

She swallowed. "I was running an errand."

He stepped to within less than a foot of her, and his nostrils flared. "Have you been sneakin' off?"

"No." Blandina and Lady Clark had been aware of her whereabouts. She'd neglected to tell him for this exact reason.

"Then how do you explain my rowboat?"

Hannah's stomach dropped to her bare toes. She'd forgotten about the rowboat. She'd never returned it to its rightful spot, nor flipped it over.

His lips curled into a snarl that displayed his overcrowded lower teeth. "Where did you go? Who did you meet?"

"There was a shipwreck about a week back. I saw it sink with my own eyes."

His jaw tightened.

"I couldn't sleep listening to their cries for help, so I helped Mayor Simmons and his wife pull survivors out of the water."

His face reddened, and a vein pulsed in his neck. "You spoke to these men?" He grabbed her arm and shook her. "Were they

English?" His voice grew shrill. "Did you tell them who you are?"

"There wasn't time to chit chat." Her topknot fell loose when she pulled away from him, and she shoved her hair out of her eyes. "Most of them were in shock."

"Are you daft?" His fingers curled into fists. "You can't be walking down to the water at night, a budding young girl. There are men without morals." He shook a fist under her chin. "Men with impure thoughts."

She didn't flinch. "How could I stand by and watch them drown?"

"You...they...grrr." He punched the clapboard beside her head. Inside, something fell off the wall, and glass shattered.

"Blast!" He shook his hand and crowded the air with a string of expletives.

Hannah stood completely still until her heart started beating again. She swallowed and sucked in a steadying breath.

He grasped his injured hand and kicked the dirt. "You are a young woman. You cannot go traipsing about the island and talking to strangers. You are my responsibility. I'm trying to protect you. Protect us."

"Your knuckles are bleeding." She opened the door and waved him inside. "Let me tend to them."

He peered down at his hand as if noticing the blood. He continued his rantings, but followed her.

Hannah scooted to the side to avoid stepping on the broken glass of her mother's favorite vase. Papa had given it to Mama as a housewarming gift when they moved to Nevis. Mama had proudly displayed the cut glass in the main foyer with a fresh bouquet for all to see.

"Blast. See what you've gone and done." He stomped down the hall, crunching over the glass in his well-worn Hessian boots. "That vase was worth a week's wages." He stopped short and slashed his uninjured hand up through the air. "I'll bet it's yer mama's ghost punishing you for yer disobedience."

Hannah bit her tongue against a sharp retort. Uncle Reuben was merely lashing out. He fell into step beside her, and she could smell spirits on his breath.

It wasn't even afternoon yet. She led him into the kitchen and caught a flash of Blandina's skirt as she slipped out the servant's entrance. Hannah couldn't blame the girl for wanting to avoid Uncle Reuben's temper. "Sit on the stool."

He complied with a grunt. His eyes searched the room. "Where's Blandina? Shouldn't she be seein' to our noon meal?"

"She's probably gathering vegetables from the garden."

"Blandina." He twisted to yell out the back door. "Bring me somethin' to drink."

With her uncle at the table, Hannah dipped a cloth into some iodine she pulled from the shelf. She used it to blot his bleeding knuckles.

"Perdition, that stings," he hissed and tried to yank his hand away.

Hannah held firm. Her lips parted to inform him of her encounter with Mr. O'Halloran.

He cut her off. "Women. The whole lot of you cause nothin' but problems. Stealing my boat. Stealing my peace." His brows snapped together. "I've a mind to keep you here under lock and key." His lips thinned into a tight line. "I don't want you going into town anymore."

"Pardon?" She lifted the cloth from his fingers and stared at him.

Blandina drifted into the room, left a mug of ale on the table, and slipped back into the kitchen.

"You mind what I say." He pointed a finger at her. "Any more instances of you sneaking out, and I'll put a stop to you helpin' out at that school." He gulped down a swig of the ale.

The air left her lungs, and she closed her lips. She loved

teaching. He wouldn't take that away from her, would he? The children adored her, and she them. How could she leave? Bradlee's face fluttered through her mind, along with her promise to help him speak in front of a class. She couldn't go back on her word.

"It's time you stayed home and learned to manage a household." He grunted his own approval of his statement.

Now wasn't the time to confront Uncle Reuben on his misdeeds. Not with the chance he could take away her greatest delight in a fit of rage. She focused on Uncle Reuben's injury and not the tightness in her chest. Blotting the raw knuckles, she said, "I'll make certain Blandina or Hattie runs the errands in town." She tied a strip of cloth around his hand and curled her fingers around his. "I'm making a difference in the lives of the children. Don't you remember today's verse from Hebrews thirteen, 'Do not neglect to do good and share what you have, for with such sacrifices the Lord is pleased.'" She leaned in closer. "Besides, how am I going to learn how to manage a household here with no one to instruct me?"

He snorted and gulped back the rest of his drink.

"If you wish" —she swallowed, hoping this was the excuse she needed to spend more time in Bradlee's company at the Clarks— "I shall ask Lady Clark for specific instruction as to how to manage a household. Perhaps, I can spend a few afternoon hours in her company."

Blandina entered the room and refilled his cup.

He caught the material of Blandina's skirt, and the poor girl jumped, almost spilling the pitcher.

Hannah didn't blame Blandina for being nervous around her uncle's temper, especially of late.

"This better not be watered down." His lips curled.

Blandina's eyes widened, and she shook her head in an almost imperceivable motion.

"You poured me the good stuff, the way I like it?"

She nodded.

He released her, and she scurried back into the kitchen.

"I won't let it affect my chores here." Hannah straightened. "I don't see another way."

He crossed his arms with a frown. A long silence fell over the room. Finally, he said, "Fine."

Hannah's heart leapt, and she pinched her lips closed to keep from smiling.

He huffed a deep breath, and his expression softened, taking off the years. It reminded her of the man she'd known long ago —a lost soul, but one with a good heart.

He patted her hand. "You may train under Lady Clark's tutelage and still help with the teaching, but stay out of town, especially with a bunch of desperate shipwrecked men millin' about the streets." He stood, towering over her. "Tell Blandina to draw me a bath and see to my fresh clothes." He ran a hand over his belly. "And have her make me a meal before I go."

He pushed back his chair, then paused. "Has my letter arrived?"

Hannah closed the lid on the iodine. "I haven't seen it. Do you know the name of the ship with which it sailed?"

Uncle Reuben blanched.

"It better not have." He grasped what little hair remained on the sides of his head. "Dash it all! That blasted estate manager." The small blue veins in his nose swelled until she thought they might pop. "If your dowry sank with that ship, I'll be buggered." He strode toward the door.

"What dowry?" She scooted around the table "What estate manager? Does he know my family?"

"I'm going out." Uncle Reuben slammed the door behind him.

She stared at the empty entranceway with a hundred unanswered questions swirling in her mind. Why had his behavior of late become so odd? She knew it had something to do with the letter he was awaiting, the items that kept disappearing, and him not wanting her to speak to people in town. And a dowry? Who's dowry? Hers?

Hannah groaned. She needed answers, but from Uncle Reuben's elusive behavior, she didn't hold out hope she'd receive any from him.

CHAPTER 13

Too knackered to lift my pen...
~ *Journaled the 19ᵗʰ of April, 1829*

*B*radlee's exhaustion seeped deep into his joints and bones, more even than when he'd hiked the Pyrenees mountains of Spain or trekked the plains of Africa. He and Colin sprawled in the shade of the trees on the Clarks' porch and watched the view of the ocean peeking through the branches. Bradlee praised God for the Sabbath after a long Saturday spent scraping barnacles off the side of a boat. Every muscle in his upper body ached, especially after sitting in one spot that morning listening to the reverend's sermon.

Captain Dailey hadn't been jesting about his revenge. Scraping boats was a nasty, sweaty, and smelly job, but it was the mental taxing that worried him the most. As he dangled inches above the water, his body refused to relax. Every muscle tensed as he envisioned sharks circling underneath the surface, waiting for him as they had the night of the wreck.

Colin groaned as he reached for the cup of tea and scones Hattie had made for them. The effort must have been too much for his friend, for his arm collapsed, hanging limp over the arm of the chair.

Outwardly, since he ached too much to move, Bradlee probably appeared as resigned as his friend. But inwardly, his thoughts and emotions had churned like the thundering surf ever since Colin relayed the comments from the tavern owner and the cockfighting spectators.

"How dare they say such names? If this were London, I'd call them out."

Colin lifted two fingers. "Before you go naming me as your second, you need to realize this is not England. Polite society's rules do not apply here."

The breeze ruffled Bradlee's overly long hair. He puffed the strands out of his eyes with his breath to save his arms from having to move. "What were the names they called her? Red legs? White beggar?" He ground his teeth.

"It sounds like her uncle is in deep and doesn't have a pocket to let." Colin groaned as he shifted in his seat, then stilled as if the effort was too great. "I daresay, Miss Barrington could hold her own if her uncle finds himself in debtor's prison. Did you see how she haggled with Mr. Maroon? It would be easier to draw blood from a stone than to get a coin from that man's clenched fists, but she convinced him. Even made him glad to do it."

"She was brilliant." Bradlee smiled over her bold words, *If you give me your decision now, then because we're friends, I'll give it to you for a half-penny less. But you know Mr. Thompson will pay a pretty penny because Mrs. Marchmain has been asking her husband for an indigo cloth for a new gown.* She'd peered up into Mr. Maroon's face with a smile on her soft lips. She had the amazing ability to appear soft and supple, yet strong and confident at the same time.

"We have to do something," Bradlee said. "We cannot stand by knowing Miss Barrington is being treated poorly. She's a gently bred woman, the daughter of a baron." Bradlee winced as he sat up straighter.

Colin only moved his eyes to glance his direction. "We?"

"You. Don't you find Miss Barrington a delightful woman?"

"Quite."

"She's witty and caring."

"Indeed."

Bradlee carefully turned his head to see Colin's face. "And good with money, as you pointed out. You two have frugality in common."

Colin's lips twisted. "Out of necessity, not because I desire it."

"She's wonderful with the children at school. You should have seen how she gained their attention. She's offered to help me improve my public speaking to take my exams. You should come with me to the school on our break."

"You want me to give up rest to watch you learn how not to swoon?"

Bradlee flicked his gaze to the porch ceiling. Why must Colin be so difficult? "So you can spend time with the lovely Miss Barrington." He ignored the protests of his muscles and sat up, turning his body to better face Colin. "She's quite appealing in a unique way. Miss Barrington makes the debutantes of London look like cookie cut-outs."

"She does have a nice figure." Colin studied the scenery. "Lithe and strong. Enough to row a mile out to sea and back."

The tightening sensation in Bradlee's chest returned.

"Good hips, too, you know—for childbearing." A crooked smile inched up one side of Colin's mouth, but his gaze darted to Bradlee as if to gauge his reaction.

Bradlee unclenched his jaw, refusing to fall for Colin's bait. "She's a lady. You shouldn't be noticing her hips."

Colin shrugged. "I'm studying to be a physician. These are

the things we notice. I can also tell you her coloring is good and her skull is nicely contoured."

"A woman who's knowledgeable with poultices would be an asset to a physician, and you must admit, marrying a baron's daughter would be an advantageous match. One to make your parents proud."

From his slouched position in the chair, Colin raised a brow. "Perhaps."

Bradlee frowned. This wasn't going the way he'd expected. "What's the matter with you? Why are you acting so strangely?"

"Me?" Colin tried to sit up. He sank back into the chair with a groan. "Why are you suddenly interested in playing matchmaker?"

"Miss Barrington saved our hides from being a shark's supper. She helped us find employment, and she has tended to my ankle. We are in her debt and must do something to help her situation."

He half expected Colin to argue. *She saved us from your mess. It's your ankle she's tending. You marry her.*

Instead, Colin said, "What exactly did you have in mind?"

Bradlee blinked. Was it a good sign Colin hadn't disagreed? Could it mean he was willing to consider marrying Hannah? Bradlee sat back in his chair. He needed to drop the suggestion slowly. "I don't have the foggiest. If I had access to funds, we'd have passage to England. I'd bring her—and a companion, of course, for appearances."

Colin chuckled.

"What?" Even the muscles in Bradlee's forehead ached as he frowned.

"You finally understand what it's like to be in my situation."

"Your situation?"

"Having people who need your help but no finances to aid them."

Bradlee stared at Colin's smug smile. He and Colin had been

through a lot together in the past year. He knew his friend hid a loyal and kind heart behind layers of sarcasm, but he didn't know he had people he wanted to help but couldn't.

"Who?" The question popped out of Bradlee's mouth before he could reconsider.

Colin heaved a sigh. "My sister. She's asthmatic, which means she suffers bouts where it is difficult for her to breathe. It's why I decided to attend university and become a physician. I hope to cure her ailment."

Guilt gnawed at Bradlee. "I didn't know Emmeline had a condition."

He grinned. "It's why I put up with insufferable people such as yourself."

"You adore me." Bradlee settled back into his seat. "Admit it."

"I have to remind myself daily, 'Be slow to fall into friendship, but when thou art in, be firm and constant.'"

Bradlee scrunched up his face and eyed Colin.

"Socrates." Colin blinked at him, then shook his head. "Quite right. There is a captivating quality to your madness. It's like watching that bird you spoke of that pecks at the alligator's teeth. You can't take your eyes off it, wondering how it hasn't already become the alligator's supper."

"Crocodile." Bradlee studied the weathered wood grain on the arm of the chair. "The bird is a plover, and it's not an alligator. It's a crocodile."

Colin pinched the bridge of his nose. "You remember that, but not the great quotes of Socrates?"

"Why should I remember the words of a man long dead?" Bradlee waved a hand to dismiss the subject and winced at the movement. "There must be something we can do."

"For Socrates or the bird?"

"Neither." Bradlee groaned and glanced heavenward. "I'm speaking of Miss Barrington."

"The only way to change Miss Barrington's situation is to get her off this island."

"And to get her off the island, we need money." Bradlee sighed. "I'm thankful for the work, but we toiled for so long for so little coin. At this rate, it will take us two months to pay for passage."

Colin offered a pinched smile. "And another month if you plan to pay for Miss Barrington's, plus another for the chaperone. So make that four months, and another two months to cross the Atlantic if the sailing is good. That gets us to England, if we're fortunate, for early December, which is after your exams."

"Unless." Bradlee forced the words past his lips. "If you marry Miss Barrington, then we won't have to pay for a chaperone."

Colin lurched upright, wincing with the effort. "I knew you were playing matchmaker." He jabbed a finger in the direction of Bradlee's chest. "Whether or not I marry Miss Barrington will be my choice. I'm not like you. I don't make spontaneous decisions, especially ones that will affect me for the rest of my life."

"So you're saying you'll think on it?"

Colin leveled him with a glare.

"All right. All right." Bradlee put up his hands. "I'm just grasping at anything in order to get back in time to take the exam." Bradlee rested his head on the back of the chair and squeezed his eyes shut. "If I don't, I'll disgrace myself and my entire family."

"Your father certainly boasted far and wide about you becoming a professor. The shock will kill him."

Dread soured Bradlee's stomach, and he closed his eyes. "There is a way to get the money." Bradlee's breathing stilled. His father would happily send funds if he agreed to marry Miss

Radcliff. "I had merely hoped you'd fancy Miss Barrington and immediately take to the idea."

Colin scratched his chin. "I'm not saying it's entirely out of the question. Merely that I need more time to get to know the chit."

"Time is a luxury I do not have." Bradlee ran a hand over the top of his head. "And I cannot ask you to do something I wouldn't do myself.

Bradlee's future spanned out in his mind's eye—the day-in and day-out life of a professor droning on, repeating the same lecture about the viability of plants in different degrees of acid soil. Every morning, he'd break his fast with his wife, who'd discuss which gown she planned to wear to the country dance, and in the evening when he arrived home, she'd ask his opinion whether to plant roses or lilies in the flower beds. Meaningless polite chatter. Was that to be his future? The humid air suddenly became stifling, and a sweat broke out on his brow.

"Dash the roses and lilies to perdition. I don't care where they're placed." Bradlee struggled to stand.

Colin eyed him as if he'd taken leave of his senses. Perhaps he had.

At least Colin hadn't flatly said no. There was hope in that. Bradlee merely needed more time to get him to see reason. Unfortunately, time was running out.

CHAPTER 14

Competition heightens my interests but often finds me in appalling circumstances.

~ Journaled the 20th of August, 1828

"*T*he heat is getting to me." Bradlee grunted a few moments later. He stood and grabbed his crutch, which was leaning against the porch wall. "I believe I shall go inside and see if Hattie has something cool to drink."

He tucked the crutch under his arm and hobbled inside. On his way to the kitchen, he passed the salon, and a flash of pale pink caught his eye. He paused and backed up a step. There on the sofa, her legs carefully tucked under her, sat Hannah. She was dressed in a fitted gown with capped sleeves, and her hair was piled up on top of her head and curled into ringlets. Sunlight pooled around her, illuminating her gentle profile. He might have believed he was peering into any formal salon in London except for a grouping of miniature tools spread before her on the table.

She studied something in her palm. Her delicate brows were drawn together, and a sliver of her pink tongue peeked out from between her lips. So intent on whatever object she poked with a small tool, she didn't hear Bradlee approach.

He leaned against the doorframe and admired the dimple that formed in her cheek whenever she frowned at the piece in her hand. What a fetching picture she presented. He'd seen the Roman sculptures, the works of Rembrandt, and Peter Paul Ruben's paintings, but nothing comprised the beauty and inner strength of this fair island girl. Colin should be jumping at the chance to marry her. If Bradlee didn't push him to take risks, he'd never be offered the chances to enjoy life.

Hannah's eyes shown bright blue next to her tanned skin and dark fringed lashes. She was a mixture of both worlds, relaxed yet elegant, exotic yet familiar. She held the object closer, set down one tool and picked up another.

And she was resourceful. He should call for Colin to join them, but instead let his curiosity get the best of him. He rested his crutch against the wall. "There's something different about you."

She glanced up, her lips parting in surprise, but her eyes sparkled.

She was happy to see him. A rush of pleasure tingled his body, and the knot in his chest melted.

He held up a finger. "Give me a minute, and I'll figure it out." He studied her. "You've gotten some sun?"

She shook her head with an I-know-you're-funning-me smile.

"Perhaps, you've grown taller?"

"I stopped growing years ago."

He hobbled a few steps closer, his leg feeling well enough to put a little weight on it. "I know." Colin was a fool. "St. Elmo's fire has taken the form of a beautiful woman."

She heaved a heavy sigh. "It's my mother's old gown, and Hattie has done my hair." She lowered her hands to her lap, still holding the watch and tool. "Lady Clark has graciously offered to show me how to manage a household, and with that comes presenting myself as a lady."

He raised her chin with his index finger so she could see the admiration in his eyes. "You have always been a lady, through and through."

She stared at him for a long moment. The invisible pull between them intensified.

He cleared his throat and gave himself a mental shake.

Hannah arched a brow. "Don't believe for a moment that such flattery shall get you out of standing in front of the class tomorrow."

He ignored the remark, unwilling to let his thoughts go there, and directed his attention to her slender hands. "What are you working on so intently?"

Hannah held the piece toward him. He lowered himself down to the couch, holding in his grunt of pain and leaving a good deal of space between them.

"It's a watch I found in the ocean." Her clear eyes found his. "Water had gotten into it, and I'm attempting to get it running again."

He peered down at the tiny gears, dials, and a mainspring.

"I thought there might be a problem with the balance wheel."

He leaned in closer. "Indeed."

"But that wasn't it, so I reset the mainspring."

"Good choice." He breathed in the sweet scent of vanilla and molasses clinging to her hair.

"That wasn't it either."

Even the delicate curve of her ear was exquisite.

"I'm not certain what to try next." She glanced up at him. "What do you think?"

He refocused on the watch.

"Perhaps salt from the ocean has dried, gumming up the works?"

"I've already taken the time to clean it." Her chest heaved

with a large sigh. "Do you think it could be the escapement mechanism?"

"Most certainly." How did she know so much about mechanics? He'd always admired a woman with a mind. Had he mentioned her intelligence to Colin?

One side of those honeyed lips pulled up into a lopsided smile. "You don't know a thing about watches, do you?"

He peered into the abyss of her eyes. "Not the foggiest."

She laughed and handed him a tool. "Hold this while I try to align the escapement." She picked up a smaller tool and held the watch right under her nose. "Do not move. It takes a steady hand."

Bradlee didn't move, nor did he breathe. He'd listed all the reasons why Colin and Hannah were perfect for one another. However, pictures of his own life with Hannah flashed through his mind—setting up a nursery, growing old together. *God? Why are You making this more difficult?*

Hannah straightened. "I think that did it." She swung the back closed and flipped the watch over. Sure enough, a faint ticking sound emanated from within, and the hands on the face began to move.

"It running." Her smile illuminated the room.

It drew a similar one from his lips. "How did you learn so much about watches?"

"We used to have a watchmaker on the island. He showed me how to fix some of my papa's old watches." She rose. "Mr. Fitzroy said his was no longer working. I'd be happy to take a look at it."

Bradlee shook his head to pull his mind back under control. "Colin, yes. Let me call for him." He stood, but this time he couldn't contain the grunt of pain from his sore muscles.

"That reminds me." She grabbed a tin from off the coffee table. "I figured you'd be sore after a day of physical labor, so I brought you and Mr. Fitzroy something to ease the ache."

"I'm not that sore." His pride struggled to hide his pain, but another groan escaped as he reached for the ointment.

His fingers brushed hers. "Hannah to my rescue, once again."

~

*H*annah slowed her steps, even though she risked angering Uncle Reuben by being late for supper. The sun seemed to express what was in her heart as it streaked the sky with bright pinks and yellows that reflected upon the ocean waves. Her steps felt light, and her heart still fluttered in her chest. She may live to regret allowing herself joy over something so simple as being in Bradlee's company, but she couldn't help but cling to thoughts of him.

It was foolish to fancy Mr. Granville. They were from different worlds. But was it wrong to savor the moment? To allow her heart to dream?

As Hannah slipped in through the servant's entrance, Blandina scurried about the kitchen preparing supper. Uncle Reuben preferred to maintain what, in London, would be considered city hours and ate after the sun set, before he ventured out for the night.

Hannah slipped an apron over her mother's dress, careful not to ruin it. Bradlee had appeared pleased by the change in her appearance. The flash of admiration which darkened his eyes to the color of rich molasses delighted her. She'd felt like a lady of the *ton*, even though the day dress she donned was the simplest of all her mother's gowns. She'd searched long and hard for her Mama's best gowns, those made of satins or lace with fine zephyr overlays, but they seemed to have been misplaced.

A spoon clattered on the stone floor. Blandina hunched over, and the sliced vegetables she'd been mixing spilled on the ground.

Hannah dashed to her side and laid a hand on her back. "Is it the babe? Is it your time?"

Blandina's eyes were glazed over with pain, and she held her breath.

"Shall I run for Hattie?"

She shook her head.

Hannah knelt by her side as her friend slowly exhaled.

Tears leaked out of the corners of Blandina's eyes. She pressed a hand to her lower back and rose. "It's not my time yet. I still have a month. Hattie said it's my body practicin' for da coming of da babe."

Blandina scooped up a handful of the spilt vegetables, but Hannah stopped her. "You go and lie down. I will finish dinner."

The girl hesitated, and her eyes shone with concern, but whether it was for Hannah or herself, Hannah couldn't tell.

"I insist."

Blandina stared at her, then nodded. Hannah opened the door for her. "If you cry out. I'll be there at a moment's notice. There is nothing to fear."

Her eyes flashed with gratitude, but the look faded into the deep sadness she'd seen so often in Blandina's gaze.

Hannah closed the door behind her and turned to clean up the mess. The spilt food was too precious to throw away, so Hannah scooped it up, washed it off, and returned it to the bowl.

The front door opened, and Miss Albina Kroft's laughter drifted from the foyer.

Hannah stiffened. Miss Kroft must be joining them for dinner. Uncle Reuben must have rowed over to the island of St. Kitts where she resided. The lightness she'd felt earlier faded. Miss Kroft's presence meant either a night of carousing or fighting for her uncle and the woman. She'd hoped to have the discussion with him about their finances and his mention of an estate and a lost dowry.

Fortunately, most of the dinner had already been prepared, so she dished rice and beans onto plates and set the small bits of chicken on top to make it appear more than it was. She frowned at the meager portions. Uncle Reuben would be furious if dinner didn't show well for his guest. She shifted the chicken from her plate to Miss Kroft's. Hannah could suffice with rice and beans tonight.

She balanced the plates on her arm and pushed through the door. The hinges squeaked, and she made a mental note to oil them later. She placed the meals on the table and set another place for Miss Kroft, just in time for her uncle and guest to stroll into the room.

"I'm famished." He stopped, and his gaze drifted slowly down Hannah's form and back up to the curls in her hair.

"Why, Hannah, darling." Miss Kroft hung on Uncle Reuben's arm, dressed in a fitted satin gown that reminded Hannah of an overfilled wineskin ready to burst at the seams. Her squared bodice was cut so low that Hannah feared if she inhaled, her bosom may spill out. "What brought about this change?"

"Uncle Reuben requested Lady Clark instruct me on domestic tasks. Such duties required me to dress properly."

Uncle Reuben slowly nodded with a frown. His hand rested on the back of Miss Kroft's chair, but she had to clear her throat before he pulled it out for her to sit. Hannah lowered into her seat and kept her gaze on her plate to avoid their uncomfortable stares.

Miss Kroft speared a piece of chicken with her fork. "If you need any advice, I'd be happy to help teach you the ways of a lady."

Uncle Reuben's fork stopped midair.

Hannah forced her head up and eyed her uncle. "Shall we say grace?"

Uncle Reuben's face reddened, and he set his fork down. "Of course, go right ahead."

He and Hannah bowed their heads. Hannah thanked God for His provision and asked for a blessing upon their food. The scraping of Miss Kroft's fork against the plate and her chewing could be heard all the while.

During the meal, Hannah listened to Miss Kroft, who apprised them of all the latest happening and gossip on the larger Leeward Island. When the sound of her droning stopped, Hannah peered up from her rice and beans to find her uncle still staring at her. He quickly averted his gaze.

Two angry splotches of red spread across Miss Kroft's cheeks until even her nose and ears appeared flushed. "Hannah has blossomed into womanhood—overnight it seems." She grabbed the open bottle of wine on the table and refilled her glass, then leaned across the table to fill Uncle Reuben's.

Hannah focused on her plate and not the uncouth way Miss Kroft's chest pressed against her bodice. She was a beautiful woman, but her demeanor caused Hannah to cringe. Did her uncle not see it?

Uncle Reuben shoveled another fork full of rice into his mouth and spoke while he chewed. "Indeed." He swallowed, wiped his mouth, and blotted the sweat from his brow with his napkin. He peered at Hannah. "Those uppity English relatives may not want you, but you turned out right fine. Despite everything you've been through, you have become a remarkable woman." His eyes softened, reminding her of the man he used to be. "Your parents would be proud."

Hannah swallowed past the tightness forming in her throat. Would her parents have been proud of their girl? Or would they see the dirt under her uneven nails and her too-tanned skin and be disappointed? Would they be appalled at the way she romped unescorted all over the island? But what other choice did she have? They hadn't thought to provide for her after their deaths.

"Huxley." Miss Kroft bristled whenever the conversation

didn't revolve around her. "Hurry and finish your meal. I do not want to be late and miss out on all the revelry."

Hannah peered at her uncle. "I've been meaning to ask you about what you said the other night. You mentioned a dowry—"

Uncle Reuben choked on a big bite and washed it down with the entire contents of his tankard. He set the mug down and pounded on his chest with his fist. "As Albina said, we are in a hurry. We'll have time to discuss things later."

Albina questioned him with her dark eyes.

He shoveled the remainder of his food into his mouth and rose to leave, but he hesitated. His lips thinned, and he stared down at Hannah. "This change is good. You look like the lady your parents would want you to be." He furrowed his brow and nodded. "How things should be."

"Indeed." Miss Kroft's lips thinned, and her tone grew ominous. "It's past time she was treated like a woman of marriageable age."

The rice stuck to the sides of Hannah's throat as she swallowed.

A twisted smile deepened the color of Miss Kroft's painted lips. "I think I'll introduce her to some fine gentlemen."

CHAPTER 15

The sweet scent of molasses from the boiling houses mingles with the ocean breeze, and the scent of rum, molasses's fermented form, exudes from the breath of men.

~ Journaled the 22ᵗʰ of April, 1829

A jolt passed through Bradlee as Hannah announced, "And now, class, Mr. Granville and Mr. Fitzroy would like to talk about the continent of Africa and the native animals they encountered, including the ferocious lion."

His knees quaked as he followed Colin to the front of the room. Lady Clark flashed him a reassuring smile as she passed him to stand at the back of the classroom, but it did nothing to calm the tremors that moved though his body, culminating in his hands. He clasped them behind his back so no one could see.

Hannah stepped aside and whispered, "Remember to breathe and keep your gaze just above their heads." She sat on the front row with an encouraging smile.

He could do this. He had to do this.

Bradlee glanced at Colin, who nodded for him to start.

Bradlee cleared his voice and faced the class. Fifteen sets of eyes stared at him. His mouth went dry, and he coughed to work up some saliva. However, the coughing only increased his light-headedness.

Lord help him, he was going to faint. He'd make a fool of himself swooning in front of a roomful of children.

Hannah cleared her throat, and his gaze snapped to her. She imitated a deep inhale and exhaling motion.

He sucked in a shaky breath, and the dizziness faded. He peered at her expressive eyes and relaxed. She'd scoured through all the books in her parents' library and the Clarks' to find ways to fight his fear. He merely had to remember what she'd told him to do. Number one, breathe. He inhaled another deep breath. Two—know the material. He'd studied Africa and spent six months there. He could easily speak of his travels.

He cleared his throat. "I—uh—have been to the continent of Africa which—ah—resides..." Blood pounded in his ears, and his face warmed. All those little faces stared directly at him. Waiting. Assessing. Wondering what was wrong with him.

Hannah held a hand just above her head.

Ah yes. Look just above their heads. That was the third.

"Africa resides below the continents of Europe and Asia." He pointed to the round world globe Colin held up. "While I was there, I was fortunate enough to explore some of its unique terrain."

A hand raised.

He nodded at the child.

"What's terrain?"

A bead of sweat dripped down the side of Bradlee's face, and his shaking intensified.

Colin stepped forward. "Terrain is a fancy way of saying the ground you walk on." He slapped Bradlee on the back. "Why don't you tell them about some of the animals I befriended in the Savanna?"

Bradlee's eyes sought Hannah's once more, and he inhaled and exhaled. What was it she'd said? *If you get stuck, pretend you're speaking only to me.*

His lips trembled. "Well—uh—my colleague—er—friend, Mr. Fitzroy, had to rescue me from an angry rhino, and we spent six hours clinging to tree branches while the rhino stomped about beneath. Do any of you know what a rhino looks like?"

When their heads shook, Bradlee proceeded to draw one on the blackboard.

Even though he'd started off rough, stuttered a few times, and sweated through his shirt, he eventually found a rhythm. He used the stage as an opportunity to highlight how Colin saved them from numerous scrapes, which not only took some of the focus off Bradlee, but also showed his appreciation for his friend. He hoped to impress Hannah with Colin's abilities, courage, and intelligence. Bradlee saved their encounter with a lion for last and even had the class impersonate a lion's roar.

"Well done." Lady Clark stood. "Class, let's thank Mr. Granville and Mr. Fitzroy for a lovely presentation."

At the motion of her hand, the class chorused. "Thank you, Mr. Granville and Mr. Fitzroy." Little Henry's voice trailed a few seconds behind the rest. Lady Clark dismissed the class for recess.

Hannah approached Bradlee with a wide smile. "You did it."

He blew air past his lips. "Thanks to your advice, I didn't swoon."

"How did it feel?"

"Wretched and excruciating at first, but by the end, did you hear them? They laughed at my jests."

"You did splendidly." She inclined her head with an approving nod. "A few more times, and you'll be able to stand confident and poised for your exams."

The blood drained from Bradlee's face. He had to do it again?

She turned to Colin. "And Mr. Fitzroy, I had no idea you could make your own fishing poles and hunting spears. How did you know what plants were safe to eat and how to make the water safe to drink?"

Colin perked up and explained what he'd learned through his medical studies as they strolled outside. It was time for them to report back to their barnacle cleaning duties at the docks. The powerful midday sun warmed his face as he stepped into the schoolyard. The children chased each other, some pretending to hold spears and others roaring like lions.

Bradlee stopped and listened to their play.

"My grandpa is from Africa, and he's been to da Sahara like Mr. Granville."

"I want ta be like a lion. Dey will hear my roar thirty miles away. Tat is da entire island."

Bradlee's chest swelled. The children were reenacting his stories. He turned to reach for Hannah's arm, but stilled. Colin held her in a deep discussion on the benefits of modern medicine.

The air deflated from his lungs.

He wanted Colin and Hannah to talk, get to know one another, and fall in love. He wanted them to live happily in England. Bradlee's jaw tightened. He was a selfish cur. It was the only explanation for the sudden impulse to shove Colin out the way and keep Hannah's approving gaze all for himself.

~

*H*annah slid off her worn slippers for the journey home in order to not wear the soles any thinner. The scent of coconut filled the air as she passed a slave who'd shaken down the coconuts from a nearby palm tree and hand-scraped out the white pulp to eat. One of her students meandered by, prodding a goat into town, most likely to be sold at the market.

"Afternoon, Elijah," she said as she passed.

"Afta-noon, Miz Barrin'ton." The boy issued her a small bow.

Moving at his pace, he'd barely get to the market by dusk.

Hannah rounded the bend and walked up the drive toward her home. Shadow neighed and stomped her foot, drawing Hannah's attention to the additional horses tied outside the stable. Was Uncle Reuben entertaining guests? He usually wasn't home at this hour.

A strange sense of foreboding slowed her steps as she crept to the front entrance. She opened the door as quietly as possible.

"There's Miss Hannah now." Miss Kroft rose from the settee in the front salon.

Three men dressed in red military uniforms stood. Their eyes roved over her form, inspecting every inch of her. The heavy scent of spiced rum hung in the air. Several glasses rested on the table, a half-empty bottle nearby.

"Miss Kroft?" Hannah hesitated in the entranceway. What was she doing here? Who were these men? Where was her uncle? "To what do I owe this surprise? Where's Uncle Reuben?"

Miss Kroft sauntered across the room. "Welcome, darling. Your uncle is out, but he doesn't mind my entertaining."

Hannah doubted Uncle Reuben would allow any stranger within his home.

"Come and meet my friends. They are all ranking officials stationed at Brimstone Hill. They've crossed the inlet to meet you." She planted her hands upon Hannah's shoulders and turned her to face the men. "Isn't she everything I said?"

Miss Kroft walked her into the salon and pushed her into the nearest chair. The men sank back into their seats, their gazes never straying from Hannah's form.

The oldest of the three, with streaks of gray in his beard and jowls that dangled under his chin, leaned forward. His cold eyes consumed her as if she were a source of warmth.

Another of the men, this one with a scraggly beard and stains on the knees of his white breeches, tossed back the contents of his glass and licked his upper lip.

The cleanest of the three peered at her with a hooded gaze like a reptile sunning itself on a rock.

Hannah was a trapped rabbit about to be made into a stew, Miss Kroft pinning her down for the kill.

The reptile-gazer asked, "Does she come with a dowry?"

The breath left Hannah's lungs, and she tried to rise, but Miss Kroft's hands remained firm on her shoulders. *God's thunder.* Miss Kroft was attempting to marry her off.

"This isn't England." Miss Kroft chuckled. She perched her hip on the low backrest of Hannah's chair and lazily swung her leg. "With few women livin' on this isle, it's not unheard of for a man to pay for the honor of marriage. Especially when the woman is a beauty."

Hannah twisted around to glare at Miss Kroft. "Is my uncle aware of what you're doing?"

She shrugged and ignored Hannah's question. "She'll inherit upon her guardian's death."

The greasy man nudged the younger one with his elbow. "Word has it, Huxley is a guzzle gut, and at the rate at which he drinks, he'll be cocking up his toes before long."

Hannah gasped at the man's audacity to enter her home and speak ill of his host.

The youngest's eyes narrowed, then rose. "Aye, she's beautiful, but I won't be taking on a drunk nor paying off his debt. This has been an abominable waste of my time. Excuse me. I have other affairs to attend." He strode from the room.

"She knows how to cook and mend," Miss Kroft called after

him. "And she's gifted with herbs and poultices too. Knows how to cure a wretched headache."

He slammed the front door.

Hannah used the distraction to slip from Miss Kroft's grasp and stand. She lifted her chin and addressed her without looking at the men. Her cheeks and ears burned. "I shall not be subjected to whatever insufferable scheme you are planning."

Miss Kroft grabbed her wrist as she tried to stalk away. "Do not be rude to our guests."

"You have overstepped." She forced an iron-control firmness to mask her mortification.

"Come now, dear. I'm merely planning for your future."

Her body engulfed into flames. "Your motives are far from honorable." She broke free of Miss Kroft's grip. "I must ask you and your friends to leave." She flicked a glance at the two remaining men. "Good evening, gentlemen." Hannah stormed out of the room and into her chamber, locking the door behind her.

Gentleman—bah. She shivered, still feeling their lude gazes upon her body.

"She merely needs to grow accustomed to the idea." Hannah heard Miss Kroft apologize to the men for Hannah's behavior. "She's usually biddable. I'm not certain what's come over her."

The greasy man's voice reverberated down the hall. "I enjoy a little spitfire to warm my bed."

Hannah's stomach lurched. If that man laid a finger on her, she would surely wretch. She yanked on the foot of her bed in an attempt to drag it in front of the door. A lock at the moment didn't seem enough of a barrier. *Lord, please get me out of this mess.*

The side door opened, and the thud of her uncle's boot traversed down the hall. "What in blazes is going on here? Albina, who are these men?"

"Huxley, darling. Come and meet some gentlemen from

Brimstone Hill." Albina's voice held a desperate edge to it. "They're potential suitors for Hannah. They've heard of her beauty and have even offered to pay for her hand."

Hannah stilled. Surely Uncle Reuben would fly into a rage.

He cleared his throat. "She's not of marriageable age."

"You are blind. She blossomed into a woman years ago." Miss Kroft snorted. "Did you truly think she filled those gowns overnight?"

"Hannah's father was a baron, and she is a gently bred woman. These men are below her station."

"Hey now—" the greasy man's voice interjected.

"They are ranking military officials in his majesty's navy and in want of a wife." Albina's voice grew shrill. "I'd like you to try and find a better husband for your hoity-toity niece on this island."

Her uncle said, "Are you lookin' to take a wife, or are you lookin' for a bit of muslin?"

By the accusation in his voice, Hannah pictured Huxley had rounded on the men.

The greasy man piped up. "I'd prefer the latter, but I'm willing to become leg-shackled to stop having to shell out shillings whenever I'm in the mood for a tup." He cackled with laughter.

"Out!" Huxley released a bellow that shook the dust from the rafters. "Get out of this house, this instant."

There was a shuffling of boots, and then the front door slammed.

"Once again, you ruin everything," Miss Kroft wailed. "They were willing to pay handsomely for her hand. If you want me to share your bed, then you're going to have to provide for me."

"Lower yer voice, Albina."

Miss Kroft complied, but Hannah could still distinguish her words through the thin walls.

"Marrying her off is the easiest solution."

"To the likes of them? I think not. Hannah has been my responsibility all these years. I won't be sellin' her like a slave."

A chill ran down Hannah's spine at his ominous words.

"Well, you're going have to make a choice. I have certain standards, and livin' in the poor house isn't one of them." Miss Kroft's tone turned deadly. "Your well has run dry. You can either marry her off for some good coin or write to the man and have him send more funds."

Hannah held her breath and leaned closer to the wall. What man? What well? What funds? She expected him to rail at Miss Kroft's madness and send her packing.

"Or you can do both." Miss Kroft's skirts swished as she moved. "What's the point in keepin' the chit? Soon she's going to need to marry, and you're going to be alone."

"She's an innocent. She doesn't deserve such treatment."

Her tone switched to a purr. "She's not going to warm your bed. Who's going to take care of you when she's gone?"

The silence that followed screamed in Hannah's ears. Her knees gave way, and she curled into a ball on the mattress.

God, what am I to do?

Never had she felt so alone. Blandina had shut her out. Bradlee and Colin must leave by midsummer to return before the exams. Lady and Mr. Clark longed to evangelize on St. Kitts and other isles, but remained here because of her. And now Miss Kroft was convincing her uncle to marry her off to unknown and ill-bred men. Nevis was her home, but even her home didn't seem to be hers anymore. *God, please help me pay for passage to England. Help me find my family. They must be out there somewhere. Help me find a place to belong.*

"I think you need to go." Uncle Reuben's voice was a low whisper through the door.

Hannah raised her head and wiped her tears.

"But we're expected—"

"Go without me."

Relief washed through Hannah. Uncle had chosen *her*.

"You're a fool." Miss Kroft's voice hissed. "Mark my word, you're going to wish you listened to me."

Hannah scurried to the window in time to see Miss Kroft wave down one of the men still readying their steed. In a flurry of skirts, she climbed into the eldest man's gig, and with a flick of the reins, they rode in the direction of town.

A fist pounded on the table. Her uncle groaned and popped the cork off another bottle.

~

*T*he following morning, Hannah pried open her secret compartment under the floorboards and removed the bag of coins she'd strived so hard to save. Several years' worth of savings. She counted the coins. It was almost enough to pay for a second-class ticket. Another month and she'd be on her way to England.

She knocked on her uncle's door, and then waited patiently at the kitchen table for him to emerge.

He shuffled down the hall, still wearing the same clothes he'd donned yesterday. His shirt was half untucked and his jacket wrinkled. Lines from the bedclothes marked his face, and his hair stuck up like a rooster's tail on one side.

"We need to have a talk." Hannah patted the table where he normally sat.

He plopped into his chair. "Hound's teeth. I'm not in the mood to talk."

"I should have spoken up earlier." She passed him the mug of her elixir, and he downed half its contents.

"I ignored the signs," she said. "The lack of work, the items that have gone missing, your not wanting me to go into town."

"You're making my head throb with your riddles." He

clutched the mug with both hands as he sipped. "What are you getting at?"

"You mentioned a dowry?"

"It was nothing." He stilled, but his eyes studied her closely. "Only the ramblings from a nightmare I had. Your parents were on the ship. They were bringing your dowry, but the storm came up and it all sank."

Her heart ached for Uncle Reuben. He too still suffered from nightmares. The troubled dreams probably resurged due to financial strain, which was the next topic she must broach. "Mr. O'Halloran said you owe him money."

He slammed the mug down, and its contents splashed over his hand and onto the table. "I told you to stay out of town."

"That was before you made me promise." Hannah used her napkin to wipe up the spill. "I hoped he was mistaken, but I overheard you and Ms. Kroft talking last night."

"Confound that blasted woman."

"She's a bad influence." Hannah tried to keep the anger from her tone and remain calm. "You heard her last night. She's an evil woman who wants to sell me to the highest bidder."

"I didn't stand fer such nonsense."

"I know. You've always watched out for me." Hannah flashed a small smile. "Perhaps it's time I watched over you. I think I can help."

He shook his head. "You're a young chit, still green. You don't need to be worrying your head. I have everything under control."

"I've been selling my poultices at Mr. Maroon's store."

"Under my nose?" He frowned. "How'd you sell stuff without my knowing and without going into town? I've got it in my mind to throttle you for your disobedience."

"Hattie has been dropping off the poultices and bringing me my earnings ever since you prohibited me. I haven't disobeyed."

"You've been selling stuff without my permission."

She ignored his fussing. "I've been saving up for a couple years." She placed the bag of coin on the table and forced her fingers to release her dream. Last night, he'd chosen her, now she would make her choice and help him. For twelve years he'd taken care of her—a single man taxed with the well-being of a young distraught child not of his own. But now she was older. Perhaps, it was time she set aside her own needs and take care of him.

Uncle Reuben's eyes bulged.

"I was going to purchase passage to England to try to find more of our relatives."

His gaze flew to hers, and she wasn't certain whether it was hurt or fear that flashed in his eyes.

She pushed the money toward him. "I want you to have it."

His mouth fell open, and he blinked.

"It will mean postponing my trip." Bradlee's face flashed in her memory, and she swallowed past the tightness of her throat. She would sacrifice for her uncle because he'd cared for her when she'd needed it most. "But I can wait a few more years."

Tears rolled down his cheeks, and he shook his head. "I can't take your money."

"Yes, you can. If you need more, then we'll sell some of the books in the library or some of the paintings on the walls." *The memories of her parents.* She exhaled a deep breath. Her parents were no longer here. They hadn't provided for her. Sacrifices had to be made for the living. "God will provide." She leaned in closer. "I only ask that you swear off spirits."

He put his face in his hands and wept. His elbows slid until his forehead rested on the table.

She laid a hand on his shoulder. "You were there for me, and now it's my turn to be there for you."

His shoulders shook with sobs. "You're a good soul." His voice cracked. "I don't deserve the likes of you."

CHAPTER 16

The Nevis hot springs attract many Englishmen seeking
healing for their ailments. If sugar no longer remains
their white gold, perhaps the island's future resides as a
healing retreat for tourists.
~ *Journaled the 5ᵗʰ of May, 1829*

*S*everal weeks later, Hannah once again sat in the front
row of the class, encouraging Bradlee with a smile.
This time he didn't stand rigid and pale. He didn't have Colin by
his side ready to interject in case he froze. Colin observed from
the back of the class beside Lady Clark.

Bradlee had taken all the recommendations she'd found
among the books and applied them. He moved around the floor
and gave a fair impression of King George IV, at least she
thought so based on what she'd seen in drawings and carica-
tures. She'd never actually seen their King. Bradlee leaned back
and hoisted his pants over a pretend round belly, and the kids
chuckled. It seemed he was becoming accustomed to speaking
in front of the class, and she couldn't be prouder.

His gaze rested upon hers, and heat filled her cheeks at the pleasure she found in their depths. There was something in the way he looked at her, as if he could see past the dirt and sand to the person she used to be, the one raised to mingle with the Quality. He made her feel like a lady, feel as though she belonged in his world. Hannah smoothed her mother's skirt and rose. In the last few weeks, she'd enjoyed dressing like a lady in front of Bradlee.

She and Colin had been helping him prepare for the public speaking portion of his exam—*the great go,* as he called it. Practicing in front of the children had been the perfect solution. When he finished, she faced the class and hoped they didn't notice her heightened color. "Class, you may be dismissed."

They hurried out of the room.

"I must say, there's not a drop of sweat dripping from your brow." She struggled to not swing her arms, Lady Clark had instructed her, as she moved to his side. "You are not only on your way to being able to face a panel of professors, but you'll soon be able to address parliament if you'd like."

"Let's not go that far." Bradlee shook his head with a smirk. "I'm much improved, thanks to your suggestions, but each time my stomach still somersaults, my hands get sweaty, and my blood rushes in my ears."

She studied him for a moment. "How do you feel when you start one of your adventures?"

"Excited." He pushed back his jacket and rested a hand on his hip. "Eager."

"No. How does your body feel? What does it do?"

"My heart pounds."

"What else?"

"My hands get sweaty." He glanced at the ceiling while he thought. "My stomach gets a little queasy."

She fiddled with her father's ring. "Aren't those the same descriptions you just felt when you were nervous about speaking?"

His brows lowered, and he shook his head. "No." He paused, and his face softened. "Yes. They're similar."

Her hand dropped back to her side. "Monday when you get up to speak, I want you to tell yourself you're starting an adventure and you're excited, not nervous. Let's see what that does."

He rubbed his chin. "All right. I'll give it a go."

"Hannah?" Lady Clark waved from the doorway. "Can you and the men finish cleaning up? I must pay Johnny's mother a visit. I shall meet you back at the house." Her voice trailed away as she slipped out into the schoolyard.

Colin, who'd been speaking with Lady Clark, walked toward them.

"Don't you have to go back to the docks?" Hannah asked Colin.

"Thank heavens, no." He dropped into a wooden seat. "Capt'n Dailey has sailed to Trinidad and will be back in two glorious days."

She rounded on Bradlee. "How splendid. What do you plan to do with your free time?"

"Nothing," answered Colin's voice behind her. "Wondrous, glorious nothing."

Bradlee eyed Colin.

Colin jerked upright. "What? What are you thinking?"

"A hike." He peered down at her. "If you'd be willing to take us?"

Colin groaned. "I want to sleep late and have some time to rest without protesting muscles and exertion."

"You don't need alone time. Newton's first law clearly states objects at rest tend to stay at rest. Objects in motion tend to stay in motion." Bradlee shuffled over and slapped Colin on the back. "What you need is to keep moving."

Colin wrinkled his nose. "I'll have you know, my alone time is for your safety."

"Bah, you'll thank me later." He turned back to her. "What do you say, Miss Barrington? Are you up for being our tour guide?"

Her stomach fluttered. Was it from nervousness or excitement or both? "Are you certain you'll be able to walk the terrain?" She glanced at his ankle.

"It's been feeling much better, thanks to your ministrations. I merely keep the crutch for sympathy."

"And to wake me with a poke each morning." Colin smirked.

"Indeed." Bradlee grinned. "It works rather well in getting him out of bed."

Saturday there was no school, and her uncle had promised to go looking for work over on St. Kitts. He'd be gone for the day. "All right then. A hike to the hot springs it is."

They made light work of cleaning the classroom, and soon the three of them were headed back to Lady Clark's for tea.

Bradlee and Colin both offered their arms. Hannah moved to take Bradlee's arm but thanked Colin for his offer. However, Bradlee yanked his arm away.

"I'm always forgetting about my injury." Bradlee backed away a step. "Please, take Colin's escort. I will only slow you down."

Hannah stared at him. "I thought your ankle was much improved? Are you certain you want to hike to the hot spring tomorrow?"

He nodded. "Most definitely. I merely want to give it a good day's rest to make certain it's at its best."

Colin shrugged and extended his arm again. The two of them strolled down the lane with Bradlee crutching himself a step behind.

His hasty withdrawal seemed odd. Had she done something wrong? She walked in silent contemplation.

Bradlee hobbled up beside Colin. "Did you know that Colin here" —he thrust his chin in Colin's direction— "also very much enjoys reading?"

His comment yanked her from her thoughts, and she peered at Colin. "What sort of books do you enjoy?"

"Medical books for school, but for pleasure I tend to follow scientific journals."

"Anyone in particular?"

"I enjoy the works of the Cornish chemist, Sir Humphry Davy. He has this new lamp that I believe will revolutionize electricity. Have you heard of him?"

"I'm afraid not, but I don't have much on contemporary figures. The most recent book in my parents' library is at least twelve years old, if not more." And soon even those may be sold to pay down her uncle's debts.

Silence fell among them once again until Bradlee nudged Colin's elbow. "I daresay the class laughed harder at your earlier jest then my last remark." He leaned around Colin to glance at her. "Don't you agree, Miss Barrington?"

Colin frowned. "What jest? I was completely serious."

"See." Bradlee chuckled. "Colin has an amazing sense of humor. I noticed you enjoying Colin's quick wit."

Hannah tucked a loose strand of hair behind her ear. "I find you both amusing."

Colin issued Bradlee a sideways glance.

Something about Bradlee's strange manner sounded alarms in her mind. Was it merely his public speaking nervousness still spilling out of his system?

Bradlee persisted. "Colin's quick to bring a smile to a person's face. I noticed you smiling quite a bit at his antics."

Why was Bradlee so eager to point out Colin's best qualities as though he wanted her to fancy Colin instead of him? Had she imagined the special way Bradlee looked at her, how his gaze sought her when he grew nervous in front of the class? Had she been missing her parents' love for so long she no longer remembered what it looked like? Did she mistake her feelings? His feelings? What of that day in town when he'd allowed her to read his journals under the Banyan tree? Was she the only one who felt the pull between them?

Colin kept his gaze steady on the Clarks' house and hurried, as if intent on a mission.

"I couldn't find a more amusing companion." Bradlee crutched faster to keep up. "He's made my grand tour a ripping good show."

"How lovely for you." She couldn't keep the clipped tone from her voice. Thank Heaven, they'd reached the Clarks' household. To think she'd been excited for their afternoon off. Her stomach fluttered each time she thought of spending the afternoon in Bradlee's company. However, now she suppressed the urge to stomp on his foot.

Colin led her up the front steps and opened the door for her. He rounded on Bradlee as he made his way up and cleared his throat. "Pardon me." Colin held out a handkerchief. "You have a bit of flummery on your lips."

Bradlee smirked and pushed the cloth aside. "See, ever so clever." However, she heard him mutter under his breath, "Insufferably so," as he crutched his way to the door.

Her fingers curled into her palms. The desire to scream or run from the room heated her body like the noonday sun. She knew her hopes had only been a dream, a beautiful bubble that was sure to pop. But why did Bradlee have to ruin her dream prematurely by attempting to pawn her off on his companion? Was it out of guilt? Did he feel sorry for the poor island girl, so he was trying to get someone to take her in and see to her well-being? As if she were a stray animal?

She'd always known deep down Bradlee wasn't going to swoop in, declare his love, and offer for her hand in marriage. She wouldn't be whisked away to the distant land of her memories where she would be revered instead of being called *red leg* or *white beggar*. It was an unrealistic fantasy, but it had been fun to believe in the what-if. Each time he looked at her in that way of his, each time she basked in his smile—hope had flared in her chest. Was hope such a bad thing?

If the ache in her heart was any indicator, then it would seem so. Bradlee never wanted her, not for himself. He may have treated her like a lady, but he believed her to be beneath him. Hope was merely a castle in the sky. The reality was that there had never been a what-if.

She couldn't look at Bradlee without the rise of tears, so she turned to Colin. "Please excuse me. I have duties to attend more fitting my station." She strode to the kitchen with her usual long stride, not the dainty steps Lady Clark had instructed.

"Fitting her station? What was that about?"

She heard the confusion in Bradlee's voice.

"You're about as subtle as a stampede of buffalo." Colin's wry tone followed. "Leave her be. I believe I saw Mr. Clark out back in the stables."

The smell of freshly-baked scones permeated the kitchen. Hattie was peeling yucca roots and walked Hannah through things to oversee for teatime. The cups and saucers were laid out on a platter, water boiled on the stove, and the tea leaf and sugar bowl filled.

"I have somethin' fer ya." Hattie set the peeler down, opened a tin canister, and pulled out a small burlap bag. "Mr. Maroon gives his regards and says dat elixir is flyin' off da shelves."

Hannah thanked Hattie, sat down at the table, and opened the sack. The shiny coins spilled out on the table. It was more than she'd ever collected before—more than she'd ever seen in one place, except for the stash she'd given her uncle—but it was now all she had. She began to count them.

Lady Clark swept into the room. "Hannah, I thought you'd be entertaining the gentlemen and serving tea. You didn't have to wait for me."

A pang of guilt washed over her. Her lips parted to explain, but Lady Clark nodded to the stack of coins on the table.

"Is that the money from your poultices?" She pulled out a chair across from Hannah and sat.

Hannah nodded. In total, she had three pounds.

"Business appears to be good." Lady Clark tilted her head. "I bet you're close to being able to purchase a ticket. How much have you saved up?"

Hannah stared at the small stacks of coins. She'd been close. This would have put her over.

Lady Clark leaned in closer. "I'd think you'd be smiling. Aren't you happy your poultices are selling, and you'll soon be off to locate your English relatives?"

She nodded. "Yes, indeed. It's merely that I won't be leaving anytime soon. Uncle Reuben got himself into a fix, and I gave him my savings to keep him—us—from ruin."

Lady Clark gasped. "I'm so sorry. I know how long you'd saved." She squeezed Hannah's hand.

"It's fine. I will save again. Now that my poultices and elixirs are becoming well known, it shall only take me half the time." If she was lucky, it would only take a year instead of two.

The sympathy in Lady Clark's eyes was almost Hannah's undoing. She turned to peer out the window and blink back the sting of tears. Bradlee walked across the stable entrance carrying a bale of hay. Colin followed with a saddle. Mr. Clark wiped his brow with a rag and leaned up against one of the stalls.

Lady Clark moved to the window and called the men to clean up for tea. She pushed away from the sill and turned back to Hannah. "Those young men are hard-working, to say the least."

Hannah, too, was hardworking. If only she could earn a living like a man, she'd regain the money to travel in a month or two, like they were.

"I haven't seen the likes of them amongst the Quality in quite a while." Lady Clark chuckled, and her eyes danced. "But then, I haven't been among the *ton* in quite some time now, have I?"

She sipped from her tea, and her eyes grew distant. "My first husband, Richard, God rest his soul, wasn't much of a worker. He was a good sort of fellow with a kind heart but believed hard work was for common folk. I never could quite agree with him. Doesn't it say in Genesis that man shall toil the land? I never recalled it saying some shall work while others live off another's spoils. If Richard had ever fallen on hard times, he'd have been lost. I commend those young men, for when they fell upon hard times, they didn't moan and complain about the unfairness of it all. They rolled up their sleeves and got to work. It takes a unique gentleman to be able to switch so easily between both worlds, the upper crust and the commoner, and especially one who treats others equally. If only all folks on this island could have the same respectability."

Equally. Indeed, Bradlee had treated her as an equal until it came to marriage. Then, he'd made his standards clear, and she didn't meet them. She touched her father's ring. How far she'd fallen from being the daughter of a baron. Perhaps it was best she didn't go to England. She wouldn't want to disgrace her family name.

Hattie pulled the scones out of the oven and placed them on the tray. They stood and relocated to the salon to await the men.

A throat cleared in the hall, and Bradlee stood peeking around the doorframe. His hair was damp and tousled as if he'd washed and quickly toweled it dry. A clean linen shirt clung to his shoulders, and a pair of buckskin breeches hugged his thighs.

"May I join you?"

"Certainly." Lady Clark gestured to the open spot on the sofa next to Hannah. "Please have a seat."

Hannah scooted over to make room. Maybe she should move to another seat so she wouldn't have to smell the fresh scent of his skin or feel the vibration of his voice when he spoke.

A jaunty smile quirked the corner of his mouth. "Is there something on my face?"

She lowered her gaze.

"Do I need to wash again?"

"The most stringent soap couldn't wash your ugly off." Colin entered the hall neatly dressed, but still buttoning the cuffs of his sleeves.

Lady Clark straightened and, in her strict teacher voice, said, "Mr. Fitzroy, apologize to Mr. Gainsville this instant."

Colin lowered his head. "I beg your pardon, Lady Clark." He stepped up to Bradlee. "My sincerest apologies." He bowed low, almost grazing Bradlee's left side and whispered, "for your ugliness."

Hannah bit back a smile as Colin reclined in the wingback chair across from her. She knew it wasn't right, but she reveled in the justice all the same.

Bradlee waved his hand at Lady Clark. "Do not fret, Lady Clark. Mr. Fitzroy's attempts to downplay my handsomeness to make himself look more appealing are pitiful. I take no offense."

She pursed her lips. "I daresay, I shall never understand male banter."

Such remarks could only be said when one was completely secure of the other's devotion. Colin and Bradlee behaved as brothers. Hannah had witnessed the like in the classroom between male siblings on plenty of occasions.

"Miss Barrington appreciates my misplaced attempts at humor." Colin laced his fingers and arched a brow at her.

"She's merely indulging us." Bradlee draped his arm around the back of the sofa.

The skin on the back of her neck and shoulders tingled at his nearness, and she cursed her traitorous body.

Hattie delivered more tea and scones, which the men

devoured as if they hadn't eaten in days. Hannah sipped from her cup and enjoyed the interactions between the two friends and the obvious fondness Lady Clark had developed for both of them.

Mr. Clark joined them and added to the repartee with a few remarks here and there. He chuckled at their merriment, to the point that his spectacles slid down his nose. Despite her earlier anger, Hannah's heart warmed as she watched the people she'd come to adore most in the world interact as a family. She desired this feeling more than anything.

She glanced out the window. The day was growing late, and the sun hovered on the horizon. She felt Bradlee's gaze upon her, warming her skin.

"You've grown quiet," he said in a low voice while the Clarks conversed with Colin.

"It's getting late. I should be going." She scooted forward in her seat.

Lady Clark's head swiveled in Hannah's direction. "Won't you stay for supper, dear?"

Colin leaned back in the chair and folded his hands. Under arched brows, his gaze flicked between Bradlee and herself as if her answer might change the trajectory of their lives. Maybe it would. The hope glinting in Bradlee's eyes didn't help. Her traitorous heart threatened to climb out of her chest. Her lips parted, and the word *yes* balanced on the tip of her tongue.

Mr. Clark adjusted his spectacles to peek at her over the rim. "How fares your uncle? He called upon me a couple weeks ago at the parsonage. Told me he was quitting drinking."

"I'm hoping things will start to look up for him," she said.

She caught Bradlee and Colin glancing at each other in a silent exchange.

The reminder of her uncle's woes broke the enchantment of the moment and sent her crashing back into reality. She expelled a deep sigh. "I'm afraid I cannot stay for supper, but thank you for the invitation."

"I'll walk you home." Bradlee stood.

"No, thank you." Her uncle wouldn't be pleased to see her with an escort, and she didn't need to give her foolish heart any more fodder for her dreams. "Stay and rest your ankle."

Colin rose. "I'd be delighted to do the honor." He held an arm out to Hannah.

"Truly, you are most kind, but I shall be fine." She side-stepped toward the door. "Save your walking for tomorrow's hike."

"Dusk is setting. It might be unsafe. I'd feel better if you had an escort." Bradlee attempted to follow her, but Lady Clark stayed him with a hand. She gave her head the barest of shakes with a look that told him to let the matter drop.

Bradlee's brow furrowed, and he locked gazes with Hannah. "I insist. At least, let us walk you to the bend in the road."

Heat flooded her face and burned the tips of her ears at the mixture of questions and accusations darkening Bradlee's normally warm eyes. What had Lady Clark relayed to them that they would know only to walk her to the bend? Had they heard about her uncle's suspicious nature? Had the rest of the island?

Colin moved to her other side as if she were under sentinel watch.

"Only to the bend, and Mr. Fitzroy may escort me. You must rest your leg." She stepped out into the cool ocean breeze. The sun had grown low on the horizon and cast long shadows of the palm trees across the drive.

Both men stepped onto the porch, but Colin extended his arm for Hannah.

She accepted his assistance, but her gaze darted back to Bradlee. He appeared torn.

Colin slapped him on the shoulder. "Buck up, chap. It's not like I've been promoted over you at work and have also stolen your opportunity to walk a fair lady home." He walked Hannah down the small set of stairs and chuckled. "Actually, that is exactly how it is."

"Next time you tell me to buck up"—Bradlee gripped the porch rail with both hands—"I'm going to break your leg and tell you to walk it off."

Colin tipped his head toward Bradlee but spoke to her. "You know that voice that keeps you from saying things you shouldn't?"

Hannah nodded.

"I lack it when I'm around Mr. Granville."

"Colin?" Bradlee's tone held a warning.

"Yes, my lord?"

"You're dismissed."

Colin smiled at Hannah. "He's terminated me five times in the past week. I'm afraid it's becoming a daily occurrence."

"Miss Barrington?" Bradlee's voice turned wistful.

She peered over her shoulder to find him staring at her as if the rest of the world ceased to exist. His eyes pleaded for things to be all right between them.

"I shall see you tomorrow?"

She should have kept walking, let her heart heal before it became injured beyond repair, but dash it all, she still wanted to spend time in his company. She raised her chin. "Rest up, for tomorrow we climb a waterfall."

Bradlee's smile nearly split his face. "Jolly good." He bit his lower lip and strummed his fingers on the railing.

Colin paled, and he dropped her arm. "What's this nonsense?"

Hannah turned and strolled down the lane, her steps lighter than when she arrived.

Colin scurried to catch up. "I never agreed to climb a waterfall."

He badgered her with questions until they reached the main

road, and Hannah could still feel Bradlee's gaze upon her back. The clip-clop of a horse's hooves could be heard coming around the bend, and Colin drew her to a halt.

Too late, Hannah recognized Shadow's gray mane and swayed back. She shoved Colin toward the hedge of sea grape trees.

"Confound it." He gripped a branch and remained steady on his feet.

"Houndzz tee-th!" Her uncle's voice slurred. "Is th-this what goes-s on behind my back?"

CHAPTER 17

I daresay, the kill devil is an astute nickname for rum. If
it doesn't kill you, it will bring the devil out of you.
~ *Journaled the 6th of May, 1829*

*H*annah whirled around.

Uncle Reuben tossed the reins to Miss Kroft,
who sat beside him, and sprung from the wagon. He staggered
to get his legs underneath him, then lunged at Colin.

Hannah stepped back to avoid being tackled by her unstable
uncle. His eyes held a wild expression under heavy-laden lids.
His face was flushed, and the sweet smell of rum followed him.

Miss Kroft released a squeal and half rose.

Colin easily sidestepped to miss the attack, and Uncle
Reuben tumbled into the sea grape trees. He grabbed a branch
to keep from falling.

"Uncle, how could you?" She placed fisted hands on her hips.
"You gave me your word."

Bradlee appeared at her side and pushed her behind him,
protecting her from her uncle.

Uncle Reuben snarled, his eyes jumping between Colin and

Bradlee. "Are ya heres to kill us off? You-you thinks you can just be rid of us, but I'm not going down without a fight."

"Sir, you're mistaken." Bradlee extended his hand to extricate Uncle Reuben from the branches clawing the back of his shirt.

He ignored Bradlee's hand. "If yer not sent by Mr. Fogurt, th-then yer heres t-to take advantage of my ward." He lunged at Bradlee.

Bradlee pushed Hannah toward Colin with one hand and caught her uncle with his other.

Uncle Reuben struggled against Bradlee's frame. "Ya think ya can come here with yer f-fancy ways an-and tailored clothes, an-and steal my niece. If ya think ya can come here and take advantage of s-some naïve island girl, yous've got another think comin'.'"

Hannah gasped. "Uncle!"

He broke free from Bradlee and rounded on her. "Don't think I'm too f-fuddled to know you've been sneakin' through the window. That's why the dinghy was out of place." He raised his hand to tap his temple, but almost poked his eye out in the process. "It's why you've st-started puttin' on yer mother's gowns and dressin' up pretty."

Heat flamed her cheeks, and she closed her eyes. Her uncle would ruin what little reputation she had by his drunken disgrace, and his public accusations only made things worse.

"I told ya to stay away from town."

"Sir, my name is Bradlee Miles Granville, and Miss Barrington has done nothing improper. In fact, she rescued us from certain death and has been most hospitable—"

"Hospitable?" Uncle Reuben's fingers curled into fists.

Bradlee glanced at Colin, who immediately slipped off to the side behind her uncle.

Uncle's voice turned shrill. "Hospitable? Ya cad. How dare ya prey upon my niece? I know yer type, coming here thinking ya won't be accountable fer yer actions outside of England. You think ya can do what ya please with whomever ya please. I was a similar young lad when I arrived here."

"Mr. Huxley, I can assure you—"

"Assure me ofs what? That yer intentions-s are honorable?"

Miss Kroft snorted from her perch in the wagon.

Hannah grabbed Uncle Reuben's arm, but he tore it from her grip.

Colin pulled her aside and blocked her path, hemming her between him and the hedge. She rose on her toes to peek over his shoulder.

Bradlee raised his hands. "I give you my word, the word of a gentleman."

"A gentleman's word." Uncle Reuben spit the words and staggered closer until he stood toe-to-toe with Bradlee. A bit of spittle formed on his lower lip. "What pretty speech h-haves you given her? Did ya promise to marry her? Or did ya say you'd whisks her off ta London and set her up withs her own townhouse? Tell her she'd lack fer nothin'?"

Bradlee's jaw tensed, and his eyes narrowed. "You speak out of turn. It is only out of respect for Miss Barrington that I don't call you out here and now."

Colin's gaze bounced between Bradlee and her uncle, his hands raised as if to intercede when necessary.

"You can't tek her from me," Uncle Reuben yelled. "Hannah is *mine*."

Miss Kroft tipped back a flask and swallowed. "Unless yer lookin' to make an offer. But yer gonna have to pay a pretty penny fer the likes of her. Ladies are hard to come by in the isles."

Hannah's molars ground against each other. She turned back to see Uncle Reuben fly at Bradlee with a drawn fist. He blocked the punch with his crutch.

Uncle Reuben howled in pain and shook his hand.

Colin moved to restrain her uncle, but Bradlee shook his head. "Get her out of here."

Hannah struggled against Colin's arms hauling her back toward the Clarks' house. "Leave me be. I need to calm him."

"You need to be safe."

No sarcastic response, no witty reaction? She was shocked at the seriousness in Colin's voice, but she resisted anyway, thwarting his progress.

Bradlee dodged the punch, keeping his weight on his good foot.

"You blackguard." Uncle Reuben swiped a second time at Bradlee.

The momentum of the swing pulled her uncle's unstable legs out from under him, and he pitched forward, hitting his head hard against the ground. His eyes opened with a dazed look before they rolled back in his head, and his body fell slack.

"Uncle!"

~

*H*annah sat in the back of the wagon with her uncle slumped against her shoulder. Part of her wanted to shove him off her and rail at him for lying and drinking. The only money he could have used was the money she'd given him. Her savings wasted on spirits. The other part of her wanted to curl into his shoulder and cry. Where was the uncle she remembered? How could she bring him back? It seemed as if he had a sickness that no poultice or elixir could heal.

Colin rode up front with Mr. Clark and Miss Kroft, who appeared more interested in Colin than in Uncle Reuben's well-being. It didn't seem a coincidence that Miss Kroft had appeared and Uncle Reuben had resumed his drinking.

Bradlee sat across from Hannah, leaning against the wagon rail. Once Mr. Clark had assured her that Uncle Reuben had merely passed out from too much to drink and should suffer no ill effects except for a raging headache come morning, Bradlee had insisted upon seeing them home.

He rubbed the top of his ear. "I know he's your uncle, but the things he said were inexcusable."

Hannah hoped her chagrin didn't show on her face as she traced the tiny cornflower motif on her mother's gown with her finger. "When he's foxed, he doesn't realize what he's saying."

"Hannah." Bradlee waited for her to meet his gaze, and, once she did, his amber eyes locked on hers and wouldn't release them. "I need to know if you are safe. Sometimes spirits change a man."

The hurtful things her uncle had said echoed in her ears, and the memory of waking with him standing over her entered her mind. She forced her eyes away and peered down at her uncle's sausage-like fingers.

"He wasn't always this way." She exhaled a deep breath. "He used to get up early. I'd ride out with him to examine the fields. Uncle Reuben would lean down and whisper in my ear, 'See how the cane grows? That's the work of God's hand, and we get the pleasure of gazing upon it.' He'd say the same thing when the sun rose. 'There isn't an artist in all the world who can paint like the hand of God.' He always spoke highly of my parents and how much he missed them. We grieved them together. He told me my parents gave him the best gift anyone had ever offered him before they died." Tears stung the back of her eyes, but she blinked them away. "I asked him what the gift was, and he said it was me. I was his saving grace."

She sniffed and lowered her voice to a whisper. "That was before he met Miss Kroft."

∾

*B*radlee's heart wrenched at the sight of Hannah holding back tears, and he struggled not to pull her into his arms to absorb her pain. She was a strong and compassionate woman. Not only had she lost her beloved parents, but she helplessly watched her uncle decline into a degenerate.

He pitied her uncle, but Hannah's memories didn't change Bradlee's concerns. There was no doubt in his mind that Huxley could injure Hannah in his drunken state. He'd proved it today, even if his punch had been intended for Bradlee's head and not Hannah's. The man's words before he'd passed out raised the fine hairs on Bradlee's neck. *You can't tek her. Hannah's mine.*

As the wagon stopped in front of a weathered home, Miss Kroft, with her tight spiral curls springing out above her ears, wrenched around. "Hannah, darlin', run in and help Blandina prepare a meal for our guests."

Hannah stiffened, but as her gaze drifted to Mr. Clark, Colin, and then to him, her shoulders lowered, and she brushed the road dust from her gown.

Bradlee jumped out and aided her down. "I will help see to your uncle."

She wouldn't make eye contact, but nodded before slipping inside the house.

Miss Kroft held out her hand and supplied him with a slow seductive smile. "What a dear. It's 'bout time we had a few gentlemen in our midst. We haven't been introduced."

"Forgive me." Mr. Clark gestured to Bradlee as he climbed down from the wagon. "Mr. Granville and Mr. Fitzroy, may I introduce you to Miss Albina Kroft, from St. Kitts."

"You must come in and join us." Miss Kroft curled her fingers around his biceps. She craned her neck around and yelled, "Huxley, time to wake up. You have guests."

Her bellow must have permeated Mr. Huxley's unconscious

state, for he jerked into an upright position in the back of the wagon and murmured, "Yes, dear."

Colin's lips twitched, but Bradlee stuffed down the urge to knock Hannah's uncle back out.

Miss Kroft's dark eyes glared at the half-lucid man. "He can't hold his drink. I begged him to stop after a couple, but he kept sayin', 'one more.'" She fanned her face with her hand and leaned heavily on Bradlee's arm as if she might collapse.

"Now, now. There will be no fainting, for I didn't bring my hartshorn with me." Mr. Clark gripped her other arm and pushed her back up. He released her and inclined his head toward Huxley in the wagon bed. "Mr. Fitzroy, would you be so kind as to aid me in getting Mr. Huxley inside?"

Colin swung one of Mr. Huxley's arms over his shoulder, and Mr. Clark came alongside on the other, and the two of them half-carried, half-dragged the man inside.

Miss Kroft's fingers stroked Bradlee's arm as she walked. He recoiled from her touch, happy to deposit her inside and be done with the woman.

The original craftsmanship of the house was easily discerned from the intricately carved moldings and tasteful design. Yet it showed years of neglect. A few pieces of artwork had been stripped from the place, evidenced by the faded outlines on the delicate wallpaper. Had Hannah been the one to sell her parents' heritage piece by piece? How must it have pained her to give up what little memories she had of her previous life? A flash of anger ripped through him at the injustice.

Miss Kroft opened the bedroom door. No one had drawn the curtains, but even in the dim light, he could make out the outline of discarded clothing and strewn papers on a nearby desk before Miss Kroft redirected him into the salon. Hannah may remember her uncle's goodness, but all Bradlee saw was a slovenly wretch.

Colin and Mr. Clark not-so-gently dragged the man into the

bedroom and dropped him onto the four-poster bed. Huxley's hand grasped his head, and he moaned before his eyes fluttered shut. Within seconds, the sound of heavy snores emanated from the room. Colin stole away, but Mr. Clark knelt, presumably to pray for the man's soul.

Miss Kroft turned to Colin and Bradlee as a cat would stalk its prey. "Thank you, kind gentlemen." She slinked her arms through theirs and dragged them onto the sofa next to her. "You have come to my aid in my time of need. How might I repay yer good deeds?"

Bradlee forced himself to remain on the sofa solely for Hannah's sake. His rapid departure might embarrass her further. He leaned back to peek around Miss Kroft and caught sight of Colin's face. His brows were raised halfway to his hairline, and his lips parted as if too shocked to toss out his typical sarcastic comment.

"Please tell me about yourselves." Miss Kroft said. "I can tell you're British, but from where?"

Mr. Clark emerged from Huxley's room.

"Unfortunately, we cannot stay." Bradlee eyed Colin, who rose at the silent command. "Lady Clark is expecting us, but we appreciate your kindness." He bowed to Miss Kroft. "Perhaps another time."

Mr. Clark rocked back on his heels and addressed Miss Kroft. "I do believe Hannah and Blandina can take care of things from here. Would you care for one of us to escort you home?"

Miss Kroft's lips pursed. "I will ensure they have everything in order before I leave, but thank you kindly, Reverend."

Hannah pushed through the kitchen door carrying a tray with lemonade.

Colin handed Bradlee his crutch, and the two men crossed to the door. Colin opened it, and they both stepped out, but Bradlee paused in the doorway. "Might I have a word, Miss Barrington?"

Miss Kroft pupils flared. "Whatever for?"

Hannah rounded the corner. A faint blush stained her cheeks, apparent even under her tan.

Mr. Clark squeezed her hand. "Good night, dear. You know where we are if you need anything." He tipped his hat at Miss Kroft. "Good evening, Miss Kroft. I'll check on Huxley's condition in the early morning." He stepped past them and down the step toward the road where he waited.

Bradlee smiled at his nicely phrased warning.

Hannah stepped outside and closed the door behind her. She pushed her hair back out of her face. "If you don't want me to join you tomorrow, I will understand."

"Don't be daft." Bradlee peered into her eyes. He wanted her to see the truth of his words. "There is nothing anyone can say or do that will change our opinion of you. Meeting your guardian has only confirmed what a strong, courageous—"

"Don't forget, saintly," Colin said.

"—saintly…" He flashed a *be-quiet* glare at Colin.

Colin scowled but wandered to where Mr. Clark stood at the edge of the sea grape trees.

Bradlee focused once again on Hannah. "As I was saying, you are an amazing woman. Very few ladies could hold up under such trying conditions, yet you keep your head high."

Her fingers toyed with her papa's ring. The innocent gesture held more allure than any of Miss Kroft's wiles. Hannah's long lashes swept up, and her vivid blue eyes appeared even brighter against her tanned face. Her teeth tugged on her bottom lip, and Bradlee's heartbeat changed its rhythm.

"I hold you in the utmost respect," he said, "and I'm honored to consider myself"—he swallowed to ease the dryness of his mouth—"your friend."

Friend? Was that how he felt?

Her smile grew tight. "And I you."

Bradlee cleared his throat. "I need to be certain…"

Hannah searched his gaze.

"I just want to know..." Would his words create for her further embarrassment? He blurted out his sentence. "Are you safe here?"

Hannah's hand released the ring and dropped back to her side. "Of course."

"I'm certain the Clarks could put you up for a time. Colin and I could sleep in the stables."

"I can't."

He frowned. "Whyever not? If it's due to your uncle. I shall speak to him directly."

"My guardianship was deemed by the governor until I marry." She shrugged. "Mrs. Simmons and Lady Clark have tried to take over my care, but the record stands. The only loophole is to pass my guardianship to other relatives."

"Which is why you want to travel to England."

She sighed. "It doesn't matter."

A movement of the curtains distracted them. Miss Kroft drifted away from the window into the recesses of the room. Bradlee gritted his teeth. There wasn't even a slight chance she would hold their confidence and not tell Huxley.

"There must be something we can do." Bradlee speared a hand through his hair.

A sad smile flittered on her lips. "We can discuss it tomorrow." She opened the door and brushed past him.

He stood for a moment, his mind digging for a solution. Colin and Mr. Clark waited for him to join them.

Bradlee readjusted his crutch and hobbled up the lane. Mr. Clark gathered a head start.

Colin fell into step beside Bradlee. "My, Miss Kroft was a treasure, wasn't she?" Sarcasm flooded his tone.

"Indeed." Bradlee wheeled his crutch to keep a fast pace. "The kind you want to bury."

"How does Miss Barrington live with those…" Colin drew in his chin. "For lack of a better term, miscreants."

"I'm uncertain," Bradlee said, "but I shall ensure it is not for any longer than she must."

Colin jogged a few steps to keep up. "Where are you off to in such a determined state?"

He kept his focus on the path ahead. "I'm off to pen a letter."

Colin stopped.

"A non-passenger cargo ship leaves tomorrow," Bradlee yelled over his shoulder. "The sooner I agree to my father's terms, the sooner Hannah can be rid of those…degenerates."

"Wait a second." Colin grabbed his arm and yanked Bradlee to a stop. "It's obvious you have feelings for Miss Barrington, despite your attempts to hide them. Are you certain you want to engage yourself to another?"

Bradlee continued on toward the house. "I don't see another way."

CHAPTER 18

Hot and cold water seemingly from the same source.
How can this be? Yet, it seems to be what one might
expect from this strange island.
~ *Journaled the 9th of May, 1829*

"*Y*our chariot awaits, milady." Bradlee welcomed the vision strolling up the lane toward him. His heart caught. Perhaps it was because, as of this morning's sailing of the *Oxbow*, Hannah was officially beyond his reach, but she looked exceptionally lovely. She'd worn one of her sturdier dresses for the hike, but she didn't need glittery ball gowns or sparkling jewels to appear beautiful. Her wholesome complexion radiated like gold, and her blue eyes sparkled brighter than aquamarine gemstones.

He should write some of this in his journal. Lord Byron himself would be impressed by the romantic drivel he conjured when in Hannah's company. Heavens, imagine the apoplectic fit his father would have if he moved to Nevis and became a poet?

"What is so amusing?" Hannah waved a greeting.

Colin removed his straw hat, borrowed from Mr. Clark, and

swept it through the air in an elaborate bow as if to a queen. "Lovely morning to you, Miss Barrington."

An amused giggle brought a smile to her lips.

Bradlee gritted his teeth, but he no longer had a right to be jealous. "I didn't think you believed any morning was lovely."

Colin plopped his hat back on. "Indeed. A lovely morning would mean I was still in bed and not gallivanting around on one of your perilous expeditions, but it doesn't mean I won't wish others a lovely morning." He took her satchel and placed it beside Bradlee's on the floorboard before offering Hannah a hand up into the carriage. "I try to be the reason why someone smiles today."

"If not, then the reason why they drink," Bradlee grumbled.

Hannah's lips pinched, and her eyes shimmered with suppressed laughter.

Bradlee's chest swelled with pride. He'd drawn it from her this time. The fact that she appreciated their humor was one of the many things that endeared him to her, but he must no longer keep an account. Miss Radcliff, his fiancée, didn't find his humor quite as amusing. He crossed behind the wagon. The back of his neck heated, but not from the morning sun. He hoisted himself up and sat on Hannah's right side. The satchel with his journal and pencil rested on the floorboards.

"How fares your uncle?" he asked.

"Still sleeping." The laughter in her eyes faded. "I left an elixir waiting for him for when he wakes."

"Where to?" Colin peered at her.

Hannah pointed a slender finger up the drive. "Head north along the main road toward Tamarind Bay."

Colin snapped the reins, and the horse-drawn wagon jerked forward. Sand and shells crunched under the turning wheels beneath them. She directed Colin to steer the horses up the slope toward Mount Lily. The foliage around them thickened, and the green monkeys' babble amplified as the creatures jumped about in the treetops.

"I should have told you yesterday," Bradlee said. "Colin and I have been offered more work helping to unload cargo at the docks. We'll be starting next week. The extra hours should provide the funds so we may return in time for the exams."

"That's wonderful." She twisted her head back and forth to smile at both of them. "See, God is making a way."

"It also means we won't be able to help out at the school any longer."

"Oh." She sobered.

"I shall maintain his progress with public speaking by having him sing sea shanties while he works." Colin bumped her with his shoulder.

The force caused her to knock into his, and his arm tingled from the touch.

"Who knows?" Colin mused. "Perhaps I'll even put out a hat for passersby to toss in a coin or two."

Hannah adjusted her bonnet and lowered her gaze. "You've done exceptionally well over the past few weeks. I daresay you are ready to face the dons."

"It's thanks to your doing." Bradlee owed her so much, he should be happy to sacrifice his future for her happiness. Then why did it pain him so?

Silence fell among them.

Would she miss their company?

Bradlee caught her staring at his arm. He lifted his hand and rubbed the white scar that ran across his tanned forearm. "I got this falling out of a tree as a boy."

She met his gaze. "It must have hurt something fierce."

"Indeed, it did. My bone protruded clean through the skin." His lips tightened. "Forgive me. I don't mean to offend your sensibilities."

"Why would that offend me?" Her brows drew together. "It's not my arm of which you speak."

He chuckled. "I merely didn't want you to swoon from the gruesome thought." Half the ladies in London would be over-wrought by such talk, but not Hannah. It was another thing he liked about her. She wasn't squeamish.

"Good heavens. One must have an extremely delicate consti-tution to faint over merely discussing a broken bone." She shrugged. "However, seeing it would be quite another story. I've had to set many a child's arm when the local surgeon is travel-ing. It's not for the weak-stomached."

Colin peeked around her. "Thanks to this chap"—he jabbed his thumb at Bradlee—"I've set my share of bones too."

"You exaggerate." Bradlee shifted in his seat to face Colin. "You only had to set my shoulder after the Indian chase. Well… and yes, there was my ankle in Spain." He smiled back at Hannah. "We were at a café in Andalucía. Everyone was dancing and stomping. Someone climbed on the table, and others followed suit." He chuckled at the memory. "I got a bit carried away with my stomping and sprained my ankle—same one as now." He raised his hurt foot.

"Oh my." Hannah's expression was priceless, a combination of sympathy and laughter.

Colin cleared his throat. "Don't forget I had to re-align your nose after you got into a tavern fight in Brussels."

"You were in a bar fight?" Hannah drew back as if she didn't recognize him.

"That was a misunderstanding." Bradlee raised one hand and put the other over his heart.

Colin lowered his voice. "He mistook a woman for a bloke."

"In my defense"—Bradlee raised his hands—"she had a high forehead and dressed in breeches."

"Most unfortunate," Hannah said, fighting back a smile.

Colin whistled. "She planted him one good facer. I can still hear the pop. She rearranged his face as well as a prized pugilist."

The reminder caused his nose to ache, and he rubbed its bridge between his thumb and index finger.

"With so much adventure and so many grand experiences," Hannah said, her eyes lighting with a winsome glow, "my life must seem so boring."

"Not at all." He shook his head. "You barter for goods, set children's arms, and heal their aches and pains. Plus, your future isn't predetermined."

Her eyes darkened before she lowered her gaze.

Was she thinking of England? It still wasn't too late to locate her relatives. Soon, his father would send funds and Bradlee would put them toward her fare to England. His lips parted to tell her so, but it would be best to wait for his father's response. He didn't wish to get her hopes up and then squash them. She'd been let down already by so many she loved. He didn't want to be added to that list.

His pinky touched hers, and he waited for her to glance up at him. "Besides, it's the people who make the adventure interesting."

He held her gaze, and the rest of the world disappeared. He hoped she could sense his open admiration. He thanked God for this woman. She'd saved his life and healed his ankle. The question remained whether she'd stolen his heart. He moved his hand away.

The road sloped upward, and Colin leaned forward for a tighter grip on the horse. Vines and branches stuck out from the surrounding trees. Bradlee shifted his body to shield Hannah from the protruding objects and pushed some aside with his hand.

Her closeness and vanilla scent teased his senses. She flinched as a low hanging vine dangled in front of them.

Bradlee knocked it away with his arm. "Are you all right?"

Her nod was barely noticeable, her lips mere inches from his.

Bradlee swallowed.

Hannah directed her attention back to the road. "We're almost there. There's a spot where we may pull the wagon over coming up around the next curve."

A gentle breeze picked up as Colin guided the wagon into a small clearing.

Bradlee hopped down, taking their satchels with him and slinging them both over his shoulder. He'd missed exploring. He felt like a horse about to be released from its bridle to run free in the wild once again.

Colin jumped out and tied the horse to a nearby tree.

Bradlee aided Hannah down, his hands encircling her narrow waist. He beamed a smile at her. "This is going to be splendid."

Her eyes illuminated as if she'd caught his enthusiasm. "I can tell how much you enjoy traveling and seeing new sights. Your ankle must have felt like a tether." Her teeth tugged on her bottom lip. "I do hope it's well enough. The hike will not be easy."

He bounced on his toes, testing out his legs, and felt no pain. "It's well enough." He shook out his hands and tilted his head to each side until he heard a soothing crack. "Let's begin."

Hannah led, with Bradlee and Colin trailing. Big tree ferns lined the ground under the thick rainforest canopy, and a cool-mist swirled about their feet. Small birds flittered along the trail ahead, darting in and out of the underbrush.

Bradlee removed his journal from his satchel and asked about the curious creatures. "What kind of birds are those?"

"Those are not birds." Hannah tracked one with her eyes. "They're bats."

"Bats?" Colin abruptly stopped and his face paled.

"I thought bats were nocturnal." Bradlee pulled out his pencil and jotted down a short description.

"These remain active during the day up here in the rainforest. There are larger ones, though. They come out at night." She turned to Colin. "There's nothing to fear." She continued to where the path began a steep incline and hiked her skirt to her ankles. "They only eat insects."

Bradlee tucked his journal and pencil under his arm.

"Watch your step." She picked her way through what became a latticework of tree roots intertwined along the ground.

Bradlee lengthened his stride to catch up with her.

"There is a machete in my satchel. We'll need to mark our path." She didn't check over her shoulder to see if it was him. She just seemed to know.

For some reason, that pleased him. He removed a good-sized knife like the ones the guides used in Africa from her bag and carved a line in a nearby tree.

"See that red flowering plant?" She pointed past the tree. "It's called a heliconia. It flowers in a thicket."

He glanced at the jagged crimson bloom and handed her the machete for a moment so he could note it in his journal. What he wanted to study was the lovely guide beside him. He yanked Colin between them. "Have you gotten a good look?"

Colin eyed him as if he'd gone mad. "Quite."

Bradlee plucked a smaller bloom and pressed it within the pages of his book.

"How is your ankle?" Hannah glanced down at his foot.

He tucked his journal away and breathed in a whiff of her vanilla scent. "It's fine."

"I'd forgotten how root-covered the path gets. We can walk slower or turn around at any time."

Concern for him tightened the skin at the corners of her eyes and mouth. When had a woman other than his mother cared for him? Truly cared? Blast. Had he made a terrible mistake? He shook his head, more to quell his doubts than to answer her question.

She trekked up the path, pushing off trees and holding onto nearby branches to aid her. The path narrowed, with one side sloping into a deep gully. He marked the path and admired how she climbed with expert agility.

Something rioted in his brain against Huxley's treatment of Hannah. He'd done the right thing requesting funds from his father. How could he leave knowing Hannah had to deal with the likes of Reuben Huxley? Everything about her guardian struck him as despicable. Bradlee needed to protect her. And he'd do so by marrying Alice Radcliff and becoming a professor like his father wanted.

Perhaps, it was God's will.

How do you know My will when you don't pray?

The question posed to his heart struck a chord. He hadn't been praying like he should. Was that why his future seemed so bleak—so uncertain?

Lord, forgive me.

"Hear the water?" She glanced back over her shoulder.

He stopped, more from the radiance of her smile than to pause and listen to the nearby rumbling of rushing water.

She rounded the bend and, sure enough, water splashed down over rocks like a billowing white curtain. She tilted her head back and eyed a narrow climb leading straight up over moss-covered rocks. "This is where it gets a bit tricky." She tugged on a long fig tree root protruding from the ground.

Hannah Barrington certainly didn't shy away from a challenge. He grinned to himself as he marked another tree with the machete. She'd be an excellent partner to travel and explore different regions alongside.

Colin groaned and peered up the sharp incline.

She tied her skirts about her calves, giving them full view of her trim ankles, and slipped off her slippers. "I warned you we'd be climbing a waterfall." She grabbed a thick vine and stepped into the water. "Don't worry. The water is relatively warm."

Bradlee stopped her. "Let me go first to make certain it's safe, and then, I can help you up."

Colin shook his head. "The two of you are perfect for each other. You're both insane."

Bradlee removed his boots and set them aside. He gripped the vine and walked himself up the slippery face. Once up, he signaled for her to join him. "Be careful. It's a bit steep."

She followed the same path he'd taken, except when she neared, Bradlee snaked an arm around her midsection.

"Let me assist you." He smiled down into her upturned face. Her bonnet had long ago slipped off and hung down her back. Tendrils of damp hair had escaped her topknot and hung in waves about her face.

When he lifted her, she let out a small squeak.

He hauled her up by his side. Her chest rose and fell from winded exertion.

God, help me remain a gentleman. Because this woman affected him like no other.

CHAPTER 19

The jungle of Nevis peak hangs thick with vines and
fronds the size of elephant's ears. Velvety moss covers the
ground and trees lush and soft to the touch.
~ *Journaled the 10th of May, 1829*

*H*annah's chest heaved as Bradlee set her safely down
on the ledge. His touch left her breathless as much
as the exertion of the climb. She struggled to settle her foolish,
hammering heart.

*Do not forget. He leaves soon, and you will remain here alone to
mend the tears in your heart.*

Colin grumbled the entire way until Bradlee yanked him
onto the ledge.

"The source of the waterfall is this way." She walked the
narrow path between a cliff and a pond of pooled water. The
cooler surface of the rock face absorbed the heat from her hand.
If only it could draw the heat from her face and body.

"How did you find this place?" Bradlee asked.

"Papa heard about it from the natives. He brought me here."

"He hiked you up this treacherous path as a young girl?"

"We had servants back then to aid us." She chuckled. "I had a fascination with rainbows. He told me he knew the source of all rainbows, so I begged to come here."

The sound of crashing water grew louder, the air more humid. The canopy of trees opened up, and a band of white water dropped over the cliff, splashing into the clear pool below. The sunlight peeked in through the branches and sparkled in the mist, creating a perpetual rainbow.

"Wow." Bradlee's husky voice whispered a few inches behind her.

His warm breath tickled the damp hairs on the back of her neck, and the sensation raised goose pimples on her arms.

"This might have been worth it." Awe filled Colin's voice.

Bradlee strolled to the falls edge, and they followed. He held his hand under the gushing flow. The overspray splashed their faces. She flinched and pulled back, even though the cool water felt splendid on her warm skin.

"It's magnificent." His head tilted back to see the source. His eyes blinked away droplets of water.

"Turn around." She gently tugged his arm.

He wiped his face with his hand and pivoted. His eyes widened, and his lips parted.

The thick green canopy opened up to a sight of blue sky blending seamlessly into the turquoise ocean. It was splendid, but seeing the look on Bradlee's face filled her heart with joy.

"Incredible." His voice rang with awe. "There are no words for such a view."

She licked her lips. "I've only come up this way a couple of times, but every time I do, it takes my breath away."

"I've got to sketch this. Do you mind if we rest a moment?"

"I'd be delighted to take a breather after that climb." Colin didn't waste any time lying down in a sunny spot, tucking his pack under his head, and closing his eyes. "Wake me up when it's time to go."

Hannah chewed her lip. "Perhaps the hike was too much."

"Colin will be fine. I don't feel the least bit sorry for him after this past week. He lorded his promotion over me and commanded me to perform the most demeaning duties." Bradlee scanned the area and found the least damp spot on the mossy rocks still close enough for them to dip their feet into the pool of water. He didn't wear a jacket, but removed his handkerchief from his back pocket and spread it out upon a rock. "For you, milady."

He extended his hand and aided her down before sitting beside her. They dipped their feet into the cool water. After some time, she brought her knees up to her chest and rested her chin upon them.

Bradlee pulled out his notebook and began to write and sketch.

He'd defended her honor against her uncle and treated her as if she were special, a true lady. However, a lady of the Quality wouldn't be climbing through the rainforest. If he truly believed her to be a woman of stature, he wouldn't be out here with her unchaperoned. The reality was, she wasn't of his rank. Her parents had told her she was a baron's daughter and would someday become a lady, but they died, and she'd let them down. She must face the truth. She was nothing more than what the islanders called her, a white beggar.

Bradlee was polite, but she mustn't let herself be fooled. She never would be part of his world. She sighed.

He nudged her shoulder. "You're frowning? How can you view the wonders of God's creation and frown?"

Bradlee found beauty in nature. He was made for adventure, not to be a stuffy professor. Why didn't his father realize it?

She chuckled and bumped him back. "I was thinking."

"What about?"

She eyed him shyly. "Must you be a professor? Would your

father be disappointed if you took another route, one that could be lucrative?"

Bradlee's face perked up, but a moment later his eyes clouded. "My father is determined I shall follow in the footsteps of my great uncle." His jaw clenched. "Anything else to him is unseemly. I might as well be a gravedigger."

She folded her legs beneath her and shifted to face him. "But God didn't make you to be a professor, at least not the type that sits in a damp, dusty room, teaching the same lecture over and over. Doesn't your father see that?"

"He used to." He sighed. "He used to encourage our exploration, have us question things, rationalize our reasoning, but when my ideas and, eventually, travels extended beyond what he considered safe boundaries, he changed his attitude. He became more controlling and decided upon specific expectations."

"Might he merely be concerned for your wellbeing?"

"His expectations have become greater than his love for me."

Her heart ached to heal his hurt, but no poultice could mend the rift between him and his father.

He rolled his lips and stared past her to the waterfall's endless pour. "What lucrative route were you thinking?"

Her stomach churned like the whitewater. Would her idea sound foolish? She'd never confided her backup plan to anyone. "It's only if I'm not able to locate my English relatives." Or if they rejected her as an unwanted poor relation. Then she would have to make a life here. "I intend to grow medicinal herbs and indigo. I've already planted a garden. I believe my elixir is going to be a big seller. Perhaps you or Colin would be interested in distributing them if I shipped them to you? I'd offer you a cut of the profits."

"Fifty-fifty?"

"Sixty-forty," she said, "and you pay for the shipping."

He threw back his head and laughed.

The boisterous sound caused birds to take flight and Colin to roll unto his side.

"You drive a hard bargain. It's another thing I enjoy about you." His face fell as if remembering something.

The waterfall gushed and swirled the pool about their feet.

He sighed. "Colin has connections for the herbs, and I know a merchant for the shipping—Nathaniel Winthrop. I can put you in contact with him."

"Perfect." She issued him a curt nod. "It's settled then."

"I'm officially the middleman." His usual wry tone held a deep sadness. "It's not going to save me from my boring fate."

She scooted closer. "Initially, it might take some time to make money, but it's going to sell. It must."

"I believe it will." He released a whoosh of breath. "It's merely that it doesn't matter. My father has it in his head that the only respectable profession for a second son is to become an Oxford professor."

"Is that God's will for you?"

Bradlee stared into the swirling depths of the pool. "How do I know what God's will is for my life?"

It was a question she often asked herself, and she could only give him the same answer her parents and Mr. and Lady Clark always told her. "Pray."

Bradlee continued to stare into the water as if lost in his thoughts.

A returning bird broke the silence with a loud whistle.

Hannah swished her feet in the cool spring water. "Do you feel prepared for your exams?"

"There hasn't been much time to study. Scraping barnacles off a ship takes a lot out of a man. I return to my bed at the Clarks' home too tired to think. Hopefully, I'll have time to study on the return trip."

She scratched the bridge of her nose with her index finger. "I was thinking about your writing and missing journals. The ocean might have washed away some of the details, but the stories are still in your head. Maybe you should switch from writing a documentary for scientific purposes to more of a fictional novel debut. Perhaps, if your professors saw how your writing makes the world seem a little smaller, they would allow your adventures to be turned into a book, and you could be a writer."

His brow furrowed. "I could never fully put into words the reason why I chase adventure and have the desire to chronicle them." His warm molasses eyes widened, lighting with excitement. "You just did—to make the world a little smaller. You're brilliant." He smiled and strummed his fingers on his thigh. "It would be my way of bringing cultures together—through story. I could provide a better understanding. A means of seeing things from others' perspectives."

He peered at her with a combination of boyish delight and the dauntless resolution of a noble pioneer. Her heart unfurled like a sail catching a gust of wind. She summoned all her restraint not to throw her arms around him and beg him to take her with him. How would she bear life without him?

His gaze grew intent, reminding her of his description of a hunting lion. His hand cupped her shoulder, and his thumb stroked the tender skin along her collarbone. "Once again, you have saved me."

Her heartbeat doubled its tempo.

Colin stretched his limbs behind them and grunted. He dusted the dirt off his sleeve. "You owe me an entirely new wardrobe upon our return. I don't get paid enough for this."

Bradlee stood, tucked his journal back in his sack, and yanked Colin to an upright stance. Something jumped out from underneath him.

"Egad!" Colin reared back. "What in perdition was that?"

Hannah spotted the creature first. "Calm down. It is merely a cane toad."

"Aren't those poisonous?" Colin's mouth dropped open.

She chuckled. "Only if you lick their skin."

Bradlee bent down to study the toad closer. "You're thinking of the poisonous dart frogs. This is a toad."

"I'm not taking any chances." Colin backed away.

"We're not done yet." Hannah pushed to a stand and moved to the rock face. "Just a little farther."

Colin's head dropped back. "Ugh."

The rock face wasn't as challenging to climb, for the natural breaks in the rock almost served as a sort of crude stairway. At the top, several small streams merged into one that led down to the waterfall. A hint of sulfur floated on the breeze.

Hannah glanced around for the large banyan tree and discovered it beyond a thicket of tree ferns. "This way. There's one more thing I want you to see. Have your sample jar ready."

They followed her down the path. Purple and yellow hibiscus flowers dangled from the trees, adding color to the rich greens of the landscape, and a few hummingbirds buzzed by, darting from flower to flower. The cloud humidity swirled around them, giving the surroundings a dream-like setting.

Two island pigs squealed and darted out from under the protection of a large elephant ear plant. Colin quickly caught up with Hannah and took her arm as one would a shield.

She glanced over her shoulder at Bradlee's smug face. "Come and feel this water." She waved him over. "It's a tad different from the last." She pointed through a faint mist to a stream gurgling through a small gully over rocks and fallen branches.

He crouched down, stuck his hand in the water, and quickly yanked it back out. "It's hot." His brow furrowed, and he dipped his fingers in again. "It's as warm as cup of tea." He waved at Colin. "Feel this."

Colin eyed Hannah as if checking to make sure it was safe. She nodded, and he too dipped his hand into the stream. "Zounds, it is hot."

It mustn't have been too warm, for he didn't remove his hand.

Bradlee cupped some of the water and brought it to his nose. "It smells like boiled eggs."

"It's the sulfuric content." Colin removed his hand and wrinkled his nose. "Sulfur always smells like rotten eggs."

"Many people believe the hot springs have healing abilities." Hannah pulled up some lemongrass to keep as an herb and stuck it in her satchel. "The Artesian Hotel has one and boasts of royalty visiting to utilize the bath's curative properties. I daresay there's not much truth to it, or death and illness wouldn't be so prevalent on the island."

Bradlee shrugged. "Shall we test the theory?" He rolled up his pant legs further and stepped in. The stream bubbled over his toes, and a lazy smile crossed his face. "It certainly feels nice, like stepping into a steamy warm bath."

Colin crossed his arms. If you come down with some sort of strange ankle rash, don't ask me to tend to it."

"I won't have to, now that I've gone into business with Miss Barrington." Bradlee flicked a glance at her.

"What have you gone and done while I was sleeping?"

Bradlee swiped a hand through the air. "I'll explain later." He dipped the sample jar into the water and screwed the lid on tight.

"Can we go now? I don't want to be stuck on this mountain at night with bats and poisonous toads and such." Colin didn't wait for an answer. He trudged back the way they came, down the natural stone steps, and over to the root climb.

Bradlee sighed and offered Hannah his arm. At the steep descent down the waterfall, Bradlee bent and grabbed hold of the root. "I'll go first and lend you a hand."

She nodded.

He pushed off and rappelled down the steep slope with the athletic agility of a native.

Once down, he talked her through where to get the best footing. As soon as she was within reach, he scooped her into his arms and gently placed her feet on the ground as if she were a priceless artifact to be handled with utmost care.

The day had been better than she'd ever expected. Bradlee had opened up to her about his father and his future. Not once did he push her toward Colin or sing Colin's praises. Had he finally realized she and Colin didn't suit?

Bradlee might not see her as marriage material, but he was willing to do business with her. Perhaps over time he'd realize there was something special between them, something he could only find in an orphaned island girl. She could only hope.

~

*A*t the Clarks' home, Hannah loathed the day coming to an end, not only because she dreaded parting company, but also because she must go home and face Uncle Reuben. He'd been sleeping when she left the house. If he'd been awake, he probably would have barred her from joining Bradlee and Colin. Her anger had gotten the best of her this morning. If her uncle could lie and misuse her money on spirits, then she shouldn't have to obey his ridiculous notion to not speak to a soul. Before she could reconsider, she'd stormed out the door and didn't look back.

Now she forced her hand to turn the knob on the side door. Was it awful to hope for him to still be feeling the effects of his drinking and not have noticed her disappearance?

The door jerked open, pulling her along with it.

"Where have you been? Off with those men again?" He pressed her shoulders against the wall. "What have you told them? What have you done?"

"Nothing. I've done nothing." Hannah shrank back. She'd never seen him look this crazed.

He growled into her face. "Word will spread. It will get back to him, and we'll be ruined."

"What will spread?" Her uncle wasn't making any sense. "Who is him, and why would he ruin us?"

His fist pounded the wall. "There are things in play you don't understand."

She pleaded with her eyes. "What don't I understand? If you'd only tell me, I can help."

He grabbed her upper arm and yanked her away from the wall. "You'll help me by staying put." With a hard shove, he propelled her into her room.

She caught herself just before her head hit the dresser.

The door slammed behind her, and the key turned in the lock. "For yer safety I want you stayin' put. I want you away from those men, the Clarks, *and* that school of theirs. You hear me?"

She jostled the handle. "Uncle Reuben. Don't do this. Talk to me."

His boots stomped back down the hall.

Hannah had never seen him so irrational. She sank onto the bed. Better to wait for his ire to cool. She didn't fear the door being locked, for she always had the window.

Several minutes later, the rusty hinges of her shutters squeaked closed, and hammering commenced.

Hannah darted to the window. "You intend to hold me prisoner? Uncle Reuben, you mustn't do this. Talk to me. We can work this out together."

"You brought this on yerself, gallivantin' around, talkin' to folks. This is the only way to protect us."

"Protect us from whom?"

He didn't respond.

Each pound felt like a nail beaten into her heart. "Why?" She sank onto her bed, and tears slid down her cheeks. "Why would you do this to me?"

CHAPTER 20

...The majestic Alps blanketed in snow,
Graceful giraffes roaming the Savannah,
The sun's rays kissing the ocean,
I've seen such splendor in my midst,
But none compares to dearest Hannah.
~ *Journaled the 12th of May, 1829, with a note for Lord Byron
to begin seeking other employment.*

Hannah paced the length of her room. She'd pounded on her door until her palms felt raw. The only response was the slamming of another door, most likely his bedroom. Uncle Reuben had lost his mind. There was no other explanation for his maddening behavior.

Hours passed without any sound from her uncle. Blandina slid a plate of cheese and bread under the door.

"Blandina." Hannah pressed her eye to the keyhole. "Please, you must help me. Find the key and unlock the door."

She could make out flashes of black and white as Blandina's hands wrung her apron. "He'd be awfully mad. He's not hisself,

Miss Hannah. He'd beat da devil out of me. I would do it fer you, but I can't think only of meself."

Hannah stilled. Poor Blandina. She too was in a terrible predicament, except for her there was no escape. She was Huxley's property. Hannah sat back on her hands. "You must think of the babe."

Blandina's footsteps retreated back down the hall.

Weariness from the hike and emotional exhaustion sank in. Hannah rose and collapsed onto her bed as her room grew dim in the twilight. Was this to be her prison? Surely, he would let her out on the morrow, but would he truly never allow her to return to the Clarks, or to the school? If she'd known today was going to be the last time she laid eyes on Bradlee, would she have done anything different?

No... Yes.

She'd never regret spending the day with Bradlee and Colin, but if only she could have told them good-bye, thanked them for making her feel like a lady, and let them know she'd be praying for them during their exams. She'd enjoyed Bradlee's company, but his arrival had stirred up feelings she shouldn't have. She'd dared to think about what her future would have been if her parents were still alive.

If her parents had raised her and she'd grown up as a proper lady should, she would have been a suitable spouse. She and Bradlee would have traveled together, maybe as missionaries teaching in different parts of the world. He'd introduce her to his family, and they would accept her with open arms. Or, perhaps she and Bradlee would settle down somewhere and have a brood of children. They'd all have his sense of humor and goofy smile. They'd play storm the castle, and he'd allow the children to climb all over him. He'd pretend to surrender, but have a resurgence and tickle them all into submission.

Her dream required her to be something she was not. She hugged her pillow to her chest and peered out the hole she'd broken in a slat of her window shutter. Breaking the wood only caused her uncle to nail two cross boards over her window, but at least she could still see through the hole. The full moon shimmered like its reflection on the oceans, only it blurred due to the haze of her tears.

A life with Bradlee was impossible, but it had been nice to dream. His warm amber eyes ignited a kinship where she felt accepted and loved—as if she'd come home. Not to the house where her uncle resided, not to a prison of his making to hide from a mysterious man who, for all she knew, could be a delusion in her uncle's crazed mind.

A life with Bradlee would be different. The home of her dreams would be a place where she warmed in front of a huge stone fireplace, where she ran through lush green grass, and where loved ones wrapped her in a warm embrace and kissed her forehead.

God, I know you have a plan for my life. You have been faithful in providing for me even when the coffers are empty. Please take these feelings for Bradlee from me. It hurts to be reminded of what I could have had.

She wiped tears from her eyes with the back of her wrist.

Help me to remember I belong to You, that I'm not an orphan. I'm a co-heir with Christ. If I share in His sufferings, then I may also share in his glory.

She chuckled a weak laugh. Lady Clark read to her so often from Romans eight that the word had become incorporated into her prayers.

Hannah poured out her heart to God until the moon rose high in the sky. She must have drifted off to sleep, for her eyes sprung open at the creak of the floorboard.

The astringent smell of rum permeated her bedroom.

She fumbled for a match to light a candle. The flame blazed to reveal a shadowy form kneeling on her floor.

CHAPTER 21

...The man lacks a spine, and I fear his motives are far from honorable.

~ *Journaled the 16th of May, 1829*

Hannah's stomach dropped like a stone.

Uncle Reuben startled at the light and quickly slid the loose floor board back into place with his hand. Scrunched in his other palm was the sack with the little money she'd brought in from her poultices after she'd given him everything else she'd saved.

"That's mine." She sat up in bed, clutching the covers.

He pushed off the floor and rose with a grunt. His expression appeared pained in the flickering light—the whites of his eyes shown in bright contrast with his dark pupils. He lifted a bottle to his lips and stumbled backward until he leaned against her dresser.

He set the bottle on the dresser, but kept his hand on it. "I should have drowned that night."

She didn't move.

"I was supposed to captain their ship. I was the best

captain in the Caribbean Sea. I lost my vessel gambling, but yer papa took pity on me and chartered me to captain his schooner."

He stared at the amber liquid in the bottle. "That night, I was in my cups and in no condition to sail. Yer father was livid. Threatened to terminate me on the spot, and I'm not sure why he didn't. He thought he could manage with my crew. It was a short trip. No one expected a storm gale to come through, especially not one so strong."

He pounded his fist on the dresser, and she jumped.

"I should have been at the helm." He lumbered over to her bed and sat on the end. The mattress sank under his weight.

Hannah pulled her knees to her chest and scrunched against the headboard.

"I could have kept them alive. They were good people, and I was nothin' but a lowlife." He gulped another ragged swallow from the bottle. "I figured I could try to make up for my sins by watching over their wee daughter. So, I gave up sailing and got a job overseeing, but I failed at that just like I've failed at taking care of you." He wiped a hand down the side of his face and leaned his head against the wall. "Now they think yer dead too, and I can't let them find out otherwise."

"Who thinks I'm dead? Why? Help me understand."

"It's my shame." His face crumpled. "Now we have to pay the price."

"What price?"

Hannah stared at the broken man silently weeping. Time ticked by as she waited for a response.

"We needed money." His voice trailed off in a whisper.

"Uncle?"

Nothing.

Should she leave? She'd only be forced to return in the morning, thanks to the governor's decree. After a while, her uncle's breathing deepened and evened out. He'd fallen asleep with his head leaning against the wall. She waited for what seemed like an eternity, and then slowly rose.

She leaned over his form. His eyes were closed, and her money lay curled in his grasp. She'd earned it, and he'd only proven he would waste it on spirits. She fingered the burlap bag and gently pulled.

His grip tightened. He dropped the now empty bottle, which landed on its side on the mattress, and grabbed her wrist.

Hannah froze.

"I'm not a bad person, but I've made some terrible mistakes. Ones I can't atone for." The sour stench of his breath hung over her.

The haunted sound of his voice sent chills through her. "Let go of me."

"That's just it. I can't let go." Even as he said the words, he released her arm. "Albina is right. You need to marry and be out of our hair, but I can't let you. I need you."

"You don't need me." She backed away, out of his reach. "You need God."

He seized the empty bottle and wiggled off the bed to a stand. "I need you to save me."

"Only God can save you."

His mouth tightened, and his voice rose. "I need you to do as yer told and stay put."

She refused to shrink back in fear. "He's a forgiving God."

Her uncle strode to the door.

"Wait. Don't—"

He stumbled into the hall, slammed her door, and locked it once again.

The creak of the front door drifted in the distance, then slammed as it shut. She rushed to the window and peeked through the broken slat.

His form stumbled down the lane in the pale moonlight. He

clutched another bottle in one hand and the coin to purchase her hopes in the other.

~

*T*he porch door squeaked, and Lady Clark stepped outside with Hattie in tow, carrying a tray of scones and tea. A week had passed without any word from Hannah. She hadn't even appeared at the school, and her disappearance set Bradlee's teeth on edge.

"Has there been any word yet?"

"I'm afraid not." Lady Clark's face grew solemn. "Would you gentlemen care for tea?" Lady Clark didn't wait for their answer, but waved for Hattie to set the tray on the side table. She started to pour as Hattie returned to the house. "One lump or two?"

"Two." Colin straightened from his reclining position in the rocking chair.

Bradlee shook his head. "I'm not in the mood for tea."

"It will do you good." She passed them each a cup and saucer and settled into a nearby chair.

"It isn't like Hannah to miss church." Bradlee scooted to the edge of his seat.

Colin sipped from his cup. "Nor to miss school."

"I find it unsettling too." Lady Clark frowned. "I figured she might have more chores with Blandina about to give birth. I even sent Hattie to check on them, but all Hattie could discover was Blandina's time hasn't come yet." She stirred her tea and set the spoon aside. "Hannah sent word shortly after that she is no longer allowed to teach at the school or come to the house until after you men have sailed."

Bradlee groaned and sank his head into his hands.

Lady Clark stared at the teacup clutched in her hands. "I shouldn't have allowed her to go unchaperoned. The rules here are lax, and she's grown up traipsing around the island, but Hannah is the daughter of a sugar baron. I should have treated her in accordance with her station."

"It's my fault. I asked her to accompany us." Bradlee lifted his head. "How do we know nothing ill has befallen her in the hands of her uncle? The man's a drunkard and unstable. I checked with Mr. Maroon at the general store, and she hasn't even sent him any poultices. I fear she may have come to harm."

"It's as if she's completely disappeared." Colin set his cup down.

Bradlee tugged on his earlobe. "We've even gone so far as to walk past her house to catch a glimpse of her, but the shutters are drawn even when the sun is setting. The house remains closed up tight."

Lady Clark sighed. "The note was written in her hand, so we know she's alive."

"I need other reassurances." Bradlee rose and paced the room. "Can we send someone to speak with her?"

"Mr. Clark has attempted to speak with Mr. Huxley, but he's become a recluse." She sipped her tea. "He hasn't even been frequenting the taverns. He sends Blandina, poor girl, to purchase spirits."

Colin shook a finger in the air. "What of that woman— Crafty or Crofty? Perhaps she knows something?"

"Miss Kroft has moved her attentions elsewhere." Lady Clark set her cup down.

"There must be something more we can do." Bradlee paused and turned to face Lady Clark.

"I can speak to the mayor and see if there's any legal action we may take. Hannah was placed in her uncle's care until she marries, but now that she's over eighteen, perhaps there's a way."

Bradlee pointed his thumb at Colin. "Colin and I will continue to survey the house on our way to and from the docks and on our breaks. We might be able to get a word with the slave girl."

Lady Clark scooted forward in her chair. "And we need to pray for God's protection and intervention. The Almighty has a plan. We must trust He will make a way."

CHAPTER 22

...The blackguard!
~ Journaled the 24th of May, 1829

*H*annah folded the book she'd already read four times and peered out through the broken slat in the shutter. The tiny breeze did nothing to cool her heated face, but the wind felt lovely all the same. Summer had swooped down upon the island, and her once fresh and beautiful home had become a stale sweatbox.

Without her regular routine, the days blurred into one another. Huxley—she could no longer refer to him as her uncle now that she knew the truth—had kept her locked in this prison she used to call home for over a week. She pleaded with him to see reason, but he refused to relent.

All those years she'd trusted him, relied on him. How could she have been so blind to his faults? She'd convinced herself his drinking wasn't that bad. Plenty of islanders overly imbibed spirits. At least, he'd never been found face down in the gutter, soaked in the stench of his own vomit, as she'd witnessed on many occasions. Even still, she never imagined it would come to this. She'd been a fool.

Little Freda Smith trotted up the lane toward town. Hannah missed the children and the Clarks. What surprised her the most was her desire to see a pair of teasing amber eyes that warmed her heart and danced with a spirit of adventure.

Bradlee and Colin had gone out of their way to pass by the house on more than one occasion. One afternoon, Bradlee stopped and stared at her window as if seeing through the closed shutters and into her heart.

She tore out a precious page of one of her books and jotted a note to let him know she was being held captive and to inform the mayor. She pushed the note through the slat a bit too far and it dropped beneath her window. Surely he saw it fall, but when she peeked through the hole, Bradlee's eyes were closed and head bowed as if saying a prayer. He opened his eyes and took one last look at her window before moving on without the note, which lay in the tall sea grass below her window.

She wanted to scream, but Huxley would hear her and come running. He used her friendship with Blandina as a weapon, threatening to beat the girl or have the baby taken away. Hannah flopped back on the bed and pressed her palms against her eyes. There must be a way out of this mess.

Later that day, Huxley found the note blown onto the front stoop and promptly removed all books, papers, and writing utensils from her room. The following day, he spied Colin trying to speak to Blandina and threatened to shoot them if Bradlee or Colin came on his property again. Neither Bradlee nor Colin had passed by in the last week. Had they sailed already? May was almost at an end. Certainly, they would have saved up the funds by now.

Now, Huxley became even more distrustful and slept on a pallet outside her door.

"I'm the only one who will protect you," he said. "I'm the

only one who wanted you, and I'm the only one who stepped up to take care of you, so we need to stick together."

"You lied to me, pretending to be my uncle to spend the last of my parents' money. You are a blackguard, and now that I know the truth, the governor's decree no longer stands."

Huxley released a string of expletives unfit for a woman's ears and turned Blandina away when she came to bring Hannah her supper. The following morning, he wept outside her room, and once again, begged her forgiveness after sliding a double portion of eggs under the door.

His condition appeared to only grow worse. Fear bled him like an application of leeches, stealing his sanity. He grew more restless and uneasy by the day. Anytime a sound commenced, she heard him jump up and run to the windows. What he was looking for, Hannah had no idea.

She tried on many occasions to ask him who the "they" was, and why "they" were after him, but he refused to discuss the subject, and asking only made him angry. The only thing she could imagine was that he believed the duns were coming for him to tote him off to debtor's prison. However, when she mentioned having him or Blandina take her poultices to Mr. Maroon to be sold to pay down his debts, his answer was a firm no.

The only time she could glean information was when he drank himself into oblivion. He'd ramble on about an evil solicitor or overseer of some sort, one who'd robbed him of the funds due to him. He murmured about people trying to kill them and how they must hide and pretend to be dead. His mad rantings were often followed by bouts of guilt, and he'd beg for her forgiveness.

He no longer went into town except when desperate for supplies, and his appetite had waned. The fun-loving uncle she remembered from her childhood had been replaced with a haggard, overly-suspicious man, who bordered on lunacy.

Hannah needed answers and an escape plan, but she must bide her time and not risk putting Blandina or the baby in harm's way.

When he'd once again bled dry the last bottle of rum, Huxley left to go into town, saying he'd be back later. Hannah heard the key turn in the lock and his footsteps crunching over the crushed shells. She ran to her bedroom window and watched him saddle Shadow and ride down the lane. She waited for him to round the bend before donning her mother's best gown and slippers.

"Blandina." Hannah whispered, but there was no reply. "Blandina?" She raised her voice. This time the sound of her waddling steps approached.

"Yes, Miss Hannah."

"I need for you to unlock the door."

"Ya know I can't do dat." Her voice shook. "If he finds ya gone, he'll hurt the baby. He told me so hisself."

"You can come with me."

"Dey'll send me back. I'm his property."

"I'll find a way to convince them."

A rap sounded on the main door.

Blandina gasped.

Hannah froze.

Huxley wouldn't knock. His rantings echoed through her mind, *They think yer dead. If they find out yer not, they'll kill you fer sure.* She shook the ridiculous thoughts from her mind. She would not catch his madness.

"Lawd have mercy upon us." Blandina whispered and her footsteps waddled down the hall.

Hannah watched through the keyhole as Blandina paused near the front door. She rested one hand on the wall and another on her rounded belly. Her chest rose and fell in deep breaths as if she were winded.

The rap sounded a second time, and the high-pitched squeak of hinges meant Blandina swung the door wide.

"May I help ya?" Blandina's voice sounded strained.

"Is your master at home?" a gruff baritone voice asked.

"Naw, sir, he's out." Her grip on the door tightened. "What's dis regardin'?"

"I'm not obliged to say." Silence fell between them. "Send someone to fetch me as soon as he returns."

Boots crunched down the crushed shell walk as Blandina shut the front door. Hannah scurried to the window to peek through the slat. A strange man of thick build dressed in full garb, despite the heat, mounted his horse.

The dust from his steed's hooves swirled down the lane as he rode off.

Blandina approached her door and a sickening feeling squeezed Hannah's stomach.

"He handed me dis card." Blandina slid it under her door. "I believe he's from da spungin' house."

"Spunging house," Hannah repeated in a whisper. So it was true. Huxley was in debt, and the duns had come to take him to a lock-up. They'd hold Huxley until he found a way to pay his debts, or he'd go to prison.

Her stomach dropped like a boat down the backside of a wave. "I need to know how bad it is." She jiggled the door handle. "Your life depends on it too. I'm merely going to look through his things. Afterwards, we'll make a plan together."

There was a long pause. Blandina walked away and Hannah's shoulders slumped. Didn't Blandina understand? They could both be in danger. She needed to know if it was only financial ruin or if there was something more nefarious.

The sound of a key sliding into the lock jerked Hannah upright. The door swung open and Blandina stood there with one hand on her stomach. Her face was tight and beads of sweat had formed on her forehead.

"Thank you." She hugged her friend in a tight squeeze. "I won't let anything happen to you and the baby. I promise. Just stand guard and let me know the moment you see or hear him coming."

Blandina nodded, but worry shone in her dark eyes.

Hannah entered into his room where stale spirits tainted the air. His curtains swayed in the breeze, for his shutters hadn't been nailed shut. Her legs itched to slip out the open window, but she'd promised Blandina. Instead, she moved to his desk. Stacks of papers lay strewn in untidy piles. She began to sift through them, careful to make everything appear untouched. Letters from bill brokers were mixed in with promissory notes. Her head ran the numbers and, before she was even halfway through the pile, the figure was upwards of a hundred and sixty-four pounds. The money she offered him wouldn't even have covered half the sum.

"He's in deep." She opened a drawer and sifted through more notes until she found a box tucked way in the back. She pulled on the lid, but the lock stayed tight.

Blandina let out a low moan.

Hannah glanced at the door. "Are you all right?"

"Yes'um." Her voice was tight. "It's jus practin'. My time hasn't come yet."

"Try to rest while you keep watch for me, and let me know if you need anything."

"Yes'um."

Hannah felt through the rest of the drawer, and even those of Huxley's dresser, until she found a small key that matched the chest. She unlocked it.

It contained a stack of letters.

Hannah sank onto the bed and read each one. She gathered that he'd poorly invested in one Captain Fielding about the same time as her parents' deaths. Fielding had promised a great return from the illegal trading of slaves, but the man ran off with the money and was never heard from again.

There were letters written to Huxley from Governor Vaux, who made vague statements regarding allowing him this favor in exchange of a cut, and another correspondence between Huxley and a man whose name was written only as Mr. F. It appeared Huxley had been extorting Mr. F for money, for he sent regular quarterly payments. A recent letter sank Hannah to her knees.

The final funds shall not be dispensed until you can show proof of her demise, or that she is no longer an issue.

Huxley's rantings had been true? He'd lied about her death to extort a man for money, but who? A relative?

"Someone's comin'," Blandina called from the salon. The words were followed by another moan.

Hannah quickly set the room back to rights, tucking the box back where she found it and placing the key in its hiding place.

A knock sounded on the door, and Blandina waited for Hannah to return to her bedroom before she opened it.

"Good afternoon." Bradlee's husky tone reverberated from the entranceway, vibrating a tingle through Hannah's fingers and toes. "Please tell Miss Barrington that Mr. Granville and Mr. Fitzroy have come to call."

Hannah pushed open her door and ran to the foyer. "Bradlee." She threw herself into his arms, not caring how unladylike it appeared or whether it was proper. Her body shook with the information she'd absorbed, and her need to be held overrode good sense.

Bradlee crushed her to him, not seeming to mind her inappropriate display. "Are you all right? Tell me you're safe. I cannot bear another minute of worry." He pulled back and cupped her face between his hands.

"I've missed you." Tears burned the back of her eyes from his soft touch. "I wait and watch for you every day through the broken shutter, but then a week passed, and I didn't see you. I feared you'd sailed."

A smile swept over his face, but it quickly inverted into a frown. Deep concern etched lines on his face. "We saw your uncle leave and then the stranger knocking."

He'd been watching over her? She fought down the overwhelming desire to release the pent-up torrent of emotion she'd held back for so long. Instead, she steeled herself for his reaction to the new information she'd learned. "Reuben Huxley isn't my uncle. He admitted as much."

Bradlee's lips parted in a silent gasp.

"Thank heavens." Colin sighed. "He'd make an odious in-law. Holiday gatherings would be a bear."

Blandina eyed Hannah, then slipped away into the kitchen.

"If your uncle isn't truly your uncle, that means you no longer are required to stay here. You can reside with the Clarks."

Hannah nodded. "I've so much to tell you." She squeezed his hands. "I'm so grateful you're here." She glanced at Colin. "But how? It's mid-afternoon, you're usually at the docks?" Hannah searched Bradlee's face.

His eyes clouded. "We've—uh—saved enough money for our passage."

Her knees threatened to collapse as if a heavy weight fell upon her shoulders.

"The *Boadicea* begins boarding at first light and sails in the afternoon."

His words sliced through her heart, and her fingers curled tighter around his shirt. She wasn't ready to say good-bye.

A crash sounded in the kitchen, followed by a low moan.

Hannah's head whipped around. "Blandina?" She forced herself to release Bradlee, then rushed down the hall, past the dining room, and into the kitchen. Bradlee and Colin's footsteps pounded behind her.

The tea service tray lay upside down with the teapot and cups shattered beside it. A puddle of water, which could barely be considered weak tea, spread across the floor. Hannah darted around the prep table to where Blandina rested on her knees, one hand clutching the table and the other her stomach.

Hannah dropped beside her.

"Did she cut herself?" Bradlee's brows drew tight together.

Colin nudged around him. "Are you blind? The woman is in labor." He peered at Hannah. "How long since her last contraction?"

"I don't know. Less than ten minutes ago."

Blandina's moan grew into a screeching cry. Her eyes shut as if to block the pain, and she clutched her belly with both hands.

Colin's eyes widened. "The baby's coming."

"Hound's teeth." Bradlee elbowed Colin. "You're the physician. What should we do?"

"Physician-in-training." Colin's face paled despite his recently tanned skin. "And physicians don't typically birth babies. It's not proper. We need a midwife."

"Everything is going to be fine," Hannah whispered into Blandina's ear. She slid a comforting arm around Blandina's back and glanced at the men. "Hattie isn't a midwife, but I know she's helped birth many a slave child. She'll know what to do."

Bradlee nodded and darted out the back door.

Colin stared at the empty doorway. "For once, I'm grateful he's mobile."

Blandina moaned again.

"Those contractions are close." Colin frowned. "We need to get her to a bed. Where's her quarters?"

Hannah gripped Blandina tighter and pulled her to a crouched stance. "My room is closer."

Colin nodded and held Blandina's other side as they gingerly walked her into Hannah's room around the corner. They were nearly there when Blandina stopped. She cried out, and water-soaked her skirts and puddled about their feet.

Hannah gasped.

"It-it's normal," Colin said, but fear shone in his eyes. "Her water has broken. The baby could come at any moment." He pressed her to keep moving and settled Blandina onto Hannah's bed.

Hannah propped Blandina's back up with the few pillows she could gather.

"We're going to need blankets and towels."

She removed her blanket from the wardrobe and a bowl and damp towel from the kitchen while Colin spoke to Blandina. When she returned, she handed the blanket to him.

"The towel is for the mother."

Blandina's chest heaved, and her breathing became rapid. Sweat dripped from her brow. Hannah's hands shook as she mopped the sweat with the damp towel.

Blandina's body scrunched, her knees rising as she screamed, "Da babe is comin'. Da babe is comin'."

Colin draped the blanket over Blandina's legs. "Miss Barrington, I need you to look under, remove any of her undergarments, and let me know if you see the crowning of the baby's head."

"Me?"

He nodded. "I know it's improper, but it's more so for a man."

Her stomach plummeted to her toes, but she knelt at the foot of the bed and lifted the blanket. She struggled to remove Blandina's wet unmentionables, praying all the while for God's wisdom and intervention.

Blandina's entire body tensed again, and she released a barbaric cry. At that moment, the top of a head appeared between her thighs.

Hannah gasped. "I see it. I see the baby's head." Black hair clung to the top of a reddish-pink scalp.

Hannah poked her head out from under the blanket.

Colin peered out the window. "Thank God." His shoulders sagged.

A moment later, Hattie ran into the room, her large bosom jostling with every step. Bradlee rushed in behind her.

Colin exhaled. "You're just in time. We can see the head."

Hattie placed a gentle hand on Hannah's shoulder, and they swapped places. She spoke to Blandina. "Easy nuh, Mama. Yer bout to have yerself a wee little pickney, but ya still got some wuk to do."

Tears filled Hannah's eyes as Blandina shook her head. "It hurts somethin' bad."

Hannah turned her head into Bradlee's chest. He automatically opened his arm and held her close. She inhaled his masculine, metallic scent mixed with sweat, and some of her tension melted away.

"Why don't you and Mista Granville mek some bush tea for us, but stay in hearin' range case I needs ya." She eyed Colin. "Mista Fitzroy, ya stay and gimmi help."

The Adam's apple at Colin's neck bobbed as he audibly gulped.

Blandina grasped the sheets, pulling them into tight cords, and released an ear-piercing wail.

"I want ya ta push." Hattie stuck her head under the blanket.

Hannah and Bradlee stepped into the hallway, all too willing to escape the scene. In the kitchen, Hannah removed the bush tea herb from her cabinet and put some water on the stove to boil. The image of the baby's head continued to flash through her mind.

Its skin had been white.

CHAPTER 23

The mother antelope paid the ultimate sacrifice. Her
blood spills out onto the African plain, nourishing the
grasses and saplings, while the lion's wide tongue licks its
chops. But her children live for another day.
~ *Journaled the 29ᵗʰ of September, 1827*

*M*aybe she was mistaken. Hannah stared at the
slightly rusted tea kettle. Perhaps African babies
were born with white skin, and it darkened over time.

Steam rose from the spout, and she removed the kettle from
the hot surface.

Deep down, she knew the truth, and it sickened her
stomach.

Bradlee bent over and picked up the wooden tray from the
floor. "Where might I find a broom and dustpan?"

Grateful for the distraction, she removed the supplies from
the closet and aided him in cleaning the mess. The screams and
Hattie's coaching continued in the other room. Hannah's hands
shook as she picked up the broken handle of what used to be a
teacup.

"Do you have other cups to serve the bush tea Hattie requested?"

Hannah sighed. That had been the last of the china. "We shall make do."

He dumped the broken pieces into the trash while Hannah wiped up the spilled tea.

Another scream shook the rafters.

Both Bradlee and Hannah froze.

Hannah bowed her head and prayed for quick and safe delivery.

"How long does it take for a woman to give birth?" His thoughts had taken the same direction as hers. He scraped a hand through his thick hair.

"I-I don't know." She rose and wrung out the rag, glancing in the direction of her room. Her friend was hurting. Blandina had no husband, and if Hannah's guess was correct, Blandina would have even worse problems once the baby was born. How could Huxley do such a thing to a young girl? She'd heard of masters taking advantage of their slaves, but Blandina was barely six and ten, at least two years younger than herself.

She turned back around, and Bradlee stood inches from her.

His amber eyes brimmed with compassion and concern. "Everything is going to be fine."

Warm relief flooded her chest more from the reassurance of his presence than his words. Lord, how she'd missed him.

The intensity of his gaze almost had her believing him, but he and Colin would be gone tomorrow. The captain had been kind in his pay for their hard work. She bent down to soak up the remainder of the water. "Blandina is in need of our prayers."

As if in response, the hearty wail of a baby sprang from the other room.

Hannah inhaled a gasp as Bradlee's face broke into a smile. He lifted her off the ground, laughing, and spun her around.

Hannah joined in the mirth as he set her feet back down on the floor.

"It's a boy," Colin yelled from the room.

"A boy." Bradlee smiled down at her. "Jolly good."

"Miz Hannah?" Hattie's voiced pitched higher than usual. "Come and hold da baby."

Hannah's smile faded. Something was wrong. Bradlee released her, and she scurried to her room, ignoring the weak feeling in her knees. She tapped lightly on the door, and it opened. Colin's pale face appeared with his hair sticking out in all directions. He thrust the tightly wrapped child into her arms and closed the door.

"Is something the matter?" she asked through the wood, but no one answered her. Only murmurings could be heard on the other side. She tugged the loose end of the blanket and tucked the babe into the crook of her arm, trying not to panic at the sight of bloody fingerprints staining its edge. It was normal for there to be some blood in childbirth, or so she thought. It would be the kind of thing she'd know if she'd grown up with a mother.

She cuddled the baby in her arms and stared down at the tiny pink face, swollen eyes, and miniature lips. He was beautiful.

He released one weak last cry and promptly fell asleep.

"Poor thing." She lightly patted the blanket and ambled into the kitchen. "You've been through quite an ordeal. I daresay, I'd want to nap myself."

She peeked up to find Bradlee staring at her as she held the baby. His possessive gaze flashed the way he'd described a lion's eyes at night in his journals, and his chest rose and fell as if he might roar like one.

Hannah swallowed back the confusion of emotions she didn't quite understand but couldn't keep herself from feeling. "Come and meet the newest member of the household."

Bradlee moved to her side, so close his breath caressed her skin. "He's so small, so perfect."

Hannah smiled. She agreed entirely.

"He's also very pale." He held Hannah's gaze, and she could read in his expression that he also guessed Huxley to be the father. It wasn't so unheard of in the islands for a master to lie with his slave woman, and Hannah's so-called guardian's sins continued to mount.

The baby released a contented sigh, and Bradlee chuckled. "I want at least five of my own." His index finger lifted the infant's hand, careful not to wake him, and his tiny fingers curled around Bradlee's. "Make that six or seven."

Their smiles radiated down on his small form, content to watch his peaceful sleep.

Bradlee stole a glance at her. "Do you—er—want children?"

"Oh, yes. It was lonely being an only child." She tilted her head to see a different angle of his sweet little face. "I'd like an entire brood of them, like the mayor and his wife have."

Bradlee's grin widened, and she leaned against his side. There they stayed, watching over the baby, for a long moment.

"Miz Hannah!" Hattie's voice seemed frantic. "We need more blankets and rags. Hurry."

Hannah passed the child to Bradlee, not missing his surprised expression, and dashed to the linen closet. She grabbed every blanket she could and ran to her bedroom.

The door was open, and Hannah gasped at the sight of Hattie's bloodied hands and apron. She grabbed the blankets from Hannah's arms and waved her inside. Colin sat at the base of the bed in between Blandina's legs. Blood soaked the sheets and bed and covered his hands up to his elbows. He grabbed a fresh blanket and packed it where Blandina's lifeblood seeped out.

Hattie pulled Hannah's desk chair to Blandina's side and motioned for her to sit. She leaned down and whispered into

Hannah's ear. "We got ta stop dis bleedin', but she needs a friend ta be by her side right now. Keep her talkin' about the baby and such."

At Hannah's slight nod, Hattie moved next to Colin to hand him more clean linens and remove the soiled ones.

Hannah sank into the chair. Blandina's lids only opened partway, revealing dark eyes glazed over with exhaustion. Her friend had been through so much at such a young age...the agony of childbirth, and even before that. What had she been forced to endure? *Oh, Blandina.* Hannah gulped back tears.

Blandina's head lolled to the side to face her. "Where's my son?"

"Mr. Granville is taking good care of him just outside the door until you're strong enough to hold him." She leaned forward and grasped Blandina's cold hand between her two warm ones. "He's beautiful, perfect, with all five tiny fingers and toes. What will you name him?"

"Moses." She blinked so slowly Hannah wondered if her lids would re-open. "Moses, because he's going to be raised by another mama."

Hannah shook her head. "You're going to raise him."

As if Hannah hadn't spoken, she said, "But someday he's gonna lead people." She swallowed and gripped Hannah's hand tighter. "Don't let him see him. Promise me you won't let him see Moses. He'll kill him. His mind isn't right." Tears welled up in Blandina's eyes and coursed down her cheeks. "Promise me."

"Of course." Hannah nodded. "I'll take him straight to Lady Clark's, and when you're well..."

"I'm gonna go be wit da Lord. He can't touch me on da other side." Her clouded eyes peered into Hannah's. "I didn't do anything to draw his attention. You know dat, don't you?"

Tears spilled down Hannah's cheeks. "I didn't know he was the father. I should have, but I was blind. I'm so sorry." Her voice cracked. "I should have protected you. You're my friend."

"Yer my friend. I have been blessed ta have ya in my life, but I want ya ta watch yerself too." She paused as if to gather her strength, and Hannah could hear the ragged intake of her breath. "Now dat I'm not gonna be around. I fear fer ya. He's plagued wit demons. Git away from here. Tek Moses wit ya." A tremor ran through Blandina's body. "Protect Moses." Her voice rose barely above a whisper. "Find him a good home wit good folks."

"Don't leave me." Hannah sobbed. "Stay here. Stay with me. We'll have another picnic at the beach or go swimming in the hot spring like we used to."

Blandina closed her eyes and her mouth curved in a weak smile. "I will see ya in heaven."

"The blood is lessening." Colin peered over the blanket at Blandina, but he appeared more fearful than relieved.

"That's good, isn't it?" Hannah's bottom lip quivered. "Did you hear that, Blandina? You're going to be fine."

Colin slowly shook his head and rose.

Blandina expelled a deep breath, and her hand fell slack.

Hannah's mouth opened in a silent gasp, and she stared, disoriented by Blandina's relaxed state.

She couldn't be dead.

She remembered the last time they made breakfast together. Blandina had been more relaxed than Hannah had seen her in a long while. She'd even teased Hannah about the look in her eyes when she spoke about the Englishmen. Hannah had always figured it was the shame of the pregnancy that made Blandina quiet. Hannah had assumed the father was the neighboring slave who'd lingered around.

If only she'd known it was Huxley. He'd made Blandina fearful in his presence. He'd estranged the girls' friendship by stealing Blandina's innocence, forcing her into early womanhood.

Hannah felt for her father's ring and clung to it as memories clenched her stomach.

She and Blandina had been playing a card game on the floor, laughing and giggling as girls did, when Huxley called for Blandina to see to cleaning his room. Blandina stiffened and stared at Hannah with a clouded expression. She set her cards aside, rose, and tended to his needs. It was soon after that when Blandina turned quiet. Hannah had tried to engage her in conversation, but Blandina hadn't responded. She hadn't been the same after that day.

Hannah covered her mouth as more memories surfaced.

She and Blandina had been tidying the kitchen when Huxley had called for Blandina. She'd grasped Hannah's arm in a tight grip.

"Ow." She'd peered at her friend. "Do you want me to see what he wants?"

Blandina shook her head furiously and removed her apron with shaking hands. "I'll tend ta him. You go and see ta yer garden."

At the time, Hannah found the whole exchange strange, but now...

Colin ran his fingers over Blandina's unseeing eyes to close them, and pulled the bloodied sheet over her head.

Oh, Lord. Had Blandina been protecting her?

A choked sob burst from her lips, and a torrent of tears flowed down her cheeks, dripping off her chin. Colin stood by helplessly, covered in Blandina's blood.

Hattie shooed him to go clean up. "I'll give you a minute alone." She stopped in the doorway. "She's in God's care now. He'll tak good care of her." Hattie's eyes shown bright with tears as she followed Colin.

Hannah closed her eyes, but felt her tears splatter onto the sheets. She tried to hold back the sobs but couldn't.

God, why? She was a child, a scared little girl, like me.

She sensed Bradlee's presence before she opened her eyes.

He pulled her to a stand and wrapped her in his arms.

She clung to him and sobbed into his chest. "I p-promised to keep her safe. I promised—" her tears choked out her words.

"Shh." His hand stroked her back, and he rested his cheek against the top of her head.

She didn't know how long he held her in the warm comfort of his embrace. It could have been ten minutes, or it could have been an hour, but it was long enough for her to absorb some of his strength.

When her sobs subsided, she inhaled a shaky breath and pulled her head back. "Where is Moses?"

Bradlee brushed away a strand of her hair dampened to her face by tears, his voice gentle as he asked, "Who is Moses?"

"The baby. Blandina named him Moses before she…"

Bradlee nodded as if to save her from saying the word. "Hattie is holding him in the kitchen."

Hannah reluctantly stepped out of his arms. "I promised Blandina he wouldn't see the baby."

She didn't have to explain who *he* was. He guided her into the kitchen, where Colin and Hattie had washed up.

Hattie must have attempted to wash some of the blood off Colin's shirt, for it was no longer stained bright red and now hung wet upon his frame. His hands rested on his hips as he stepped forward. "I'm sorry. I did everything I knew to do. If only I knew more." He turned his head to the side and swiped a hand down his face. "I'm sorry."

Hannah squeezed his other hand. "She was fortunate to have been in such capable hands. Blandina knew she was dying and had made peace with it. She wasn't scared to go." Tears sprung to Hannah's eyes once more, and her voice cracked, but she forced the words out. "She told me she'd see me in heaven."

Colin sniffed and blinked away tears. "Thank you for telling me."

Moses scrunched up his face and let out a tiny wail. Hattie shifted him in her arms and patted his tiny bottom.

"Hattie." Hannah peeked down at the precious bundle in her arms. "Will you take Moses to Lady Clark and see if you can help her find a wet nurse and a good family who'd be willing to raise him?"

"I surely can do dat, Miss Hannah."

Hannah placed a hand on her arm. "Be discreet about it. I don't want word getting back to Huxley."

She nodded, bid everyone farewell, and headed out the door.

Bradlee cleared his throat. "Did Blandina have any family or anyone we should notify?"

Hannah shook her head.

"We need to get you away from here before Huxley returns." He tilted his ear toward the road as if listening for horse's hooves.

"I can't leave her." She closed her eyes to hold back a fresh round of tears. "Not until I've tended to her body."

Bradlee frowned and rubbed the back of his head. "I don't—"

Hannah opened her eyes and lifted her chin. "I won't leave my friend. Not in there. She deserves better."

"Do you have a burial ground?"

"My parents are buried in the grove. I'd like Blandina to be buried near there."

Bradlee tapped Colin on the arm with the back of his hand. "We'll get to work."

They exited through the servant's entrance, and she walked to the shed and pulled out shovels.

What if they hadn't been here to help? What would she have done then?

God, I may not understand why things happened the way they did, but You do. Thank you for Bradlee, Colin, and Hattie being here. Thank you that Blandina can now find rest and protection in your arms. Please help us to find a good home for Moses and pour Your blessing out on his life.

Hannah set to work, washing all the blood out of the linens and towels. She willed her fingers to work faster. They needed to be gone before Huxley returned. However, remembrances of Blandina feeding the chickens out the window, giggling with Hannah behind the shed, blowing soap bubbles from the wash-tub, and screaming in the pains of childbirth, slowed Hannah's arms into rote movements. As she hung the laundry out on the line, Bradlee and Colin carried Blandina's body from the house. Hannah followed them to the grave. The poignant scent of freshly dug earth enveloped her. She prayed over Blandina's soul and baptized the grave with more tears.

Bradlee and Colin gently lowered her body, still wrapped in one of the bloodied sheets, and covered it with clumps of dirt. Hannah stood by with silent tears before leaving to gather flowers to place on the grave. However, the beauty that was Blandina was no longer part of this world. Alongside Hannah's parents, she'd be a missing part of Hannah's heart forever.

～

*B*radlee wiped the sweat dripping down the sides of his face with his arm. He reeked of sweat and earth, and dirt stained his shirt and trousers. Colin looked and smelled much the same as they placed the last few rocks on Blandina's grave.

Hannah rose from the garden. The setting sunlight illumi-nated her hair in a yellow halo and set her bronzed skin aglow. A bouquet of flowers, their colorful heads bobbing in the light breeze, were clutched in her hand. She glanced up, and their eyes met.

He'd seen the majestic mountains at sunrise and the stun-ning savannah at sunset, but he'd never seen anything like the woman striding toward him. Something stirred inside. He'd always been a fidgety child and a restless youth, but ever since meeting Miss Hannah Barrington, he'd felt a deep insatiable hope, a thirst that demanded to be quenched, an itch that ached to be scratched. And when he'd seen her earlier with a tiny babe snuggled in her arms, his knees had gone weak as an unidentifiable longing caught fire and blazed through his entire being, branding deep in his soul.

He admired the sureness of her steps as she strolled up the steep incline toward the grove, carrying herself humbly, yet at the same time in a regal manner. She was different than other women, a unique lady of the highest order. It wouldn't matter if she were the orphaned child of a slop seller or the Queen of Scotland. He'd never meet another like her.

He needed to protect this rare, unprecedented find. However, the only way he'd known to protect Hannah was to agree to marry another. He'd posted the letter to his father, and it was probably halfway across the Atlantic by now. He and Colin had earned enough money to return to London. Bradlee would take his exams, collect the money from his father, and leave the next day to sail back for Hannah while Miss Radcliff and his mother readied for his wedding.

His jaw set. It didn't matter that he didn't love Miss Radcliff. What mattered was Hannah's safety. Two questions remained. Could the Clarks keep Hannah safe from Reuben Huxley until the next ship arrived? And, once she was in England, how would he be able to live with Hannah so near, yet completely beyond his grasp? His heart clenched so tightly it might have stopped beating.

"Are you all right?" Her thin brows lifted as she studied his face.

She stood within an arm's reach, tempting him to pull her close and taste her lips—drink her in so he'd know what he'd be missing for the rest of his life. He cleared his throat. "I'm fine."

"Thank you, both, for everything you did today." Her eyes misted, and she chewed her bottom lip. "I don't know what I would have done if you hadn't been here."

Colin wiped his hands on his dirty trousers. "I'm glad we were." The shadows under his eyes created a haunted look. "I merely wish we could have done more."

"You were a blessing." Hannah bent down and arranged the flowers. She stared at the mound for a long moment with the sound of the crashing waves, chirping birds, and chattering monkeys in the distance. Her head turned toward the sunset, which tinted her skin a pinkish-orange. "Hattie will be serving supper soon. You must be famished."

Bradlee picked up the shovel to return it to the shed.

Colin grabbed the other and held out his hand. "Here, let me take them."

Hannah tucked a strand of hair behind her ear. "What happens now?"

He widened his stance. "You're going to pack what you need and come back with us."

"You sail in the morning." She raised her chin in that courageous way of hers, but he glimpsed a tinge of uncertainty in her eyes. It amazed him it was only a tinge. Her life was like a sand-castle that she kept rebuilding, even though the waves washed it away each night.

"There are two options. Either you will stay under the Clarks' protection until the money I requested from my father arrives. The Clarks will then purchase you and a chaperone a ticket to England." He stepped closer and peered down into her upturned face. "If you don't come on the next boat, then I will return for you." He heaved a deep breath and forced the next sentence. "Or, you can marry Colin and come with us now."

"Colin?" Her head reared back.

"A spousal ticket will cost less because the two of you shall share a room, so I'm certain our combined funds, plus what the Clarks offered, should cover it. And Colin has agreed."

"Agreed?" Her voice held an edge to it. "People agree to a bargain. Is that all I am to you? A business deal?"

He stiffened. "No, that's not what I mean. Colin has determined the two of you will suit."

She shook her head. "No. We don't suit. I do not love Colin and Colin does not love me." Her chest heaved as if she'd run a race. She looked down at her hands and whispered inaudibly.

He could have sworn she'd said.... His heart pounded, and he leaned in closer. "Pardon?"

She cleared her throat and met his gaze. "Why won't you marry me?"

The unexpected question hit Bradlee like a blow to the face. He stood there, stunned, unable to think. His heart pleaded to declare his undying love, but his brain screamed a loud and clear warning.

He couldn't engage himself to two women.

"Never mind." She turned and strode toward the house.

Bradlee dogged her steps. "Wait. Let me explain."

She stopped and wrapped her arms about her midsection. The shimmer of tears in her eyes clenched his chest.

"I might be engaged."

Her eyes widened as hurt and betrayal flooded their depths.

"It was the only way." He reached out to touch her, but she stepped away. "My father refused to send any more funds unless I agreed to his terms—his future. I wouldn't relent, but then your uncle—er—guardian showed his true character, and I had to do something. Above all else, I had to keep you safe. The Clarks will see to your safety and passage once the funds arrive."

Hannah closed her eyes and tears spilled, leaving shiny tracks over her cheeks.

His fingers grasped her hand. "I never meant to hurt you. I would do anything to help you."

"If you will not, or cannot, marry me, then..." She pivoted back around, and her voice shook. "It's better to have an ocean between us."

"Hannah, I..."

She marched up to the house and grabbed the knob.

He gripped her elbow. "You're not safe here. You saw the color of the baby's skin. Huxley lied..."

"He's not the only one who got me to believe a lie." She wouldn't look at him.

He inhaled a deep breath. "Please, come with us. I won't sleep knowing you are in the same house as that lecher."

"I'll stay somewhere else tonight." She pulled the door open. "Thank you for your help today, but please go. Your supper will be growing cold."

"Hannah—"

"Aren't we leaving?" Colin called, edging up the lane. "My stomach is screaming for Hattie's goat water stew."

Bradlee glared at him.

Colin held up his hands as if surrendering. "All right. Don't call me out and meet me on a grassy knoll at dawn merely for being hungry."

Hannah closed the door between them.

He tried to open it, but the lock clicked.

"Hannah, open up." He banged on the door and waited, but there was no response. "Don't shut me out."

Waves crashed in the distance, and the monkeys laughed at him from the trees.

"Confound it. Open the door."

A seagull's cry jeered overhead.

He only wanted to help her. How had he made such a mull of things?

CHAPTER 24

I find myself in an impossible predicament of my own
making, but I cannot stop seeing her with a babe in arms.
His tiny features held snugly to her bosom. I peered into
a potential future, and it left me forever changed.
~ *Journaled the 31st of May, 1829*

Grief weighed down Hannah's limbs, and her vision
blurred with tears as if she were swimming through
murky water, but she had to hurry. She was definitely
not up for facing Huxley. Thank God, he hadn't arrived
home yet.

She scrambled to pack a bag. Tonight, she hoped to stay with
the Simmons family. Lady Clark would wonder why she didn't
go there, but she would only go to the Clarks once Bradlee
sailed. A clean cut healed better than a jagged wound, and the
emotional toil of what she'd just been through had left her
hollow and fragile, as if a single thought could shatter her like
her mother's precious vase.

Lord, give me strength.

The ache of all she'd lost might not subside, but perhaps her mind would clear. With her last ounce of strength, she stuffed two other gowns into her satchel and peered about the room in case she'd forgotten something.

Her bed glared up at her, Blandina's lifeblood staining the sheets, spilled for her and baby Moses.

She wanted to rail against the injustice, at the same time she wanted to curl into a ball and weep until numb, but she forced her body to function and her mind to think.

The letters.

She would need the letters to prove Huxley's wrongdoing and that he wasn't her uncle.

Hannah slipped from her room and locked her door to buy her a few precious moments before Huxley realized she was missing. She entered Huxley's room, crept straight to his dresser, and removed the key. She then moved to his desk and pulled out the locked box.

Hoof beats pounded up the lane, followed by men's voices outside, thankfully not Huxley's. Hannah crept to the window and peeked around the curtain. *Blast!* It was Miss Kroft and her cicisbeos. Hannah tucked the box under her arm and waited for them to dismount. Once they entered the house, she'd sneak out the window and make a run for it.

The front door opened and Miss Kroft's laughter echoed from the foyer. Hannah wasted no time. She quickly checked her escape path and dropped her satchel out the window. She slid one leg over the ledge and ducked under the sash.

Her head was yanked back and her scalp burned as if it had caught fire. She yelped as the hand pulled her back into the room.

"Where do you think yer going?"

~

*B*radlee punched his pillow to fluff it. He flopped over and propped his aching foot on the bed rail. With a deep sigh, he laced his fingers behind his head and stared at the ceiling. Colin's light snores whistled through the night air.

"Lord, all my life, when I've gotten into one mess after another, I've always been able to work my way out of it. This time, Lord, it seems the obstacles are too many to count and too great to surmount. I need Your help."

If only he'd prayed for wisdom before he'd sent the letter to his father. In his hastiness to become Hannah's hero, he ruined his chance with her. The thought burned like acid in his stomach.

He conjured an image of Alice Radcliff. They'd always been friends. She was a pleasant girl with a sweet smile, but she didn't excite him any more than the thought of choosing paper for the walls or fabric for curtains. Whereas, the sight of Hannah holding a small babe in her arms raised goose pimples and weakened his knees.

"Why, God? Why would You allow my heart to be drawn to a woman I cannot be with?"

Only silence filled the night air.

Colin rolled over in his bunk. He cracked open an eye. "Maybe God wants you to marry Miss Barrington?" His voice was slow and slurred with the remnants of sleep. "Did you ever think of that?"

"What do mean?"

"All I know"—Colin closed his eyes and stuffed the pillow under his head—"is God put us here for a reason. Miss Barrington suits you. She's not a proper London socialite like what you make Miss Radcliff out to be. I still have yet to see her with my own eyes, but God doesn't set someone up for failure." Colin yawned. "It's pride, fear, and stubbornness that lure us into disasters."

Did Colin have a point? Hadn't Hannah said something similar at the waterfall? Not exactly, but the result was the same. He hadn't consulted God about his future because he'd been right certain he could work out the future he wanted on his own. Or perhaps because he hadn't felt he'd had a future at all.

Colin's breathing deepened, and his snoring resumed.

Sleep seemed even further out of his reach, so Bradlee slid his journal off the nightstand. Rereading his adventures usually helped to focus him. He turned up the oil lamp and opened to their hunting and fishing excursion with Little Horse and the Sioux Indians along the White River. He flipped to the more recent pages. He'd documented the shipwreck and Hannah's daring rescue to save his and the seamen's lives.

Even in the dark, he'd known she was a unique woman—strong, resourceful, courageous, and selfless. He turned to the next page, where he'd sketched her likeness sitting in the banyan tree. His finger slid along the edge of the page, longing to caress the delicate curve of her cheek, yet not wanting to smear the charcoal. Hannah was as beautiful inside as she was outside. She wasn't dressed in the latest fashion. She didn't need trinkets and baubles to draw out her beauty. The only jewelry she wore was the leather strap holding her papa's ring close to her heart.

On the next page, he'd written about her knowledge of watches and timepieces and how intuitive her thought processes were. She looked at things as if dismantling them with her mind, figuring out how they worked down to the last piece. She'd peered at him much the same way.

He'd written an entire page on the gracefulness of her walk. The facing page began as a documentation of the tropical bird plumage, but changed into the way Hannah twisted her hair up into a topknot and the cute way she scratched the bridge of her nose when thinking. He loved how she picked up leaves, berries, rocks, and other objects others would pass up, because she had plans to make use of them. Several pages later, he discussed the island's bartering system and how adept Hannah was at negotiating. No matter what topic he started out writing—the stately palm trees, the vibrant birds, the radiant heat of the sun—it morphed into a dissertation on the beauty and wonder of Miss Hannah Barrington.

Obviously, he was taken with her, but was this more than just being smitten?

Marriage to Miss Radcliff meant exactly what the men of the *ton* called it—leg shackling. It represented a loss of freedom, an end to his adventures. But maybe marriage never appealed to him because he wasn't interested in the woman he was supposed to marry? Marriage to Hannah held a different meaning.

She didn't seem the type to sit around filling her days with embroidering or paying social calls. She was like him. She thrived on seeking purpose and meaningful work. And even if she did choose to sit around and embroider, would that be so bad, as long as she greeted him every morning with her smile? The thought of marriage to Hannah didn't suck the life out of him. It breathed life into his being.

But would he grow restless over time?

He was notorious for going headlong into a project and then losing interest. Would that happen with Hannah? Would he miss traveling to exotic lands? Did he love her more than he loved adventure? His heart rattled his rib cage and screamed, *Yes! Experiences aren't fun without someone else to enjoy them with.*

Bradlee slammed his journal closed.

Colin muttered, "Go to sleep."

All of his reasoning was mute, for he'd already written to his father. He'd given his word and engaged himself to another. Tomorrow, he sailed for England, deserting his heart on an island, knowing Hannah surely hated him for shunning her love.

God, fix my mess. I've gone and gotten myself into another jam, but to You, this is just a small scrape. Please make a way.

∽

*P*ain caused Hannah's eyes to water as she was jerked upright by her hair.

"Curse Blandina. I'll have her hide fer letting you out." Huxley's voice from behind her rang with an ominous tone. He ripped the box from under her arm and tossed it on the bed. "So you know the truth of it now."

She prayed for the strength to face Huxley one last time. Reasoning with a madman would be a challenge, but God made her resourceful. He would be her shield and rampart. He'd help her find a way out of this mess. "If you let me go, I will ask Mayor Simmons to show leniency."

He pushed her down the hall, keeping a tight grip on her hair as they passed the front door. Miss Kroft's laughter rang out, jarring Hannah's ears. Huxley shoved her around the corner into the salon. She tripped on the hem of her mother's gown, but caught herself before falling.

Two of the military gentlemen from the other night sat with Miss Kroft on the sofa. The smell of spiced rum hung thick in the air. Her fingers curled in one of the men's hair, and her bosom hovered near his face. The older man shifted his hooded gaze to Hannah. His nostrils flared, and his lips twitched as he regarded her form.

Miss Kroft waved her over. "Come here, Hannah, so Admiral Gomer can get a closer look at you."

CHAPTER 25

Barnacles attach to the underside of a ship, eroding the whitewash and causing the vessel to drag, and, by Jove, they are dreadful to remove.
~ *Journaled the 1st of June, 1829*

*H*annah refused to budge. Instead, she turned to face Huxley and gasped. Dried blood darkened a crack on his lip and a split on his cheekbone. One of his eyes was blackened and so swollen he could barely see. His face looked as raw as a slab of meat from the butcher. She didn't need to ask who'd done this. The duns had found Huxley, and they'd demanded payment.

"It was never supposed to come to this." Huxley's face was so swollen, she couldn't read his expression.

The admiral rose from his seat, his jowls swaying as he slurred his words, "I'lls take h-her."

"How could you sell me to a stranger?" Her gaze pivoted back to Huxley. "What happened to the man who taught me to swim? The man who carried me on his shoulders and hiked with me up to the natural springs?"

Remorse laced his tone. "If you want to live, you need to go with him. It's better for you to be gone."

Her jaw clenched. He'd just sold her to save his hide. "Better for whom?"

He winced. "You must disappear or you'll wind up dead."

His rantings finally made sense. The mysterious Mr. F's handwritten note flashed in her memory. *I need proof of her demise.* Did Huxley believe he was saving her? His greed and poor choices had brought them to this point. After all the years they'd cared for each other, how had they come to this?

Admiral Gomer fumbled to untie a full change purse from his waistband and tossed it to Huxley. His aim was off in his drunken state and the bag landed at Huxley's feet, sliding on the stone floor until it connected with his worn boot. "That should take care of it."

Huxley's defeated gaze pleaded with her for forgiveness before it dropped to the floor. He slowly reached for the bag.

The admiral hoisted his pants over his rounded belly and directed an order at Hannah, "I hope yer thinzgs are packed. I'm ready to turn in for t-the night." He turned as if dismissing her and peered down at the other soldier.

Huxley drew open the string and began to count the coins.

The sight of the man she once called uncle counting the coin he'd used to sell her turned her blood to steam. She swatted at the bag, sending coins into the air.

As Huxley dove for the money, she planted a fist into his already blacked eye. He crumpled to the floor.

"By the devil!" She heard one of the men shout and another burst into laughter.

Her exit no longer barred, Hannah darted from the room and out the main door. She sprinted around the side of the house, pausing only to snatch her bag from where she'd dropped it under the window, then darted into the barn. She swung open Shadow's stall and gave the horse's rump a good smack, sending her in the direction of town.

"Afta her! Dere she goes down the main road." The Admiral shouted and struggled to untie his horse.

Hannah slipped out the back of the stable and darted down the path to the beach. The same path she'd traveled a thousand times, yet never in this much of a hurry.

The beach held little place to hide, but they would have easily overtaken her on the roads. The underbrush was too thick for her to pass through quickly or quietly. She could try to hide there, but it would be risky. There would be no place to run if they found her.

Her bare feet kicked up sand. She was leaving tracks easy to follow. What if she continued to mislead them? Hannah ran down the beach toward the mayor's house. Huxley would try there first, especially after her comment about asking for leniency. Without the letters, it would be her word against Huxley's. She couldn't risk the mayor sending her back into Huxley's care.

She waded into the surf. Blue crabs raised their pinchers, outraged by her invasion.

A streak of lightning illuminated the sky. The echo of thunder followed. A strangled cry ripped from her throat. *Lord, help me.*

Distant voices yelled, but she couldn't discern any movement on the shore.

She inhaled a deep breath and dove under the waves. Cool inky blackness surrounded her as she swam under the water in the opposite direction of the Simmons'. Hannah stayed parallel with the breakers, only surfacing for the barest of breaths. She would swim to the cove where she could sneak undetected back onto land. There she could follow a goat path through the cane fields. Something brushed her leg. Sharks mostly stay beyond the reef. *Please, Lord keep the sharks beyond the reef.*

CHAPTER 26

I cannot bear to stay, yet I cannot bear to leave. A thousand times I berate myself for being a fool.

~ Journaled the 2nd of June, 1829

Hannah's shoulder and hip ached from sleeping on the hard bench seat. She pried her weary eyes open and groaned as she recalled the event that brought her to seek shelter in the Lord's house. If only it had been a bad dream.

A horse neighed outside.

She bolted upright. Sun streamed in through the cracks in the shuttered windows, illuminating the specks of dust in the air like floating sparkles. It was Sunday morning. Mr. Clark and the parishioners would be arriving soon.

The latch jiggled.

She crouched low, ducking behind the back of the pew.

The door swung wide. Bright light streamed into the room, outlining Reverend Clark's silhouette. He hummed a hymn as he shuffled into the room, his Bible tucked under his arm. He moved straight to opening the shutters, not noticing her presence.

She relaxed, slumping forward in her seat. Should she make her presence known? How much should she tell him about what transpired last evening?

"Hannah, darling." Lady Clark's voice rang from the back of the sanctuary.

Mr. Clark turned with a start. His bushy white brows rose as he peered at her above his spectacles.

Lady Clark's hand moved to her breast, and her eyes turned heavenward. Hannah thought she saw the mouthed words, *thank you*, before exhaling a deep breath and smiling at Hannah. "You are here bright and early this morning." She exchanged a glance with her husband.

Mr. Clark finished opening the last window. "Getting in some early prayer time with the Lord?"

Hannah straightened. Her crouched position must have made it look like she'd been praying. Perhaps they wouldn't realize she'd slept here. She rubbed the side of her cheek to wipe away any imprints from sleeping with her hands folded under her head. With her foot, she pushed her satchel under the bench seat.

Lady Clark approached and rested a hand on Hannah's shoulder. "You poor dear. You've been through such an ordeal."

Did she know? Did Huxley knock on their door last night searching for her?

"I'll have you know, we've already found a splendid family for baby Moses." Lady Clark smiled, but her gaze held traces of sympathy, concern, and a flash of what might have been relief. "You may know them—the Carlson family from St. Kitts. Mr. Clark knows them well from preaching at our sister church, St. Michael's parsonage. Mr. Carlson is of Scottish descent, and Mrs. Carlson is several generations of freed mulatto. They have not been able to bear children and welcome Moses as a blessing. The wet nurse has agreed to go with Moses to stay on their farm."

Lady Clark's brow furrowed. "I'm so sorry for your loss. I know you and Blandina were close."

Hannah swallowed around the lump in her throat. She longed to ask about Bradlee and Colin, but feared she'd burst into tears.

"If you're up for it, would you mind helping us tidy up before service?"

Hannah hesitated. People would be arriving shortly. Huxley might learn of her presence. "I'm afraid I must go." She tried to rise but Lady Clark's hand kept her in her seat.

"I know you've been through an ordeal, but when we're going through trials, we must trust God will pull us through." Lady Clark's strong gaze implored her to stay. "God is an ever-present help in trouble. Seek his refuge."

Hannah's insides quaked, but she nodded. When Lady Clark turned her back, she attempted to shake some of the wrinkles out of her gown and fix her hair back into its fallen topknot.

"If you could sweep the palm branches off the front steps, I'll finish letting in the air." She strode to the other side of the room and opened the shutters.

Mr. Clark set up at the podium, crossing out and rewriting a few points to hone his message.

Lady Clark cast her a sideways glance. "Last night's storm was a frightening one."

"Indeed. It shook the rafters." Hannah forced her eyes not to peer upward at the wooden boards she'd watched shake only a few hours ago.

She opened the small closet, removed the broom, and quickly swept the steps. At every shadow of a passing bird or sway of a tree limb, Hannah jumped. When parishioners began to arrive, she quickly found her seat and kept her head bowed.

The mayor and Mrs. Simmons arrived with their brood of children. "Hannah, so lovely to see you this morning."

Hannah glanced up.

Mrs. Simmons's voice held a bit more emotion than usual, but her youngest yanked the tight braids of his elder sister, Gracie, causing her to cry.

Perhaps Mrs. Simmons's voice was tight due to the strain of keeping all those children under control. Hannah waved the crying girl over, asking if she might sit next to her this morning. The tears stopped, and the child scooted up against Hannah's side.

The rest of the church filed in, taking their seats, and, after a few announcements, Mr. Clark began his sermon. "Let me read to you from First Peter chapter two. 'But ye are a chosen generation, a royal priesthood, a holy nation, a peculiar people; that ye should shew forth the praises of him who hath called you out of darkness into his marvelous light.'" Reverend Clark leaned his forearms onto the podium and scanned the gathered crowd of islanders. "God has chosen us to be his children. He has made us co-heirs with Christ, and it comes with glorious treasures in heaven, but also a heavy cross to bear."

Hannah's thoughts drifted to Bradlee. Did he know he was so much more than a second son? He had wisdom, courage, and a caring heart. Even if his father considered him a disappointment, his Heavenly Father certainly did not.

"We share in Christ's sufferings so that we may also share in His glory." Mr. Clark's gaze rested upon her, and she offered him a small smile. He continued, "Even in trials, it is important for us to remember we are not fighting *for* victory, we are fighting *from* victory. Jesus secured our triumph over evil when He died on the cross. We must not act as victims, for we are victors. We must be bold and take on new challenges with faith. Remind the devil that we are God's, and, as First John tells us, the evil one cannot touch us."

Hannah wished Bradlee were here to hear those words and be encouraged about taking his exams. Perhaps she could ask

Mr. Clark to post his message in a letter to Bradlee, but would it make it to him in time?

When the sermon ended, everyone rose, but Gracie tugged on Hannah's arm and pointed to her mouth. She smiled with two big gaps in the bottom.

Hannah bent down to the girl's level. "My heavens, where did your teeth go?"

Gracie beamed as she explained how they fell out. When she finished, Hannah noticed a crowd had gathered around them. She stood and shifted to face all the sorrowful expressions watching her. Did they know Huxley had sold her to the highest bidder? Were they here to turn her over—regretfully? They still didn't know Huxley wasn't truly her uncle.

Mr. Maroon stepped forward and grasped Hannah's wrist.

She gasped and stepped back, not yet ready to surrender, but he turned her hand over and pressed several large silver coins into her palm.

"Even though ya drive a hard bargain, you have been a blessing ta me. I'm gonna miss seein' yer face at da store." Mr. Maroon flashed his white smile and stepped away.

Her brows drew together, and she stared at the money.

Mrs. Simmons approached, and Gracie wrapped her arms around her mother's skirts. She rested a hand on Gracie's back and, with the other, placed a bag of coins in Hannah's hand. "It's not much, but you deserve a better life than what is available here."

Hannah peered at all the faces. What was happening?

Mrs. O'Dell, the dress shop owner, handed her more coins. "All the best to you, dearie."

"I don't understand." Hannah looked to Lady Clark.

With a nudge from her mother, Gracie ran to the first pew, grabbed Hannah's satchel, and handed it to her.

Lady Clark stuffed another heavy pouch of coins into Hannah's bag and folded Hannah's fingers around the other money. "We heard what happened to your uncle and what he planned to do."

Hannah hung her head. They already knew her shame.

"Look at me, dear." Lady Clark waited for Hannah to make eye contact. "Your uncle is a broken man. You have done nothing of which to be ashamed. You have carried a burden for your guardian for too long. All of us here believe you deserve a better life than the one Huxley has offered you. We hope you'll purchase a ticket to England with this money. There's a ship leaving in a little while, and Mr. Maroon offered to drive you to the docks." She reached into her reticule and retrieved a sealed envelope with an address written on the front. "When you arrive in England, take this letter to the inscribed address and ask for the Duchess of Linton. She is my niece. Give her this letter, and she will provide for you."

Tears blurred Hannah's vision. She accepted the letter with her free hand, biting her bottom lip to keep from bursting into tears. All these people who could themselves barely keep food on their own tables were sacrificing precious coin for her well-being. Blinking to clear her vision, she glanced at all the caring faces. "I'm overwhelmed. I don't know what to say. Thank you isn't enough."

"It's our pleasure, my dear." Lady Clark stepped back and threaded her arm through her husband's. "Mrs. Marchmain is already on board. She's offered for you to be her daughter's companion for the voyage. I do believe Mr. Granville and Mr. Fitzroy will also watch over you, even though they left before we could tell them. You must hurry, though, for I fear the *Boadicea* will be shoving off in the next few hours."

Mr. Clark lowered his spectacles. "Remember, God loves you. He's your protector. You fight from victory, and we're all rooting for you." He squeezed her hand. "Now, hurry along and go with God."

Had Reverend Clark's message been meant for her?

Suddenly, the words contained a whole new meaning. Tears coursed down her cheeks. She wrapped both Lady and Mr. Clark in a tight embrace. "Thank you both for"—her voice cracked—"everything." They held each other for a long moment before she stepped away and turned to the people she never realized until now had been her surrogate family, more so than her guardian. "Thank you all."

Mrs. Simmons brushed away tears from her cheeks. "Hurry along before the ship sails."

Mr. Maroon exited the church and waved her to follow.

Hannah nodded and turned to leave. With one last glance over her shoulder and a handblown kiss to the friends she'd most likely never see again, she stepped through the church entrance and into the daylight.

She tucked the letter into her satchel, along with the remaining coin. A ripple of excitement spread through her midsection. God was providing. She was going home to England, the place of her birth.

Her fingers found their way to her father's ring hidden under the bodice of her dress. *Papa, I'm going home.*

Would Bradlee be pleased she was traveling with him across the Atlantic? Or would her presence only complicate their feelings?

CHAPTER 27

The palm trees conform with the wind. During storms,
they bow their heads to the point of touching the ground.
Only the fiercest of gales cause them to break.
~ *Journaled the 3rd of June, 1829*

*H*annah stepped up to the window of the ticket
counter. Her chest heaved, and she panted from the
quick pace she'd traveled to arrive on time. Blinking to clear her
still-dazed mind from the recent change of events, she trusted
God's guiding hand, for He had made a way. "I'd like to
purchase passage on the *Boadicea*."

A rugged man sat tilted back on the hind legs of his chair
with his booted feet perched on a small shelf. He flicked back
his straw hat and peered at her from under the brim. His eyes
narrowed, and he removed his feet from the ledge, setting the
chair down. "Ya have the means to pay fer yer passage?"

Hannah glanced at the sign for the price. "Is it forty-six
pounds?"

The man rose to a stand and licked his lips. "In your case, it's
fifty-four."

In her case? She tried to meet the man's gaze, but his eyes shifted. "Passage to England on the *Boadicea* is fifty-four?"

"That's what I said, ain't it?"

"But the sign says—"

"I don't care what the sign says." The man scrunched up his face "Fer you, the charge is £54."

Hannah swallowed and counted out the coins she'd been given. Hopefully, the meager amount remaining would be enough to hire a hack to bring her to the Duchess of Linton's residence. Her hands shook as she placed them in small stacks on the counter. She opened another pouch and counted out a few more coins, enough to feed her and uncle—er, Huxley, for a year. It was a gift, and she was expected to use it to begin a new life in England. She straightened her shoulders and swallowed guilt that didn't belong. "Fifty-four pounds exactly."

A wicked smile split the man's face as he removed his hat, scooped the money into it, and rolled down the window's shutter.

Hannah stared at the closed window with parted lips for a moment before she pounded on the wooden slats with her fist. "You forgot to hand me my ticket. Open up."

"Tell yer no good uncle. His debt to me is paid."

She stilled and sucked in a breath. Huxley wouldn't ruin this for her, too. She moved to the side door and tried the handle, but it was locked. Her fists pounded on the door. "I paid for the passage. Please, I must be on the ship." She glanced at the *Boadicea*. The crew was preparing to set sail. She pounded harder.

The door opened, and the man glared at her with a cutlass in hand. "I don't 'ave any beef wit ya, but move out of me way, or I'll run you through. I've got a ship ta catch."

She backed away until she bumped against the neighboring building. The man eyed her as he slipped by, then scurried to the pier and into the dinghy loaded with passengers for the

Boadicea. The events of the previous evening, compounded by her lack of sleep and the man's duplicity, crumbled her composure. She closed her eyes, and fresh tears slid down her cheeks.

What was she going to do? *God, was this not Your will?* How would she tell the Clarks and all the others that she'd lost their money? She crumpled into the sandy dirt with her head in her hands and sobbed.

"What's got ya so glum, missy?"

Hannah peeked through the cracks in her fingers to see Captain Dailey in his long baggy pants standing in front of her. He waved a handkerchief in front of her face, and she used it to wipe away her tears.

"I paid for passage on the *Boadicea.*" Her voice cracked. "B-but the man behind the counter took the money and didn't give me a ticket."

"Swindled ya, he did." His dark eyes shown with sympathy. "Well, yer not the first one, and ya probably won't be the last, but there's more than one way to pluck a bird."

Hannah wrinkled her forehead. "Pardon?"

He offered his hand and helped her to stand. "Come, now. I haven't been much of a churchgoer, being at sea fer most of my life, but I have read God's word, and if I'm not mistaken, in Revelation somewhere it states, if God opens a door then no bloke is gonna shut it, and if God closes a door then, there ain't nothin' that's gonna open it."

The lack of sleep must be getting to her. "I'm not certain I'm following."

He tucked her hand into the crook of his arm and escorted her toward the pier. "As I said, there's more than one way to scale a fence."

Hannah shook her head to clear it.

"The devil may think he's closed the door, but I know better." He raised a hand. "Hoy there, Fuerte."

A dark-skinned burly man with gold rings in both ears turned his head.

"Miss Barrington missed boarding her ship. I was hoping ya might be able to lend her a hand."

"As long as she don't mind riding wit da cargo." The burly man lifted a barrel onto his shoulder and passed it to a lithe man standing in a rowboat below the pier. "Dat was the last of it." He dusted his hands.

Captain Dailey patted Hannah's hand. "See now. The good Lord provides. Mr. Granville will take care of ya once yer on board. I expect the two of you will be smellin' of April and May and posting banns soon enough. I saw the way he looked at ya."

"It's not..." She tried to shake her head, but he nudged her toward Mr. Fuerte.

"Off with ya now. We'll certainly miss yer bonny face in these parts, but we all do grand things fer love."

Mr. Fuerte held the ladder while she climbed into the dinghy. She settled into a tight space in the bow while Fuerte sat in the middle with the oars, the lithe man at the stern. Cargo was stacked so high between them that Hannah could barely glimpse either man. She did get a last look at Captain Dailey, who raised his hand in salute before Fuerte rowed them out to the ship.

Crewmen from the *Boadicea* lowered ropes and hoisted the dinghy up until it was level with the rail. The men proceeded to unload the cargo and carry it below deck. A man holding an open ledger, who appeared to be taking inventory, inclined his head toward Hannah. "She a passenger?"

Hannah swallowed. Was she? She'd paid for her fare, but without a ticket they'd assume she was a stowaway.

"Aye." Mr. Fuerte nodded. "She missed da last dinghy, but lucky fer her got a ride wit us."

The sailor helped her aboard. "You'll need to see the first

mate to check-in and find yer room." He pointed his quill toward a man near the helm.

She thanked him and Mr. Fuerte before strolling in the direction of the helm. Her hands clung to the strap of her bag with a tight grip. Passengers littered the deck and crowded along the rail, securing their last glimpse at the isle before the ship sailed out of sight. Were Bradlee and Colin in the mix? Her traitorous heart skipped a beat.

Bradlee was engaged. If he hadn't been beyond her reach before, he certainly was now. She pushed aside her longing, locking the memory of the way he looked at her as if she were a lady, deep into the recesses of her heart. Despite herself, she still scanned the backs of everyone's heads. A light-haired man stationed behind the rigging caught Hannah's eye. Was he Colin? If so, then, where was Bradlee? How would they feel about her presence?

A cluster of people crowded around the first mate, who appeared busy giving orders to his men and dealing with the demands of the other passengers. Lady Marchmain stood among them, the peacock feather in her hat waving in the breeze.

Hannah crossed the deck toward the crowd and Lady Marchmain. The man she thought might be Colin turned, and a long-chinned man with spectacles met her gaze.

Hannah clutched her hands at her midsection and squeezed past him, but felt his eyes upon her as she walked away. She continued to scan the passengers as she passed. Too tall. Too dark. Too stout. Her heart hammered. Why did it even matter if she saw Bradlee? Perhaps she merely needed the comfort of a familiar face. However, there would be no familiar faces in England until she located and grew to know her family. She forced her gaze straight ahead and excused herself by a few sailors.

A man slammed into her shoulder, knocking her satchel off as he passed.

She pulled the strap back up and rubbed her aching arm. When she glanced up again, she stood face to face with the man from the ticket counter.

"Well, what 'ave we 'ere?" He slapped the stomach of the bearded crewman beside him. "We got ourselves a stowaway."

Heads turned, and faces peered at her. Hannah felt her blood drain to her feet, and her stomach landed somewhere around her ankles. His was one familiar face she'd hoped to never lay eyes on again.

The bearded crewman grabbed her arm in a tight grip. "Where's yer ticket?"

~

*B*radlee heard the commotion behind him and peeked over his shoulder, expecting to see a runaway slave or one of the shipwrecked men who didn't have means for passage home. He pitied the poor soul.

A hulking, bearded man blocked his view, but Bradlee despised the grin on the other seaman's face. His smug expression reminded Bradlee of a large cat strutting around, pleased with its kill. The poor stowaway wouldn't receive any mercy from this fellow, nor the bearded man, if the line of his jaw indicated anything. Bradlee leaned right for a better view. It wasn't a man's arm that the bearded man held, but that of a woman. He put a hand on Colin's shoulder and raised onto his toes for a better look.

The air left Bradlee's body as if he'd been punched in the stomach. His grip tightened on Colin's shoulder.

"Ow." Colin turned around. "For heaven's sake, what's gotten into you?"

Bradlee knew the moment Colin saw her, for he stiffened.

"Is that…?"

"It's Hannah."

"What is she doing onboard?"

Someone said, "Get the captain."

Another yelled, "Throw her overboard."

The bearded man yanked her in the direction of the helm. Her face paled, but one wouldn't believe she was afraid, for she held her chin up as one born of noble birth.

Bradlee pushed his way through the crowd, fighting to get to her, struggling like a fish swimming upstream.

The shouts from the crowd grew rowdy. "Let 'er stay. She can 'ave my bed," a seaman in the rigging yelled.

"Give the bit o' goods to the crew and let us 'ave a bit of fun wit 'er."

The bearded man shoved Hannah toward the captain. She lost her footing and landed, sprawled out, in front of him.

"No!" the bellow ripped from Bradlee's throat as he broke through the circling group.

She must have recognized Bradlee's voice, for her head whipped around, spilling loose tendrils of hair over her shoulders in golden-brown waves.

"Hannah." He lunged for her, but smug-grin-man blocked him with his body, sneaking a blow with his elbow into Bradlee's abdomen. Bradlee's breath expelled from his lungs, and he doubled over in pain, but his gaze locked on Hannah's. She'd raised herself onto her knees. Her features were tense as if ready for a blow, but when her gaze met his, a flicker of relief passed through her eyes.

Colin hoisted him to standing. "Get up. Hannah needs our help."

Bradlee leveled his friend with an *as-if-I-weren't-aware-of-that* glare.

The captain peered down at Hannah from under the brim of

his bicorn hat. "Stowaways are not tolerated on my ship, only paying passengers."

"But, Captain, sir." Hannah tilted her face up and rose to her feet. "I have paid for passage."

Colin eyed him with a confused sideways glance.

Bradlee shrugged. He knew nothing of her boarding or how she would have obtained the funds.

"Then where's your ticket?" The captain raised a brow.

Hannah turned and pointed at the man with the smug grin. "I paid this man the money, and he has my ticket."

The captain and the crowd shifted to peer at the man. Smug-man's arrogant smile never faltered. "I've never seen this woman in my life."

Bradlee pushed forward. "I can vouch for the woman's character. If she says she paid for a ticket, then it is so."

Smug-man turned to face him. "Who are you to call me a liar?" He balled his hands into fists.

Mrs. Marchmain stepped to the captain's side, drawing the crowd's attention. The curled peacock feather on her hat fluttered in the wind. "The gentleman is Mr. Bradlee Granville, the son of the Earl of Cardon."

While everyone was distracted, the heel of the smug man's boot slammed down on Bradlee's bad foot. Pain shot up his leg. *Son of a slop seller.* He held in his grunt and gripped Colin's arm.

Mrs. Marchmain peered down her nose at Hannah. "This woman is my daughter's companion. I know for a fact she was given the funds to purchase a ticket."

Smug-smile crossed his arms. "How do you know she didn't keep the money fer herself?" He glanced around at his supporters. "Are we going to believe a woman?"

"Throw her in the drink," someone yelled. "If she sinks, she be tellin' the truth. If she's lyin', she'll float."

The captain lifted his hat, ran a hand through his hair, and then set it back on his head. He nodded to his first mate. "Check her bag."

The first mate yanked Hannah's satchel away and dug through its contents. "Only a few farthings, sir."

The captain cleared his throat. "Give her a shake."

Bradlee straightened, ready to rush to her rescue, but Colin stilled him with a hand.

Hannah's eyes widened as the first mate slid his thickly-calloused hands under her arms. She yelped and clutched his shoulders as he raised her off the ground and shook her, knocking her loose bun free.

"Now, him." The captain rounded on the smug man.

The first mate set Hannah back on the ground, and she twisted her hair up, setting it back to rights.

Smug-man wavered, and he backed up a step. "Let's not be hasty."

Those same brawny fingers clutched smug-man's shoulders, lifted him into the air, and shook him.

The clinking of coins jangled.

Hannah raised her chin, and her blue eyes shown brighter. "There will be at least £54 in his purse. It is the amount he charged me for passage."

The first mate set him back down but kept a firm hand on his shoulder.

The smug man paled. "The money was mine. Her uncle owed me. It was only fair she should pay her debts first."

The captain's nostrils flared. "Are you tellin' me the money that should have gone into the ship's coffers, you kept for yerself?"

"S-she owed me the money. Debts should be paid down first."

Colin commented in Bradlee's ear. "Why is it that people with brains the size of peas have mouths the size of cabbages?"

"We have rules for thieves, especially those who skim from

the ship's ledgers." The captain clasped his hands behind his back. "Take his money and have him find his own way back to shore."

The no longer smug man pleaded as the crewmen stripped him of his purse and carried him to the boat's stern.

The captain bowed to Hannah. "I beg your pardon for your harsh treatment. Please accept my apology and an invitation to join me for supper in my quarters."

Lady Marchmain fluttered her fan. "How gracious of you, Captain. We'd be delighted to dine with you this evening. Won't we, Miss Barrington?"

Her answer was interrupted by a man's scream and the loud splash that followed.

Her gaze flew to Bradlee's, and he could read the expression on her face. *That would have been her.*

He ached to enfold her in his embrace and whisper into her hair that he would never let anything happen to her. However, they were not alone, and they were no longer on an island where society had grown slack in its rules. He could only peer into her eyes and hope his steadfast gaze would suffice.

"Come along, Miss Barrington. My daughter is waiting for you in the cabin. Time to get you settled and ready for supper." Mrs. Marchmain smiled at the captain. "We must look our best for our host."

Hannah followed Mrs. Marchmain, but not without one long look over her shoulder at Bradlee.

A thousand questions burned in his chest, but they had to wait. Surely, they would run into one another on the ship. He must be patient to discover how she was able to board the *Boadicea.*

Patience, however, was not his strong suit.

CHAPTER 28

Who knew propriety could be so irritating?
~ *Journaled the 15th of July, 1829*

Finding time to converse with Hannah proved most challenging. Mrs. Marchmain and her daughter, Louisa, strolled above deck regularly after high tea and again around half past four, always with Hannah in tow. Other than a warm greeting, he couldn't find a proper way to engage in an exchange with her. He'd even feigned interest in Miss Marchmain and offered to escort her around the top deck, which resulted in his ear hurting from Louisa Marchmain's ceaseless chatter and Mrs. Marchmain now eyeing him as a potential suitor for her daughter, who'd be coming out at the start of the season. He could practically hear the wedding march ringing in the older woman's head.

The turns about the top deck, however, allowed for Colin to converse with Hannah, since it was not uncommon for companions to talk openly. Knowing Colin strolled arm in arm with her did nothing to ease Bradlee's tension. *Confound it.* He'd spent half his time on Nevis trying to pair the two of them together, but now he stuffed his hands into his pockets so he wouldn't wrench Colin away and take his spot.

They'd been at sea a week when Bradlee had, once again, paraded above deck listening to Louisa's aimless rambling while Hannah and Colin walked behind them in deep conversation. Bradlee's jaw hurt from clenching his teeth, and his neck felt stiff as if someone tightened a crank until his shoulders moved toward his ears. He was in a beastly mood when they returned to their cabin, and nearly bursting with questions.

Colin flopped onto his bunk and laced his fingers behind his head with a smile.

Of course, he'd be enjoying Bradlee's misery. Bradlee closed the door for privacy and turned up the oil lantern. "What did she say?" He sat on the other bunk and leaned forward, resting his forearms on his thighs.

"The Marchmains are treating her fairly. Miss Marchmain speaks incessantly, but I'm assuming you've discovered that already."

"Quite." He scooted closer. "Why did Hannah board?"

"She was vague, but it sounded as if her guardian attempted to marry her off to settle his financial debts."

"The blackguard." Bradlee jumped to his feet and paced what little ground there was to cover in the cramped cabin. "I knew that elbow-crooker couldn't be trusted. Attempting to sell his ward to the highest bidder is the lowest of low." His ankle pained him after that bugger tromped on his foot, but he suffered through and raked both hands through his hair. "Did the Marchmains pay for her fare?"

"The Clarks and townsfolk scraped together the funds to pay for her passage." Colin fluffed his pillow. "It's an emotional subject. I'm not certain I'd bring it up. It nearly brought her to tears."

Bradlee pivoted and ran a hand down his face. "Did she say what her plans are once she reaches England?"

"Lady Clark handed Miss Barrington a note to give to her niece. I suspect Lady Clark's relative shall look after her."

"We must find out for certain. We owe her our lives. If there is anything we can do to aid Miss Barrington once we arrive, I plan to do it. We'll have access to credit as soon as we set foot on British soil."

"Ah, funds." Colin's sigh resounded with relief. "At last, I will be able to don something that isn't threadbare."

Bradlee sat down on the opposite bunk. "Did she say anything else?" He hated the wistfulness in his voice.

"That was all."

Was she still angry, or had she forgiven him? He cleared his throat. "She didn't ask about me?" He sounded desperate. *Blast.* He was desperate.

Colin propped himself up on his elbows. "She did ask if you'd been writing."

He nodded and tried to appear nonchalant. "Jolly good." But his heart pattered like a schoolboy who'd won a smile from the girl he fancied. He had been. Writing his book was one of the few things he could do to fill the time while he waited for her to pass with the off-chance possibility he might be able to speak with her. He'd hoped to see Hannah in the common dining area, but the Marchmains had been dining each night with the captain.

Bradlee opened his journal to where he'd last written about a young traveler and his adventures in the African plains. He'd written each word with the desire to hear Hannah's approval and to see the wonderment on her face, but would he ever gain the chance? His pencil scribbled words across the page as Colin drifted off to sleep, but Bradlee's mind puzzled over his dilemma. There had to be a way to speak to Hannah alone. He needed to hear reassurance from her lips that she was going to be fine. Then maybe he could be too.

~

*H*annah had no business thinking about Bradlee, but she couldn't stop loving him. Time had melted her anger, and even though he was beyond her reach, she allowed herself a break from the incessant talk of London fashions and the upcoming season to let her thoughts drift to him. She'd become adept at allowing her mind to wander while still maintaining enough awareness to add the occasional *hmm, ah,* or *I see,* whenever Louisa paused in her monologues. She contented herself just to be near Bradlee.

As she strolled behind him and Louisa, she admired the way his linen shirt conformed to his broad shoulders and the rhythm of his smooth, easy stride. She remembered their hike together and the way he looked at her with an energetic glow in his eyes and a teasing smile on his lips.

"Miss Barrington, proper ladies always sit up straight. They never slouch." Mrs. Marchmain peered at her from beneath the peacock-feathered hat.

Hannah straightened her spine and pulled back her shoulders. "Thank you for the kind reminder."

Mrs. Marchmain, despite her stark demeanor, seemed to have taken it upon herself to make Hannah acceptable to society, insisting she sit up straight, walk with poise, and speak without an island accent. She averred that, if Hannah was going to reside in England, she must act and appear as an English gentlewoman.

Hannah soaked up the information, hoping to make a good impression upon Lady Clark's niece and her own relatives—once she located them. Soon, she began asking more questions regarding etiquette than Louisa. After a week of interpreting Mrs. Marchmain's stern glances during meals with the captain, Hannah learned which fork to use, how to sip her soup, and to slowly eat as if food were of no interest to her. Hannah almost fell over when Mrs. Marchmain praised her on her conduct one evening. She wasn't certain whether Mrs. Marchmain's heart was softening or if the woman's gruff manner was growing on her.

Over the last several weeks, as the air grew cooler and the sea darkened. Bradlee joined Miss Marchmain on her daily strolls above deck, much to Mrs. Marchmain's delight and encouragement. Hannah learned how much could be communicated in a single look. Even though Bradlee and Hannah barely exchanged a full sentence, the tender way he glanced at her was enough to weaken her knees. She imagined a designated meaning to each gaze. If he twitched a brow, he was asking about her wellbeing, to which she'd comment to Colin or Louisa, or the air for that matter, "Lovely day, isn't it?" or "I believe the sky is turning gray. Is a storm expected?" depending upon her mood or situation.

When his eyes glittered, it was merely because he was pleased to see her, and she'd offer a small smile.

But on the occasions when his eyes became glazed and heavy-lidded, she'd curled her fingers around her ear as if tucking back a loose strand the way he'd done to her on Nevis. She'd let her hand rest briefly over her chest as a symbol she'd forever keep the thought of him close to her heart. It was a fanciful daydream, but it offered her hope and a sense of security when her future remained as unsettled as the ocean's surface.

Their third week at sea, on a gloomy day made even gloomier by Louisa's decision to forgo her stroll above deck, a knock sounded on the cabin door.

Hannah rose to answer it.

"Tell mama I'm not interested in embroidering today," Louisa said. "My fingers ache from the endless days of being trapped inside my cabin, pulling a needle through cloth." Louisa flopped down onto her bunk. "Tell her I have a headache or my stomach is queasy." She pulled a pillow over her face, which mumbled her next words, but Hannah understood them to be, "or something of that sort."

Hannah unlatched the door and swung it open.

Bradlee stood in the passageway, his easy smile broadening when he saw her. "Good afternoon, Miss Barrington." He stepped closer. "Lovely to see you."

Hannah soaked in his presence. Oh, how she missed the freedom of the island, where they could speak their mind. "And you, Mr. Granville."

Louisa popped upright at the sound of Mr. Granville's voice. Her pillow dropped to the floor. "How splendid of you to call. I'm terribly sorry to miss taking a turn above deck with you this morning, but the weather wasn't cooperative. Has the rain stopped? I do hope so. Being confined to this tiny cabin has frayed my nerves, and the ocean swells have turned my stomach so much so that I couldn't even partake of tea—"

"I have a surprise." He blurted out the words when Louisa inhaled before she could begin rambling again.

Hannah tilted her head. Bradlee's eyes sparkled, and his thumb and pinky alternated a rapid tapping against his thigh, which he often did when excited.

"How thrilling. Let me get my wrap." Louisa removed it from the peg and wrapped it about her shoulders. "I do love surprises. Did you know I love surprises? Papa once threw a surprise birthday party for me…"

Louisa continued to ramble, but Hannah stopped listening. She peeked out the door, looking for Colin, assuming he would escort her.

Bradlee kept his attention on Louisa, but he leaned in and whispered through the side of his mouth, "He's sleeping."

Hannah fought back her smile—especially when Bradlee offered an arm to both women. Was she wicked for enjoying Colin's absence—for savoring a moment with the man she loved, who'd soon be married to another? She missed the way Bradlee set her at ease and made her smile.

His scent washed over her like fresh spring water, and she couldn't resist leaning in a tad closer to drink of it. Louisa accepted his other arm, and the three of them strolled a bit awkwardly down the narrow halls. Hannah knew she should relinquish his arm, but she was reluctant to do so until they reached the stairs and she had no other choice.

Above deck, the sun peeked out from the clouds, and Hannah lifted her face to enjoy its warmth. Bradlee offered her and Louisa his arms once again, and Hannah was grateful not only for the opportunity to be close to Bradlee, but also for his warmth. She was underdressed for the chillier temperatures, but lacked warmer wardrobe options. Her chilled skin absorbed the heat of his body, and she leaned in closer, feeling the ripple of his muscles under her fingers.

"You must both close your eyes." Bradlee's eyes danced as he glanced her way.

Louisa giggled like a schoolgirl. "I shall expire from anticipation. I cannot imagine what the surprise might be."

Hannah couldn't hold back her smile as she closed her eyes. She didn't care what the surprise was, since it had afforded her a chance to cling to Bradlee's side. He turned them and drew to a halt. She wished he would not let this moment end.

"You may open your eyes."

Louisa gasped.

Hannah raised her lids to witness a double rainbow illuminating the darkened sky, its vivid colors blazing. Her lips parted, and she sucked in a breath. Even the indigo, the hardest color to catch, shown a vibrant purple-blue.

Her pulse quickened.

Bradlee had done this for her. Well...he hadn't created the rainbow. It was God's masterful handiwork, but Bradlee brought her up here because he remembered her tale about the spring being the source of all rainbows. Tears clouded her eyes, but she wouldn't move to wipe them away. She was too busy engraving this moment, with its beauty and emotions, into her memory forever.

Bradlee slid his hand about her waist. "Do you like it?"

Hannah found his hand and curled her fingers around his. Words couldn't explain it.

Louisa, who'd henceforth remained transfixed to the point of loss of speech, found her voice. "It's lovely. Absolutely delightful—"

"It's magnificent." Hannah's voice exuded reverence. Her tone filled with awe. It wasn't until after she heard her own words that she realized her gaffe in interrupting her employer, but "lovely" and "delightful" did not do justice to the miracle of God's beauty.

Bradlee peered down at her, his warm gaze melting its way to her very soul.

She straightened and released his hand. The subtle gesture of their fingers touching would be seen as a breach in propriety if caught, and as Mrs. Marchmain often explained, her reputation would suffer.

She pinned her lips together to stay the rush of emotion welling. She wanted to throw herself into his arms and pour out her heart, all her desires, all her fears, all the uncertainty. She longed to envelop herself in the safety and sense of belonging she always felt in his arms, but the longings of her heart always met with the wall of his engagement. He'd sworn himself to another. Her heart must go on without him. The dam of tears broke, and streams ran helplessly down either side of her face.

"Do you think this is the type of rainbow God used as a promise to Noah?" Louisa turned to Bradlee.

Bradlee removed his arm from Hannah's waist.

Louisa didn't appear to notice. "I do not see how Noah and his family were trapped on a boat with all the noises of the animals for so many days. After the numerous trips we've taken to Nevis, I have a whole new sympathy for Noah." Louisa's gaze flicked briefly to Hannah. "Why, Hannah, are you crying?"

Hannah quickly wiped away the tears. "I'm merely overwhelmed by the hope the rainbow represents as God's promise."

Louisa sighed. "We are a sentimental pair, aren't we? Perhaps that is why we've gotten along so famously." She fixed a coy smile on Bradlee. "It seems Mr. Granville also holds a romantic side."

Bradlee raised a finger to his lips. "If we could keep that our secret, I would be much appreciative. I'd hate to endure Mr. Fitzroy's taunts if word got out."

"Your secret is safe with us. Isn't it, Hannah?" Louisa didn't wait for a reply. "Once I caught Papa stashing a fifth of brandy in his office, which Mama would never approve of. He asked for it to be our secret, and I haven't told a soul."

Bradlee coughed into his hand as if to hide his grin. "Pardon me. It must be the dampness of the air."

"Perhaps we should return to our cabins. The wind is a bit brisk." Louisa pulled her shawl tighter. "But that is to be expected, especially with the ship nearing England. The captain said we should arrive sometime next week. I will be overjoyed to set foot once again on stable ground, but I shall miss your company. Hannah will be off to visit with the Duchess of Linton, and you shall be off to finish your exams."

"How is your writing going?" Hannah snuck in a question.

"Brilliantly." His eyes sparkled once again. "I find the stories are pouring out of me, and the ship has afforded me plenty of time to write."

"I had no idea you were a writer." Louisa peered at him as they descended the stairs back into the dim passageway. "What a lovely pastime. I do so love a good story, preferably romantic novels. Do your stories have a romantic element?"

They stopped in front of Louisa and Hannah's cabin, and

Bradlee opened the door for the ladies. "Indeed, but it is still to be seen whether love will be victorious."

Hannah's breath stilled when his gaze fell upon her as he spoke those words.

"Good day to you, ladies." He bowed and backed out of the room, shutting the door behind him.

Louisa sighed and pretended to swoon onto her bunk. "Isn't he delightful? Handsome and romantic."

Hannah nodded, but her heart clenched to the point that she put a hand to her chest to ensure it was still beating. Today made one thing abundantly clear. She'd lost her heart to Bradlee, and there was no getting it back.

CHAPTER 29

The winsome smells of home – the day's catch sizzling in lard and the hearty fare of roasting of meats and potatoes over a wood fire.

~ *Journaled the 28th of August, 1829*

The winds favored their voyage, and the captain had been correct in his prediction that they'd reach London by the end of the following week. The docks buzzed as cargo was loaded and unloaded onto ships. The smell of fish, vinegar, and lard hung in the air from a nearby inn, and the gulls screamed overhead, scanning for any dropped scraps of food or the off chance a fisherman left his catch unattended.

Men, dressed mostly in the bland colors of grays and browns, hefted people's trunks into carriages and spoke in thick accents, often dropping the letter *h*. She was used to the activity of the pier on Nevis, but it seemed mundane compared to the excitement and activity of the Bristol port. Her skin tingled. England was her country—the land of her birth and soon to once again be called her home.

The Marchmain coachman awaited them at the end of the pier, and Mrs. Marchmain waved down a hack for Hannah. Louisa shed dramatic tears as she bid Hannah farewell, and Mrs. Marchmain reviewed proper etiquette and hinted that they would be delighted to visit if the Duchess would be kind enough to extend them an invitation.

Hannah thanked them for the opportunity, and then in a last desperate attempt, scanned the crowded pier for a final look at Bradlee, but neither he nor Colin were anywhere to be found. Had they already left? In Bradlee's haste to return for his exams, had he overlooked saying good-bye? A pair of women strolled by with flower-trimmed bonnets and matching parasols. They moved in rhythm, with small graceful steps. An unrefined island girl could easily be forgotten after returning to English standards.

Mrs. Marchmain raised a hand in a subtle wave. "I knew Mr. Granville would come to wish you well for your debut." She gently spun Louisa around, and Hannah followed suit.

Bradlee and Colin strolled down the gangplank. Colin had donned a pressed jacket and neatly tied cravat, once again fitting into English society. Bradlee, on the other hand, slung his jacket over his shoulder and skipped the cravat altogether. They stopped in front of the Marchmains.

"Mr. Granville, it has been lovely making your acquaintance." The breeze rustled Mrs. Marchmain's skirts, and she attempted to pin them with her hand. "I do hope, when you visit London, you'll come calling."

"Perhaps we shall see each other at the Marshall's ball?" Louisa clasped her hands in front of her chest. "It's supposed to be a grand event with everyone in attendance—"

"And if you're ever in the Cotswolds, please visit," Bradlee spoke over her. "My family would enjoy meeting others who've resided on Nevis." He offered his arm to Louisa. "Let me see you to your coach."

He passed a stern look to Colin and flashed a glance at Hannah before strolling off.

Louisa peered over her shoulder and bid farewell to Hannah.

Hannah kept her arms in and her hands folded demurely in front. Colin widened his stance and waited for Bradlee's return.

With a final wave, the Marchmains climbed into their coach.

A loud ruckus of two men as they greeted each other with whacks on the back distracted Hannah. A nearby crewman stole a kiss from his awaiting lady love, and two children ran into their papa's open arms. She'd always imagined an exuberant homecoming. In her fantasies, her lost family would greet her arrival with warm hugs and whisk her off to welcome her to her rightful home, amid a flurry of comments and questions. It was a foolish dream, but she'd harbored the notion anyway.

She'd start this adventure on her own.

Hannah pivoted to face Colin. "I wish you the best in your studies, Mr. Fitzroy." It felt odd to be formal with someone she'd spent so much time alongside, but she was in England and should behave as an Englishwoman. She peered at the spot she'd last seen Bradlee aid Louisa into their carriage, but neither he nor the Marchmain carriage remained. Her heart clenched, but it was time she understood her place. She notified the driver of her destination and nodded to Colin. "Please give my regards to Mr. Granville on his exams."

"I shall happily do so." He stuck his hands into his pockets and shifted his weight, his gaze scanning the pier. "Farewell, Miss Barrington. Best wishes in finding your family."

He opened the carriage door, and she climbed into the rented hack. The driver assumed his post aloft and settled under the reins. The other side door opened, and in crawled Bradlee.

Hannah gasped.

Bradlee grinned.

"I thought you left—"

"Without saying goodbye?" He raised her hand to his lips. "Never. It was best for Mrs. Marchmain not to see us join you."

Because it could ruin her reputation. Her heart sank. Should she ask them to get out? Would anyone see? Did it matter? No one knew of her existence. Not yet anyway.

"Did you think I'd be able to rest until I saw you settled?" He lightly brushed a kiss on the back of her hand. "I've had a lot of time to think about—"

"Tut, tut, none of that." Colin scooted in across from them and wagged an index finger.

Hannah pulled her hand away.

Bradlee frowned.

Colin leveled him with a bored expression. "If you're going to keep casting me as the part of duenna, then, by George, I'm going to do a bang-up job of it."

His frown deepened. "Blasted pain in—"

Colin arched a haughty brow as well as any of the aristocracy. "Now, now, do remember your manners. We're back among the sophisticated."

Hannah needed this—to be around people with whom she could relax and not worry about all the looming what-ifs. "Oh, how I've missed you both."

Bradlee grinned and brought her hand to his lips once more.

Colin groaned and glanced at the ceiling as if pleading with God for patience.

Hannah giggled, unable to contain her delight any longer, despite Mrs. Marchmain's reprimands about her impropriety. It felt lovely to be herself.

Bradlee and Hannah caught up on a month's worth of communication as Colin pretended to doze in the seat across from them. He occasionally tossed out a sarcastic comment. Too soon, the hackney cab turned into a cobbled drive lined with green cut grass and leading to a great stone house with a grand columned entrance.

Hannah broke off the conversation to peer out the window. Her lips parted as a scattering of elusive memories reseeded themselves in her mind. Her heart leapt into her throat.

Bradlee glanced out his window and did a double-take. "I believe our driver is mistaken. This isn't Ainsley Park, where the Duke and Duchess reside."

"I needed to make a stop first." Hannah patted her hair to make certain it was in place and inhaled a deep breath. "This is Rosewood Manor, my home." She touched the glass with her fingers. "At least, it was my home a long time ago."

The hack rolled to a stop at the main entrance.

Bradlee squeezed her hand. "Are you sure you want to do this?"

She nodded. "More than ever." Her eyes locked on his. "Especially now that I don't have to face the memories alone."

With his foot, Bradlee nudged Colin, who had drifted off to sleep. Colin awoke with a start. "We're here? So soon?"

"We've added a stop." Bradlee opened the door. "Stay here and make certain the driver doesn't leave." He climbed out before Colin could complain. He walked around the carriage and aided Hannah down. Ever the gentleman, he tucked her hand into his arm and covered it with his own.

The air hung with the scent of sweet green silage, as if the grass had been freshly cut. She peered about the grounds and let nostalgia wash over her. "I ran through this grass as a child." She pointed toward the right side of the manor. "I used to roll down the southside hill and, afterward, my nanny would scold me for staining my dress."

They ascended the wide set of stone stairs.

"Ready?" Bradlee raised a hand toward the front door's brass knocker.

She sucked in a deep breath and exhaled. "Quite."

He rapped the handle against the entranceway.

A young butler opened the door. He held a stiff posture and

eyed them warily. "Staff and those seeking employment are to use the servant's entrance around back."

He attempted to close the door, but Bradlee caught a foothold. "We are not servants," he said in a tone of commanding authority. "You are speaking to the former mistress of Rosewood Manor, who has just arrived on the *Boadicea* from the Leeward Isle of Nevis."

The young butler blanched. He peeked back over his shoulder as if looking for someone to direct him. When nobody appeared, he turned back to them and cleared his throat. "I will need to inform Mr. Fogarty." He opened the door wider. "You may follow me to the blue salon."

Hannah entered the main foyer with its soaring ceiling painted cerulean blue with white puffy clouds and flying doves. A grand marble staircase stood straight ahead. The butler led them into a double-doored blue salon. A large stone hearth blazed with a cheery fire. He gestured to the sofa. "Please, make yourselves comfortable."

She strolled over to the stone fireplace and touched the wooden mantle topped with a gilded mirror. Crouching down to the height of a child five years of age, she ran her fingers along the chiseled stone. "I used to play with my dolls in this very spot." She closed her eyes. "I used to pretend the fireplace was a castle, and my dolls would wave to their subjects below." She truly was home. It was just as she remembered in her dreams.

Bradlee moved to her side.

She rose and met his gaze. "Once, an ember from the flames caught my dress on fire. I screamed, and a man in dark red rushed over and clapped out the fire with his hands."

The young butler cleared his throat, and they turned their attention to the door. He stepped aside, and a formally dressed middle-aged man passed through. His frock coattails almost hung down to his calves. The high points of his collar touched his earlobes, and a snowy white cravat was tied in a neat bow. He carried a thick ledger under his arm, and his fingers, on the right hand were stained black as if he'd recently been writing figures in the accounts. A pair of spectacles rested on the bridge of his nose, and he tilted his head back to peer at Bradlee and her through the lenses. "Is there something in which I may assist you?" His gaze roved over their casual dress, and his lips curled.

Hannah swallowed. She must appear a mess for the butler to mistake her as a servant and for the steward to recoil in such a manner. Their coming was a mistake. She should have waited and freshened up her appearance, but it was too late to do anything about it now. She squared her shoulders and straightened as Mrs. Marchmain had instructed her.

Bradlee didn't appear concerned. He strode over to the steward and introduced himself. He gestured to Hannah. "This is Miss Hannah Barrington, daughter of Sir Charles Barrington of Bristol."

She stumbled into an awkward curtsy. Did one curtsy to the paid help? She rather thought not, but it was too late to undo what was already done.

"She is looking to become reacquainted with her estranged family."

Mr. Fogarty's Adam's apple bobbed, and he shook his head almost imperceivably.

Bradlee sniffed. "Letters were sent upon the death of her parents, but either the letters or the replies were lost at sea, for none were ever returned. She is here to claim her heritage and inheritance."

A muscle twitched in the steward's jaw, and his nostrils flared. "The baron's daughter is dead."

Hannah's lips parted to refute his statement, but her breath stilled, and the air squeezed from her lungs. Huxley's letters had been written to a Mr. F. Was Mr. Fogarty the man with whom he corresponded?

He peered at Hannah. "Do you have any documents proving your lineage?"

Bradlee's gaze met hers.

Hannah's palms grew moist, and she blinked. How could she prove who she was? She had nothing but the contents of her satchel, which only included a spare gown.

"Anything to show you are who you claim to be?" Mr. Fogarty strummed his fingers on the edge of the ledger book.

Was Mr. Fogarty the one who wanted her dead? Had she put Bradlee in danger? Hannah chewed her lip and side-stepped toward the exit.

Bradlee turned to Mr. Fogarty. "Surely, some of the staff might be able to identify her?"

"The new master brought in his own staff when he inherited Rosewood Manor. I daresay there's not a one." He snorted. "There is an ancient head butler who stayed, but he went blind several years back. I hardly think he'd be able to identify his former mistress now."

"Then we'd like to see the master himself. He's a distant relative and may be able to recognize his cousin."

"The master is very busy." Mr. Fogarty gestured toward the door as a sign for them to leave.

Hannah slid another step toward the exit.

Bradlee dropped into a chair. "We will wait."

A haughty chuckle was Mr. Fogarty's response. "The master doesn't reside here. He has a dozen manor homes to occupy and maintain much grander than this." Mr. Fogarty's eyes swept across his surroundings. His volume increased. "And he doesn't take kindly to imposters who try to usurp his holdings." A white blob of spittle formed in the corner of his mouth.

Bradlee rose to a wide-legged stance. His chest bowed out as if ready to come to blows.

Hannah scurried to his side and laid a hand on his arm. "It's all right." She eyed Mr. Fogarty. "We'll be going." She tugged on Bradlee's arm

Bradlee questioned her with his eyes but followed.

The young butler scowled as he saw them out.

Her heart thundered, and the carriage where Colin awaited seemed much farther away than when they'd arrived. It was almost impossible to maintain the small steps expected of a lady when all Hannah wanted to do was pick up her skirts and dash to safety.

The sun passed under a cloud, and the birds quieted their singing as Bradlee grumbled about the arrogance of such a man all the way to the awaiting hack.

Colin opened the carriage door for them. "How'd it go?"

Hannah couldn't answer. The lump in her throat choked her voice as she climbed inside. She'd stepped into the realm of her childhood, laid a hand where her fingers once rested, brought back images she'd thought long dead, and then had a gate close on her hopes. Mr. Fogarty stood as guard, locking the chain and barring her from her past and future. What was she to do now? How could she search for her family when she didn't know whom to trust?

Bradlee grumbled some heated words and plopped down beside her.

The driver snapped the reins, and the hack jolted to a start.

Blinded by unshed tears, she still peered out the window, for she didn't know how to face Bradlee. The steward had made her look foolish, as if she'd been telling falsehoods, but he was a liar in cahoots with Huxley. She hadn't the time to grab the letters before she fled. If she had, then she could go to the authorities and prove their complicity. If she wrote Lady Clark, would she even be able to proposition the mayor to seize the letters from Huxley? It could take up to a year or more, if it was even possible. She couldn't impose upon the Duchess of Linton's hospitality for that long.

Bradlee explained the happenings of their visit to Colin in a gruff tone.

After he finished, Hannah pushed the words past the lump. "I didn't make it up. I remember things…the layout of the house…the furniture. It's all familiar."

"I know." Bradlee pulled her head onto his shoulder. "We'll find a way to convince them."

"It's worse than that." She briefly closed her eyes to form the words. "I found letters locked in a box in Huxley's desk the day Blandina died. Huxley was being paid to keep me in Nevis. Everyone in England believes I'm dead."

Bradlee stared at her. "Who was Huxley blackmailing? Your relative?"

She shook her head. "Names were not used, but one was signed Mr. F."

"Fogarty, the knave."

"I cannot be certain it's him, and I cannot prove anything. I left in such a rush, I didn't think to bring the letters."

Silence fell among them. Her home had never been so near, yet it might as well still be an ocean away. Her lips trembled, and she inhaled a ragged breath to keep the dam of tears from spilling.

The clip-clopping of the horse's hooves pervaded the small enclosure.

Colin grabbed Bradlee's satchel and removed his journal. "Perhaps I might lift our moods by reading your manuscript. Miss Barrington has been inquiring about it, after all."

Bradlee nodded, and Colin began to read.

She wiped away her tears and listened intently, allowing her mind to drift from the current situation to an adventure in a foreign land. Bradlee's writing drew her into the story, and she lost herself among the grassy plains in the wilds of America.

Heat flooded her cheeks whenever the hero's love interest was mentioned. However, as the carriage drew closer to Ainsley Park, Hannah found herself praying that the next visit would proceed better than the last.

She exhaled. It could hardly go worse than the encounter at Rosewood Manor.

CHAPTER 30

The large stately houses of the English aristocracy,
despite their opulence, still echo with a hollow timbre
when the doors close on the lowly.
~ *Journaled the 28ᵗʰ of August, 1829*

*H*annah was numb as she walked away from the
sweeping entranceway of Ainsley Park. The sound
of the butler closing the oversized double doors thundered
through her like a gavel might slam on someone issued a death
sentence.

Had God turned His back upon her?

She clutched Bradlee's arm to keep moving one foot in front
of the other and not melt into a puddle on the duchess's front
walkway. Colin flanked her other side, his hand hovering near
her elbow as if worried she might faint.

What would she do now that the duke and duchess were not
in residence? The butler informed them His and Her Grace
were traveling north to attend the wedding of the duke's eldest
son, Maxwell David Weld, the Earl of Harcourt. Their return

date was unknown, but the butler believed it wouldn't be for several months.

Where should she go? She had no funds, no relatives. Bradlee must return to his family and fiancée. Colin would return to Oxford. *Lord, where do I belong? To whom can I turn?*

Outside, the dutiful gardener's shears rhythmically sliced the air as they trimmed the topiaries. The peaceful fountain bubbled, and birds chirped, splashing in the water. Internally, icy fear froze the blood in Hannah's veins, and a tremor ran through her body.

Bradlee stopped and held both of her hands in his. "Do not fear. I'm not going to let anything happen to you."

Colin nodded. "He always has a backup plan in case the first goes awry." He craned his neck to peer over the top of her head at Bradlee. "Which it frequently does."

Praise God that Bradlee was here and she didn't have to face this alone.

"You will come home with me until the duchess returns." He squeezed her hands.

Her breath quivered as she inhaled. "But that is a lot to ask of your family. I'll be an imposition."

"You are never an imposition, and my mother will adore you."

She was reluctant to depart from Bradlee's company, but she couldn't ignore the obvious problem. "What will your fiancée think about you bringing me into your home?"

Colin stuffed his hands into his pockets and shifted his feet, slowly backing toward the carriage.

Bradlee turned his head and peered past the carriage down the tree-lined lane. "I'm going to speak to my father. I need to set things to rights. He will have to understand." His warm gaze met hers. "When I posted that letter, I didn't know the extent of my feelings for you, but the entire voyage, all I could think about was you. I want you by my side now and always. I finished my manuscript. I plan to submit it to a publisher. It might not be much of a living at first, but I can do odd jobs to supplement. I'm not afraid of work. I will find a way to provide for you."

Hannah's mind whirled. Bradlee wanted to be with her? Her heart, which only seconds before needed to be peeled from the cobblestone walkway, now soared like a kite to extraordinary heights. However, one question caused it to dip. "What about your engagement?"

"I'm not certain Miss Radcliff wants to marry me. It's another thing I will clear up as soon as I get home. If the banns have already been posted, I must do what I can to save Alice from embarrassment. She's done nothing to deserve such treatment."

"Her reputation could be ruined if you jilt her." Hannah swallowed.

"I know. I've been praying for wisdom." He leaned in and stared deeper into her eyes. "But don't be discouraged. God will make a way."

She wanted to believe him. She'd seen the love in his eyes, but why would Bradlee desire her over a distinguished Englishwoman? Once he had a chance to compare her with the stunning Miss Radcliff, surely, he'd find Hannah lacking. She couldn't escape the doubts. "If it's God's will, then why have so many doors shut? What if your father doesn't understand?" The Bible said that God looked after the orphans, but why would she matter to Him when there were more important people?

"God's not done yet." An easy grin swept across his features. "He got you here to England, didn't He?" Bradlee tucked her hand into his arm and led her toward the hired hack.

Her gaze lowered, and she exhaled a deep breath. "Perhaps you're right."

He arched a brow. "Perhaps?"

She nudged his shoulder. "We've yet to see how this all plays out."

"For the record, I'm good at going after what I set my heart on. I'm extremely competitive and rarely lose, for which my brother will vouch when you meet him." He opened the carriage door and aided her ascent.

Bradlee climbed in and slid next to her. "I might be being selfish, but I believe this to be the best possible of outcomes. I daresay, once my parents meet you, they will see reason and know we are better suited."

She clung to his optimism, but how could his family not see her as an outsider?

~

*H*annah awoke at an inn in Bath, unrested. The ballads of the drunken patrons below had drifted through the cracks in the floorboards until the wee early hours of the morning, allowing her mind to replay the events of the previous day and ponder the problems of her near future.

Bradlee and Colin slept in the room next to hers at the inn halfway between Ainsley Park and his home. Upon bidding her goodnight, Bradlee had squeezed her hand. "You need only make a sound, and we'll be by your side."

At least she'd felt safe. Hannah thanked God for that fact in her morning prayers before she scrubbed her face in the freezing water of the washstand basin and tidied herself for meeting Bradlee's parents. If only she'd remembered to bring her mother's gloves when she'd packed in such a rush back on Nevis.

She examined her nails. They were clean and even, but her hands were too tanned. Surely the Granvilles would notice and disapprove. Funny how she'd always thought she looked so different than the islanders. It's why they called her red legs and white beggar. But neither did she resemble the pale English gentlewomen who floated about like ghosts, their parasols tugging them with the wind. Hannah's tanned skin and lanky stride stood in stark contrast. She would never fit in.

A knock sounded upon the door.

She quickly scraped her hair up into a topknot and unlatched the door. Bradlee and Colin stood dressed and ready.

"Shall we break our fast?" Bradlee offered his arm.

Colin rubbed his stomach. "I'm famished and ready for a hearty fare after all the travel."

They found seats in the dining room. Several men held their heads and sipped mugs of strong coffee after last evening's revelry.

A buxom woman brought over steaming mugs of chocolate and plates heaping with mutton and eggs. Colin dug in and groaned with an expression of unadulterated pleasure. Bradlee and Hannah chuckled, for they understood the beauty of a good meal after a long voyage.

Bradlee paused halfway through his meal and peered at Hannah. "Colin and I, we..." His eyes jumped nervously. "We thought it might be best if we brought in some help to..." He swallowed.

Hannah laid down her fork and stared at the worried expression on his face. The food she'd enjoyed now churned in her stomach. Why would he suddenly be nervous?

"...to help make certain we make the best impression."

She glanced down at the better of her two gowns she'd donned this morning.

"Things in England are strictly proper."

Had she used her utensils improperly? She'd done exactly how Mrs. Marchmain instructed.

He leaned forward, sliding his hand across the table until his fingers almost touched hers. "Here, it is unseemly for a woman to travel alone with male companions."

"I see." She glanced around, expecting everyone to be staring at her, but only the server surveyed her in a queer manner. Mrs. Marchmain's voice resounded in her head. *Every precaution must be taken to protect a lady's reputation.* Hannah pulled her hand away and tucked it under the table.

Bradlee leaned back, but his gaze remained steadfast upon her. "The only person I could think of eligible to aid us was my neighbor."

Hannah stilled while his words soaked in. *His neighbor?* She straightened. "Miss Radcliff? The woman to whom you're engaged?"

"We don't know that for certain."

Colin must have noticed her panicked expression, for he dabbed at his mouth with his napkin. "I told you this was a bad idea."

The tops of her ears burned.

Bradlee ignored Colin. "It's one of the things I shall find out when Miss Radcliff arrives."

"She's coming here?" Her stomach flipped inside out, and her meal almost made a reappearance. Colin was correct. This was a very bad idea.

"I'd prefer to know what has been declared before I face my father. Alice understands the dynamics of my immediate family and is the epitome of proper decorum. She's a good ally and will help us prepare to make the best of appearances." He eyed Colin. "Besides, you haven't even met Miss Radcliff yet."

Alice sounded like everything Hannah was not. How was she supposed to measure up to the *epitome of proper decorum?*

Bradlee twisted in his seat to inspect the entrance. "She should be arriving at any moment."

Was God testing her? She'd left one set of problems only to encounter another. Would life ever be easy?

Reverend Clark's voice rang in her head. *You are a victor, not a victim.*

How could she be a victor peering up from the bottom of an insurmountable precipice?

She forced herself to finish her meal. Colin remained engrossed in his food, and Bradlee stayed quiet, but glanced her way often.

Chimes rang.

"She's here." Bradlee rose.

Hannah stiffened. The glow of the morning sun spilled in through the window upon the regally dressed form of a woman standing in the front entrance.

Colin settled the tab, putting the meal and the rooms on credit under the Granville name for one of the family solicitors to pay at a later date.

The blonde woman met Bradlee with a lovely smile from under a rose-trimmed, silk bonnet that matched her pelisse.

Hannah stood and smoothed the sides of her mother's wrinkled gown. She'd felt so lovely when she'd worn the dress on Nevis. Next to Miss Radcliff, it appeared dated, worn, and faded.

Colin turned to see the elegant Miss Radcliff accept Bradlee's extended hands. His reaction didn't help Hannah's nerves one bit. Colin took one look at the woman, and his eyes softened. A wistful expression arched his brows.

Bradlee summoned them over with a wave. "Come and meet my dear childhood friend and neighbor."

Hannah nudged Colin to get him moving.

"Miss Radcliff"—Bradlee gestured toward Hannah—"may I introduce to you Miss Hannah Barrington and Mr. Colin Fitzroy."

Hannah bobbed what she hoped was an acceptable curtsy.

Miss Radcliff issued them each a stately nod of her head. "It's a pleasure to make the acquaintance of any friend of Bradlee's." Her gaze drifted over Hannah's figure. "I do believe the gowns shall fit. We seem to be of a similar height."

And that is where the similarities ended. Hannah tried not to squirm under her assessment.

"I thought as much. Thank you for coming so quickly." Bradlee clasped his hands behind his back and rocked onto his heels. "I do hope we didn't keep you from anything pressing?"

"Only endless hours of addressing invitations for mother." Miss Radcliff released an airy sigh. "She's decided to throw another pre-season party and plans to invite half of England."

Bradlee chuckled.

Miss Radcliff smiled back at him. "I know."

Know what? Miss Radcliff's shared smile with Bradlee filled Hannah's neck with heat. At least Colin also appeared not to be following their insider jest.

"Mama is beside herself with planning seating charts and wardrobe changes. She's set the entire household into turmoil." Miss Radcliff's tone turned dry. "Let the festivities begin."

Bradlee tilted his head back and laughed. "We better get started, then, so you don't miss the preparations."

"I have every intention of making a day out of this. I owe you a debt of gratitude for saving me from Mama's nagging." She tugged at the edge of her kid glove. "I daresay, it is good to see you. You've been missed." Her index finger pointed to his hair. "I see you've decided to set a new trend?"

He raked a hand through his hair. "I thought long hair was the style."

"It's too long to even be considered a Caesar cut."

"While you take Miss Barrington under your wing, Colin and I have plans to remedy it by visiting the barber."

Colin's lips curled. "I daresay the gardener might need a go at it first with his lopping sheers."

Miss Radcliff covered her mouth with her glove to hide her giggle.

Colin appeared to grow in height a couple of inches, as if proud of drawing Miss Radcliff's laughter.

Heaven help them all if Colin was taken with Miss Radcliff, because the already awkward love triangle would be even more disastrous if it became a love square.

"Did I mention Hannah saved both Colin and me from being eaten by sharks?" Bradlee flashed Hannah a smile.

"You did not." Miss Radcliff's eyes turned to Bradlee and narrowed. "However, I do not find it surprising for you to end up in such a scrape. I must hear the tale."

"Miss Barrington will be much too modest in her retelling. She soared in like St. Elmo's fire. A splendid sight, indeed, but I shall have her finish the story."

Miss Radcliff threaded her arm through Hannah's and nodded to the maid Hannah hadn't noticed standing in the corner with several gowns folded over her arm. "Which way to your rented room?"

Hannah eyed Bradlee.

He shooed her. "You're in good hands."

She glanced over her shoulder at Colin, pleading for him to intervene, but his eyes were fixated on Miss Radcliff.

This was a terrible idea.

CHAPTER 31

A smashing idea…
~ *Journaled the 30ᵗʰ of August, 1829*

*A*s much as she didn't want to, Hannah had to admit Miss Radcliff was a lovely woman inside and out. She'd chosen a gown in a sunny pale yellow for Hannah.

"Try this one on. I believe it will draw out the highlights in your hair. Ruth will help you with the buttons and style your hair."

Hannah stood still as Ruth, the lady's maid, tightened the stays until Hannah thought her ribs might crack. Her hand moved to her stomach as she fought to fill her lungs. The corset only allowed shallow breaths. "Is it supposed to be this tight?"

"Yes, mum." Ruth tied it off. "You have an ample bosom and narrow waist, if I may say so. Might as well show it off." She picked up the gown and pulled it over Hannah's head.

Hannah tried to aid the maid with the buttons, but Ruth insisted upon buttoning all of them. Hannah fidgeted, feeling like a helpless child.

"Did you not have a lady's maid on…" Miss Radcliff's head tilted. "On which isle did you say you resided?"

"Nevis. One of the Leeward Islands."

"Ah, Bradlee wrote you are the daughter of a sugar baron."

Hannah's voice squeaked, "He wrote to you about me?"

"In the missive he sent yesterday. Bradlee isn't much for correspondence, nor writing."

"Oh, but he is. He's an amazing writer." She couldn't help the enthusiasm in her voice. "The descriptions in his journals are magnificent."

"Truly?" Miss Radcliff smiled. "I had no idea he held such a talent."

Hannah paled. She shouldn't have spoken of his writings. Especially, if his fiancée wasn't aware of his accomplishments. However, she didn't have much time to dwell upon it, for Ruth gently pressed her to sit in a nearby chair. She undid the knot that held Hannah's hair and let it drape over her shoulders.

Miss Radcliff squeezed a handful. "It's so thick."

"You are too kind." The polite platitude she'd heard Miss Marchmain often respond fell from her lips. She glanced at Miss Radcliff without moving her head as the maid brushed the long strands. "You and Bradlee have been longtime friends?"

"Indeed." A lively smile split Miss Radcliff's face.

Hannah's heart dropped like a cannonball.

"Ever since he removed a snake from my slippers." She strolled to her valise and removed a handheld mirror and a small case. "Later I learned he and his older brother were the ones who'd put the snake there in the first place." Her tone held no bitterness, only warm fondness. "So tell me about island life. I'm curious to know if it's the same as what I've read in books."

Hannah described the beauty of the island and its culture as Ruth worked on an elaborate coiffure, braiding sections of her hair and interweaving them together. Hannah spoke of the natural beauty, relaxed culture, and the school, feeling wistful as she described how she would miss the children.

"My sister is in dire need of a governess." Miss Radcliff interrupted her. "Oh, forget I mentioned it. I know you are awaiting the return of the duke and duchess of Linton, and you're much too lovely. I'm certain the single gentlemen within their acquaintance will line up outside the duke's study to ask for your hand. Governess positions are for the austere."

Perspiration dampened Hannah's palms. By the way she spoke and the shared looks, certainly, Miss Radcliff expected to marry Bradlee.

Miss Radcliff waved her gloved hand. "Pardon my interruption. Do go on. Nevis sounds quite lovely. Did your parents ever meet Alexander Hamilton? He was born there, wasn't he?"

"Indeed, he was. Papa had run into him in passing when he was a young lad, but Mr. Hamilton died in an unfortunate duel before my family settled on Nevis. I have enjoyed his works, *The Federalist Papers*. Our library held both volumes."

Miss Radcliff clasped her hands. "How splendid! We are kindred spirits. I would love to discuss your thoughts regarding a republic. It seems so foreign for people to govern themselves. I never have anyone with whom to hold an intelligent discourse, for my mother disapproves of my bluestocking ways."

Ruth stepped back, and Miss Radcliff held a gilded handheld mirror up for Hannah to inspect.

Hannah's lips parted with a silent gasp, for it was her mother's face that showed in the reflection. Tears sprung to her eyes, and she blinked them away.

"Do you not like it?" Miss Radcliff's brows drew together.

"It's splendid. It's merely that...I've never..." Her fingers touched her face. "This is how I remember my mother's face. She was so beautiful, so elegant..." For a moment, Hannah lost the ability to speak.

"Your mother must have been lovely, because you look stun-

ning. Bradlee is going to be flabbergasted by your transformation."

How odd that Miss Radcliff would say Bradlee's name and
not Colin's or both?

Miss Radcliff opened a box and removed a necklace. "This
will add the final touch to the masterpiece."

Ruth moved to untie the leather strap around Hannah's
neck.

"Wait." Hannah's hand covered the ring. "It was my father's. I
never take it off."

"I beg your pardon, miss." Ruth's face paled. "I didn't know."

"If it's all the same, I would like to keep it on."

Miss Radcliff eyed her neckline and the slinky gold jewelry
sparkling in her hands. "Are you certain? This piece is—er—
better suited."

Hannah stared at the ugly leather strap tied about her neck.
It had been her solace and sense of comfort all these years. But
where had it gotten her? It hadn't saved her from pain and
heartache. It hadn't protected her from trials and hardships.
Stale questions seeped back into her mind. Why hadn't her
parents included her in their will? Why hadn't they provided a
means for her in case of their deaths, or at least a small stipend?
Were they naïve and not willing to believe death possible? Or
did they not love her as much as she remembered? Perhaps her
future welfare hadn't been important enough to them to be
bothered worrying about.

Should she take it off? The other necklace glittered and
shined, but part of her couldn't let go. After all these years, it
was the one item that reminded her who she was and to whom
she'd once belonged.

"Your necklace is lovely, but I'd prefer to keep mine."

Miss Radcliff handed the necklace to Ruth to put away. "I
understand. It has sentimental value." She searched another

compartment in her valise. "I have a simple gold chain. Would you consider hanging the ring on it instead of the strap?"

She nodded. "I'd like that." Hannah carefully untied the knotted leather and accepted the chain from Miss Radcliff's hands.

"Consider it a gift. I haven't worn it in an age."

Hannah shook her head. "Miss Radcliff, I couldn't possibly accept."

"Posh, I would be offended if you didn't, and anyway, please call me Alice. I do feel like we could become fast friends."

She thanked her and nodded, but wondered how friendly Alice would be toward her if she knew Hannah was in love with Bradlee.

Ruth attached the clasp behind her neck, and the transformation was final.

"Stand up and let me have a look at you." Alice gestured for her to rise.

As Hannah stood, the pale-yellow superfine material shimmered a golden color. The light fabric swished around her ankles.

Alice held up a pair of matching kid boots and gloves. "They may be too large or too snug, but try them on while I find Bradlee and Mr. Fitzroy." She stole from the room with one last smile from the doorway.

Hannah ran her hands down the soft fabric and held it out in a pretend curtsy. It reminded her of when she used to dress up as a child in her mother's luxurious gowns. The ones Huxley must have sold long ago to purchase spirits. Her mind couldn't help but calculate the value of all she'd donned. The grand sum seemed staggering, enough to feed them for half a year at least. Hannah exhaled a breath. She no longer resided with her former guardian, but she still might be scraping for pennies.

∾

"*A*ny news from home?" Bradlee flipped back the side of his newly purchased jacket from the tailor and hooked his thumb into the waistband of his pants. The jacket was a tad snug, but he considered himself lucky not to have to wait for a suit to be made. A customer had never come to pick up his order.

A guffaw of laughter sounded from the tavern. The guests were beginning to wake. Soon this would not be an acceptable place for a gentlewoman. Alice's eyes strayed to the doorway.

She fanned her face and pointed at where Bradlee should stand for the best view of the staircase. "My father fell ill but is rebounding. It delayed my coming out, but now mama is headlong into preparations for the season."

He leaned his shoulder against the wall, hoping to appear nonchalant, even though beads of perspiration formed on his forehead. Surely, if they were engaged, Alice would have said something about making preparations. "Any other announcements? News of a celebratory nature?"

She glanced at the ceiling while she thought. "The baker and his wife gave birth to their first child."

His breath quickened. Alice hadn't mentioned anything about their being engaged. If his father had received the letter, then surely he would have spoken to the Radcliff family and posted banns. "Alice, we've been friends a long time."

She met his gaze.

"There have always been expectations, and I hold you in the highest regard."

She leaned closer.

"But, the grand tour has matured me. I no longer see the world as I used to. I've changed—honed who I am."

A smile grew on her lips. "Indeed, it shows. You are not the same boy who used to tie my braids together."

"I know better who I am." He cleared his throat. "And who I am not. Alice, I—we…"

Movement on the stairs drew their attention. Colin emerged from his room, fiddling with the sleeve of his jacket.

Bradlee gritted his teeth. "Colin."

"Lovely to see you too." Colin smirked as he descended the stairs. His high pointed collars were raised to accommodate a neatly knotted cravat.

Colin had offered to tie Bradlee's, but Bradlee couldn't be bothered with the suffocating thing. It would take time to adjust back to the tight form-fitting styles of London fashion after the loose casual clothing from the Leeward Islands.

"It's a good fit." Colin rolled his arms. "The sleeves are a bit long, but nothing a quick alteration won't fix." He turned to Alice as if to get a lady's opinion.

"Indeed." Her gaze drifted over Colin's form. "A splendid fit."

Colin frowned at Bradlee as he took his place beside him. "I wish you'd let me tie the cravat. You look like a common tradesman."

"You may tie it as we're pulling up the lane for home. There is no purpose in suffering longer than necessary."

A door creaked open, and all gazes rose to the top of the stairs.

A golden goddess emerged in a flowing yellow gown with her hair swept up in an elaborate coiffure. Her face glowed as she descended with her chin held high. However, as she drew closer, Bradlee could see the nervousness in her clouded eyes as her gaze flittered around the room. She had no idea how beautiful she looked, enough for Bradlee's fingers and toes to tingle as if he were about to rappel from a cliff or launch across a chasm. He should have tied his cravat.

Her gaze met his, and her shoulders relaxed. Those inviting lips parted into a shy smile, and only then did he realize he was grinning like a fool. She stopped in front of him. Never had he wanted to clear a room so badly. He clasped his hands behind his back so he wouldn't pull her into his arms and declare he'd loved her from the moment she'd decided to row back out to save more men.

"You look stunning." His voice sounded huskier than he intended.

Hannah's smile widened.

He chuckled at his own awkwardness and scratched the corner of his jaw bone with his thumb.

"She looks lovely." Alice eyed Colin. "Doesn't she, Mr. Fitzroy?"

Colin's gaze shifted to Hannah. "Um, yes, indeed. Exquisite."

Bradlee's brows drew together. Had he been staring at Alice?

Hannah must have noticed it also, for she said, "Did Mr. Fitzroy mention he adores reading?"

Alice's face perked up, and she examined Colin with further interest. "Is that so?"

"He's studying medicine and has even sat in on one of Sir Humphry Davy's lectures." Hannah stepped out of the way for Alice and Colin to draw closer.

Colin offered Alice his arm, and they strolled outside. Bradlee grasped Hannah's hand and promenaded her in a circle for everyone to see the lovely woman he proudly displayed on his arm, then they followed in Colin and Alice's wake.

The coachman brought around Alice's carriage.

"I adore Sir Humphry's writings." Alice's voice rang with enthusiasm. "He was a brilliant man and quite handsome, I must say."

"You said was? Past tense?" Colin leaned away.

A footman lowered the steps, and Bradlee aided Hannah inside.

"He passed in Switzerland several months ago while you were away. I daresay the scientific community lost a great innovator that day."

Colin aided Alice into the carriage and seated himself across from her. Ruth, the maid rode aloft with the driver.

Alice remained riveted on the conversation. "I would love to hear your thoughts on his lecture."

Bradlee watched the exchange with mild interest. He should have known the pair would get along famously. Alice had always been interested in academic pursuits. She'd enjoyed reading and lectures, whereas he'd preferred field study and travel. As Alice and Colin debated whether Sir Humphry Davy was a genius or a madman, considering he'd blown off two of his fingers in a failed experiment, Bradlee used the time to admire Hannah's transformation.

Their eyes met, and he employed the same tactics of nonverbal communication he'd developed during the ship's voyage. He issued her the barest of smiles and held her gaze from under heavy lids. *Love me*, his eyes pleaded. He didn't know whether his letter had arrived or if his parents were waiting for his return before informing the Radcliff family, but either way, it seemed banns hadn't been posted, and he had a chance to explain things to his father. His father would be livid, but a least there wouldn't be a scandal, and Miss Radcliff would be spared embarrassment.

Hannah tucked a pretend strand of hair behind her ear, and her gloved fingers came to rest over her heart. He might be misinterpreting her gesture, but each time it appeared as if she was sealing his love deep within.

She'd held up amazingly well for someone who left all she'd ever known to come to a strange country where nothing had gone as planned.

A shiver ran through her body.

"Are you chilled?"

She nodded.

He removed his jacket, leaned across, and draped it around her shoulders. "The weather is a trifle cooler than in Nevis."

She snuggled into its warmth, and he wished it was his arm wrapped around her. There was no denying the physical attraction between the two of them, but it was more than that. He'd fallen in love with her courage and her resourcefulness. Despite the hardships she'd endured, Hannah didn't become discouraged. In fact, adversity made her stronger, but it didn't harden her heart. She believed she could save everyone, whether it was drowning sea travelers, her deplorable guardian, or restless school children. If she could survive all she'd been through and still be of good character, then she would be the perfect mate for him, because he had many more challenges to face.

The first being his father's expectations. If only he could get his father to see her the way he did.

God, please make a way.

Hannah's eyes widened, and her gaze flicked between Colin and Alice. The discussion between them had grown heated.

Colin leaned forward in his seat. "Davy admits his assistant, Michael Faraday, was his greatest discovery."

"The Davy lamp has saved countless coal miners' lives." Alice's voice grew shrill, and she met his glare with only a foot between their heated faces. "You cannot discredit a life."

"Whoa, now." Bradlee raised both hands. "I can see you're both passionate about science. However, perhaps you two can call a truce, as we're nearing Ywain Manor."

Hannah paled as if about to face the gallows.

Both Colin and Alice sat back in their seats and crossed their arms. Colin's flushed face turned to peer out the window while Alice stared at Colin's profile, as if to flay him with her eyes.

So much for matchmaking the pair.

With grand timing, the carriage turned down the lane. The large estate made of Cotswold stone brought a nostalgic smile to his face. It was good to be home after a year and a half's time. A large willow tree drooped its branches over the stream that ran under the bridge. The horses' hooves clopped across the small overpass.

He pointed out the window, hoping to take Hannah's mind off what lay ahead. "See that willow tree?"

Hannah's hands were tightly clasped in her lap as she leaned closer to the window.

"I dislocated my shoulder falling out of it, but I beat my older brother, Samuel, to the top." He pointed to the main house. "There is Ywain Manor. I'll spare you the details because father will probably launch into a diatribe on its history. He believes it was a holding of Sir Ywain, knight of King Arthur's round table. However, what father will neglect to mention is that it may be the holding of his baseborn brother of the same name who was also a knight of King Arthur."

Alice sighed. "It's as if you're looking for disgrace."

"Both were honorable men."

"Your father would disapprove of such a discussion," Alice said.

Bradlee leaned closer to Hannah. "Samuel and I often pretended to be knights. He'd be Sir Ywain, the knight of the lion, and I'd be his half-brother, Sir Ywain, the adventurous."

"Admit there are similarities." Colin eyed Alice. "Sir Ywain was also reckless, wild, rash, thoughtless, and half-mad."

Alice gasped.

"Never fear, Alice," Bradlee said. "I take no offense to Mr. Fitzroy's insults."

Colin arched a brow. "I'm not insulting you. I'm describing you."

The corners of Alice's lips curled into a smile. She rolled her lips as if to subdue them.

"Watch yourself." Bradlee issued him a warning. "Or I'll give you a piece of my mind."

Colin raised a hand and shook his head. "Oh no, I couldn't take the last piece."

Alice covered her mouth with her hand while Hannah fought to subdue her own laughter.

Bradlee wanted to wring Colin's neck, but one look at Hannah's relaxed expression and her dancing eyes, and all was forgiven. He couldn't let Colin get away clean with such a remark, however. "Revenge may be beneath me, my friend." He leaned back in his seat as if biding his time. "Nevertheless, accidents will happen."

"As I've become keenly aware, ever since making your acquaintance."

"Perhaps I shall remain another year at university so I may enjoy your company longer."

Colin paled, and Hannah burst into another fit of giggles.

The clip-clop of the horses' hooves slowed, and the carriage stopped in front of the main entrance. The front door swung open, and the butler stepped out to greet them.

Hannah straightened her shoulders and smoothed her skirts as she often had under the watchful eye of Mrs. Marchmain.

Bradlee wanted to scoop her hands into his and tell her everything was going to be all right, but now that they'd arrived and the confrontation impending, he lost a bit of his certainty. He inhaled a deep breath. He had no other choice.

It was time to face his father.

CHAPTER 32

The delightful longing of home, marred only by family
expectations.

~ *Journaled the 30ᵗʰ of August, 1829*

*H*annah sat on a tufted sofa in the gold salon, hoping
the yellow gown would help her blend in. She had
been greeted warmly by Bradlee's mother and eldest brother,
Samuel, who'd joined them in front of the largest stone fireplace
Hannah had ever seen. Thick timber beams ran across the high
ceiling, and an enormous wrought iron chandelier dripped with
beeswax candles.

Tea was served, and Bradlee relayed the events of his grand
tour to his mother and brother, with Colin occasionally adding
his perspective. His brother sat attentive, listening to Bradlee's
tales with only the occasional flinch when Bradlee mentioned
looming lions, the Indian attack, and the ship running aground.
His mother sat straight as a ramrod the entire time, also
showing limited emotion except for the occasional clasping and
unclasping of her hands during the tense moments of the story.
Bradlee's brother resembled his mother with lighter eyes and

high cheekbones, but while his brows were thick, hers were thin and regally arched. It appeared she and Mrs. Marchmain had similar schooling on etiquette.

Even though everyone seemed engrossed in Bradlee's retelling, Hannah often felt their gazes sliding in her direction as if to discern more about her. He'd reached the part of their tumbling into the shark infested waters when a barrel-chested man with grayed temples, resembling Bradlee in facial features only, hobbled into the center of the room with the aid of a cane.

"What's this?" He stamped the end of his cane on the floor. "Has my scholarly son arrived home from his grand tour?" He patted Bradlee on the back. "Welcome home, son. I'm so proud of your accomplishments. I've been bragging about your accolades at the club."

Bradlee forced a smile and awkwardly stood as his father clamped a hand on his shoulder. "About that—"

"Samuel had his doubts if you'd see it through to the finish, but I knew once you hopped aboard the ship bound for the States that you'd pulled through your exams." He turned to face Colin. "You must be his bear leader, Mr. Fitzroy." Lord Cardon dipped his head in a curt bow. "I hope he wasn't a handful. You have my sincerest gratitude for being his guide and returning him home safely. Hopefully, now that he's gotten that spirit of adventure out of his system..." His gaze fell upon Hannah.

She pressed into the back of the sofa.

"You must be Mrs. Fitzroy." Lord Cardon bowed formally. "I'm certain you are delighted to have your husband back after such a long absence." He shifted a tender gaze to Lady Cardon. "I wouldn't let him out of your sights again if I were you, either."

The blood drained from Hannah's extremities. Bradlee stood stock still, and Colin paled.

Lord Cardon shifted to Alice. "And it's always lovely when you grace us with your delightful presence. I hope you see Ywain Manor as your second home."

Bradlee snapped out of his stupor. "Actually, Papa." he gestured to Hannah. "This is Miss Hannah Barrington, from the Leeward Islands."

His eyebrows lifted. "My apologies, Miss Barrington." He bowed his head. "I assumed..." Silence fell, stifling the room like a thick blanket. "Well, I assumed too much." He straightened and rested both hands on the top of his cane.

Had they noticed she had no chaperone? Her stomach twisted. She'd overstepped in coming here, but where else could she have gone?

Lady Cardon tilted her head. "Barrington sounds familiar. What is your mother's maiden name? Perhaps we know your family?"

What should she say? How should she respond? That she couldn't remember because they died twelve years ago? Should she mention the duke and duchess, when they didn't even know of her arrival? Should she mention her guardian—Reuben Huxley? Even though he wasn't truly her uncle, would his reputation follow her here?

Lord Cardon blinked at her hesitation. He cleared his throat. "She's asking what family or lineage?" He turned to glance at Bradlee. "Perhaps, they call it something different in the Leeward Islands."

Bradlee moved to her side and rested a hand on the back of the sofa. "Her parents are deceased. She is the daughter of Sir Charles Barrington of Bristol and has returned with us to accept her inheritance."

"A sugar baron's daughter. How splendid." Lady Cardon sipped from her tea. "Lovely to make your acquaintance."

Lord Cardon rested both hands on the rounded top of his cane. "My condolences for your parents' deaths. I daresay, few sugar barons remain in the islands. Your father must have been one of the last holdouts."

"He passed quite a few years back," she said, "and yes, there are very few planters remaining on Nevis."

Lady Cardon set aside her cup and folded her gloved hands. "How did you become acquainted with our son and Mr. Fitzroy? Was it on the ship?"

"No. I…" She glanced at Bradlee, for she had no idea what would be acceptable to say.

"She rescued us from certain death." Bradlee over-dramatized the tale, making her sound more like a valiant Joan of Arc instead of a poor island girl.

"My heavens." Lady Cardon raised a hand to her lips. "We owe you more than our gratitude. We owe you our son's life." Her eyes misted as she glanced at Bradlee. "I do hope you will join us for supper. It is the least we can do after all you've done." She leaned forward. "Are you passing through?"

Bradlee cleared his throat. "I've insisted that she stay here until the Duchess of Linton returns. The duchess will be helping Miss Barrington gain back her inheritance when she returns from her stepson's wedding up north."

Lady Cardon inhaled a sharp breath, but quickly masked any expression from her face. "Oh, how delightful." She, once again, folded her hands. "We love visitors to Ywain Manor, expected… or otherwise. Bradlee, you must arrange for Miss Barrington and Mr. Fitzroy to receive a tour, but if you'll excuse me. I must inform the housekeeper to prepare the bedchambers." She stood and paused. "I'll have Seaton, our butler, instruct your maid as to where you shall be sleeping, and a footman will bring in your trunks."

Hannah swallowed. "I—"

"I already instructed a footman to unload her valise." Alice's gaze locked on Hannah. "And isn't her maid, Ruth, talented with hairstyles?" She squeezed Hannah's hand. "You must let me borrow her sometime."

Her eyes questioned Alice, *Are you certain?*

"I'll inform Seaton and see your maid begins unpacking."
Lady Cardon departed.

"It has been an eventful trip. I'm certain Miss Barrington and
Mr. Fitzroy are exhausted." Bradlee extended a hand to Hannah.
"Perhaps, we should begin the tour so they may rest before we
dine."

Samuel rose and patted his brother on the back. "Good to
see you hale, brother. Your adventuresome side never ceases to
amaze me or give me ulcers worrying over your sorry hide." His
eyes shone with fondness, and he turned to the rest of them. "It
was lovely to meet you, Miss Barrington, Mr. Fitzroy, and
delightful to see you again, Miss Radcliff. Please excuse me. I
have business to attend."

Lord Cardon hobbled after his son. "Bradlee, you go on and
show them the grounds without me. I must go over a few
accounts with your brother. I'll tell them the story of Ywain
manor over dinner."

Alice, Colin, Bradlee, and Hannah exited the salon. As they re-
entered the foyer, Alice moved to the front entrance. "I must be
going. I have invitations to finish, or else I'll receive a lecture from
Mama." She turned to Hannah. "It was very nice to meet you. If
you need anything, I'm only a few minutes away. Bradlee can show
you the shortcut through the glen." She shared a look with Bradlee.
"Just watch out for the trolls who live in the gnarled trees."

Bradlee burst out laughing. He waved a hand through the
air. "I might have told a few exaggerated tales."

A knot hardened in Hannah's stomach. Alice and Bradlee
seemed so good together. Hannah didn't belong. Alice did. They
had a past and a future, whereas Hannah had neither.

Alice turned to Colin. "I still disagree with your sentiments
regarding Sir Humphry."

Colin flashed a cheeky grin. "I'd agree with you, but then
we'd both be wrong."

Alice's mouth tightened.

Hannah glared at Colin, who then offered Alice an elaborate bow. "It was lovely meeting you."

Alice harrumphed and exited through the front door, opened by the butler. Hannah caught a glimpse of a smile on Alice's lips as she peered over her shoulder before leaving.

Colin exhaled a deep breath. "Well, my duties as duenna are over. If you could point me to my room."

"Up the stairs to the left, third door on the right."

Colin turned and strode up the curved stair.

Bradlee tucked her hand into the crook of his arm. He met her gaze with a crooked smile, and his eyes darkened. "It is just the two of us then." She glanced around the foyer for Ruth, but she'd left to do her unpacking.

Hannah attempted to steady her breathing. "Miss Radcliff is a lovely woman. I understand if you have feelings for her. It's easy to forget what you have until you become reacquainted."

He paused and faced her. His gaze bore into her, warming her from the inside out. "I haven't forgotten anything." He stepped closer until his boots met the tips of her borrowed shoes. "Especially not what you mean to me."

Hannah's heart pounded so hard against her chest that her extremities vibrated with each beat.

Bradlee glanced around before drawing her farther down the hall and into a small room off to the side. He quietly closed the door behind him and faced her. His eyes glittered, and he grinned like someone who'd gotten away with a crime.

Hannah inspected the green and gold drawing room and tried to calm her breathing. This was only Bradlee. She'd been alone with him before. Why then did she feel as jumpy as a cane toad?

CHAPTER 33

...to awaken to the smell of a dew-soaked English garden.
~ Journaled the 1ˢᵗ of September, 1829

*I*t wasn't proper for her to be alone with a man in a room. Mrs. Marchmain's warnings to her daughter and, ergo, to Hannah blared like a trumpet announcing an attack. She backed away from Bradlee. "This isn't proper. There are people in the walls."

His brows drew together, and then he released a short burst of laughter. "You must remember having servants." His hands grasped her shoulders, and his thumbs stroked the bare skin at the edge of her collarbone.

As much as she yearned for his touch, it didn't mean she should encourage such forwardness. Especially not while she resided under his parents' roof. Creating a scandal was not the way to repay them for their kindness.

His hand moved to cup her face, and his dancing eyes stared into hers.

She tensed.

"Do you know what this means?" Only a few inches separated his face from hers.

She answered with the barest shake of her head.

"It never arrived." He rested his forehead against hers and half-laughed, half-sighed, before pulling back and squeezing her upper arms.

His smile was contagious even though she wasn't following his comments.

"My letter never arrived, and my father never read its contents. If it had, one of my parents would have mentioned it."

He lifted her into the air and spun her about the room. "I'm not engaged."

She squealed as her feet left the ground, but his infectious laughter spread.

He set her feet back on the floor. "This means I can finish my exams, come back, and court you properly." His face sobered, and the thinnest thread of insecurity wove itself into his usually confident eyes. "That is, if you'll have me."

Her heart stilled. Could it be possible? A life with Bradlee as his wife? "Yes." The words leapt from her lips before he could change his mind. "Most definitely, yes."

He seized her, wrapping her in his arms, crushing her against his chest so close she could hear the wild beating of his heart. Somehow, God had made the impossible possible.

She sighed into his chest, treasuring the sensation of being snuggled in his embrace, but doubts whispered in her ears. She pulled away. "What about Alice?"

"She too is unaware of the engagement, other than the silent assumption we've lived under all our lives. I will speak with her regarding it. I don't believe she harbors any feelings for me other than longtime friendship. She will understand."

"What about your parents?"

"They will fall in love with you as I have."

He loved her? Her breath stopped, and a lightness filled her chest. She'd never fainted, but her heart beat so rapidly she felt lightheaded.

"Come on." He tugged on her arm. "I have something I've been dying to show you."

He pulled open the door and ran with her in tow down the hall. Hannah bit back her smile as they passed a maid. The woman paused in dusting a glass vase and shook her head. Bradlee exited through a large set of French doors leading into a small portico, where he aided her through the archway and borrowed a pair of sheers from the gardener, who was planting a row of mums along the steps. Bradlee descended into a small walled garden and drew up short on the pebbled path.

Hannah bumped into his side.

Red, pink, and yellow blooms burst from lush green stems, bushes, and vines. Their sweet perfume hung in the afternoon breeze. Her lips parted.

A rose garden.

She couldn't remember ever seeing one, but the scent triggered memories of her mother in a wide-brimmed hat and long gloves, standing in the sun with a basket of bright blooms.

Bradlee examined a few of the bushes before reaching into the mass of thorny stems.

Hannah held her breath. "Do be careful—"

"Ow." A drop of blood formed on the side of his hand where a thorn pierced the skin, but it didn't thwart him in the least. He snapped off a long stem, making quick work of pruning the rest of the thorns. His lips curled into a devastating smile, and he held the rose out to her. "A rose for Hannah Rose."

The thoughtful gesture melted any remaining knots in her stomach. She accepted the beautiful scarlet flower. Its delicate petals curled into a soft blossoming array. She closed her eyes and inhaled its rich fragrance.

"There is not a rose in all of England as perfect as you."

She met his gaze, not wanting him to be disillusioned by her new appearance. "I'm not perfect." She was still the same poor island girl who, only a few months past, had walked barefoot through town.

He cupped her cheek. "You're perfect for me." A twinkle glinted in his eyes. "But if you'd like, we can search all of England for a rose that matches your beauty. We can make it an adventure to scour the land in search of the one flower that might compare, but I don't think we'll ever locate it."

Her gaze dropped back to the flower as she remembered Alice's beautiful elegance. "You're being silly."

He tipped her chin up with his index finger. "Am I?"

The breeze picked up, dancing the ringlets of curls about her face and sending a shiver along her skin.

"You're chilled." He tucked her hand into his arm and turned them back toward the house. "We'll finish the tour of the gardens tomorrow." He drew her closer to his side and wrapped an arm about her for warmth.

"There you are, Bradlee." His mother opened the door to back salon.

Bradlee quickly dropped his arm and held the door as Hannah entered the house.

Lady Cardon glanced over his shoulder. "Where are Miss Radcliff and Mr. Fitzroy?"

"Miss Radcliff had invitations to address, and Mr. Fitzroy retired to his room." He closed the door behind him.

"It is just you and Miss Barrington?" She eyed him, and Hannah didn't miss the reprimand in her tone.

She'd broken one of the many rules Mrs. Marchmain pounded into her head. A lady should never be alone with a man. Hannah forced her head to remain high.

"Your father is looking for you. He's in his study." She rounded on Hannah. "Miss Barrington, perhaps you would like to rest before supper. May I show you to your room?"

"Indeed. Thank you, my lady."

Lady Cardon's gaze dropped to the rose clutched in Hannah's hand.

The urge to hide it behind her back caused her fingers to twitch. What did Lady Cardon think of her? She had the distinct feeling she wasn't making a proper impression.

"I shall see you at supper." Bradlee bowed to them both and left the room.

His mother sighed. "It's a relief Bradlee is home. My fear is he'll soon be off again." She gestured for Hannah to follow her up the back staircase. "I wish he would settle down, but he was born with a restless spirit." At the top of the stairs, she veered right down a hall lined with wainscoting. She stopped in front of a portrait hung in an alcove. "This portrait took over a year to paint, for Bradlee simply couldn't sit long enough for the artist to capture him."

A younger version of Bradlee stood next to a horse. His fingers clutched the reins, and his body leaned in a way that made it look as if he was ready to mount the steed and ride off at a breakneck pace.

Hannah admired the brushwork. "The artist did capture the mischievous gleam in his eyes."

"Indeed." Lady Cardon's face remained impassive. "Are you the settling type, Miss Barrington?"

It was an odd question to pose. Was Lady Cardon wondering if she could handle her son's sense of adventure? Was she looking for a woman to bring her son to heel? Or was she insinuating that Hannah was loose in morals?

"As soon as I determine where I belong, I intend to settle there and grow roots."

She studied Hannah for a long moment before gesturing to a door on the left. "Here is your room. Please make yourself at home. Ring the bell pull if you find you are in need of anything."

Hannah entered the spacious chamber. A large canopied bed filled one wall. A bureau was flanked by two large mullioned windows, which were outlined by heavy brocade curtains tied back with tassels. "It's lovely. Thank you again for your hospitality."

A flash of emotion shone in her eyes. Was it pity?

"I shall have a footman bring up a vase and water for your rose." Lady Cardon exited the room.

Hannah watched her go before moving to the window. She peered out at the rolling green hills and shady arbors with trees taller than any she'd ever seen. She touched the cool glass. Bradlee had played among those trees as a child. His smile appeared before her eyes, and his words echoed in her mind. *You are perfect for me.*

She loved Bradlee. There was no use denying what God had put in her heart, but the situation still flipped her stomach upside-down.

Thank you, Lord, for bringing me back to my homeland, for making a way for me to be with Bradlee. But if this is Your will, why then do I feel so out of place?

~

The nostalgic smells of his father's musky cologne and a good cigar wafted under Bradlee's nose. His father pointed to the empty wall in the foyer right outside his study. "I've commissioned an artist." The opposite wall displayed a painting of his brother Samuel in his cap and gown to commemorate his graduation from university. "This is where I shall hang your portrait."

Bradlee swallowed the guilt rising into his chest and inhaled a deep breath. It was time to confess everything.

His father smacked him on the back, knocking the air from his lungs. "I knew you had it in you. Your tutors said you were inattentive and unable to be taught, but I knew when it came down to it, you would rise to the occasion. Everyone who passes this way shall know that my sons have received higher educations, the family tradition since your great-great-grandfather, Lord Fredrick Ascot Granville, was granted the earldom. He went on to manage his lands with great care, and his younger brother Henry Granville became a professor at Oxford. You have done us proud by following in your great-great uncle's footsteps."

"About that." Bradlee ran a hand over his mouth and chin. "On my grand tour, I wrote a manuscript."

"You don't say?" His father's bushy brows lifted.

"It's quite good. I'm going to see if it might be publishable."

"Splendid." His father moved to shuffle some papers on his desk. "Oxford will be even more pleased to see one of their professors' works published." He lifted the papers and tapped the edge. "What sort of work is it? A scientific study? Historical documentation?"

"It's fiction."

"Fiction?" His father snorted. "Not the sort of drivel that fellow Lord Byron wrote, I hope." He set the papers down.

"It's a story with details from the places I traveled. It will help people to understand different cultures. Bring people together. Make the world a smaller place. I believe I can make a decent living writing." He stepped forward. "It took me three months to write a novel. At that rate, I can publish four a year. My English professor believed in my talent, and while I was still at school, offered to put in a good word for me with his friends in the publishing industry. With his backing, I know I can—"

"Why don't you publish something academic? Something Oxford would be proud of?"

Bradlee's teeth clenched. "You mean something you'd be proud of?"

"Didn't I just tell you how proud of you I am?" His lips thinned and his face reddened as he pointed to the empty space on the wall. "I just said I was going to have your portrait painted and hung on the wall to show the world my son is a graduate of Oxford."

Bradlee's gaze dropped to the floor, and he braced himself for the tidal wave of disappointment about to wash over him. "I haven't yet graduated."

Stunned silence sucked all the air from the room.

His father blinked in rapid sequence. "I believe I misheard what you said." He turned his head to bring his ear closer.

"I haven't graduated. I asked for an extension so I could better prepare for the exams."

"You went on your grand tour when you should have been taking your exams?" He pounded a fist on the desk.

"So I could research for my paper."

"You wasted your education to write fiction?" His lips quivered. "Of all the irresponsible, reckless, foolish..." The red of his face deepened to that of a pickled beet. "You're going to return to Oxford straightaway, beg the dons for forgiveness, and take the exam." He flung the stack of papers onto the floor. "What goes through that head of yours? Is there anything between your ears?"

Bradlee's chest tightened, shortening his breath. Old feelings rushed in, and he was once again a small child peering up at his father. His blood pounded in his ears and his body began to tremble. Hadn't he gotten over these spells? By Jove, he'd been able to speak in front of an entire classroom, but now the room spun. He couldn't even face his father without embarrassing himself by fainting. What had Hannah taught him?

Breathe.

His father's voice lowered to a menacing grumble. "Why can't you be more like your brother?"

He couldn't find any air. The room spun faster and he swayed on his feet.

"Get out of my sight!" His father pointed to the door. "We'll discuss this at length later."

Bradlee wasted no time darting for the door.

~

*B*radlee forced his shoulders to lower, despite their continuing to creep up toward his ears. He picked up his knife and scraped it across the braised portion of beef next to the pile of bitter Brussels sprouts. His jaw tightened, for the tender slice of meat didn't satisfy his frustration. If only their chef had overcooked it, then he could extract his angst upon his food, sawing it into tiny bite-sized pieces. Instead, he speared it with his fork and popped the piece into his mouth.

Hannah watched him over her crystal goblet. Her thin brows bunched together, and questions swirled in her eyes. Colin entertained his mother at one end of the table, while Samuel discussed the number of hired hands needed to re-thatch one of their tenant's homes with his father.

Funny how his family heartily enjoyed their meal, oblivious to his unease, yet a woman he'd known for only four months could read him so well.

The discussion with his father had gone poorly, and he hadn't even broached the topic of Alice and Hannah. His stomach twisted into a knot. How is it he could gain the respect of an African tribal leader and an American Indian chief and be welcomed in their huts and tents, yet shortly after his son's return, his father hung his head in shame?

He shouldn't have come home. His father only dragged up all his past insecurities. Now, how was he going to stand up and be tested before the dons? He should have gone straight to the publisher and only returned after he'd graduated and held a book contract. But he'd had no other choice. He couldn't take Hannah with him to Oxford.

An hour ago, his father had beamed with pride—pride Bradlee hadn't deserved.

Now, he wouldn't even make eye contact. Bradlee's stomach soured, and he sipped his drink to settle it. If only he'd summoned the courage and taken the final exam before he'd sailed for his grand tour.

"Bradlee?" His father set down his fork and addressed him. "I saw a letter from Oxford among your correspondences."

Hannah broke off from a conversation with Samuel and stared at him.

Bradlee fingered his glass, and the footman scurried to refill it. "The letter was merely my professors requesting my return."

His father's hand slapped the table, rattling the plates and glasses.

Samuel stilled his rocking glass.

"Do you still keep in touch with any of your professors at Oxford?" His father leaned back in his seat and peered at Samuel.

Samuel scratched behind his ear with his index finger. "A few."

"We may need you to write and ask for a favor. It seems Bradlee hasn't finished his exams."

Lady Cardon gasped.

Samuel's head snapped around. "And you went on your grand tour?"

"There's no need to contact anyone." Bradlee set down his fork. "I received an extension, and my grand tour was used to finish my research and collect samples for the great go."

Lady Cardon put a hand to her chest. "Thank heaven. You'll still graduate on time."

If he remained conscious during the final exam.

"I just hope word doesn't get back to the Radcliffs. We don't want them reconsidering Alice's options. She'll have her coming out this spring. You'll be expected to court her properly before the banns are posted."

Mother cast a sidelong glance at Hannah.

Hannah set down her cup and peered at Bradlee.

He didn't want to get into an argument in front of Hannah, especially not after their last discussion, but his father left him no other choice. He sat up straighter. "I have other plans."

"What other plans could surpass the ones laid out for you?" A crease formed between his father's brows. "It's all settled."

"Nothing has been settled." Bradlee gritted his teeth.

Colin relaxed back in his chair as if ready to be entertained.

His mother issued Bradlee a small warning shake of her head before changing the topic. "Perhaps it's time for the ladies to retire to the drawing room."

Bradlee exhaled. Bless his mother's soul. He didn't want Hannah to witness his father's temper.

The men stood and pulled out the ladies' chairs. They rose and were almost to the door when Father spoke.

"Bradlee, Mr. Fitzroy, you'll have to excuse us." His father leaned on his cane. "A missive arrived earlier informing us of a dispute at our northern holdings. Samuel and I must retire early to be on our way at first light to see matters settled." He strode toward the door and paused. "Bradlee, I'll expect you'll be off to Oxford to settle your matters before I return. Further discussions must wait until after you complete your exams. I know you will not let your family down." He patted the doorframe and left.

At the door, Hannah paled. He wanted to reassure her, but his own confidence slipped to a new low. She trailed behind his mother out of the room.

He had so much to tell Hannah, and so little time. He needed to dispel the doubts he saw in her eyes and reassure her of his intentions—and he needed to do so alone.

CHAPTER 34

My attitude toward Oxford's exams: they ask me questions to which I haven't the foggiest. Then, I proceed to respond with an answer to which the professors haven't a clue, and we both leave bewildered.
~ *Journaled Bradlee's first year at Oxford, the 15th of September, 1825*

The following morning, Hannah awoke in a dark room, but when she tried to draw the curtains, Ruth shooed her away and drew them herself. Hannah opened the wardrobe and selected a dress to wear.

Ruth held up a different one. "Might I suggest the chintz day gown?"

Neither held any preference for Hannah. She shrugged and stood still while the maid insisted on helping her dress. As if she hadn't dressed herself for at least the past twelve years.

Were all Englishwomen expected to be so helpless?

"Would you like me to show you down to the breakfast room, milady?" Ruth folded her hands at her waist.

"No need. I remember the way." She glanced back over her

shoulder, half expecting Ruth to follow her to ensure she made it safely.

A hand snaked around her waist and yanked her into the alcove.

She released a small yelp before Bradlee pressed a finger to her lips.

"Shh." His eyes darted back and forth down the hall.

"If someone discovers us, your parents' estimation of me will lower even further."

"You and Colin are the only guests in this wing. Besides, my mother adores you."

"She does?" She certainly had an odd way of showing it.

His gaze melted into hers, and he pressed her hands between his warm ones. "Immensely, almost as much as I do."

She wanted this to be real, to be loved by Bradlee, to be his wife and live in his world. It had seemed as if God had made a way, for He'd brought her to England and there'd been no announcement of any engagement. However, his parents' approval seemed to be another hand on a door ready to be slammed in her face. How could her lack of proper decorum possibly stand against the demure Miss Radcliff? Her gaze dropped to the borrowed gown. Not only was she a foreigner, she was a fraud, trying to fit in where she did not belong.

God, why would Your will have so many obstacles? Did I misunderstand Your plans for me?

"What is the matter?" He squeezed her hands.

"Your father seemed upset." She felt him stiffen. "Telling him about me is only going to infuriate him more."

"Don't worry. I'll get him to come around as soon as I return."

She gasped. "You're leaving? Where are you going?"

"To Oxford. It's why I needed to speak with you. They moved up the great go. The professor with whom I traveled to Africa has decided to retire. I need his approval of my writ-

ings and journals to graduate. Colin and I must leave immediately."

"Immediately?" She could only echo his word, for her
thoughts tumbled over each other. How could he leave her all
alone? Would Lord and Lady Cardon allow her to impose upon
their hospitality? If not, where would she go? She could have
survived on Nevis, but could she survive in England?

"My parents will be delighted to have you continue as my
guest." He nodded as if to encourage her. "It'll give you time to
know one another better."

Or a chance to prove her inadequacies.

"Don't look so glum. I should return in a little over a fortnight." His hands moved to her shoulders, and he widened his
stance to meet her eyelevel. "You survived a suspicious, half-
drunk guardian on an island filled with unrest. I believe you can
survive four weeks in England with my mother."

A weary smile wavered on her lips. He was right. She had
endured much worse.

"God will make a way. I'm hoping the dons will accept my
journal as credit and perhaps even help me submit it to a
publishing agency. If I can come back an Oxford graduate with
proof I can make it as a writer, Father will have to understand."
A shadow fell over his eyes.

"Something's wrong." She studied his expression, and a knot
formed in her stomach. "What happened yesterday in the
meeting with your father? At dinner, you seemed in a dudgeon."

"It's nothing."

The coil in her stomach tightened. She placed a hand on his
lapel.

"I'm merely concerned about the exams."

She relaxed and exhaled. "You'll do splendidly, of that I have
no doubt."

Her declaration seemed to loosen his tongue. "I had another
attack yesterday in front of my father." He closed his eyes as if

to block the memory. "I couldn't leave the room fast enough." He opened his eyes. "Why can I face lions and fierce Indians, but not my father and a handful of professors?"

"It's because you care." She tugged on the side of his lapel. "You respect them and you want to earn their respect in return."

"I'm not going to earn their respect by swooning at their feet."

"Didn't you just tell me God would make a way?"

A begrudging smile curled his lips. "Are you using my words against me?"

"I am, because you're right. God is bigger than our insecurities." The words from Reverend Clark's message flowed through her head. "He didn't make you a victim. He created you to be a victor. God will make the rough places smooth. I believe in Him, and I believe in you." She steadied her gaze. "You know the information inside and out. You are the bravest and most capable man I know. They are merely men. What can they do to you when you are walking in God's will?"

"Nothing."

She traced the line of his clean-shaven jaw. "Then you have nothing to fear."

"And neither do you." His gaze lowered to her mouth. "When I return, I plan to never again let you out of my sight."

He leaned down, hesitating before his lips brushed hers. She melted against him like a molasses drip down a bottle, as he sealed his promise with a tender, drugging kiss. It warmed her like the Caribbean sun, and she clung to him, absorbing his strength for what was to come and transferring hers to him.

With a weary sigh, he released her. "The sooner I leave, the sooner I can return." His smoldering gaze locked on her. "And then, we shall plan our future together."

She nodded her consent.

He backed up a step and stared at her for a long moment. "This is how I shall think of you each day and night, standing here with flushed cheeks and those becoming lips"—he flashed a grin—"still branded with my kiss."

She tried to frown, but it curved into a smile.

He turned and jogged down the hall, spinning on his heel for one last look before he descended the stairs.

A footman rounded the corner from the backstairs. "Morning, Miss Barrington." He bowed. "Lady Cardon requests your presence."

CHAPTER 35

I hear the lilt of her voice reminding me to pray for
wisdom. I see her faith and know I am stronger for it.
~ *Journaled the 9ᵗʰ of September, 1829*

*T*he clock chimed half past eight as Hannah paused on
the main stair. Through the window, she saw the
backs of Bradlee and Colin preparing their steeds. She lifted her
hand in a silent wave and sent a prayer for their speedy return.
A brisk breeze shook the trees, raining down leaves, and a
formation of geese flew south for the coming of winter. Instead
of turning their horses down the lane, Bradlee and Colin
steered them the other direction toward the glen—the path to
Alice's home.

Hannah's heart stilled. Was Bradlee bidding Alice farewell as
he had her? She remembered his kiss and shook her head to
clear it. His words had been genuine. Perhaps bidding the
neighbors farewell was customary in England. She hurried
down the stairs to not keep Lady Cardon waiting. She had so
much to learn about her homeland.

The footman swung the door wide as she approached.

Heaven forbid she knock and open the door herself. Lady Cardon greeted her politely and gestured for her to take a seat.

"It seems it shall be just the two of us." Lady Cardon sipped from her cup.

Hannah stared at the rows of silverware on either side of her plate and fingered one. Lady Cardon peered at her choice from over the rim of her teacup, one brow raised slightly. Hannah thought back to which fork Lady Marchmain instructed her to use and selected the proper one to eat her eggs. "I am grateful for your hospitality."

Lady Cardon set down her teacup. "I believe it's about time we got to know one another. My son doesn't often invite guests to Ywain Manor, especially not of the female variety."

Hannah plopped a bite of eggs into her mouth, for she had no idea how to respond to such a statement.

"Bradlee tells me you volunteered at a local school, teaching slave children reading and arithmetic?"

"Free and slave children."

"I see. And you helped him prepare for his exams? I had no idea the Leeward Islands provided such lofty schooling that a woman could tutor an Oxford student."

Hannah's throat tightened at the verbal slight, and the eggs stuck in her throat. She sipped from her drink and prayed for wisdom. God willing, Lady Cardon would be her mother-in-law. It would bode well to remain on good terms. "My parents held an extensive library, and with the weather on an island being what it is, I spent many a warm day reclining in the shade reading whatever I could lay my hands on. I do not claim to even come close to the broad spectrum of subjects Mr. Granville has learned, but I did read a book once on the precepts of public speaking and offered him some of the wisdom I'd gleaned."

Lady Cardon tilted her head. "Bradlee needed help with public speaking?"

Hannah swallowed. Would Bradlee want her to discuss his fears with his mother? "Er—I don't mean to dishonor Mr. Granville by saying something I shouldn't."

"I'm his mother." Lady Cardon shifted in her seat. "There is nothing he'd withhold from me. Go on."

She sent up a prayer for forgiveness, if Bradlee should be angry with her. "He becomes nervous when speaking in front of people. We had him practice teaching the class to help him overcome his fear."

"I see." Her brows drew together.

"His fear was the reason he requested an extension for the great go."

"I think I understand why becoming a professor may not be his ideal profession." Lady Cardon placed her hands on the edge of the table. "If you'll excuse me, I'm afraid I'm coming down with a bit of a headache." She abruptly rose and left the room.

Hannah finished her meal and found her way to the kitchens to prepare an elixir.

She prayed for Lady Cardon's health and that the elixir might suffice as a gesture of good will. She was growing desperate to find a way to turn Bradlee's mother's heart toward her.

~

*B*radlee inhaled the scent of decaying leaves as he took a turn about the grounds with Alice on his arm. He slowed his pace to match what she'd consider proper. A horse neighed, and her gaze slid over to Colin, who was holding the reins and patting the nose of his steed.

"I hope I've not misled you in anyway." He tapped his riding gloves against his thigh. "It was not my intent. You are a lovely person and a great friend. I wanted you to know before the season began."

Her face remained impassive, and Bradlee chewed his lip, hoping he hadn't destroyed her dreams or her heart.

Alice stared at the tree line. "Truthfully, I'm relieved."

Bradlee perked up.

"I care for you deeply."

His breath stopped.

"But as a friend." She released a sigh. "I've been going along because our parents seemed set on the idea." She stopped and faced him. "I think I've always known we wouldn't suit. You are too adventurous for my tastes." She gestured toward his missing cravat. "And you do not give a wit about decorum."

He chuckled, but more so out of an exhilarating sense of relief. "I find I have other priorities."

Her gaze strayed back to Colin, who was watching them. "I think it may be for the best." She peered back at Bradlee. "How shall we inform our parents?"

"I don't want to cause you any undue strain." The tension in his shoulders returned. "Leave it to me. I shall deal with it first thing upon my return."

~

*S*ince the only life Hannah had known was the neighborly way of small island life, she couldn't determine whether Lady Cardon remained aloof because that was English custom or because Hannah was unwelcome.

She suspected the latter, which was why she was shocked when, several days later, Lady Cardon summoned her to the foyer.

Lady Cardon adjusted the edge of her gloves. "I have plans to ride into town to do a bit of shopping. Would you care to join me?"

Hannah's heart thumped against her ribs. Spend the afternoon under the assessing gaze of Lady Cardon? She forced her head to nod. "That sounds lovely."

"Well then, let's be off." She strode through the door the butler held open.

"One moment. I must get a shawl." Hannah turned to take the stairs.

"Here you are, miss."

The butler held out her pelisse.

Hannah grinned and thanked him.

"It is my duty." He bowed.

Another gaff. Never thank the servants for doing their duty. Add that to the growing list of mistakes she continued to make. She must do better.

Hannah climbed into the carriage and sat across from Lady Cardon. "I'm glad to see you feeling hale. Was the elixir any help?"

"Foul tasting brew." Her lips pursed. "However, it did cure my headache, for which I am grateful."

Hannah blinked. Should she consider that a victory?

As the coach bounced down the lane, Hannah asked about the area. Certainly, the local domestic products and history would be an acceptable conversation. Lady Cardon was happy to answer her questions. She even posed a few of her own regarding the weather in the Leeward Islands and the healing qualities of their hot springs. Eventually, the banter dwindled, and Hannah found herself staring at the passing scenery.

The main street of the Cotswolds was a quaint area filled with thatched roof cottages and shops. Instead of sheets hung to separate the different vendors like the market in Nevis, each shop had a hanging wooden sign and displayed a few goods out front or in the windows.

The driver stopped in front of a bakery, and the smell of freshly baked bread welcomed her. A footman aided them down from the carriage. Hannah stood on the cobblestone street, soaking in the bustle of the town and inhaling the delicious scent of lightly burnt sugar emanating from the confectionary across the road.

"Right this way." Lady Cardon opened her parasol and strolled toward the milliner's store.

A parasol. Of course, Hannah should have remembered to bring one along. She scurried to catch up. Footsteps followed, and she turned to discover the footman trailing. Did they forget something? The footman made no sound or gesture to indicate they had.

Lady Cardon stopped in the millinery shop and tried on a few different bonnets while Hannah examined the colorful ribbons.

"Would you care to purchase one?" The milliner leaned over the counter.

Hannah barely had any funds remaining, and she certainly couldn't afford to waste what she had on something frivolous like ribbon. "Perhaps another day. Thank you."

Lady Cardon passed a bonnet to the shopkeeper.

"Lovely to see you again, Lady Cardon." The milliner slid the bonnet into a hatbox. "That will be eighteen shillings."

Hannah hid her gasp.

"Shall I put it on credit?" the owner asked.

"Indeed." Lady Cardon eyed the colorful ribbons. "Has Lucinda embellished any more wide-brim bonnets? You know the ones with the lace bow and peacock feathers." She held up a thick piece of purple ribbon dangling from a rack. "I do think she could make me one with this instead of the lace and a cluster of flowers on one side and another with the green ribbon."

"Of course, madam. The total combined would be two pounds and seven shillings." He bowed and set the ribbon aside.

"Come now." Hannah's bargaining instincts rioted. "A lower price should be arranged if she is purchasing more than one."

The man drew back, frowning as if affronted. "The price is what it is."

"That isn't necessarily true." Hannah glanced at Lady Cardon's wrinkled brow and shrunk back. "I beg your pardon. I spoke out of turn."

She waved a gloved hand. "I'd like to hear your reasoning."

Hannah licked her lips. "It should take less time to make several hats in one sitting since the tools and materials would only need to be taken out once. It also saves you the time and energy of having to sell each one separately." She peered at the seller. "Your time is valuable, is it not?"

The milliner blinked. "Of course, it is."

"Then, Lady Cardon should receive a discount for the time saved."

Lady Cardon arched a regal brow at the owner.

"Er..." The man appeared flustered, his gaze bouncing between Hannah and Lady Cardon. "Yes, indeed. Shall we make it an even two shillings?"

Lady Cardon turned to Hannah.

"That sounds reasonable." She smiled at the milliner.

He passed the hatbox to the footman, who followed them out the door to the shoemaker's shop down the road.

"I commend you on your astute observations," Lady Cardon said as they strolled down the cobblestone walk. "I must endeavor to bring you along on all of my shopping excursions."

Hannah perked up at the compliment, but at the same time it turned her stomach inside-out. "Thank you. That would be lovely." She peeked over her shoulder at the large footman carrying Lady Cardon's packages. A more ludicrous sight she couldn't imagine. She almost felt embarrassed for him, except she was coming to understand that the English aristocracy were a completely helpless bunch. They were either unwilling or unable to dress, bathe, or walk anywhere without someone's aid.

They strolled past a pub, and a door opened for a patron to exit. The smell of stale air and musty upholstery assaulted Hannah's senses. The all too familiar scent reminded her of Huxley. Well, some things were similar in England.

The church bells chimed the hour and Hannah spied a large stone church at the end of the road. She itched to set foot in it to see if she could check the annals. If her mother and father had been married in the church, she might be able to locate her nearest relative. Her plan may be far-fetched, but a least it was something. If she had to check every church in the county, she would.

The remainder of the shopping excursion proceeded well. Lady Cardon deferred to Hannah if a lower price might be achieved. On the ride home, Hannah felt Lady Cardon's gaze upon her and glanced up.

"You are a resourceful woman." Lady Cardon's face held little expression as she paid Hannah the compliment. If it was a compliment.

"Thank you, my lady." Hannah tried to keep the question out of her tone.

"My son needs a dutiful wife who will keep his feet on the ground. Someone who knows him well."

Someone who has known him all his life and grown up next door. Her insecurities clawed their way to the surface.

"I believe you have feelings for Bradlee." Lady Cardon's gray eyes pierced her defenses.

Hannah twisted the index finger of her glove. There was no point in denying it. "I had hoped it wasn't so obvious."

Tension lines formed around Lady Cardon's mouth. "What is it that you admire in him?"

If Hannah were a mother, which someday she hoped to be, she would have wanted an honest answer. She ran her hands over her thighs, smoothing her skirt. "I love his laugh and the witty way he banters back and forth with Mr. Fitzroy. I admire his bravery. He not only yanked me out of the way of a shark's jaws, but also stood up to my guardian when he was in his cups."

Lady Cardon folded her hands. "Tell me more about these happenings."

Hannah explained both tales but shied away from revealing too much about her guardian's poor character. "Bradlee makes me feel safe."

"What else?" Lady Cardon tilted her head.

A smile touched her lips. "I adore his spirit of adventure and how he enjoys seeing new lands and trying new things. I also love his creativity. His writings are both informative and engaging, as you probably already know."

Lady Cardon held up a hand. "What writings?"

She didn't know? "He's documented his travels, describing the wildlife and inhabitants in vivid detail. When I read them, I felt as if I were there alongside him."

Lady Cardon touched her gloved fingers to her cheek, and her eyes appeared distant as she stared straight ahead. "A writer."

"He's quite good. When parts of his journals were ruined during the shipwreck, he decided to take his memories and turn them into a fictional story. I believe he plans to submit it for publishing."

Lady Cardon's eyes cleared, and focused on Hannah. She studied her for a moment. A faint smile touched her lips. "Thank you for telling me."

Lady Cardon turned to peer out the window and spent the remainder of the trip in thoughtful silence.

Hannah replayed the excursion in her head, picking out her mistakes. Lady Cardon would never want a poor island girl as her daughter-in-law. Especially not one who bargained over shillings and gushed her emotions. Once again, she'd made a mull of things.

~

*a*fter their shopping trip, the relationship between Lady Cardon and Hannah lost some of its strain. Hannah spent hours in the dusty records of the nearby churches, but joined Lady Cardon for meals, tea, and the occasional stroll when the autumn weather was warm. Hannah struggled to appear more refined, but found that the more she relaxed in Lady Cardon's company, the more she slipped into her old ways.

A week into her stay, she joined Lady Cardon for a turn about the grounds after high tea, and Lady Cardon asked about her progress in locating her relatives.

"I'm afraid, I haven't had much success." She sighed. "It's a large task since I can only estimate the year they were married. Tomorrow if it suits you, I'd like to ride into Sherston to visit the vicar there."

"Go wherever you must. You have my blessing." Lady Cardon paused to catch her breath. "My heavens, you keep a fast pace."

Hannah felt the blood drain to her extremities. "Dreadfully sorry. We typically walked everywhere on the island instead of taking a gig, which often called for a fast stride to travel distances. Sometimes, I forget myself and pick up my old habits."

Lady Cardon fanned her face. "At least, I'm no longer chilled."

"That makes one of us. I can't seem to get the cold out of my bones."

"You'll grow accustomed over time."

Hannah perked up. Did that mean Lady Cardon believed she could adapt? The question that plagued her daily slipped from her lips. "Do you think I'll ever be...acceptable?" She instantly regretted her vulnerability, especially when Lady Cardon didn't respond immediately. "I mean, my manners. I would hate to embarrass you, Mr. Granville, or my family, if I should ever find them."

They walked in silence for a few steps, and the tension in Hannah's spine wound to the point of snapping.

"Manners can easily be learned. Character is harder to develop."

Hannah's lungs deflated. She'd failed. If Lady Cardon found her character lacking, she might as well pack her things. She'd never be good enough for her son.

Hannah straightened. Maybe God was still doing a work in her, but her character shouldn't be in question. She might not know the proper thing to do in every situation, but she always tried to do the right thing. "What, may I ask, do you find lacking in my character?"

"You misunderstand." Lady Cardon placed a hand on Hannah's arm. "I find your character to be beyond reproach. Your heart is good, and that's what matters most. The rest can be learned."

Hannah couldn't hold back her smile. She'd just been paid the highest compliment.

The sound of a horse's hooves kicking up dirt turned them toward the lane. It was too early for Bradlee to return. His exams would have just started.

"Henry is home." Lady Cardon started toward the stables to greet her husband, and Hannah followed.

"It's splendid to see you, my dear." Lord Cardon dismounted and passed the reins to a groom. "I'm getting too old for such a long ride."

"Where's Samuel?" Lady Cardon asked as her husband kissed her cheek in greeting.

"He stayed behind to plan a few things for the spring with the steward." His gaze caught sight of Hannah. "Miss Barrington, I didn't expect to see you. I thought the duke and duchess might have returned by now." A muscle in his jaw twitched. "I hope you are enjoying your stay."

Her unease, so recently lost, had ridden in on his horse. She lifted her chin. "I have enjoyed spending time getting to know Lady Cardon."

Lady Cardon threaded her arm through her husband's and pulled him toward the main house. "Indeed. I do not know what I would have done without Miss Barrington's company." She glanced back at Hannah before addressing her husband. "I'm certain you're famished. Let's inform cook of your arrival. We can discuss recent events over our meal."

$\sim$

*A*fter the noontime meal, Hannah kept herself busy to allow Lady and Lord Cardon their space. She discovered a small nook in the sun on the second floor balcony of the library. She sat at the rolltop desk, pulled out a sheet of paper, and penned a letter to the governor of Bristol to see if he might know the whereabouts of her relatives or a better means to locate them.

"If she had any family, why would she be staying here?" Lord Cardon strode into the first floor of the library below.

Hannah froze.

"I had my solicitors look into her," he said. "She's an orphan with no family."

Lord Cardon had investigated her?

"She's a charming young woman," Lady Cardon said.

Hannah set down her quill and leaned forward to peek through the slats in the railing. All she could see was the balding head of Lord Cardon.

"She certainly has charmed our son. Bradlee doesn't know what's best for him. He makes decisions on a whim and doesn't think through the consequences." Lord Cardon waved his hands and paced. "He is a second son. He needs to marry for money. Miss Radcliff is a lady of means and has a significant inheritance."

"He has never been interested in Miss Radcliff." His mother's voice remained flat as if pointing out facts. "Bradlee and Miss Barrington love each other."

Lord Cardon grunted. "Like he loved hunting and lost interest after catching his first fox?" The pitch of his voice rose. "Like he loved joining me at the club? One week of socializing with my connections, and he never returned."

"This is different." Lady Cardon didn't raise her voice.

Lord Cardon stopped pacing. "He only thinks he's in love, but it will change as fast as the weather. I'd hoped his grand tour would mature him so he'd come to see that what is best for his future. What he needs is a good-paying profession and a socially accepted and dutiful wife who can proudly stand by his side, not some... some... foreigner."

Hannah leaned away. She feared this would happen. She'd tried to warn Bradlee and shield her heart.

"If he is going to continue with his whimsical plans, I will have no other choice but to cut him off. I can no longer fund his irresponsibility."

Hannah gripped the edge of the desk.

"Calm yourself, Henry. There's no need to raise your voice. The servants will overhear."

The door opened to Lord Cardon's study and closed behind them, but Hannah had heard enough. Lord Cardon wouldn't condone a marriage to a poor islander, and Bradlee would have to sacrifice his family and his wellbeing. Bradlee may love her, but would his feelings change if he knew he'd be cut off? Could she live with herself knowing she was responsible for the rift in his family?

CHAPTER 36

A fortnight has never seemed so long…
~ Journaled the 15th of September, 1829

*H*annah removed her shawl as she slipped into the house through the back parlor door. She'd hoped a brisk walk about the grounds would settle the disquiet in her mind.

The clipped tone of the butler's shoes tapping the polished floors as he strode down the hallway stopped upon his spying her reading in the drawing room. "There you are, miss." He pivoted on his heel and stood tall like the mast of a ship. "Miss Radcliff is awaiting you in the rose salon."

"Thank…" Hannah stopped herself from thanking the butler and, instead, nodded her acknowledgment.

She scurried down the hall and past the foyer. Finally, a friend. At least she hoped Alice was a friend. The memory of Bradlee sneaking through the woods to visit Alice before he left scarred her mind. The lines of who was for her and who was against her had blurred since her arrival in England.

The taffeta of Alice's skirts swished as she rose from the sofa. "Hannah, darling, how are you faring?"

She squeezed Hannah's hands, and they sank onto the couch together. The gilt buckle cinching Alice's tiny waist and the puffed sleeves on her gown were the height of fashion. That exact style had shown prominently in every boutique window when Hannah had shopped with Lady Cardon.

Her brows pulled together. "How are you faring with Bradlee and Colin having left for Oxford?"

Hannah sighed. "He should hopefully return before the end of the month."

"I would have come calling earlier"—her tone communicated genuine concern—"but Mama has had me doing countless dress fittings for the upcoming season."

"I'm happy you're here now." Hannah attempted to smile.

"So am I." Her brows lifted. "Have you had a chance to explore the house and grounds?"

"I just returned from a stroll outside." Hannah tilted her head. "Perhaps you can tell me what the gated set of doors are that seem to lead into the ground?"

Alice blinked. "Oh. You mean the family mausoleum near the old chapel."

"Yes, over on the hill."

"I'm not certain who is buried there."

Hannah gasped. "It's a grave?"

"Several graves. An entire family is buried there." Alice's eyes sparkled. "Once, Bradlee convinced me to explore inside. His brother, Samuel, told him there was treasure buried in secret compartments in the walls. As you know, Bradlee cannot miss out on a grand adventure, so he persuaded me to go with him. We snuck into the darkened tomb, and suddenly the doors locked behind us. Bradlee jiggled the handle and banged on the door."

Hannah's hand rose to her chest. "What did you do?"

"I wailed so loudly Bradlee told me that if I didn't quiet down, I'd wake the dead. That shut my lips tight." She chuckled. "He promised everything would be all right and held me and stroked my hair until Samuel finally opened the door. It seemed like we were in there for days, but we were trapped for merely ten minutes."

"How horrid."

"It was, but Bradlee made me feel safe."

Bradlee had held her in a similar fashion in the rowboat and again after Blandina passed. He was good at helping women feel safe. All women, it seemed. Her heart constricted at the thought.

Lady Cardon swept into the room with a warm smile. "Alice, how splendid to see you. How are preparations for the season?"

"You know how Mama is." Alice sighed with a giggle.

Lady Cardon glanced around and frowned. "Has tea not been rung for yet?"

Hannah stiffened. "No. I-I can ring for it now." She half-rose, but Lady Cardon tugged on the bell pull.

"It's fine." Alice reeled Hannah back into her seat. "I'm not thirsty."

"I knew it!" Lord Cardon's voice rang from outside the door, followed by a guffaw of laughter.

"Henry?" Lady Cardon peeked her head out the door. "Please lower your voice. We have guests."

"He's gone and done it."

"Who's done what?" Lady Cardon stepped into the hall.

Lord Cardon's thick hand grabbed hers and looped her into a spin.

She yelped.

Alice peered at Hannah with wide eyes and a curious smile. She tipped her head toward the door as if to say, *Shall we?*

Hannah nodded.

They rose and peeked around the doorframe.

"Our son." Lord Cardon's chest puffed out, and his voice rang like a squire announcing his lord. His back was to Hannah and Alice as he waved a piece of paper in front of Lady Cardon. "He's finally put aside his childish dreams and become a man."

"Please calm yourself. I'm not following." Lady Cardon pulled down his arm.

"It's here. See." He pointed to the piece of paper. "Bradlee has agreed to marry Miss Radcliff and become a professor, as we've always hoped."

Alice gasped.

Hannah's heart dropped like a coconut from a palm tree. She clutched the edge of the doorframe to pull herself back into the salon and leaned against the wall, for her knees would no longer support her weight. The letter had arrived. *Oh, Bradlee, if only you'd cleared things up before leaving.*

"Miss Radcliff?" Lord Cardon cleared his throat. "I didn't know you'd come calling. I must apologize, for I've spoiled your surprise." His boots clicked upon the floor as he approached. He scooped Alice's hands in his. "Let me be the first to welcome you to the family. I shall be proud to call you, my daughter."

Alice smiled but seemed pale—at least paler than normal.

Hannah felt her future happiness fade like the morning mist.

"This calls for a celebration. You and my wife must make the arrangements for an engagement party. I shall leave you two to do the planning." He released her hands and strode down the hall, humming a tune as he went.

Alice's smile wobbled as she glanced Hannah's way.

Lady Cardon re-entered the room with stiff movements. "We always believed the two of you would be lovely together. You've always gotten along so well." She read the letter in her hands. "I'm merely surprised Bradlee didn't mention it while he was home." She glanced up at Hannah. "Granted, it was for such a short stint. Perhaps he meant to surprise us, but then why the letter?" Her eyes narrowed, and confusion registered in the lines on her face. She held the letter closer. "It appears to have been dated several months ago. I daresay, my husband overlooked that fact in his delight. He's long hoped for Bradlee to settle down."

Alice fanned herself with her gloved hand. "I'm afraid I can't stay for tea." She sidestepped out into the hall. "I must return home—er—to tell mama the delightful news."

Lady Cardon stood. "I shall see you out."

When their backs turned, Hannah sped down the hallway and up the back stairs to the safety of her room.

She dismissed Ruth, who was prepared to dress her like a doll for afternoon tea. Hannah was no longer in the mood for tea or company. She sank onto the bed and clutched a pillow to her chest.

Lord, what was she to do?

The echo of Lord Cardon's declarations rang in her ears. *Bradlee only thinks he's in love, but it will change as fast as the weather. He makes decisions on a whim. He doesn't know what is best for him.*

What if his love for her was a passing fancy? What if he only believed himself in love with her? If they married, would he wake up one morning wishing he'd married Alice?

He is a second son. He needs to marry for money. I shall have no other choice but to cut him off.

How could she ask him to give up the things she'd longed for most in this world—a family, a sense of belonging, people who care?

She loved Bradlee too much to ruin his life.

Had she wanted to be part of Bradlee's life so badly that she'd convinced herself it was God's will when it wasn't?

On quaking legs, she rose and pulled a sheet of paper from the desk drawer.

. . .

*D*earest Alice,
  If your cousin is still seeking a governess, I would be delighted to apply for the position.

CHAPTER 37

"The unexamined life is not worth living." – Socrates
"For a man to conquer himself is the first and noblest of victories." – Plato
~ Journaled by Bradlee while studying

The carriage jolted over a bump in the road, and Hannah gripped the bottom of her seat tighter. Once again, she was alone in the world. At least on Nevis, she was familiar with the people, the climate, and the dangers. Here, everything was unknown.

Hannah inhaled a deep breath. She could do this. A governess post was a blessing. She adored children and teaching. Her wages could be put toward hiring a private investigator to locate her family. She scratched a speck of dirt off her mother's gown. And most importantly, she would save Bradlee from future regrets.

Alice and Lady Cardon had tried to waylay her until Bradlee's return, but Hannah knew she wouldn't have the strength to resist his persuasiveness, nor the ability to keep her wits about her once she saw his face.

Her heart had clenched when she'd wished Alice and Lady Cardon well. Despite her desire to be in Alice's shoes, aside from herself, there was no one she'd rather have marry Bradlee. Alice was a wonderful person, and if things had been different, they could have been close friends.

"You will be in good hands." Alice had squeezed her hand as she passed Hannah the written address of her cousin's home in Charlcombe, outside of Bath. "My cousin and her husband can be a bit socially ambitious, but she has a good heart. Her boys are adventuresome." She smiled. "But you are familiar with that sort of behavior."

Hannah's heart twisted at her reference to Bradlee.

"If you need anything, please don't hesitate to write or visit." A weariness underlined Lady Cardon's eyes. "I had hoped things would be different."

"Your hospitality and allowing me to use the family coach are enough." Hannah raised her chin to force the words around the lump in her throat. "This is for the best." She turned to leave.

A half-day's ride later, the coach rolled to a stop in front of a stately home. Its modern Greek-revival style front contrasted with the old stone of the protruding west wing and the stables on the opposite side. The footman opened the door.

Hannah hesitated. Bradlee wasn't here to save her. She didn't have Blandina to confide her worries to, nor Lady Clark to encourage her. This was her own adventure. It was up to her now.

With a deep breath, she alighted from the carriage and peered up at the large white front with its tall grooved columns. Would a governess use the main entrance, or should she go around to the servant's door?

The footman held out her satchel, and Hannah hooked it over her shoulder. A breeze rustled the falling leaves. She rubbed her bare arms to warm them. Hopefully, her body would adapt quickly to the cooler temperatures. Already, she was drawn to hearths, sunlit windows, and even candle flames, seeking warmth like an iguana sunning on the rocks.

The front door opened, and two young boys, their mops of yellow hair hanging in their eyes, brushed past the butler. They ran down the steps into the yard.

"I found it. It's mine, give it back." The littlest of the two tugged on the taller boy's wrist.

The eldest yanked his hand away and held a large toad above his head. Its long brown legs jutted out behind it. "I want to look at it."

"It's my frog." The youngest jumped to reach the creature, but his brother held it higher.

"Actually, it's a toad, not a frog." She strode toward them.

The boys' heads snapped in Hannah's direction.

"On Nevis, we have a lot of cane toads. They eat the beetles that hurt our crops."

Two pairs of blue eyes and one smaller set of reptilian brown blinked at her.

"Did you know toads secrete poison?"

The taller child released the toad as if he'd been burned. Hannah caught it midway to the ground and cupped it in her hands. She pointed to the bulges on the toad's upper back. "These are the glands that hold the poison, but it isn't harmful to humans, unless, of course, you eat it."

"Ew." The oldest child wrinkled his nose.

Hannah chuckled. "I believe toad legs are shorter than frog legs." She inhaled a quick breath. "I have an idea." She handed the toad back to the children. "You should find a frog and see which one can jump the furthest. You can measure the length with a yardstick or a piece of string."

The boys' eyes widened. "Let's go." They dashed around the side of the house toward an area past the stable, where the brown heads of cattails nodded in the breeze.

The butler cleared his throat, and there was a slight curve to his lips. "The mistress is expecting you. I will escort you to the parlor."

Hannah forced a composed expression as she entered the manor and absorbed the ornate beauty of the marble statues and massive paintings gracing the front foyer. Gilded frames encased depictions of foxhunts and men on horseback. The lavish riches of the English astounded her, for she'd never seen the like on Nevis.

The butler pushed open a door and stepped aside. "Miss Barrington has arrived, madam."

Cornflower blue wallpaper in a diamond pattern lined the walls above hand-carved wainscoting, and gold painted furniture shined against the complementary backdrop. A petite woman with white-blonde hair curled in ringlets stood by the far window. She turned, and her hand dropped. The lace curtains swung back into place. "At first, I was concerned about your appearance."

Hannah's breath stilled.

"I wish Alice would have mentioned it. No one wants a pretty governess, nor a foreigner from the islands—highly unusual." She peered at Hannah, and a polite smile spread across her lips, much like an expression Alice would display. "However, I saw your interaction with the boys, and I must thank Alice for her recommendation. I should have known my cousin wouldn't steer me wrong." She gestured to a chair. "Please have a seat. I'm Joanne Lister. You've met my children, Percy at six years, and Lewis at four. They are dears, but quite active."

Hannah smiled. "In my experience, most boys are."

Mrs. Lister's light hair and pallid complexion made her appear other-worldly. "Your accent is quite unusual. It's English, but it almost sounds French." She scooted forward in her chair. "It reminds me. There are a few expectations and rules we have for a governess. You will be expected to teach the boys French, along with arithmetic, history, and writing."

Hannah nodded. She spoke passable French, which she'd learned from the creoles on the island and former French planters who'd remained in the Leeward Islands after Britain established its control.

Mrs. Lister folded her hands. "You are to interact strictly with the children, myself, and Mrs. Gael, our housekeeper. You are to remember your station is above that of the staff, but you are not to mingle with any of our guests."

She paused, and Hannah nodded her understanding.

"The schoolroom is on the third floor, and your room is right next door. I expect the children to have lessons in the mornings and afternoons. They may earn playtime at midday and before the evening meal, if they behave. They take their meals in the schoolroom unless my husband requests for them to join us. Do you have any questions?"

"If I'm in need of any supplies?"

Mrs. Lister rose and rang the bell pull. "Our housekeeper, Mrs. Gael, will order any materials you need, but I think you'll find our schoolroom well stocked."

A robust woman with her reddish-gray hair pinned back in a tight bun appeared in the doorway.

"Miss Barrington, meet our housekeeper, Mrs. Gael. She will show you to your room." Mrs. Lister strode to her desk. "Welcome to Tuvis Manor, Miss Barrington. That will be all."

Mrs. Gael didn't speak much as she climbed the stairs to the third floor, but when she did, it was of household rules. "Midday meal is served at the noon hour sharp, and tea shall be taken in the schoolroom. A footman will come along shortly with your bag."

Hannah's room was small but adequate, with a bed, a small writing desk, and a narrow wardrobe. A far cry from the large guestroom she'd slept in at Bradlee's home, but it held a spectacular view of the terrace and the arbors beyond the stables. She spied the boys below, slapping their hands on the ground, most likely to encourage a frog and toad to jump. She didn't mind their activeness. Hopefully it would serve as a distraction to take her mind off Bradlee.

~

*F*or the most part, her wishes came true. Bradlee continued to plague Hannah's thoughts, and she prayed for success with his exams and understanding when he returned to find her gone. Her lessons kept her mind occupied, and the boys kept her busy. She often converted her teachings into competitions to appease the boys.

At the end of the week, the weather turned warm as summer issued its last hurrah, and by midday, the chilly schoolroom heated up warmer than the natural hot springs on Nevis. Despite her having opened the windows to allow in the air, the boys struggled to maintain focus in the heat. When the temperature became unbearable, Hannah decided it best to take the boys for a stroll along the grounds or into the woods.

She carried a book of the different types of regional trees, and the boys raced to bring back all sorts of leaves to identify within the book's pages.

"What about this one?" Lewis held up a large leaf with rounded, fingerlike projections.

Percy yanked it out of his hand. "We've done that one already. It's an English Oak."

"Very good, Percy." She bent down to eye-level with a frowning Lewis. "Lewis, tell me what kind of seeds they grow."

His round face perked up. "Acorns?"

"Indeed, you are correct." She beamed him a smile as she straightened.

He wrapped his little arms around her skirts in a spontaneous hug before dashing off to collect more leaves.

Voices carried on the wind, and she glanced over to see the

boys' parents playing a game of pall mall with some guests. All but one of them laughed and carried on with the game. The man's gaze turned her way as he leaned on his mallet.

Hannah froze. She wasn't supposed to interact with the guests. She called Percy and Lewis over and instructed them to wash up for afternoon tea and lessons. The boys' shoulders slumped, but they turned toward the house.

"Race you," Percy said over his shoulder as he darted toward the back entrance.

"That's not fair." Lewis ran after him.

An odd tingling caused Hannah to look over her shoulder.

The man's gaze still rested on her.

She gathered her skirts and scurried after the boys.

Percy veered off. Instead of running to the house, he sprinted toward the guests.

Hannah called his name, but he paid no heed.

"Papa!" He danced around the man leaning on his mallet. Lewis joined him.

Mr. Lister stood out from the guests with his Corinthian stature and fashionable dress. He patted his boys on the heads to settle them, but his gaze strayed to Hannah.

Mrs. Lister stopped in the middle of her turn. She eyed Hannah.

"I beg your pardon. We didn't mean to interrupt." Hannah waved the boys over. "Percy and Lewis, it's time to resume our lessons."

"My children are never an interruption." A dashing smile flashed across his features. "You must be Miss Barrington, our governess."

Hannah curtsied. "Pleased to meet you, sir."

He nodded. "The pleasure is mine. I daresay our game needed an interruption."

He attempted to hold her gaze, but Hannah peeked at Mrs. Lister and received a cold stare. Hannah held her hands out to the boys. Their small fingers slid into hers, and she strode toward the house. Her feet itched to hurry, but the children's little steps couldn't keep up, so she forced a slower pace. After she opened the door, the boys turned back toward the guests.

Mr. Lister peered at them before swinging his mallet. The ball rolled through the wicket.

"Bye, Papa." The boys waved, and he returned it, but his eyes honed in on her.

CHAPTER 38

I cannot bear to be apart much longer. I miss the way she sees everything with a purpose. How she adapts to any situation, and the adorable way she scratches her nose while she ponders. One more exam and the torture shall be over.

~ Journaled the 1ˢᵗ of October, 1829

The following evening after putting the boys to bed, Hannah sought Mrs. Gael to see if there were any art supplies. Percy had shown promise of artistic talent in his drawings, and she wanted to see how he handled a brush. She descended the stair and paused at the rail when she heard voices below.

Joanna Lister clung to her husband's arm and peered at him with open admiration. She stopped him in front of the door. "Will you stay and dance at least one dance with me?"

"You know how I don't like to miss a hand of cards." He ushered her through the door.

Hannah descended a step, believing they'd left, but Mr. Lister turned. He spied her on the stairs, and their gazes met.

She didn't move.

He flashed her a wicked smile followed by a bold wink.

Hannah gritted her teeth. She'd witnessed such outlandish behavior on the island, but she did not expect to be subjected to it here. It was obvious Joanne Lister adored her husband and desired his attention, yet his eyes wandered. Hannah wanted no part of it.

Mr. and Mrs. Lister spent many an evening traveling into Bath for various balls, routes, and soirees. Often, they didn't return until midmorning the following day. Mrs. Lister spent her days entertaining guests or paying calls. Mr. Lister spent his time hunting or partaking of spirits on the terrace with the male guests.

Hannah did her best to remain on the third floor. She arranged the boys' schedules to avoid interaction with the Listers. She was even able to convince Mrs. Gael to bring the boys down to bid goodnight to their parents before bed. During her second week, Mr. Lister, however, paid a surprise visit to the boys during their lesson. The boys adored their papa and were delighted to explain all they'd learned. Hannah stood quietly at the front of the room, but squirmed under his overly long gazes in her direction. He often brought treats from the kitchen, cookies, scones, and muffins, which the children devoured.

"Ah, Miss Barrington, I haven't forgotten you." He unwrapped a napkin and handed her a large sugar cookie.

"Thank you, but I do not want to spoil my evening meal."

He set the cookie aside. "If only I were comprised of such a strong will. Alas, I am a weak man." He broke off a part of the cookie and popped it into his mouth. "I quite forgot you hale from the islands. Sugar is probably commonplace for you."

"I was born in Bristol, but lived most of my life in Nevis." A piece of hair slid from her topknot.

"Indeed." He reached up to tuck it away, but Hannah reared

back. He chuckled and dropped his hand back to his side. "I'm a close acquaintance with an admiral in His Majesty's Navy who was stationed at Brimstone Hill."

The dark eyes of the admiral Albina had brought home to meet her flashed in her memory.

"I asked him if he'd heard of a Miss Hannah Barrington. He said there was a woman with the same name, an orphaned daughter of a sugar baron from Bristol."

Hannah's throat convulsed, and her hand squeezed her father's ring.

"Poor girl had a drunken lout of an uncle who fell on hard times and tried to sell her to my friend." His right brow twitched. "My friend was too miserly to pay for his conquests."

Hannah's blood drained to her feet, and lightheadedness beset her. Would she ever be free of her guardian's shame? Must it always be hers to bear? She straightened. "Why are you telling me this?"

His eyes darkened. "Because if you are in need, I may be able to help." His gaze shifted to her hand at her chest. "There could be an arrangement."

"You are mistaken."

He trailed a knuckle down the bare skin of her arm below her capped sleeve. "Pity." He strode over to the boys licking the crumbs from their lips and tussled their hair. "Be on your best behavior for Miss Barrington, and more treats shall come your way." He bid them farewell and left the schoolroom.

Hannah leaned against the chalkboard and folded her hands to keep them from shaking. She should pack her things and leave immediately.

"Are you all right, Miss Barrington?" Percy squished one side of his face. "You look white like mama."

"Are you gonna swoon?" Lewis asked. "Mama says she used to swoon whenever papa smiled at her."

Percy rose from his seat. "I can get her smelling salts. I know where she keeps the hartshorn." He started toward the door.

"No." The command came out harsher then she'd intended.

He froze. His bottom lip trembled.

She softened her voice. "Thank you, Percy. It is sweet of you, but I'm fine. There's no need to bother anyone. Besides, it's time to do some reading. Do you like adventure stories?"

She opened a tale of the knights of old and sat on the rug. The boys settled in next to her. Their blonde heads snuggled against her sides. How could she leave these precious little boys, whom she'd become so fond of in the last couple of weeks? And where would she go? Her wages wouldn't be paid until the end of the month. At least here she had a room and three warm meals a day.

~

The rest of the week fared without incident until Hannah awoke in the dark to a thumping sound coming from the direction of the hallway. She jerked back the covers. Had someone tumbled down the stairs? Did one of the boys get out of bed? Were they hurt?

She stuffed her hands into the sleeves of her wrapper, tied the sash, and felt her way down the hall through the darkness. A cloud passed and unveiled the dim light of the moon through the window above the back stairs. Sure enough, a dark figure lay on the landing on the second floor.

Hannah rushed to the person's side. It wasn't one of the boys, but their father who lay at her feet. "Mr. Lister? Are you all right?"

He groaned, and the stench of spirits fanned around him. He scooted into a seated position. "Help me stand."

She hooked her arm through his and, using the wall for extra leverage, heaved him to his feet. How many times had she done a similar thing for Huxley?

"You're a strong woman." He burped, and the smell of fermented fruit wafted under her nose. "Not quite as strong as my favorite brandy, but prettier...prettier than my wife. She repulses me."

Hannah had suffered through Huxley's drunken rants. She wasn't about to endure another. "Good night, Mr. Lister. Hold the rail so you don't fall down the remaining stairs." She turned her back on him.

He grabbed her arm.

"You're not going to help me to my room?"

"Shh." Hannah's ears strained for any sound. "You'll wake the children."

"I'm a trifle foxed." He flashed her one of his wicked smiles. "You must aid me, make certain I find my way."

"It would be improper."

He stepped closer, much too close for her comfort. She stepped back, but bumped into the corner of the wall. "If I fall again, would you tend to me?" He touched her cheek.

She jerked her head away.

"Lister?" Joanne's voice called from the room across the hall. She lifted an oil lantern high above her head.

They winced at the light.

Mr. Lister twisted around, and Hannah used the opportunity to slide away from him. He swayed, but grabbed hold of the rail.

"What is going on here?" Mrs. Lister's tone grew harsh. "Miss Barrington? I told you to stay on the third floor."

"I thought one of the boys had fallen down the stairs."

Mr. Lister sauntered toward his wife. "I dipped a little too deep tonight with our guests. I thought I was headed to bed, but apparently, I was on the third floor. My feet slipped, and Miss Barrington came to my aid." He glanced back her way. "I'm appreciative of her kindness." He kissed his wife's cheek and sauntered past her to the next room. "It's best if I sleep this off." He opened his door and hesitated.

Mrs. Lister stared at Hannah, her eyes reflecting the oil lamp's flame.

"Are you coming to bed, dear?" Mr. Lister leaned against the doorframe before entering his room.

Joanne Lister's eyes narrowed, and her voice hissed, "Come morning, you are dismissed." She spun on her heel and chased her husband.

CHAPTER 39

Even agricultural studies lead me to think of Hannah and how she might enjoy the methods for growing her herbs.
~ *Journaled the 1st of October, 1829*

"This 'ere is the Queen's Square." The wagon driver pointed to the right. "Plenty of shops and such along this way." He tipped his straw hat to Hannah. "Best of luck to ya, miss."

The pigs in the back squealed as the wagon jerked to a stop.

Hannah thanked Mr. Mason and jumped down from the open seat. The road to Bath had been longer than she'd anticipated. Fortunately, Mr. Mason happened upon her trudging down the lane.

He waved and snapped the reins, bent on selling his load of pigs at market.

She was resourceful and a survivor. Bradlee had told her that before he'd left for the great go. This would be the true test. With barely two coins to rub together, she needed to find work or she would be sleeping on the streets.

Footsteps sounded behind her. A school-aged boy with a cap

dipped to just above his eyes sauntered up beside her. Quick as a flash he yanked her satchel from her arm and took off running down a narrow street.

"Stop thief!" Hannah dashed after him, but the boy was quick and knew the area. He slid through a broken slat in a fence and zig-zagged through the back allies. Hannah clutched her side and heaved in deep breaths. She scanned the area and listened for any sounds, but the lad was nowhere in sight.

God, why? Now she had nothing but the clothes on her back. She sucked in a breath, then realized...*Lady Clark's reference!* Without a reference, how was she going to find work?

The sun was high in the sky as she entered one establishment after another. Each asked for a reference, but she could only mention her brief employment with Lady Lister and pray they wouldn't consult her.

Lady Lister wouldn't heed her explanation of the previous night's events. Tears had stained the woman's cheeks, and she'd pointed Hannah to the door. "I cannot stand the sight of you. Go, you...you...hussy. Do not shadow my doorstep again." There was no chance Lady Lister would speak well of her. The butler tossed Hannah out before she could finish a sentence.

The baker shook his head and pointed to the door.

"I'm a quick learner." She stood before the dressmaker.

The woman pursed her lips. "Do you know 'ow many women seekin' work I turn out in a week? Ones with references —good ones?"

Hannah shook her head.

"There ain't any jobs." She showed Hannah the door. "Yer better off movin' on to another town."

The sun began to set, and the chill returned to the air as Hannah used the one coin she'd had in her pocket to buy a loaf of bread. She wandered down Broad Street and onto Walcott. The alluring warmth of a small fire in a back alley drew her.

A woman with a wool cape draped over her head warmed

her hands. A small sneeze sounded, and Hannah noticed a child's dirty face standing beside the woman.

"May I join you?"

The haggard mother shook her head, waving the cloth and fanning the flames. "Leave us be."

"I have bread. I'd be happy to share."

The small child's neck craned.

"Are you from the parish?"

"I'm looking for work."

"Ah, yer one of us." She waved her over. "Are ya widowed?"

Hannah shook her head. "I'm an orphan. My name is Hannah, Hannah Barrington."

"Milly Hendricks. This here is Isabel."

Hannah smiled at the young girl. "What a pretty name."

"Named her after her grandmother. You said you have bread?"

She removed the loaf from her satchel and broke it into thirds. Milly and Isabel wasted no time devouring the food. The light of the fire cast deep shadows under their hollow eyes.

"How did you end up...?" Something moved in the corner. Hannah spied a rat and stiffened.

"On the streets?" Milly drew Isabel close to her side and wrapped the cape around her. "My husband passed about six months ago."

"God rest Papa's soul." Isabel crossed herself.

Milly frowned and leaned closer to Hannah. "It's God who's resting. If he were watching, then none of us would be here on the streets begging fer scraps."

"I've been in similar situations, and God has always been faithful." Hannah tried to give the little girl hope.

"He wasn't faithful when I prayed for Him to heal my husband. He wasn't faithful when I prayed for those men not to come and take our house." Milly laid down on the ground next to the fire, pulling Isabel down with her.

A tabby cat pounced on the rat with a screech.

Hannah jolted, but Milly and Isabel didn't react. Her heart thudded in her chest, but the pair's breath soon deepened as sleep fell upon them. Hannah lay her head on the hard ground and forced her eyes closed.

God, I believed You'd make a way, but here I am on the streets. Do You see me, or are You resting? The tears flowed over her cheeks. *I put my hope in You, but I can no longer hold back the floodwaters. It's been one disaster after another. I'm in desperate need of Your rescue. My faith is failing.*

She choked back a sob. Her father's ring rolled out from under her shirt, and she reached for it. A small rainbow flashed upon the hard dirt. The light from the fire reflected off the ring and formed a small array of colors. Her mind was transported back to the pool by the waterfall, with Bradlee beside her as the rainbow shimmered in the mist. And then she was on the deck of the *Boadicea*. She had leaned against Bradlee's side in awe of God's creation.

As her body lay on the hard ground, God planted a familiar Bible verse into her heart. *And I will remember my covenant, which is between You and me and every living creature of all flesh; and the waters shall no more become a flood to destroy all flesh.*

She scooped the ring into her hand and held it close to her heart.

~

A stick nudged Hannah's shoulder. "Get up." Footsteps thudded near her face. "You too. The whole lot of you need to rise and shine."

Her eyelids felt heavy as lead after the fitful night of sleep she'd had. Once the fire had died, a chill had seeped into Hannah's bones, and she'd shivered until her teeth rattled so loudly that the chattering woke her. The only way she'd been able to get warm was to inch over to Milly's side and absorb her warmth.

Now, she opened her eyes to a pair of high-shine black boots inches from her nose. A hand gripped her upper arm and hauled her to a stand. "There'll be no sleepin' in these streets." The constable's shiny buttons gleamed in the morning light. He grabbed hold of Milly and yanked her upright.

"Mama?" Isabel reached for her mother.

"You too. Everybody up." The constable ushered them toward his wagon. "We're going for a ride."

Hannah's stiff muscles protested as he swung open the back door, where four other women sat with their heads hung low. "Where are you taking us?"

The man ignored Hannah's question and pushed her backside up into the wagon. He handed her Isabel, who hid behind Hannah's skirts until Milly joined them. The door swung shut, and the click of the lock echoed in Hannah's brain.

"Where is he taking us?" she whispered to Milly, who sat and pulled Isabel into her lap. The wagon jerked to a start and rumbled down the road.

"To the poorhouse." Milly sighed. "At least it will provide food and a roof over our heads."

Hannah sat, clutched her father's ring, and closed her eyes.

"Take that off and hide it if you want to keep it." Milly pointed at her hand.

Her fingers squeezed the ring tighter. She'd never taken it off before. With shaky fingers, she unclasped the gold chain and tucked it inside her corset.

The wagon rolled to a stop, and the constable opened the door. "All right, out you go."

He herded them toward the front door of a three-story stone building and pounded his fist on the wooden door.

A plump woman dressed in mourning blacks opened the entryway.

The constable tipped his hat. "A few more lost souls to lay upon the kindness of the church."

The woman stepped forward and yanked Milly and Isabel into the hall. "Were you born in Bath?"

"Aye," Milly nodded. "And me daughter."

She grabbed Hannah and pushed her next to Milly. "What about you?"

Hannah stared at the woman's deepening frown lines. What would happen if she said no?

Milly nudged Hannah. "Her too."

The woman's lips pinched. "My name is Mrs. Smith. I'm the caretaker of the women's ward." She grabbed a folded cloth from a shelf and shoved it into Hannah's arms, along with a box. "Fifth room on the left down the hall. Any personal items go in the box." She pointed at Isabel. "Change and take her to the mill, then report to the yard to see to yer duties."

Hannah's heart thudded until she could barely hear Isabel's whimpers. Racking coughs sounded from the rooms they passed. The dimly lit hall with its narrow windows barely allowed in the light, and a cold draft swirled around her ankles. The putrid smell of sickness hung in the air, and Hannah covered her nose with her hand.

The cramped room they entered held eight narrow beds and made her long for the tiny room with a desk she'd had with her governess position. They changed quickly under Mrs. Smith's watchful eye. The baggy gray uniform held no pockets and reminded Hannah of the gowns she'd worn around Nevis. She hid the ring in her topknot before tucking her hair under the provided white cap.

Milly escorted the screaming Isabel to the mill. Hannah stepped into the yard, but Isabel's wails could still be heard. "Mama, don't leave me."

The gray mist clouded Hannah's vision and seeped into her heart. *Lord, Your promises are true. You are the same yesterday, today, and tomorrow. Be with Isabel and Milly.* A rhythmic pounding filled her ears, and the shapes of bone-thin women appeared in the mist. A woman shoved a mallet into Hannah's hands and instructed her to crush the bone into fertilizer.

The heavy mallet weighed several stones, but Hannah swung it at the pile over and over. She thought she'd finished when everything was crushed, but another woman arrived and dumped more dried skeletons of rats, pigs, and chickens into her pile.

A woman with chopped hair and missing teeth leaned her way. "You think these are just animal bones, do ya?" She struck her pile with the heavy hammer. "What do you think they do with the bones of the sick and the elderly? I've seen it. I recognize a human skull."

"Mind your mouth, Greta, and do your duty." One of the overseers shouted as he paced the yard.

After she passed, Greta leaned in again. "They don't even ring the church bells fer a death anymore, cuz it would be ringing every hour."

Hannah swallowed and focused on her work, but that night as she crawled exhausted into bed next to an unnaturally thin girl named Polly, her mind focused on memories of Bradlee before she collapsed into a deep sleep. The same routine resumed the following day and each night thereafter.

⁓

"*T*ime to get up," Mrs. Smith hollered as she banged a wooden spoon on a pot. "You've got work to do." She opened the door to Hannah's room and banged the pot inside. "Everyone up."

Hannah covered her ears and groaned. A week had passed, and now she didn't know which ached more, her hungry stomach or her tired muscles. The other women in the room rose from their beds with a woeful sigh to start the day. How did her life become a series of disasters? Had she dreamed too big, aspired too high? Was God putting a red leg, white beggar back in her place?

A shiver ran over her skin. Cold weather must be settling because last night had seemed chillier than the previous. She propped her head up with her elbow and gently shook Polly, who'd somehow slept through Mrs. Smith's cacophony.

The girl didn't rouse.

Hannah shook harder.

The poor girl was chilled to the bone.

A sickening dread turned Hannah's blood to sludge. She threw back the covers and scrambled out of bed.

Greta, Milly, and a couple other roommates gathered around Polly's unseeing eyes.

"Poor thing." Milly shifted Polly's slack body onto her back. "She was too thin to survive here. A wafer she was."

Greta closed Polly's eyes with her fingers and pulled the sheet up over her face. "Go tell o' Ms. Smith." She instructed a woman named Nan.

A couple of women crossed themselves, then donned their uniforms as if nothing had happened.

Milly nudged Hannah. "Get dressed, or you'll miss your morning meal."

"If you can call a moldy slice of bread, a meal," Greta grumbled. "We're all gonna end up like poor Polly."

Milly shooed the woman away. Hannah's hands shook to the point that Mille had to help tie her cap.

"Kate, walk with Hannah to the dining hall, would ya?" Milly passed her off to the hollow-cheeked woman. "I've gotten permission this morn to visit Isabel. I don't want to miss it."

The torn look in Milly's eyes awoke Hannah from her stupor. "Of course. Don't worry about me." She attempted a weak smile, but the muscles in her face seemed to have forgotten how. "I am a survivor. Give Isabel my blessing."

Milly nodded and slipped from the room.

Kate trudged down the hall, keeping Hannah by her side. They stood in line for their slice of stale bread and sat to eat.

Hannah peered down the row of women. Their long, tired faces held empty stares as they gnawed at their meager meal.

These women, like her, had been orphaned—maybe not by their parents, but by society. They, too, had been left behind to fend for themselves without any preparation for their future. She glanced up to see row after row of tables, the women at them thin, haggard, gray. Passing time until death. The front of the room held young girls, knee-high to almost womanhood, who shared the same forgotten fate.

Where was the rainbow? Hadn't God promised? Why did the flood waters still rise?

I have not forgotten you.

Hannah gasped as the words, clear as day, entered her mind.

I sent My son to die for you. He endured the cross because of My love for you. I have made a way.

Images of her uncle and Albina flashed through her mind. Her brow furrowed. They'd been with her, but they'd not been *for* her.

More faces flashed, one after another. Lady Clark, Blandina, Mr. Maroon, Mrs. O'Dell, Mrs. Marchmain, Alice, Colin... Bradlee.

They are for me, but they are not with me.

A man's face appeared in her mind. His eyes were compassionate and filled with love. On his brow rested a crown of thorns.

I am for you, and I am with you.

Hannah dropped her head into her hands and wept like a child.

"Is she all right?" a woman whispered from across the table.

Kate shushed her. "She was Polly's bed mate."

"First time seeing death, I take it."

"We all crack at some point in this hovel," Greta murmured.

Hannah let the tears course down her cheeks as sobs wracked her body.

I didn't make you a survivor, the Lord whispered. *I made you a conqueror, and you fight from victory.*

She sucked in a shuddered breath and raised her head.

The women surrounding her no longer were her fellow workers or roommates. These women were her sisters, and they needed her help.

The ladies stared at her with blinking eyes. Their gazes shifted to peer over her shoulder as rapid footsteps padded behind her.

Hannah glanced over her shoulder to see Milly's pale face. She skidded to a halt behind Hannah and dropped to her knees in tears.

"It's Isabel. She's sick." The woman's voice cracked. "Please, I need help."

CHAPTER 40

Lord, calm my spirit. Give me the wisdom to finish the
final exam and a speedy return home.
~ *Journaled the 2ⁿᵈ of October, 1829*

*B*radlee shook out his hands and bounced on his toes.
He murmured dry facts about agricultural processes
and dead philosophers while he tilted his head from side to side,
cracking his neck and rolling his shoulders.

"Mr. Granville, you may enter," one of the dons called.

He inhaled a steadying breath, and his fingers closed around
the cold knob. Two more days of public exams, and he'd return
to Hannah. He missed the dimple that formed in her cheek
when her mind worked a solution to a problem. He loved the
excitement in her eyes as she negotiated a bargain, and the way
she looked at him as if he was assured victory made him want to
wrap her in a tight embrace and never let go.

Because of her inspiration, he'd been able to submit his journals as credits and forgo part of the writing portion. Because of
her tips for public speaking, he'd been able to stand in front of

the panel and pass the examination thus far. He pushed the door open.

Three professors sat at the front of the classroom in long black robes. Each had their heads down, flipping through pages of paper.

The ancient floorboards creaked beneath his weight with every step. He stopped in the grid pattern cast upon the floor from the sunlit mullioned windows on his left. The occasional passing student shrouded him in a shadow as they scurried across the grassy mall outside.

"Mr. Granville." Professor Walker closed a book in front of him, and Bradlee recognized his journal cover. "We must say your examination thus far has shown remarkable improvement." He adjusted his spectacles and peered down at the page before him. "Shall we begin?"

Bradlee swallowed a deep breath and peered just above their heads. Whenever his knees or hands began to shake, he reminded himself he was merely excited and remembered Hannah's words. *You are not a victim. You are a victor.*

The dons pummeled him with questions for the next hour. Bradlee dug into his memory to extract the answers. Sometimes the responses readily bobbed to the surface. Other times, he held his breath and dove deep until he dragged them to the surface, feeling dizzy from the strain of effort.

A shadow fell across the floor as Bradlee sought how to calculate the theoretical shear strength for tungsten. He glanced out the window.

Colin? What was he doing here?

Colin pivoted on his heel, marched a few steps, and turned again. He clutched a piece of paper in one hand and raked a hand through his hair, causing it to jet out in different directions like a crazed man. He waved his hands and moved his lips as if talking out loud—to himself.

"Do you know this student?" Professor Walker eyed Bradlee while the other two peered out the window at the madman.

"I—er—yes. He's—"

"What does he want?"

Bradlee glanced back out the window. "I haven't the foggiest."

Colin froze, as if sensing all eyes were on him. He turned and faced the window. His eyes locked on Bradlee. *I must speak with you,* he mouthed.

Bradlee shook his head.

Colin held up a letter. "It's Hannah," he yelled through the glass.

Bradlee staggered back a step, his blood turning to ice.

"Is something amiss?" Professor Walker leaned over the table.

"I believe so." His dry throat turned his voice to a croak.

Professor Walker waved Colin inside and instructed Bradlee to open the door.

Colin did a little hop-step and dashed to the hall entrance. His footfalls pounded down the passageway, and Bradlee swung the door wide.

Colin skidded past the door, his soles sliding on the highly waxed floors. He slowed to a stop and tugged on the bottom of his frock coat. "It's Hannah." He pressed the letter into Bradlee's chest as he strode into the room. "She's gone missing."

"What." He scanned the letter.

Dearest Bradlee,

Hannah has disappeared. I should never have mentioned the open governess position. It turns out my cousin's husband is a libertine...

Bradlee eyed Colin. "Alice wrote this?"

He nodded.

"How did you...? Why would she...? You read my mail?" Bradlee shook his head. "Never mind. Where is Hannah now?"

"No one knows." Colin paced again. "She was dismissed, and no one has seen her since."

"How long ago?"

"Over two weeks."

"Mr. Granville." Professor Oswald cleared his throat. "This is highly irregular."

Bradlee turned to the men who held his future in their hands. "There has been another unforeseeable circumstance. I'm afraid I must leave."

Professor Walker reared back. "If you leave in the middle of the public examination, you will take an incomplete and not graduate."

His father would forever believe him a disappointment. He'd promised God he'd become a professor, but God wouldn't want him to stand by while one of His lambs was lost.

And not merely any lamb, but Hannah. *His Hannah.*

She didn't know a single person in whom to turn. Winter was approaching and the nights held a chill. Did she have shelter? Hannah was resourceful. Would she go to the city to find employment? His heart dropped. The city was another beast, with crime, pickpockets, brothels, and the like. *Lord, protect Hannah.*

Bradlee straightened and inhaled a sense of determination. "Something more pressing has come along. I beg your pardon, but I must go." He turned on his heel, and with a pat on Colin's back, they both dashed from the room.

"Mr. Granville!" Professor Walker hollered after him. "Mr. Granville..."

~

*H*annah tucked the covers around Isabel. Mrs. Smith peered over her shoulder. The poultice Hannah had made from the garden plants was already helping Isabel's breathing. The paste was smeared across the girl's chest and reeked of peppermint oil.

Mrs. Smith dusted her hands. "That settles it. You are granted special rights to treat the sick until further notice." She issued a curt nod and left the room.

Patting Isabel's shoulder, Hannah rose. "I'm going to make you some tea. I'll be right back."

Hannah strode into the kitchen, the necessary herbs stuffed in her cap like a sack. Small children scrubbed pans over the wash buckets, and a woman from room three wiped the counter free of crumbs.

"May I have a cup of hot water to make tea?"

The woman snorted. "Who do you think you are? The queen?"

Hannah's mother's voice rang in her head, and she responded without hesitation. "I am Hannah Barrington, child of God."

The woman snickered.

Amid everything, Hannah had forgotten who she was and to Whom she belonged. Hannah Barrington was a resourceful negotiator. She was not merely a survivor, but a conqueror, and she was God's beloved daughter.

"Well, don't let me stop you, yer highness." The woman curtsied and stepped aside.

"How about I help you finish your task while I wait for the tea to boil?"

The woman reared back. "You want to help?"

Hannah nodded.

"Well, I'll be."

They worked together, and soon Hannah was coaxing Isabel to drink the bitter tea. "It might taste bad, but you'll feel better."

The child sipped the liquid. The rumble of her cough assured Hannah the illness hadn't yet settled in the girl's chest. Hopefully, she'd gotten her the herbs in time.

After Isabel finished the tea, she rolled over, and Hannah stroked her hair. Hannah stood and faced Milly. "The tea will help her to sleep. A couple days of rest, and she should be back to her usual self."

Milly twisted her cap in her hands. "Are you certain?"

Hannah nodded. "I treated a friend for similar ailments. The best thing for her is sleep."

Tears misted in Milly's eyes. "Thank you. She's all I have left."

"Milly." Hannah bit her lower lip, uncertain how to say what she needed to convey. "I believe God put me in your path for this moment. He's shown me some things. I—I think God wants me to tell you that He sees you."

Milly's face crumpled.

Hannah opened her arms, and the woman fell into them and released a torrent of tears.

"I needed to hear that." She hugged Hannah tighter, and her shoulders shook with sobs. "You are a blessing."

～

*B*radlee knocked on the door to his father's study.

"Enter," his father's voice boomed.

He pushed the door open to find Father standing and facing the window with his hands clasped behind his back. He turned at the sound of Bradlee's footstep and the latch clicking shut behind him.

"What is the news?" His brows rose. "Have you graduated?"

Bradlee stood with a wide stance in front of the man whose approval he'd tried all of his life to attain. This time his knees didn't shake. This time the room didn't spin. He met his father's level stare with one of his own. "No."

A disappointed scowl twisted his father's face and he bellowed, "How could you let your family down? How could you be so irresponsible?" His father's rant went on for some time, until he paused as if considering something else in which to lecture Bradlee.

"I had only another day left." Bradlee straightened. "But I was called away on an emergency."

"What sort of emergency would take precedence over your graduation?"

"Hannah has gone missing."

"Hannah?" His arms crossed. "You mean Miss Barrington? The orphaned island girl with no connections?"

"The woman I plan to marry."

Red flooded his father's face the same way red wine filled a challis. "Not if I have any say in the matter. I'll cut you off entirely."

"Do what you must, but you cannot choose my path for me. I am not my great grandfather. I've tried to do it your way, and I've tried to do it mine, but both lead to disaster. It's time I accepted a different path—the one God has placed before me."

His father's head reared back, and he blinked several times as the anger seemed to drain from his body. "I only want what's best for you, and being a professor is a good and honorable profession."

"You are right."

His father's brows lifted.

"It is a good profession, but I would not only dread it, I would be terrible at it." Bradlee sighed. "God didn't give me the disposition to stand in front of a room of students and teach the same thing day in and out. He's instilled other strengths within me, like a desire to unite cultures and people through my writing."

"But what about the letter you wrote claiming you'd marry Alice Radcliff?"

"I wrote that letter because I believed at the time it was the only way to help Hannah get off the island. I love her, and I'd do anything for her, even if it means sacrificing my future."

"You see becoming a professor and marrying Miss Radcliff as a sacrifice?" His father shook his head.

"It isn't in line with how God made me."

His father stared at his desk. "We don't all get to choose our paths."

"No, we don't always." Bradlee saw his father in a new light. His father had no say as a firstborn child. He was raised to take over the earldom. Did he wish he could have followed his dreams? "I love you, and I in no way intended to disappoint you, but more importantly I cannot disappoint God. I'm sorry. I should have explained my actions long ago."

He peered at Bradlee. "I do not agree with your choices, but they are your mistakes to make, and you must live with the consequences."

Bradlee stepped closer to his father. "All is forgiven?"

A long pause stilled even the air Bradlee breathed.

"I believe so." His father appeared dazed, but he'd taken it well.

"I must ask your leave." Bradlee swallowed. "I need to find Hannah."

His father chewed his lip, but nodded. "You love this woman?"

"With all my heart."

A loud exhale blew past his father's lips "Then, you have my blessing. Let me know if there is anything your mother or I can do to help."

The tightness in Bradlee's spine relaxed, and his chest filled with a sense of victory. "Thank you." He turned and strode from the room.

His mother stopped her pacing in the hallway and peered at him with wide eyes. Beside her, Colin and Alice also waited for his news.

"Well?" Colin scratched the back of his head.

Bradlee issued him a curt nod. "I have his blessing."

Mother blinked. "But all that screaming and yelling?"

"We came to an understanding." He pushed back the sides of his jacket and hooked his thumbs into his waistband. "I understand his reasoning, and he now understands mine."

Mama clasped her hands to Bradlee's cheeks. "How splendid."

He beamed a wide smile as he pulled her hands away, before glancing at Colin and Alice. Usually arbiters of fashion, they both looked disheveled, as if they hadn't slept in days.

They stared at him with a remaining question in their eyes.

He nodded. "Let's go find her."

CHAPTER 41

But ye are a chosen generation, a royal priesthood, an
holy nation, a peculiar people; that ye should shew forth
the praises of him who hath called you out of darkness
into his marvelous light.
*~ Journaled after Bradlee's reading of 1Peter 2:9, the 15ᵗʰ of
October, 1829*

*H*annah stood in the corner of room two. The
youngest of the girls sat at her feet, and the rest
circled, squeezing in tight to hear the story. Isabel sat up on her
bed, looking better. The dark circles under her eyes had faded.
Hannah had begun telling Isabel bedtime stories each night,
stories filled with God's redemption and hope. Soon, girls came
from other rooms to listen. The women joined them, gathering
in the doorways and down the hall. Even Mrs. Smith came to
listen.

Tonight's tale consisted of an adventuresome knight who
closely resembled Bradlee, and a forgotten, foreign heroine who
rescued him and his witty apprentice from a shipwreck. The
girls held still as they listened, transfixed by her story. She'd

reached the part where the heroine had been turned out with no place to go.

Pounding sounded on the front door.

Several of the girls startled, and then giggled at their response.

Mrs. Smith raised her hands heavenward with a sigh. "Who in their right mind would come calling at this late hour, and right when I was wantin' to hear the ending?"

"Where was I?" Hannah asked the youngest girls at her feet.

Anna, who was barely six years, raised her hand. "She was livin' on the streets like me, and-and-and my ma befores w-we ended up 'ere."

Hannah loved to hear the girl try to talk, despite her stutter. "Very good, Anna." She smiled and scanned the faces of the room. "The baron's daughter curled up on the hard ground with only a thin gown for her covers. Her warm breath swirled the cold mist—"

"Hannah!" A male voice shouted from the foyer.

Her breath caught. It couldn't be. She was hearing things. Bradlee was at Oxford finishing his final exams.

"Hannah!" The call was louder this time, closer, and most definitely Bradlee's voice.

"Bradlee?" Her heart fluttered like a hummingbird taking flight.

The ladies moved as a wave, pressing to the side, and Bradlee's muscular form squeezed his way through the throng. "Hannah, thank heaven, I found you."

"You're here." *How? Why?* She pressed her hands to the sides of her face as if to hold her thoughts together, but her heart exploded with joy. "How did you find me? You should be at Oxford finishing your exams. What of your father?"

He gingerly stepped among the younger girls, excusing himself as he went.

The girls stared at him in awe, as if the hero of the fairytale had come to life.

For Hannah, it had. Never had she seen such a wonderful sight. Was he truly here, or was her grip on reality slipping? His warm amber eyes bathed her in love and hope, but she was afraid to reach for him for fear he might only be a dream.

"Alice wrote and explained the mishap. I came as quickly as I could." He scooped her cold hands into his warm ones, but a second later, he yanked her into his embrace.

She clung to his jacket and soaked in his strength. Bradlee was real. He was with her.

He kissed the top of her head. "I love you. You're never leaving my side again. Do you hear me?"

Reality crashed over her. She shook her head and pulled back. "Your parents will cut you off. Alice is more suitable. I can't ruin your life."

"There will be no cutting off." Lady Cardon scooted around a woman from room four.

Alice followed her, shaking her head. "I have never been, nor will I ever be, in love with Bradlee." Her gaze slid to Colin, and she issued him a shy smile. "Bradlee and I do not suit."

Hannah's hair left a streak of bone dust on Bradlee's cheek, and she brushed it away with her thumb. She glanced down at her dirty gray uniform. She didn't fit. She'd been between classes on Nevis, and now, she was beneath him, a working girl in a poorhouse. "Look at me. I don't come with a dowry or fancy gowns. I can't afford your world travel and adventure. All I have to offer is me."

Bradlee cupped her face. "You are all I need. I will take you as you are. You belong with me, and I plan to spend the rest of my life proving you are my greatest adventure."

His gaze fell to her neck, and his eyes clouded.

Was he already having doubts?

"I'm sorry you've lost your father's ring. I know how much it meant to you, and I will find a way to get it back." He stuck his hand into his jacket's inside pocket and pulled out a tiny box. "But I hope you will wear mine on your finger."

A simultaneous gasp sucked all the air from the room. The girls clasped hands and stared wide-eyed as he held up a sapphire ring.

"Hannah Barrington, will you marry me?"

Her breathing ceased.

His eyes challenged her to say yes.

Her lips quivered. "Yes." She nodded. "Most definitely, yes."

He claimed her mouth with a possessive kiss, melting away any remaining doubts.

Hannah clung to him, thanking God for making a way.

The children jumped to their feet, cheering and dancing.

Bradlee chuckled into her lips, and they both peered out at the crowd. Tears glistened in the women's eyes, and they hugged each other with joy. Even Greta accepted a hug or two.

Bradlee slid the ring on her finger and raised their joined hands high in the air.

The room erupted once more.

CHAPTER 42

The Spirit itself beareth witness with our spirit, that we
are the children of God. And if children, then heirs; heirs
of God, and joint-heirs with Christ... Romans 8:16-17
~ *Journaled after Bradlee's daily devotional, the 7th of October,*
1829

*B*radlee pressed his back to the door of their room at
the inn. "We should stay for another week."

"The innkeeper will believe we're hibernating for the
winter." Hannah laughed and twisted her hair up into a topknot
and secured it with the leather strap.

He pushed off the door and moved to sit on the bed beside
her. He couldn't resist planting a kiss on her delicious neck any
more than he could have waited to marry her. Any bystander
who'd peeked out his window the night he proposed would
have been astounded by the sight of the entire women's wing of
the poorhouse filing into the Walcott parish and awakening the
reverend.

He thanked God for Colin and Alice's forward-thinking in

obtaining a special license and a ring while they searched for Hannah those long and harrowing six days.

His hands caressed her shoulders, still a mite too thin, but he would rectify that. If only he had spoken to his father sooner, he could have prevented her enduring such hardship. "I'm sorry for what you went through."

"Don't be." She leaned into his chest. "My experience strengthened my faith, and it opened my eyes to my calling." She peeked up at him. "You saw the hope in the women's and children's eyes. I want to continue to offer them hope. I want to help destitute women."

"That is a lovely idea." He planted a kiss behind her ear.

"I'm not certain how I shall go about it, but I know God will make a way."

He never wanted their honeymoon to end, but he'd also never wanted their wedding to end. He'd thought he couldn't have felt more love for her then when she said, *I do* in front of the priest, his mother, Colin, Alice, and an entire roomful of women and girls. He pushed her capped sleeve further down her arm and trailed a row of kisses along the graceful slope of her shoulder. He loved her even more now and would even more so tomorrow.

"If you keep this up, we shall never reach your brother's holding before nightfall." She twisted to glance at him.

The sight of her barren neck, as lovely as it was, wrenched his heart. "I'm dreadfully sorry about your father's ring." He shifted to face her.

"I—"

He placed a finger on her lips. "I know how much it meant to you. I promise I will find it and buy it back no matter the cost."

She shook her head. "I still have the ring."

"You do?" He furrowed his brow.

"I had to hide it." She undid her topknot, and rich golden

waves of hair spilled over her shoulders. Holding up the chain, she dangled the ring between them. "I hid it in my hair."

Bradlee laughed and grabbed the ring to inspect it closer. "I never had a chance to see it up close." His heart skipped. He stared at what was not only her father's ring, but also the Barrington seal. "You've had this all along?"

She nodded. "My father gave it to me for safekeeping the night he died."

"All this time?"

Hannah peered at him, clearly puzzled.

"Darling." He held the ring up. "This is the sugar baron's seal. All along, you've held the proof of your inheritance."

"Truly?" Her eyes narrowed on the ring.

"Your father didn't forget you. He gave you the key to unlock your inheritance. It's been with you all along—next to your heart. He left you his signet ring to proclaim you are his heiress."

Tears gathered in her eyes.

Bradlee pulled her into his embrace and stroked her hair.

"My love, you are his beloved daughter."

EPILOGUE

*O*ctober rolled into November, and even though the air grew cooler, Hannah's heart remained warm. She sat curled in a chair with a Bible in her lap. Bradlee sat in the chair next to hers with a Bible in his. A fire crackled in Ywain Manor's large stone hearth. He extended a hand across the small table separating them and laced his fingers with hers. Her pulse quickened.

Did Lady Clark's heart still beat like this after so many years sitting next to Mr. Clark during their morning devotionals?

Lord Cardon paraded into the room waving a package. He was followed by Lady Cardon holding a letter.

"It has arrived!" He thrust the brown paper package into Bradlee's chest. "You've done it."

Hannah slipped her hand out from Bradlee's and let the pride she held for him be expressed in her smile.

They gathered around as he opened the first edition of his novel titled, *The Jewel of Africa*. He held up the leather-bound book, and the gold embossed lettering shone in the light.

Lord Cardon clapped a hand on his shoulder. "My son is an author."

"We're so proud of you." Lady Cardon cupped his cheeks in her hands and smiled.

"Let me get a look at it," her father-in-law said.

Bradlee passed the book to his father, who thumbed through it, pausing to read a few sentences. "Hannah was right. You make us feel as if we are in Africa with you."

Lady Cardon passed a letter to Hannah and seated herself on the sofa across from them.

Hannah didn't recognize the penmanship.

"Where is the next book taking place?" his mother asked.

Bradlee strummed his thumb and index finger on his knees. "In the wild grassy plains of America."

His father glanced up from the book in his hands. "Will there be Indians like the ones you've told us about?"

"Indeed."

"Are you going to add the tale about the Indian woman trying to make a home with Colin and become his wife?" Lord Cardon's belly jiggled as he chuckled.

"Most definitely."

Hannah shook her head. "You know Colin will be livid."

Bradlee flashed her a smile. "That's the idea."

She flipped the letter over and noticed a red seal with the Linton emblem stamped upon it. The Duchess of Linton had returned.

"Open it and see what it says." Her mother-in-law nodded her encouragement.

Bradlee shifted closer.

Hannah bit her bottom lip and used her fingernail to open the seal. She pulled out a piece of fine paper with neatly written script.

"Read it aloud." Bradlee squeezed her hand.

She cleared her throat.

Dearest Hannah,

Our deepest apologies for not being here when you arrived. The Duke and I had traveled north to witness our son Max marry a delightful woman in Northallerton, and thus missed Aunt Tessa's letter informing us of your coming.

My aunt and Reverend Clark both speak highly of you, and I feel like you are part of our family from their letters. I do hope you will come and pay us a visit. Much has occurred since your first arrival. Mrs. Marchmain has written inquiring about you, and Lady Cardon has informed us of your nuptials."

Hannah glanced at her mother-in-law. "You've corresponded with the Duchess of Linton?"

"I have. She is a delightful lady. You and Bradlee were on your honeymoon when her first letter arrived. Go on."

Hannah cleared her throat and continued.

"Please accept my congratulations and expect a wedding present to arrive soon.

I do have some tragic news from another letter Aunt Tessa sent. It seems your past guardian, Reuben Huxley, was found dead."

Hannah's breath caught. Huxley had done a lot of vile things, but part of her mourned for the occasional goodness she'd witnessed in him. Would his tormented soul ever find rest? She looked to her husband. Bradlee rose and moved to her side, propping his hip on the armrest of her chair and curling a protective arm around her shoulders.

She forced herself to focus on the letter again.

It is uncertain whether he stumbled off a cliff or whether foul play was involved, but she assured me that the constable is looking into the matter."

A chill ran through Hannah, and she said a silent prayer for his soul.

Aunt Tessa took it upon herself to go through your guardian's things and mailed us some letters she discovered, requesting for our solicitors to look into the matter. They have asked you to meet them this Saturday at Rosewood Manor. My husband and I will also be in attendance and look forward to finally meeting you.

Yours truly,

The honorable
Lady Georgia Weld
Duchess of Linton

"My word." Her father-in-law blinked successively. "You have an engagement with the duke and duchess?"

~

$\mathcal{T}$he Cardon coach pulled into Rosewood Manor, where numerous carriages lined the drive. The coachman stopped next to a six-horse drawn coach with the footman and driver dressed in fine livery and the letter *L* emblazed upon the side.

The Duke and Duchess had already arrived.

Hannah peered at her former home with nervous anticipation. Why would the Duchess summon her here?

Bradlee leaned against her side and peeked through the window. "It seems we're the last to arrive to the party."

She curled her fingers around his arm and clung to his strength. How could he remain so calm when she felt like a thousand insects were gnawing at her insides?

Bradlee alighted and helped her down. He maintained a possessive arm around her waist and pressed a kiss to the top of her head. "This homecoming shall be different."

She certainly hoped so.

The front door burst open. A constable and his man gripped Mr. Fogarty's arms behind his back and forced him toward the side of the house, where a barred wagon was stationed.

Mr. Fogarty's flinty gaze caught sight of her. His teeth bared, and he twisted his head in her direction. "She's the fraud!" He struggled against his bindings. "I've done nothing wrong."

The constable shook his head. "I daresay, the earl thinks differently after inspecting the ledgers and seein' how much you skimmed off the top."

"The real heiress is dead." He dug in his heels and writhed his body. "This is preposterous. She's an imposter." Bits of spittle sprayed with each *p* sound.

"We'll let the magistrate decide." The constable swung the rear door to the wagon wide and shoved Mr. Fogarty inside.

Fogarty pressed his face against the bars and peered at

Hannah. "I paid that lout of a guardian a sum equal to your dowry to make you disappear."

Bradlee's hand tightened on her waist and hurried her to the front door. Instead of the young pompous butler they'd seen before, an elderly man in deep red livery held it open.

"Milady, welcome home." His voice shook with emotion.

As Hannah drew closer, she could see that the butler's vision was blocked by a cloudy film, and his jowls had sagged with age, but she knew his face.

"Stodges?"

Tears formed in his rheumy eyes. "At your service, milady." His hand lifted as if wanting to touch her, but hesitated and dropped it back to his side.

Hannah clasped his hand and cupped it to her cheek. "It is so good to see you."

He blinked back tears, but several escaped and rolled down his cheeks. "And may I say how good it is to know you're alive and where you rightfully belong."

She squeezed his hand and turned to Bradlee. "Stodges is the man I told you about. He saved me the day my gown caught on fire."

Stodges's chest puffed out, and he seemed to grow younger before their eyes. "You were just a wee mite back then."

She patted Bradlee's arm. "Bradlee, let me introduce you to Stodges, my father's steadfast and loyal butler."

Stodges bowed. "Master Granville, a pleasure to meet you."

Bradlee nodded. "The pleasure is all mine."

"The duke and duchess are awaiting your arrival." Stodges turned. "Right this way."

He led them down the hall into a large drawing room. He didn't need to feel his way, for it seemed he'd made the route thousands of times over the years. He pushed the door open and stepped aside. "Your Grace, Mr. and Mrs. Granville have arrived."

"There she is." Her grace, Lady Georgia Weld, the honorable Duchess of Linton, strode to Hannah and scooped up her hands. "How lovely to finally meet you."

"Your Grace." Hannah bobbed a curtsy.

The duchess's lavender taffeta skirts swished as she gestured to her husband. "Harrison, please come meet a fellow Nevisian resident and dear friend, Mrs. Hannah Granville and her husband, Mr. Bradlee Miles Granville."

Bradlee bowed.

The duke stepped next to his wife and returned the bow. Despite his graying temples, his eyes shown with youthful energy and admiration for his wife.

"An honor to meet you." Hannah dipped into a curtsy.

The duchess's brow furrowed. "I'm still terribly sorry we weren't around when you first arrived."

"We had no time to notify you of our arrival." Hannah hadn't known what to expect of meeting with royalty, but natural warmth flowed from the duchess, and she took to her grace instantly. "Congratulations once again upon your son's nuptials."

"Max married a lovely woman. We couldn't ask for a better daughter-in-law." The duchess locked arms with Hannah. They strode together into the salon and sat on the sofa.

The Duke of Linton and Bradlee entered the room after them. The duke rested his arm upon the mantel, and Bradlee leaned against the stone where they could observe the ladies chatting.

"I was beside myself after receiving Aunt Tessa's letter," the duchess said. "I'm so delighted things turned out well for you." She glanced at Bradlee.

Stodges opened the door, and both Hannah and the duchess shifted to see who'd arrived.

The duke pushed off the mantel. "Ainsbury? It's about time you arrived. We'd hoped to get this mess cleared up and get an early jump on the hunt. I've yet to see you best me in catching a fox."

A man in his thirties strode into the room dressed in a red coat and buckskin breeches prepared for the sport. He stopped in front of Hannah and smiled. "So, my cousin is truly alive and returned after all these years."

Hannah's lips parted. *Cousin?*

Georgia stood. "Lord Ainsbury, let me introduce to you your closest cousin, Miss Hannah Granville."

He bowed. "I'm delighted to meet you finally. Had I known you existed, I swear I would have sent for you. My father resided in India when you were born and hadn't kept in the best of contact with his siblings."

Two other men entered the room, greeted the duke and duchess, and took seats. Hannah couldn't take her eyes off her relative.

He beamed at her. "My sister has made me promise you shall come and meet the rest of the family after the will is read."

Hannah sucked in a breath. *Family?*

The two men opened files and pulled out paper. "Let's begin with the will." One of them held out a paper the length of his arm and peered at it through his spectacles. "The will and testament of Sir Charles Edmund Barrington..."

Her eyes strayed to Bradlee as her pulse picked up speed. Her father had left a will.

As the solicitor read the will leaving Rosewood manor to his daughter, Hannah Rose Barrington, tears formed in her eyes. She'd never been forgotten. Huxley had tried to tell her she was unwanted, others called her red legs and white beggar, and somewhere in the mix she'd forgotten who she really was, but God reminded her what He called her—*daughter.*

People had tried to hide her inheritance and place doubts in her heart. Huxley, Fogarty, and even Governor Vaux had wanted her to be the victim, but God helped her to rise up. He placed warriors as her front and rear guards through Bradlee, Blandina, Lady Clark, Alice, even the Duke and Duchess of Linton.

The solicitors finished the reading and stood.

Hannah, too, stood—in victory, for she not only had an earthly inheritance, but also a heavenly one.

God had made a way in the wilderness and created streams in the wasteland.

The Duchess of Linton inhaled a deep breath. "Praise God. What was once hidden has been brought to the light."

Her new cousin smiled down at her. "Rosewood Manor is your home. I apologize for my steward's mismanagement. I will send you funds to make up for what he skimmed from the ledgers."

She shook her head. "I'm merely grateful to have a family." She bit her bottom lip. "You're not upset about foregoing ownership?" She could only imagine what he was feeling after she arrived from out of nowhere and laid claim to his property.

"The duchess allowed me plenty of forewarning so I wouldn't find it a shock." He shook his head. "Besides, I have plenty of roofs to keep over my head. It's hard enough to maintain what I have. I'd much prefer to rejoice knowing my cousin is alive and well." He smiled. "Now, who shall give the tour of your home, you or I?"

Hannah thought her heart might burst. "I would love for you to do us the honor."

Lord Ainsbury exited the room, followed by the duke and duchess.

Bradlee offered Hannah his arm. "May I be the first to welcome you home, Mrs. Granville."

"Home. Such a lovely word." She hugged Bradlee's arm as they strolled from the room after her cousin. "But not as lovely as family."

"Speaking of family." He peered over his shoulder and

lowered his voice. "We mustn't allow Colin and Alice to get ahead of us in setting up a nursery."

"They've only been married for a week." She bit back her laughter. "Besides, must the two of you turn everything into a competition?"

He flashed her a dashing smile that still quickened her pulse. "A little competition keeps things interesting."

Hannah's heart nearly burst with anticipation. As her newfound cousin reintroduced her to her childhood home, she found it hard to concentrate.

She licked her lips and prayed once again for patience, for she could barely wait until evening when she would be alone with Bradlee to inform him his life was about to get a lot more interesting. Her hand moved to her temporarily flat stomach and thanked God for her new family. She couldn't wait to see her husband's reaction.

Bradlee, my love, we have a bit of a head start on the competition.

Did you enjoy this book? We hope so!
Would you take a quick minute to leave a review where you purchased the book?
It doesn't have to be long. Just a sentence or two telling what you liked about the story!

Receive a FREE ebook and get updates when new Wild Heart books release: https://wildheartbooks.org/newsletter

Here's a sneak peek at the next book in The Leeward Islands Series!

The Captain's Quest

Innocent mistakes can have dire consequences.

CHAPTER ONE

The skirts of the other dancers swirled around Priscilla Leah Middleton like colorful pinwheels. The rousing music and boisterous men and women dressed in the height of fashion did nothing to diminish the prickle of unease tapping at her conscience. Why did she agree to this? Why did she listen to Nellie's whimsical woes of heartache?

The violinist concerto finished its movement, and the dancers changed direction. Distracted, Priscilla would have continued straight, but the sturdy frame of her dance partner saved her from embarrassing herself. She flashed her gratitude.

Her stately partner returned her smile, but the look didn't quite meet his eyes.

The rapping on her conscience intensified, building pressure. "It's quite a party, is it not?" She blurted out the statement, even though conversations were hard to hold while dancing.

"Quite." He glanced about the room.

Her nerves made her prattling hard to stop. "Does Lady Lemoore always entertain such interesting groups of people? I've never seen the like, politicians mixing with opera singers, military officers speaking to notorious rakes and gamblers."

"Indeed."

Her breath hitched. Would he have taken offense to her statement? Did he fit into one of those categories? She barely knew this man. "I love a good party, dancing, meeting interesting people, matchmaking among friends. It's all thrilling. Don't you think?"

He didn't respond. His gaze had drifted to the far corner of the room and he didn't appear aware that she'd spoken.

One thing she did know about this man Nellie had insisted she partner with for dance—he wasn't much of a conversationist. Priscilla willed the orchestra to end the song. Why had she allowed herself to be swayed by Nellie. *Please, Priscilla, Lord Fortin's leaving tomorrow. He must hear what is on my heart from my own lips. I must look him in the eyes and see for myself if he returns my sentiment.*

Nellie had been on the verge of tears, but Priscilla should have known to inquire about the whereabouts before agreeing. Her mother called her *sensitive* when speaking of Priscilla's ability to share others' emotions as if they were her own. Her brother called it *gullible*.

Do not destroy our chance at love. You must attend with me, Nellie had begged her. *It shall be a splendid time. Everyone of notice shall be in attendance.*

Nellie neglected to mention that by *everyone*, she meant people affiliated with the Tory party. After this dance, Priscilla would have the coach brought around. It was time they left before the headlines of the Morning Star read: *Daughters of two prominent affiliates of the Whig party seen dancing in the enemy's camp.*

A loud cheer erupted from the card room, and Priscilla startled.

"Relax." A lazy half-grin formed on the lips of her dance partner, revealing even, white teeth.

Blast, what was his name? Guy, Gould, Goulart? *Goulart*, that was it. How could she relax when their host, Lady Lemoore, decided to become politically outspoken?

He swept Priscilla cross the floor. "How does a lovely woman like yourself sneak away unchaperoned?"

She stiffened. "How did you know we're unchaperoned?"

"Your friend told Lord Fortin."

Drat. Why would Nellie mention such a thing unless she was trying to encourage a clandestine interlude? Priscilla caught sight of Nellie, basking in the adoration of the well-dressed lord guiding her across the crowded dance floor. By the dreamy expression on Nellie's face, Lord Fortin had once again wooed her with his fanciful flummery.

Could Nellie not see the man was a rogue? She needed to get Nellie away from Lord Fortin and this party sooner rather than later. Would this dance never end? "Our chaperone was merely delayed." It wasn't a lie. Her duenna fell ill with a severe headache, and Nellie's chaperone had nodded off during the carriage ride over. Nellie had convinced Priscilla to let the poor woman sleep.

Now, it seemed awfully convenient for Nellie.

Priscilla lifted her chin. "She shall be arriving shortly."

An intoxicated couple nearly collided with her, but Lord Goulart adeptly reworked the steps to avoid disaster. She had to give him credit. He was a superb dancer.

"Your father works for the War Department?"

She tensed as he drew her closer than the proper waltz

distance—a spark of interest illuminating his dark eyes. He, who ignored her earlier attempts at conversation, now wanted to discuss her father? What had changed?

Persistent brown eyes bore into hers, waiting for her answer.

"I beg your pardon, Mr. Goulart. I lost myself in the steps." She blinked at his straight nose and tight-trimmed beard. "My father used to dabble within the War Department, but he has recently retired."

"No one truly retires from that place." He raised his hand and ushered her under his arm for a turn.

"Quite right." Papa's visits, callers, and hand-delivered missives certainly hadn't slowed.

Mr. Goulart leaned in and whispered in her ear. "I adore a lady with dimples." His breath tickled her skin. "I do hope to see more of them."

Heat spread across her cheeks. It seemed flummery was catching. She'd heard many a compliment before, but not regarding her dimples. Dimples were adorable on children, but not on a grown woman.

She cleared her throat and ignored his statement. Better to return to the topic at hand. "I'd thought, after Napoleon's surrender, things would have died down, but my father still spends endless hours in his study, with ambassadors and generals filing in and out."

Mr. Goulart's eyes flared. "You don't say?" He removed his hand from her lower back and scratched his nose with his thumb. The movement somehow allowed him to cloak the eagerness she'd witnessed in his gaze. "I'd like to hear more about my competition. I'm certain, after discovering Admiral Middleton has such a lovely daughter, they call upon you as well?"

An inelegant snort erupted through her nose. "You jest."

His expression remained serious.

She bit back her laughter. "Most of the men who call upon

my father are well along in years—er, except perhaps Officer Campbell and Lord Asterly. But I daresay, they see me as an annoying intruder."

His eye twitched. "An intruder, you say?"

The song ended with three crisp notes. Mr. Goulart dropped his arms to his sides and bowed, while Priscilla held out her skirt for a proper curtsy. To her left, laughter erupted, and she recognized the hollow, wheezy tone of Lord Eversley—a key leader in the Tory party.

She gulped and mentally measured the distance to the main exit, then glanced back over her shoulder in search of Nellie.

Mr. Goulart offered her his arm and escorted Priscilla off the dance floor. "Care to take a turn about the room?"

"Actually, I must speak to my friend. I just remembered another obligation I promised to attend. I'm afraid we'll leaving."

"Stay." Mr. Goulart placed his other hand on top of hers. "I'd be loath without your company."

In any other situation, she'd enjoy the affectionate gesture and words, but tonight his gloved hand snared her like a trap.

When Priscilla didn't respond, Mr. Goulart guided her to the perimeter, away from the crush of guests. He turned her in the opposite direction of Lord Fortin and Nellie, but Priscilla tracked them in her periphery. Instead of stopping for refreshments or returning to where they'd previously stood before the dance, Nellie and Lord Fortin continued strolling. His gaze hovered upon Nellie as if she were a savory feast he was about to partake of. Could she not see the man was a knave?

"Officer Campbell is an interesting chap. He and I became acquainted in the West Indies." Mr. Goulart stopped next to a large marble pillar in a secluded corner, away from the loud banter of the party. "Have you seen him lately?"

"Who?" She'd long since lost track of their conversation.

"Officer Neil Campbell, the man you said, 'sees you as an interloper.'"

"Ah, yes." Priscilla's gaze tracked Nellie. "Last week—I believe. He paid father a brief visit."

Her jaw tightened. *No, Nellie, don't go toward the guest wing.* Her friend lacked for an ounce of sense, and Pricilla was twice the fool for involving herself. More than ever, she missed Lottie, her closest friend who'd married and moved to the Leeward Islands. Lottie would never have placed Priscilla in such a predicament.

"I thought he was supervising Bonaparte?" Mr. Goulart leaned his shoulder against the pillar. His chocolate eyes melted into hers, demanding her full focus.

Her breath caught at the intensity of his gaze.

His lips curled, almost as if he could sense the way having his full attention on her warmed her insides.

She worked to steel herself. Not tonight. She would not let her guard slip.

"Officer Campbell was known in Guadeloupe for having an eye for beautiful women." Mr. Goulart reached out and touched the strip of bare skin below her capped sleeve. "I think only of your safety. Did Campbell make known the reason for his visit?"

The doors from the balcony opened, and a buxom woman squealing with laughter entered, pursued by a robust gentleman.

Priscilla used the distraction to step out of Mr. Goulart's reach. "It's surprising you wish to speak politics with a woman." Where was Nellie? She shouldn't have let her out of sight.

He stepped closer, blocking her view of the room. "I can tell there's an intelligence about you." His gaze flicked to where she'd last seen Lord Fortin and Nellie, and he, once again, rubbed the side of his nose with his knuckle. "I appreciate a woman with a mind."

Priscilla shifted to the side and spotted Lord Fortin's wavy hair and proud swagger on the edge of the ballroom. She released a sigh. "If I were an intelligent woman, I wouldn't be here."

Mr. Goulart sent her his full, almost-blinding smile, and his deep chuckle reverberated the air around her. "And a delightful sense of humor, might I add."

Lord Fortin stepped into the dim hall near the guest's quarters, where the wall candles had suspiciously been snuffed out. His outstretched hand beckoned Nellie forward. The curls that framed Nellie's face swayed as she peeked both ways before she slipped into the shadows.

"Blast." Priscilla stepped forward, preparing to chase after them. "Pardon me. I must be going."

"You never answered my question." Mr. Goulart halted her with a hand on her arm. "What was the reason was for his visit?"

"I need to return to my friend." She attempted to brush off his fingers. "Thank you for the dance, Mr. Goulart." When he didn't release her, she gave a pointed look at his fingers still on her arm.

"Let me help you locate her."

"I'm capable of finding her myself."

"I insist. I cannot, in good conscience, allow a young woman with delicate sensibilities to traipse about unescorted. Lady Lucille Lemoore has been known to allow..." He cleared his throat. "...certain indiscretions. I wouldn't want you to happen upon anything—er, shocking."

Priscilla's insides hollowed. "All the more reason for me to locate Nellie immediately." She nodded toward the guest hall. "I last spied her over there."

He ushered her around the wainscoted perimeter. The cool breeze blowing in from the open doors of the terrace cooled her heated skin. Outside, Lady Lucille slapped a man's hand away with her fan, her seductive smile implying she didn't mind in the least. Pricilla's stomach tightened. The night was still young, what sort of debauchery would ensue when the hour grew late? They had to get out of here.

Lady Lucille rose, excused herself from the men, and entered the ballroom, passing in front of Priscilla and Mr. Goulart and leaving a scented wake of expensive perfume. Priscilla craned her neck to see a cluster of military coats filling the entrance. Lady Lucille extended her hands in warm greeting to the men, most of whom Priscilla recognized as acquaintances of her brother, Anthony.

Anthony wasn't among them. He'd be on his ship, preparing to make sail on Monday. But if his friends recognized her, gossip would spread quickly. Priscilla tripped on the lacy trim of her hem, but fortunately, Mr. Goulart's grip kept her from falling.

"They know my brother." Her chest rose and fell in rapid succession. "If they see me...I need to leave." She rounded the corner and pressed against the wall. The ledge of the ornate wainscoting dug into her lower back.

Earlier, she'd thought it was only her reputation that could suffer, and she'd been willing to endure some gossip for Nellie's sake. But, heaven's above, why hadn't she considered how this would affect her father's political connections? Why didn't Nellie tell her the party would be filled with Tories? How did she get herself into such a mess?

"Everyone's focus was on the door and Lady Lucille. No one saw us." Mr. Goulart moved to the first closed door and put his ear against it.

"Are you certain?"

He nodded and moved to try the latch, but paused. "Listen, you seem like a nice woman. Things are about to get complicated. If you don't want to be in the middle of it, I recommend you leave, but don't return home just yet."

"Don't go home?" The casual way he spoke such ominous

words froze the blood in her veins. "What do you mean? What are you suggesting I do?"

He glanced her way, and a wicked smile twisted his lips. "Go where the naïve and innocent go, someplace visible, like Almacks." His voice lowered to a murmur. "Or, *cheri*, you'll need a good alibi."

Priscilla gasped at the brazen endearment spoken in French when their country was at war with France… Merciful heaven, with whom had she been conversing?

He tried the latch, but the door was locked. Staying close to the shadows, he snuck to the next door, once again pressing his ear to it. This latch gave, and he poked his head into the room, whispering Lord Fortin's name. No answer. He repeated this process down the hall.

Something about Mr. Goulart's movements struck Priscilla as odd. He moved like a stealthy cat on the hunt. She peeked around the corner into the ballroom where the military men had begun to mingle. Laughter sounded nearby, and one of the men's heads raised and peered in her direction.

Egad. It was Anthony's friend from Eton. He'd joined their family on school holidays, since his family lived too far north to travel. She ducked back to find a quiet, dim hallway, and Mr. Goulart was gone.

She was alone, and the fine hair on her neck raised.

Priscilla's feet were moving before she even knew where she was going. She darted around a corner and collided with Mr. Goulart's back.

Lord Fortin stood in front of him, adjusting the frill of his cuff. "I have what I came for."

"We have company." Mr. Goulart peered back over his shoulder, but not at her.

"Out the back, then?"

Mr. Goulart nodded, and they both strode toward the servant's entrance.

"Wait." She whispered. "Where is Nellie?"

They kept walking, their long strides covering a lot of ground.

She raised her voice as loud as she dared without drawing unwanted attention. "You can't leave us."

Mr. Goulart held the back door open for Lord Fortin.

She grabbed her skirts and chased after them.

"It's about time."

The familiar voice skidded Priscilla to a halt. She knew that voice. She'd heard it all her life. The Royal blue of a navy jacket flashed as the door closed.

Priscilla dashed to the nearby open window and peered out, but they'd disappeared. The vanilla scent of papa's favorite cheroot still hung in the air.

What was he doing here? And why was he with those men?

Get The Captain's Quest at your favorite retailer!

GET ALL THE BOOKS IN THE LEEWARD ISLANDS SERIES

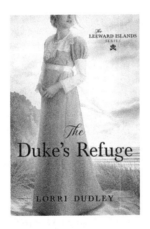

Book 1: The Duke's Refuge

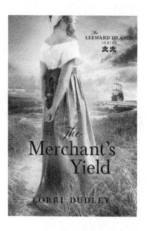

Book 2: The Merchant's Yield

Book 3: The Sugar Baron's Ring

Book 4: The Captain's Quest

ABOUT THE AUTHOR

Lorri Dudley has been a finalist in numerous writing contests and has a master's degree in Psychology. She lives in Ashland, Massachusetts with her husband and three teenage sons, where writing romance allows her an escape from her testosterone filled household.

Connect with Lorri at http://LorriDudley.com

ACKNOWLEDGMENTS

I am so grateful to God for allowing me the opportunity to write. His love is awe-inspiring.

I must thank my boys for their inspiration. The friendship between Bradlee and Colin was based on their relationship. As much as my sons tease each other, there is a tight fraternal bond between them. No matter what comes their way. I know they have one another and each other's backs. "A cord of three strands is not easily broken (Ecclesiastes 4:12)." I'm blessed to be their mom.

Thanks to my supportive and loving husband, you'll always be my hero, and to my parents, who are my constant source of encouragement. God has blessed me with an incredibly loving family, and I'm so pleased that writing has provided an opportunity to connect more with my aunts, uncles, and cousins who live all over the US. I can't thank you enough for your moral support.

It's a joy to work with such a wonderful and fun publisher, Misty Beller. You've made writing and publishing a remarkable journey. I'm excited for more. Special thanks to the Wild Heart Books team for designing another great cover and for your tremendous editing and marketing wisdom.

Erin Taylor Young, once again, thank you for your wise perspective and for forcing me to rethink situations and dig deep to bring out the best in my stories. Robin Patchen, my fantastic editor and friend, thank you for connecting me with Misty and for honing my writing. I'm so grateful for your eye for detail and finding my ridiculous errors. (I swear I know that shudder is spelled with two Ds and not Ts.) Robyn Hook, I'm so blessed to have someone with whom I can share my raw work, who'll guide me and critique my work even when your year has been so crazy. Also, big hugs and kisses to my beta readers, Kristen, Shannon, and Louise. Additional thanks to Kristen for making the awesome promo gifts.

To my launch team and blog readers, thank you for promoting my books with your friends and family, for your kind remarks on Facebook and posting reviews. You are vital lifeblood to the success of my books. I'm humbled by the outpouring of love and appreciative of your encouragement and excitement. To my church family and small group, thank you for being my cheering section.

May God bless you all abundantly.

If you love historical romance, check out the other Wild Heart books!

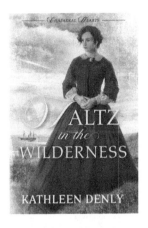

Waltz in the Wilderness by Kathleen Denly

She's desperate to find her missing father. His conscience demands he risk all to help.

Eliza Brooks is haunted by her role in her mother's death, so she'll do anything to find her missing pa—even if it means sneaking aboard a southbound ship. When those meant to protect her abandon and betray her instead, a family friend's unexpected assistance is a blessing she can't refuse.

Daniel Clarke came to California to make his fortune, and a stable job as a San Francisco carpenter has earned him more than most have scraped from the local goldfields. But it's been four years since he left Massachusetts and his fiancé is impatient for his return. Bound for home at last, Daniel Clarke finds his heart and plans challenged by a tenacious young woman with haunted eyes. Though every word he utters seems to offend her, he is determined to see her safely returned to her father. Even if that means risking his fragile engagement.

When disaster befalls them in the remote wilderness of the Southern California mountains, true feelings are revealed, and both must face heart-rending decisions. But how to decide when every choice before them leads to someone getting hurt?

~

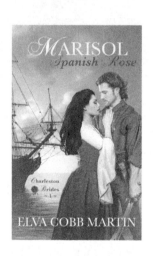

Marisol ~ Spanish Rose by Elva Cobb Martin

Escaping to the New World is her only option...Rescuing her will wrap the chains of the Inquisition around his neck.

Marisol Valentin flees Spain after murdering the nobleman who molested her. She ends up for sale on the indentured servants' block at Charles Town harbor—dirty, angry, and with child. Her hopes are shattered, but she must find a refuge for herself and the child she carries. Can this new land offer her the grace, love, and security she craves? Or must she escape again to her only living relative in Cartagena?

Captain Ethan Becket, once a Charles Town minister, now sails the seas as a privateer, grieving his deceased wife. But when he takes captive a ship full of indentured servants, he's intrigued by the woman whose manners seem much more refined than the average Spanish serving girl. Perfect to become governess for his young son. But when he sets out on a quest to find his captured sister, said to be in Cartagena, little does he expect his new Spanish governess to stow away on his ship with her six-month-old son. Yet her offer of help to free his sister is too tempting to pass up. And her beauty, both inside and out, is too attractive for his heart to protect itself against—until he learns she is a wanted murderess.

As their paths intertwine on a journey filled with danger, intrigue, and romance, only love and the grace of God can overcome the past and ignite a new beginning for Marisol and Ethan.

~

Lone Star Ranger by Renae Brumbaugh Green

Elizabeth Covington will get her man.

And she has just a week to prove her brother isn't the murderer Texas Ranger Rett Smith accuses him of being. She'll show the good-looking lawman he's wrong, even if it means setting out on a risky race across Texas to catch the real killer.

Rett doesn't want to convict an innocent man. But he can't let the Boston beauty sway his senses to set a guilty man free. When Elizabeth follows him on a dangerous trek, the Ranger vows to keep her safe. But who will protect him from the woman whose conviction and courage leave him doubting everything—even his heart?

Made in the USA
Las Vegas, NV
25 September 2021

31060360R00233